TH
NEX
WIDOW

BOOKS BY CJ LYONS

FATAL INSOMNIA MEDICAL THRILLERS
Farewell to Dreams
A Raging Dawn
The Sleepless Stars

LUCY GUARDINO THRILLERS
Snake Skin
Blood Stained
Kill Zone
After Shock
Hard Fall
Last Light
Devil Smoke
Open Grave
Gone Dark
Bitter Truth

ANGELS OF MERCY MEDICAL SUSPENSE
Lifelines
Catalyst
Trauma
Isolation

THE NEXT WIDOW

CJ LYONS

Bookouture

Published by Bookouture in 2020

An imprint of Storyfire Ltd.
Carmelite House
50 Victoria Embankment
London EC4Y 0DZ

www.bookouture.com

ISBN: 978-1-83888-712-4
eBook ISBN: 978-1-83888-711-7

Dedicated to Debra and Toni, two of the smartest, kindest, and most courageous women I've had the privilege of calling my friends. Couldn't have done it without you both!

"Deep vengeance is the daughter of deep silence."

Vittorio Alfieri

CHAPTER 1

Dr. Leah Wright cradled the boy's heart in her hand.

She glanced at his unconscious face. So young, so peaceful. Some might have said that he was dead already, but Leah wasn't one to give up so easily. What the hell had he been doing out on the street, getting stabbed in the heart, on Valentine's of all nights?

"Give it up, doc," the cop told her. He'd transported the teen to Cambria City's Good Samaritan Medical Center's ER in his squad car. Despite his racing from the scene, the kid had no vital signs when they'd arrived at Good Sam. "Just heard from my partner." He shook his head as he peeled bloody nitrile gloves from his hands. "Some people aren't even worth trying to save."

The anesthesia resident had one hand on the boy's carotid pulse, the other forcing oxygen into his lungs. His frown mirrored Leah's own fears—the kid's heart had stopped for too long; there might be nothing left to revive. "Still no pulse."

"Hang on. Wait. There. Found it." Leah used her gloved finger to plug the hole in the boy's right ventricle. Hidden by the mask she wore, her mouth twisted in determination. She ignored the sounds around her: monitor alarms, people talking, the huff and puff of the bag-valve-mask the anesthesiologist squeezed, and focused on listening through her fingertips, stretching every sense to find the life left in the boy's damaged heart. "Foley catheter. Get ready to push the O-neg as soon as I have the balloon inflated."

She guided the thin catheter through the puncture wound by touch alone. It was a strange sensation, her hands inside the chest cavity, working blind. An out of body experience—really tough traumas were all like that in a way. Time slowed, senses expanded, the entire world collapsed into a surreal tunnel vision of absolute focus.

"Now. Inflate the balloon. Slowly." She gently tugged the catheter against the heart muscle, the balloon plugging the wound from inside the ventricle. "Push the O-neg." This was the hard part: waiting for the damaged organ to start to beat. Everyone in the trauma bay hushed.

C'mon, she urged the motionless organ. Leah wasn't superstitious or particularly religious, but she felt something cold pass through her own body—someone walking on her grave, her great aunt Nellie would have said.

"Internal paddles," she ordered, ready to shock the heart back to life. As the nurse offered them to her, Leah felt a contraction ripple beneath her fingers. First one, then another. She held her breath, hoping, praying. "Wait. I've got something."

All eyes turned to the monitor. A bleep of activity. Then a flurry of more. Slow and irregular but definitely there. Was it enough?

"Anything?" she asked the anesthesia resident.

At first, he shook his head, but then jerked his chin up, meeting her gaze. "Got a pulse!"

The trauma team arrived. Leah brought the surgical resident up to date on everything they'd done to revive the kid—she still didn't know the boy's name.

"We'll take it from here," the resident said as he left. "Hope he still has some brain left after being down so long."

It wasn't Leah's fault that he'd arrived without vitals. Her team's hit-the-door to return-of-circulation time was near record-breaking.

"Good work," she told them as they filed out, leaving her alone in the suddenly silent room.

As she scrubbed clean the blood that had seeped over the rims of her gloves, she glanced at the overhead clock. Almost eight, she could still make it. Phoning home before Emily went to bed was a ritual she tried never to miss. Leah grinned. Tonight, if Emily asked her if she'd saved any lives, she could honestly say yes.

The door slammed open.

"When you gonna learn playing God isn't your job?" came the rough bark of a Bronx accent mixed with a Haitian lilt. Andre Toussaint, the chief of trauma and emergency services and Leah's boss's boss, was a short man, not much taller than Leah, with wiry gray hair. Even when he was in a good mood, he was brusque and domineering—and with thirty-seven years on the job and his position at the apex of the hospital professional hierarchy cemented, he could get away with it.

She frowned at him. "Did the kid crash on the way to the OR?"

"This isn't about one kid. It's about you treating every patient as if you're personally arm wrestling with God. It's about a flagrant disregard for the needs of the hospital and all of our patients, not to mention the community we serve. Because of your would-be rapist, we're now closed to trauma. He'll deplete our blood bank, take up nursing hours, OR staff time, and—because my team is just that good, he'll make it out of the OR to tie up our last ICU bed, probably for days. All for nothing. Because you know as well as I do, he was down too damn long."

Leah barely heard the last half of his harangue; she was caught on one word. "Rapist?" *Rapist?* The police officer had said something during the trauma about letting the kid die, but Leah had been too focused on saving his life to listen. "I thought he was the victim—"

"Surprised you had time to think, so busy raising Lazarus. Cops tell you how he got stabbed? Attacking a girl in a parking lot—had the knife on her but a good Samaritan came along, jumped him."

"I—I didn't know." Leah still couldn't wrap her mind around the fact that the kid was a rapist. He was so damn young. She remembered when they'd cut off his clothes, he'd had rolls of baby fat, his pale skin marred by acne. God, what a waste. The elation of triumphing over death was replaced by a sinking feeling deep in her gut. She swallowed hard then faced Toussaint, chin up, refusing to be cowed. She'd done the right thing. "Doesn't matter who he was or what he was doing when he got injured. My job is to care for each patient the best I—"

"Your problem?" He steamrolled over her words. "Is that you think small. Don't see the bigger picture. You should've thought about what bringing him back from the dead would cost everyone. Should've declared him, then maybe we could have saved some lives with his organs. Least then the kid's life would've been worth something." Toussaint came from an older generation of surgeons and seemed to think that his own hardscrabble climb out of the South Bronx gave him the right to preside as judge and jury over his patients—along with the other medical professionals who treated them.

Leah's posture grew rigid at his challenge. "You'd just let him die? Because of what he's accused of doing?"

"No. Not because of his crimes." He shook his head. "Because I have to think of everyone's best interests. Including that kid and his family—the quality of life he'll have. Or not have. You know as well as I do. Kid has zero chance of recovery. We don't have the resources to waste."

"I'm not a bean counter—"

"Little comfort to the next poor slob we have to turn away because we're too busy keeping your miracle-boy alive." His phone rang. "Yeah, I'm on my way." He hung up. "Got to get to the OR, finish what you started. I'll see you at next week's Morbidity and Mortality conference where you'll be justifying your actions." He pulled the door open. "You really should think about taking that job at the Crisis Intervention Center. Plenty of lost causes to fight without endangering innocent lives." Satisfied that he'd had the last word, he flapped his white coat around him as he whirled, strutting away like a bantam rooster.

Leah stared after him. The weekly Morbidity and Mortality conference gathered the medical staff to discuss cases where things went wrong in the hopes of preventing similar incidents. It was meant to be a peer-teaching event but occasionally deteriorated into a public shaming.

She left the trauma room, not making eye contact with anyone, certain her cheeks were blazing red after Toussaint's accusations. She reached the nurses' station, where she eyed the triage queue. Not bad for Valentine's Day—whoever created a mandatory date night holiday in the middle of February had never spent a winter in the mountains of central Pennsylvania. Luckily the weather was clear tonight, no snow in the forecast for another day or two. She glanced at the clock: seven past eight. "Nancy, I'm taking five."

"Tell Emily I say hi," the charge nurse replied. The ER staff always tried to free Leah for her good-night call to Emily—her own prescription for self-care to get her through a twelve-hour shift. "What did Ian get you for V-day?"

"No idea. He said it'd be a surprise."

Nancy and Jamil, the ward clerk, exchanged glances. "Oil change. Same as last year."

"I hope so," Leah said. "I hate having to deal with that stuff, especially in winter."

She headed toward the ER's back hallway and used her ID badge to key herself into the office she shared with three other attendings. She quickly dialed Ian's cell. "Is she still awake?"

"It's me, Mommy," Emily shouted so loud, Leah pulled the receiver away from her ear. "Fooled you. Daddy let me answer."

"You got me. How was your day?"

"I got Valentimes from every single person in class. Plus a special one from Daddy. And I made one for you. It's hanging on the fridge."

"Well, here's a special Valentine's kiss from me." Leah blew a loud smacking kiss into the phone. "Did you catch it?"

"Yep. Oh, Daddy helped me make a new game—musical chairs. You stack them real high but sometimes you can only use two or one legs and you have to get them just right and you have to watch the ones at the bottom because they shift as the Earth spins, but if you're real good you can make it all the way to the moon!"

"You know it was nice out today—you could have played outside instead of on your computer." Leah reminded herself to reinforce that notion with Ian—his idea of "playing" often translated into teaching Emily new computer skills instead of doing what normal six-year-olds called fun. The two of them could happily escape for hours, heads bowed together over a screen, speaking their own language—unintelligible to Leah—creating their own virtual worlds, leaving Leah behind, stranded in reality.

"When will you be home?" Emily asked.

"Not until after you're fast asleep. Which PJs are you wearing?"

"Purple polka dots! But what time?"

"Work ends at midnight. So, after that, I'm not sure. Why?"

Leah could practically hear Emily's pout over the phone. "Midnight means tomorrow. So you'll miss Valentime's."

"Tell you what. You be a good girl and go to bed without more than two stories—"

"One for me and one for Huggybear?"

"Exactly. And I'll get up early, make you a special super-duper Valentine's Day after breakfast, okay?"

"Yeah! Okay, here's Dad. Night."

There was a rattle as she handed the phone to Ian. "Good day?" he asked.

"Patient-wise, fine. Toussaint is on the warpath, though. Wants me to reconsider that job with the Crisis Center." She took a breath, trying to cleanse her thoughts of Toussaint; last thing she wanted was to ruin her few minutes of family time with talk of her idiot boss.

"It'd mean less night shifts," Ian reminded her. He taught cyber security at the college and had assumed the brunt of caring for Emily. Including mastering an assortment of skills that Leah could never dream of achieving: coiffing Emily's hair, playing princess dress up, baking allergen-free cupcakes for school birthdays. Not a day went by without Leah wondering what she'd ever done to deserve him—or their beautiful, brilliant daughter.

"Yeah, but less money." Despite her student loan debt, money wasn't the real problem. The Crisis Intervention Center was the part of the ER that dealt with victims, performing forensic evaluations—sexual assault exams, specialized interviews for the police—and then presenting that evidence in court. Right now, all the ER physicians took turns overseeing the Sexual Assault Nurse Examiners and the social workers at the CIC, but Toussaint wanted one person to take over as medical director. Leah was the newest ER attending—she'd only been at Good Sam four years—and had all the requisite qualifications, which some of the older ER physicians hadn't gotten during their training, so the pressure was on her to take the job. No one wanted it. There was no saving lives in the CIC.

"Wait up for me?" she asked Ian.

"Of course. I want to see your face when you see my surprise." He hesitated. "Then we need to talk."

"What's wrong? Did the furnace break down again?" Their budget was already strained after the last time. Leah glanced up as Nancy rapped on the office door. "Gotta go. Can we talk later? Not tonight, though—you still need to open my present to you," she said in a seductive tone, glad she'd found the time to order from Victoria's Secret.

"Right. Yeah." His tone was flat, distracted.

"What is it? Everything okay?" He was silent for a long moment. Leah rubbed her palm along her thigh, the smooth cotton of her scrubs soothing. She and Ian had been together for eight years, but sometimes—always for no good reason—a sudden wave of anxiety would ambush her, leaving her as nervous as she'd been on their first date. Fearful that with one small slip she could ruin everything, lose him forever. "Are we okay?"

"What? Of course. It's just work stuff." His tone brightened. "And you're right—tonight is for us, you and me. We'll deal with the rest of the world after. Love you."

He hung up. Leah stared at the phone, taking a few deep breaths. She had no reason to doubt Ian—he was her rock, her touchstone, easing her past the myriad of stupid, imaginary fears and insecurities that had haunted her since she was a child. She couldn't help it; her upbringing had hardwired her to always leap to the worst possible conclusion.

"Control freak," she chided herself as she returned to the ER. Her pessimistic nature made her a better ER doctor, never taking anything for granted, but she knew it also made her at times not the best wife or mother. Instead of imagining every dire catastrophe Ian might have been alluding to, she forced herself to concentrate on the smile he'd greet her with when she got home.

The rest of the night went quickly until, finally, she'd finished with her last patient and her charting, and had given her sign-out to the next attending. It was twenty past midnight by the time she was walking through the ER on her way to her car, when the clerk called her name, gesturing with a phone handset from his seat at the nurses' station. He nodded to a bouquet of red roses wrapped in cellophane and green florist tissue paper lying on the counter. "These came for you."

"From Ian?" Ian never sent her flowers for Valentine's.

"Sorry, didn't see. They were just left here, not sure when."

Leah ruffled through the roses until she found the card. The envelope had her name typed on the front. The card inside was also typed, reading: *I left a surprise for you at home.*

No signature, but if Ian phoned the order into the hospital gift shop, there wouldn't be. She inhaled the fragrant bouquet's perfume. He must have heard her frustration when they'd talked earlier, ordered the flowers to make her smile.

She headed out to the parking garage, suddenly exhausted, wanting only Ian's arms wrapped around her. She spotted her Subaru Forester parked in her reserved spot, but instead of being backed in like she'd left it, it was now parked head in. It was also gleaming clean, no trace of winter road salt.

Leah grinned. Ian had definitely been here. And gotten her exactly what she wanted. She climbed inside the SUV and set the roses on the passenger seat, where there was a receipt from the mechanic waiting for her. Oil changed, tires rotated, all the past-due maintenance performed, state inspection taken care of along with a wash. She leaned back and inhaled the almost-new car smell. Best Valentine's present ever.

Ian always knew how to make her smile. Her good mood lasted her entire drive from Good Sam to their townhouse in a converted Victorian on Jefferson Street. She pulled into their narrow driveway paved with ancient cobblestones that refused any attempt to be covered with modern materials. The sidewalk leading from the old carriage house that was now their garage was freshly shoveled and salted.

Leah found herself humming as she carried the roses past the tiny garden mounded with remnants of the snow that had fallen over the past few days. Moonlight danced with clouds, giving the dormant plants a bluish glow as shadows tangled with the snow's gleam.

She climbed the steps to the back stoop, tapped her shoes to shed any road salt, and reached to put her key in the kitchen door. It was unlocked. More than unlocked—it was slightly ajar, as if someone had pushed it shut but not hard enough for the latch to catch. Maybe when Ian had taken out the trash?

An unexpected shiver raced over her, a stray dagger of winter piercing her fleece jacket. She opened the door. The lights in the kitchen were off—also unusual. Ian always left a light for her. She flicked them on.

That's when she saw the blood.

CHAPTER 2

Leah scanned the tiny outdated kitchen. "Ian?"

There was a single streak of blood on the countertop. One kitchen chair lay on the ground below their vintage steel and red vinyl-topped table. Flecks of blood glared red against the white of a stack of napkins fluttering in the wind from the still-open door. Beside the stove, the knife block was toppled on its side, knives gleaming under the glare of the fluorescent light, half-naked where they'd slid free from their safe haven. None were missing.

Had Ian cut himself? But why put the knife back? Why not grab the first aid kit she kept in the drawer beside the sink? The thoughts rushed through Leah's mind, pushing out other thoughts she could not—would not—allow herself to think. She took one step inside but kept the door open to the night chill, leaving her blanketed by the cold, barely able to feel her face or feet. Shouldn't waste heat—the electric bill would be staggering. She should close the door… *Why didn't she?*

"Ian?" she called louder this time. Leah touched the door behind her, as if to close it, and froze there, one hand on the knob, the other holding the roses, adrenaline spiking, everything in her gut telling her to get out. She forced the primal emotions aside, focusing on what had happened here. Emily? Could she have been the one who'd gotten hurt? No. Ian would have called Leah or brought Em into the ER. So… where was he? Was Emily all right?

Then she spotted more blood streaks marring the surface of the refrigerator, not quite forming a handprint that echoed Emily's finger-painted Valentine's Day artwork from school. Leah froze, listening to her home. It was drowning in silence. And yet there was an underlying disturbance, a faint vibration, a breath held too long before sighing. When Leah inhaled, the stench of something more primal than blood filled her nostrils. Fear. Beyond fear. Terror.

Why not close the door, Leah? She'd only been inside her house for less than four seconds but was fighting the urge to flee. An escape. That was why she left the door open.

"Ian!" His name scraped against her tight vocal cords, fighting for escape. No answer. She took another step into the kitchen even as she slid her phone from her pocket.

She had to force herself to glance into the dining room. Empty. And dark. Not even a glimmer of light from the stairway. They never turned that light off at night—in case Emily had to get up to use the bathroom.

Her hand trembled as she snapped on the dining room lights.

Blood stained the walls, all the way up to the ceiling. The chandelier crystals reflected scarlet onto the cream-colored walls, danced blood-red light onto the tablecloth. One of the chairs was smashed, its legs splintered among the crystal bowl and candlesticks.

Emily. She needed to get to Emily.

"911, what's your emergency?"

Leah stared at the phone in her hand, not even remembering dialing. It was as if her brain was slashed in two: one part absorbing the details surrounding her, awareness blunted by shock and awe; the other half following well-trained instincts, taking control.

"I think someone broke into my house," she told the operator after first giving her address and name in case they were disconnected. "I got home and the back door was open. There's blood in the kitchen and my husband isn't answering. I can't find him." Her voice up-ticked, tight with fear. She forced a breath. Focus, Leah. "There are signs of a struggle."

"Ma'am." The operator's voice sliced through her panic. "Leave the house. Now. I have help on the way."

"I can't." Leah's voice was a strangled whisper. Even as she spoke she stumbled toward the staircase leading to the second floor, leading to their bedroom... and Emily's. She wanted to scream Emily's name, but couldn't force enough air past the noose that had tightened her throat. "My daughter. I need to find—"

"No. Ma'am. Leah. Listen to me. You need to leave the house. Wait for the police. They'll be there in just a few minutes."

Leah pounded up the stairs, not caring how much noise she made or whom she woke, praying only that she woke someone, that this was all a mistake, a dream, some kind of sick joke. *A surprise waiting for you*, the message on the roses said. She glanced down at the bouquet in her free hand. She dropped it, numbly watched the roses tumble down to the bottom landing, blood-red petals littering the steps.

"Get out of the house, Leah," the operator ordered.

"I can't." It was as much a plea for help as a statement of fact.

Leah gripped the phone to her ear as she reached the banister at the top of the stairs and used it to pivot around the landing into the hallway. All the doors were open. No lights except for the ghastly glow of her phone. The air stank of blood.

She turned on the hall light. Her foot squished in something, pulling her gaze down. Dark blood, sticky, enough of it to form a small puddle. More blood in ribbons and dribbles on the hardwood of the hall floor that suddenly appeared warped, extending into an unnatural distance. Tunnel vision. Adrenaline-induced, along with the roaring that had hijacked her brain. Knowing the reason for her pounding chest and shaking hands didn't help, though. She raised her gaze. Smeared handprints, one so close she could see the old scar that formed a crescent moon across the base of Ian's right thumb. She gagged, forcing herself not to scream.

"Leah?" the operator asked. "Stay with me. Are you out of the house?"

Leah barely registered the disembodied sounds coming from her phone. The plaster along the hallway was crushed in spots—too large to be fists, someone's head? A few of the dents went all the way through the ancient wire lath plaster to its horsehair insulation. A sleepwalker in a trance, she followed the trail of destruction. Emily. She had to get to Emily.

She felt as if she was in slow motion while also aware that she was moving too fast down the hall to properly assess any danger lurking behind her. Every cell in her body was screaming at her to go faster, faster. Was the intruder still here? Was he waiting for her in Emily's room? Was he behind her, ready to pounce? Where was Ian? Emily… please, God… Emily.

The blood trail led to Emily's door at the far end of the hall. So much blood. The door was ajar, Emily's Happy Hippo nightlight casting bright red and yellow dancing stars across the pink rug inside.

"Leah," the operator said. "They're almost there. Where are you? I need to know where you are so I can tell the officers."

Leah didn't answer, her attention focused on Emily's bubble-gum-pink rug and the darker red stains splashed against it. She pushed the door open wide, her hand on the knob catching some of the dancing stars, and gasped. Emily's bed was piled high with her stuffed animals, the sheets in disarray. Empty. No Emily.

But that wasn't what made her stumble back, hitting the doorjamb. She blinked, as if the simple reflex could erase what she was staring at and reset reality.

Ian sat on the floor, his back against Emily's bed. He wore the silly Curious George PJs Emily had gotten him for Christmas, their bright yellow flannel slashed and stained with blood. His head rested against one shoulder, twisted to an unnatural angle, his face bruised and swollen into a grotesque mask. One palm pressed against his abdomen, his wedding band glistening in the gleam of the nightlight.

Leah fell to her knees, crawling toward him. Pulse, did he have a pulse? But she knew before she even touched his flesh that it would be cold and lifeless.

"Emily!" Her voice ricocheted from the walls, returning to her with a hollow thud that barely made it over the pounding of her pulse. She spun around, still on her knees. Other than Ian's mutilated body, there was no sign of struggle, nothing out of place. Emily's bookcase, her toy chest, dresser, all stood intact, mocking Leah.

Then a small sound, the rustle of an animal hiding from prey, came from under the bed. Leah flattened her body, ignoring the blood she had to lie in, and aimed her cell phone into the darkness. Emily had curled herself into a ball, the smallest target possible, backed into the far corner. Out of Leah's reach.

"I'm here," Leah whispered. "Emily, look at me. It's okay."

Emily had her eyes squeezed shut, her hands tightened in fists pressed against her mouth. She didn't move.

"Emily," Leah tried again. "It's Mommy." In the distance, Leah heard sirens. She ignored them. Right now, her daughter needed her, and she was too far away.

She did the only thing any mother would do. She crawled through her dead husband's blood to get to her daughter.

The space beneath Emily's bed was so crowded Leah could barely move. It didn't help that she was hyperventilating, her chest ratcheted tight, each breath a ticking bomb threatening to explode.

Emily didn't reach for her, didn't respond when Leah grabbed her ankle. Leah tried again, stretching farther until she could touch one of Emily's elbows. Emily kept her eyes shut, her hands pressed tight against her face, her entire body heaving with silent, swallowed, half-birthed sobs.

"I'm here, baby," Leah crooned. The stench of blood contaminated what little air there was in the tiny space. She fought to control her breathing, to forget the body that lay beside them, to focus on her daughter. "Did he hurt you? The bad man?" God, if he did, if the animal who did that to Ian touched one hair on her baby girl's head—fury cauterized her fear. She belly-crawled a few inches closer to Emily, shoving shoe boxes and discarded toys and books and sneakers aside.

Using her cell, Leah examined what little she could of Emily's balled-up body. No blood. No obvious injuries. Finally, she'd edged far enough beneath the bed that she was able to wrap her arms around Emily. Leah was cramped and contorted, her head pushing against a bed slat, one shoulder nudging the mattress, and both legs sprawled behind her.

"Leah." The 911 operator hadn't given up on her. "The officers are there. They'll be coming in the rear of the house. Stay where you are. Make sure your hands are empty and keep them where they can see them. Set the phone down, it's okay, I'll still be here until I know you're with them."

A wave of hysterical laughter burbled up, but Leah choked it back. "I can't show them my hands," she told the anonymous operator. "I'm under my daughter's bed. She's here, too. I'm not leaving her."

"Which room?" The sound of computer keys drifted past the woman's voice.

"End of the hall. Where Ian—" Leah gulped, lowered her voice. Emily knew about Ian—more than Leah did—but Leah couldn't say the words, risk them penetrating Emily's protective cocoon of denial. "Where my husband is. He's on the floor."

"They're securing the house. You will probably hear them checking all the rooms. You're safe now, Leah. You can come out. You and your daughter. Just show them your hands, leave the phone."

Leah could barely hear the operator over the sounds of two men shouting downstairs and banging through the first floor. The noises did not make her feel safe—in fact, they were terrifying. Probably the point if she was a thief cowering, desperately hiding. "I'm not leaving Emily."

"Okay, hang on. Let me tell them where you are. Is your daughter injured?"

"She's in shock. But I can't find any external injuries."

Footsteps thundered up the stairs followed by the thud of doors being thrown open. Finally, the light clicked on inside Emily's room. A man made a guttural sound and swore, stepping inside only far enough to swing the door and look behind it, and then to check Emily's closet.

Leah gasped at what the light revealed. Thankfully Emily still had her eyes squeezed tight.

Ian's back was shredded with deep gouges that exposed muscle and cut down to the bone. How the hell had he found the strength to keep fighting? For Emily. Of course. Leah blinked back tears and gripped her daughter tighter.

"Ma'am." One pair of black military boots shuffled beyond the end of the bed, away from Ian. "There's no sign of the intruder. You can come out now."

Leah's body was twisted so tight she couldn't feel her legs and her muscles had locked into position, hanging onto Emily. "I can't leave my daughter. She's in shock, won't even open her eyes."

"Might not be a bad thing," he muttered as he stepped back, skirting a pool of blood. There was a hushed conversation; Leah could only hear bits and pieces. "Can't leave them—"

"Crime scene unit… Evidence—"

"Can't move the DB. CSU would have our hides and the detectives will chew up what's left."

"Wait for the sarge? It'll just be a few minutes."

Two pairs of boots approached. "Er, ma'am? We need to preserve the crime scene—"

"He means we can't drag you out, not past—"

"I know what he means," Leah snapped. She hunched her shoulder up, jostling the bed slat above her. "Can you lift the mattress? Tilt it enough so I can push the slats away and carry Emily out?"

A pause as they considered the logistics. "Yeah, that might work. You okay to wait a sec while we document the scene?"

"I still think we should wait for backup," the second man said.

Emily's trembling had grown worse. She felt cold, clammy with sweat. "As soon as you can," Leah called out. "Do you have a sterile sheet you could cover…" She trailed off, unable to complete the thought. In no universe imaginable were the words "Ian's body" part of Leah's vocabulary. No. Not. Possible.

His blood was soaking through her scrubs, she couldn't erase the image of his head resting so unnaturally against his shoulder, yet somehow part of Leah's brain refused to believe what every one of her senses screamed was real. Ian was dead. Beaten. Brutalized. Butchered.

Those were the facts of her new existence, the laws of physics that would now forever govern her universe.

Ian. Dead.

Still, her mind rebelled. This could not be happening. Not to him, not to them. Why would anyone want to hurt Ian? Why?

A rhythmic wet noise filled the tiny space. Emily. Rocking her body harder, banging her head against the bed frame as she sucked her thumb. Emily had never sucked her thumb, not even as an infant. "Baby, stop. Please. I'm here, Mommy's here."

She grasped Emily tighter, trying to pull her closer, ease her from the corner and the bed frame with its metal screws. Emily made a grunting sound like an animal and resisted, yanking away and huddling in the corner, squeezing herself into an even tighter ball. Leah somehow contorted her body to follow. Anything to not lose her tenuous connection with Emily. She squirmed farther under the bed until finally she was able to wrap her body around as much of Emily's as she could reach. She rocked in time with Emily, their heads moving in unison, their cheeks both wet with tears.

"It's okay, baby. Everything's going to be okay," Leah crooned.

It was the first time she'd ever lied to her daughter.

It wouldn't be the last.

CHAPTER 3

Detective Sergeant Luka Jericho purposefully parked his departmental Taurus at the bottom of Jefferson Street, well beyond the flashing lights of the other vehicles gathered at the scene. Despite the cold and the late hour there was a crowd of onlookers huddled in pajamas and parkas, gaping at the perfectly ordinary house halfway up a street of perfectly ordinary homes in one of Cambria City's perfectly ordinary neighborhoods.

He strolled up the hill, his pace steady and his breathing slow, almost hypnotic, an athlete preparing for a marathon. To Luka, this was the best metaphor for a homicide investigation, but it wasn't only because of the endurance needed for the long race. It was also the frenzied chaos the trampling crowd caused as they surged forward once the starter's gun released them. During his decade working violent crimes, he'd learned to slow down, ignore the urge to sprint, and instead, take the time to watch and listen. This was his last chance to observe the scene in a state as close to its pre-crime existence as possible.

As he walked, his gaze combing over the houses and the people who lived here, he kept his hands tucked deep in the pockets of his overcoat in an effort to keep them from growing numb before he'd need them to be nimble enough to take notes. Navy wool, the coat was cut in an old-fashioned English military style, giving him an air of authority while still allowing him to blend into the darkness and become invisible when he chose to. Two contradictory yet invaluable attributes of a homicide detective: a commanding presence and the ability to fade into the background.

As he observed the faces pressed against frosted windows and huddled against porch columns, Luka was certain that before tonight the calls from this block mainly concerned disputes over the limited street parking. This was an old-fashioned middle-class neighborhood with two churches anchoring the bottom of the hill and an elementary school at the top. Mature maples and sycamores old enough that their roots pushed up against the sidewalk towered over Tudor and Victorian style houses past their prime, a reflection of the entire city. Typical of many towns in the failing rustbelt, Cambria City was a paradox of rural and urban, old and new.

During the drive over from his grandparents' farm across the river he'd gotten a report from the duty sergeant. Luka hoped he'd arrived before the brass contaminated both the scene and public opinion. With any luck, he'd see what he needed to see and be gone before he had to deal with them. He'd had a taste of administration duties after first becoming a sergeant, had fought to return to the investigative side of the department. Luka wasn't a station house detective. He enjoyed being on the streets, watching the people and places and how they all fit together to tell their own unique stories.

Back when Luka worked arson, he'd solved as many cases by studying the crowd of bystanders as he had with other investigative tools. But tonight no one seemed abnormally interested in the tragedy playing out behind the now bright windows of the Wrights' home. No one appeared out of place. No one putting themselves forward, ostensibly to help. Also no one lurking, trying to avoid attention even as they fixated on the object of their obsession.

The people observing the spectacle of crime scene activity reflected the neighborhood. Elderly couples clinging to each other, worried frowns creasing their features as they observed from behind thick leaded glass. Younger couples whose worry was trumped by curiosity that drove them onto their stoops for a better look. A handful of single men who crowded the police barricade, the glow of their e-cigs and cell phones punctuating the night. Given the number of scaffolds, yellow construction permits, and panel vans scattered up and down the block, he suspected they were looking to flip houses with "good bones." Still, he needed to hear from each of them, so he was gratified when he spotted a woman almost as tall as he was, weaving through the crowd, taking notes. Naomi Harper, the youngest member of his team.

He sidled through the crowd, smiling inwardly at snatches of overheard conversation confirming his impression about the men congregated together—they were more concerned about what a violent crime would do to housing values than they cared about the man who'd been killed.

What did that say about Ian Wright? A man too busy to meet his neighbors? Or maybe Ian had had words with the house-flippers, complaining about noise or parking, the universal homeowner gripes in a quiet, well-established neighborhood like this. Luka allowed his imagination to roam freely, knowing that as soon as he made his presence officially known, he'd be faced with the reality of excavating the facts of Ian Wright's life—the good and the bad. Homicide detectives couldn't afford the luxury of never speaking ill of the dead.

Harper finished her survey of the crowd just as Luka approached the barricade. As the newest member of Luka's team, Harper was the resident gopher, fetching coffee and taking night calls. She appeared even younger than her twenty-eight years with her long, bleached braids pulled back under a knit cap. It was her first homicide investigation, and Luka could see the light in her eyes and the flush of her cheeks.

She waited for him at the barricade, impatiently tapping her pen against her thigh, unable to mask her eager expression. She'd been on the force for six years and had her bachelor's in criminal justice. When Luka met her on her first day with the squad and had been showing her the ropes, she'd hinted at trying law school—but she'd been nervous and gushing about a lot of things that he didn't hold against her.

"Hey, boss," she said, her voice pitched higher than usual. "Got a good one. Home invasion."

Luka hid his smile—he wasn't so old that he couldn't still remember those days. In fact, he'd been a bit younger than Harper when he'd started on what was then called the Major Case Squad before it became simply Homicide and now, after yet another administrative scandal and departmental reshuffling, was reincarnated as the Violent Crimes Unit. Back then he'd been a lot like Harper—eager to learn, wanting to make himself useful, always hoping to be the one who found the clue that cracked a case.

He ducked under the crime scene tape, his coat flapping behind him as he strode forward. When he straightened, he pulled his hands free of the warmth of the wool and flexed his fingers. Time to get to work. "Home invasion? What makes you think that?"

She frowned, obviously disappointed in his lack of basic observational skills. "Actor entered through the back door, that's why we're staging out here," she answered as if reassuring him that she had things handled despite his not seeing the full picture. "Homeowner fought back. Began in the kitchen, ended up in his kid's room."

Together they climbed the steps to the front porch. As Luka signed in with the patrol officer there, he scanned the list of who had already come and gone. The medical examiner's team had entered only six minutes ago. Which meant the crime scene unit had finished processing the area around the body. Perfect timing. The CSU guys were great at collecting evidence and preserving the scene but terrible at answers this early on. But, depending on which death investigator the Coroner's office had sent, they might give Luka some helpful early presumptions to work with. Case like this, anything helped.

He glanced over at the neighboring houses. "You're thinking random?"

"Sure. Why not?"

"To start with, most home invasions aren't totally random." He bent to pull Tyvek booties over his Rockports. As Harper mirrored his actions, he noted that her chosen apparel for a past midnight callout was less fashion forward and more utilitarian: black Timberland boots, jeans, a dark green parka with ample pockets. He continued his didactic, "Houses for home invasions are typically chosen to provide the greatest and easiest return on investment." He waved a hand, gesturing to the street.

Harper turned and stared past the crowd. It took her a moment, then she nodded. "Middle of the street, hemmed in by neighbors within shouting distance, harder to escape from as opposed to a house closer to an intersection."

"Exactly." The Wright residence was also a modest townhouse as opposed to one of the larger homes, so theoretically less valuables waited inside. And, given the number of elderly neighbors, why choose a younger, healthy, able-bodied couple's house to rob, especially when it was obvious at least one adult was at home? "Even the violent, thrill-seeking home invaders, where monetary profit's secondary, they still look for victims easily subdued and terrified. They aren't interested in a fight; they want domination and subjugation."

Ian Wright did not fit that profile. This was a man who'd fought back, desperate to save his daughter. Luka had no idea why Ian had been targeted, but part of him already respected and admired the man. He felt a pang deep inside; his own parents had died trying to save his little sister. Too bad they'd died for nothing.

As they crossed the threshold into the Wright home, a weight settled on his shoulders, accepting the burden that came with every case. Ian Wright, the facts of his life and the answers to his death, was now Luka's responsibility.

"Tell me about the victim," he asked Harper as he snapped on his gloves.

Without consulting her notes, she began the rundown. "Dr. Ian Wright, age forty-one—"

"Medical doctor?" he interrupted. The duty sergeant hadn't clarified when he'd told Luka what little they knew about the victim and how he'd been killed. Instead, he'd spent most of their conversation defending the actions of the patrol officers who'd responded to the 911 call and who'd sent their two chief witnesses, the wife and daughter, to Good Samaritan before any detectives had arrived.

"No, that's his wife. Works the ER at Good Sam. Husband is—was—a Ph.D," Harper answered. "Professor of cyber security over at Cambria College."

From the doorway Luka could see the dining room to his left and beyond it a glimpse of CSU techs working in the kitchen. Opposite the dining room was the staircase climbing to the second floor. Luka turned to survey the front room. The living room—or parlor, his grandmother would have called it with its large bay window and ornate fireplace. Except that, unlike the parlor at Gran's, which was strictly off limits for children, saved for "company" only, this room actually appeared to be lived in. It wasn't messy, but toys and children's books gleefully mixed with tapestry pillows and silk throws. While the living room appeared undisturbed, both the dining room and steps had signs of a struggle that had progressed from one area to the next.

"Wright was a member of CERT—the national cyber emergency response team—and consulted for the government," Harper continued her recitation.

"For who?"

"Who? You mean which government Wright worked for? Us. Our government."

"Which government agency?" Luka finally stepped forward, still assessing the story the rooms told. From the photos arranged on the mantle and along the end tables, the Wrights had been a happy family, loving couple. He liked the way both husband and wife lit up around their daughter. And how they were touching and turned toward each other in every photo, no matter how candid. Couldn't fake that kind of emotion.

"Oh." She sounded disappointed that she'd already disappointed him. "All of them. Far as I can tell from the CERT website. HHS, CIA, NSA, Homeland, DOD, DOJ."

"So smart, talented, and trusted with classified material."

"Possible motive, then."

He shrugged, not wanting to snap her enthusiasm, but also wanting her to proceed with caution. "Too early to tell. Right now, our focus is on collecting as many facts as possible—even if they are contradictory."

She frowned at that. "But if they contradict each other, how do you know what the truth is?"

"Exactly." He stopped at the foot of the stairs and crouched down. A bouquet of roses sprawled against the hardwood, petals radiating out as if they'd been thrown to the ground.

Harper rushed to explain, "Wife got them at work from the husband, brought them home with her. Card says there's a surprise waiting for her at home."

Luka grunted as he straightened. In his mind's eye, he imagined the wife, panicked about her husband and daughter, making it halfway through the house before she realized she still held the flowers. He had first-hand experience of that kind of disjointed thinking—shock and awe distorting time, twisting logic as adrenaline took over. He kept his focus on the ground as if searching for clues, when really he was using the moment to force the image of Cherise's body from his mind.

After a breath he looked up at Harper, who hadn't noticed, too busy bustling around, making her own observations and judgments of the heart of the Wrights' home. They climbed the steps following the path the CSU guys had laid, avoiding crime scene markers and the fingerprint powder staining the railing and walls. When they reached the top, Luka heard the whirl of a camera followed by a bright flash from the room at the far end. The door had a cheerfully lettered sign: *Emily's Room*.

"As you can see," Harper said, indicating the damage along the walls of both sides of the corridor, "Wright fought back."

More to the point, Luka thought, was that their actor hadn't cut and run after being confronted. Instead, he seemed determined to outlast Ian Wright to get what he wanted. "Anything missing?"

Harper shrugged. "Wife said nothing obvious. Laptops, TVs, victim's wallet all seem untouched."

Making robbery less likely as a motive.

Cursing carried down the hall, making Luka smile. His favorite death investigator from the coroner's office was on the case. Luka set off, following the sound. He'd start by viewing the body and its surroundings. Then he'd finish with the complete tour before heading over to the hospital where his witnesses and their stories waited.

"What the hell?" Maggie Chen stood in one corner of the pink and purple bedroom, yelling at a uniformed officer as she stared at his phone. "Who the fuck are you to mess with my body?"

Luka joined her, although his focus was on the corpse. Ian Wright. The man had put up one hell of a fight—it was rare to see a body this devastated from a homicide that wasn't domestic in nature.

"Luka Jericho," Maggie said, waving the phone in front of him so vigorously she threatened to jostle the protective hood free of her sky-blue hair. She was in her late twenties but fearlessly bossed everyone once she took control of a scene—Luka had once seen her outshout a watch commander at a gang shooting. The dead belonged to Maggie and she fiercely protected their right to justice—one of the reasons why she and Luka got along so well. Kindred spirits in many ways.

"Did you see what these clowns did to my crime scene?" She tapped the screen and a video began. Two officers filmed by a third, awkwardly scooting the bed out from the wall and lifting the mattress, almost but not quite dumping everything onto the poor dead man suffering in silence on the floor.

"What were we supposed to do?" the patrolman argued. "Let her and the girl wait under there all night?"

Luka kept watching as a macabre scene played out before his eyes. A woman clutching a child tight to her chest, climbing out from behind the bed with the help of the officers. The child appeared unharmed but was pale, whimpering, obviously in shock. The woman had blood smeared all over her hospital scrubs and fleece as well as her hands.

"No," he told the officer even as Maggie was opening her mouth to ream the poor guy out. "No." This was directed at the death investigator. Maggie shut her mouth, lips pressed tight, but surrendered the point with a quick nod. "You did right." He jerked his chin to the door and handed the officer his phone back. "Get us copies for the file and give Harper your statement. Every detail."

"Yes, sir." Relief filled the man's voice as he fled the room. Now it was just Maggie, Luka, and Ian Wright.

Maggie resumed her photography, meticulously documenting the scene, her movements still agitated. The CSU team had already photographed everything, but the ME always wanted their own images—something that had proven invaluable more than once when a case went to trial. Luka stayed out of her way, simply observing and waiting, and pretending to ignore her unending spew of curses.

When he'd first encountered her, he'd thought maybe she had Tourette's. The swearing was relentless and unapologetic. But then he'd crossed paths with her at the scene of an obvious suicide—a man with terminal cancer—and instead of ranting and cursing, she'd sung a lullaby the entire time, the melody haunting him even after she'd packaged the body and driven away into the rain.

After their first few cases together, Luka had asked Maggie about her on-scene outbursts. To his surprise, she'd laughed. "You think I'm unprofessional? Some over-wrought, over-emotional woman, right?"

"No, but—"

"It's okay. That's actually one of the reasons why I do it. When I started, I was often the only woman on a scene, plus I was young, no one took me seriously. After a few episodes suddenly the guys leave me space to do my job properly." She gave him a wink. "No one messes with me now."

"Gotcha. You said that's one reason?"

She sobered, took a moment before answering. "What we do, there's no way to avoid emotions. If I can get them out at the scene, then I do my job better and I can go home and sleep at night." She shrugged. "My way of coping. Plus, I think it honors the dead. So many of us die alone, and then we become just another part of the system, a cog on a wheel, processed, catalogued, inventoried. It's so impersonal. Don't you think we all deserve better?"

Luka couldn't help but agree and nodded, wishing he'd figured out a similar coping mechanism for himself.

Now he watched as Maggie finished with her photos. She crouched on her heels mere inches from the body and handed Luka her camera. He stowed it in her gear bag before joining her. She seemed more upset than he'd ever seen her before. He thought about the video, the mother and daughter. "You know her, don't you? The wife? She's a doctor?"

She nodded, her gaze fixed on the little girl's bed with its matching ballerina sheets and mounds of stuffed animals. "What she did, to get to her daughter—"

"Tell me about her. Leah Wright." At this early stage, any insights were helpful.

"Did you see this room?" she said, annoyed he was missing what she saw as obvious. "Leah's a good doctor. Not just skilled. *Good*. Gives a shit. These are good people, this is a good man, good father."

The vehemence in her voice surprised him. He turned his focus back to the victim. "He put up a fight."

"You haven't seen the half of it." She took a deep breath, the emotion draining from her face. Once composed, she reached for Ian's hand, taking it in her gloved one with the careful caress of a lover, gently rolling it over so Luka could see the man's palm and forearm. Cuts sliced in random patterns, some shallow, others deep enough that muscle extruded from between the flaps of skin. "Defensive wounds. I think Ian was doing whatever it took to keep the devil away from his daughter." A small noise rumbled from her throat—the type of noise that would make a man think twice if he heard it in a dark alley.

"DNA?" Ian had fought back, so a good chance—Luka hoped—that the killer's DNA was caught under his nails or had transferred to his body.

"We'll see. Depends on how smart and how prepared our actor was. CSU hasn't found any trace of the weapon yet. Looks like he took it with him."

"What do you think it was?" Luka asked as he forced himself to take a closer look at the gouges along the right side of Ian's neck, arm, and shoulder. He didn't touch the body—was afraid if he did the damn head might topple all the way off.

"We'll do comparisons, but I'd say a hatchet. Maybe a short machete. Something that could strike with considerable force."

She pointed to one of the wounds. "But also with a sharp cutting edge—see how it's down to the bone?"

He didn't want to, but he followed her hands as she pivoted the body forward to reveal the right shoulder. "Not much blood."

"Not much time to bleed out. My guess is the gash to the belly came as he was up against the door. Should've dropped him— would've most men." She aimed her gaze at the open bedroom door. "He fell, leaving that smear of blood. Killer pushed the door open. Stepped past Ian—explaining that handprint on the floor where Ian props himself up, maybe makes a grab at the killer's legs. Killer swings down, slashing the neck, the arm, the shoulder, whatever he can hit, all the while dragging Ian across the rug. Then Ian makes one heroic last stand, shoving the killer away while he leans up against the bed he knows his little girl is hiding under."

Luka drew in his breath, the vision she painted as visceral as a punch to the gut. He glanced up, saw the spray of blood on the ceiling. "That only pissed off the actor."

"Exactly." She made a slashing motion with her hand, the chop of a hatchet over and over. "He went into a frenzy. Just about decapitated Ian."

Luka pushed up to standing, glancing around the room. "And then what? He didn't go after the girl. Was gone by the time the wife got home. Didn't steal anything—at least nothing obvious. What the hell did he do next?"

Maggie carefully repositioned Ian Wright's body and covered him with a sterile shroud, as if tucking him in for a long sleep. Then she gestured to faint bloody footprints marked by CSU tags. Luka followed her out to the hall where the footprints stopped in front of the pile of dirty laundry. "He grabbed something to wrap over his bloody shoes or he simply stopped and took them off."

"And then?" he asked, not seeing any crime scene markers to indicate the killer's path from there.

"Then he walked away. Vanished."

CHAPTER 4

At three in the morning, Good Sam's ER was at its most quiet. Although the nurses and staff never used the "q" word. Instead, three a.m. in the ER was known as the dead hour.

Leah embraced the quiet. She cradled Emily on her lap in the finally empty exam room across the hall from the ER's glass-walled waiting area and allowed the silence to invade her mind, crowding out all thought and feeling—at least for a minute.

The frenzied moments that brought them here had already blurred together, almost as if they'd happened to someone else, not Leah. Not Emily… Not Ian. The ride in the ambulance. Leah and Emily strapped to the gurney. Emily on her mother's lap, clutching Leah, as the police officer repeated back what Leah told him while the medics avoided eye contact. Leah didn't hold it against them; it was a constant fear among first responders, that despite their best efforts, their families weren't immune to the dangers they fought.

Then being whisked through the ER, past the triage nurse who sobbed as she took a moment to try to comfort Leah, into this room, a quiet side room usually used for sutures and orthopedic procedures. The policeman—he told Leah his name several times, but she still couldn't remember it—waited with them.

"Daddy, Daddy, Daddy," Emily kept crying as she clung to Leah, her volume a rollercoaster climbing from a whimper to a shriek and back again.

Rita, the charge nurse, entered, a collection of paper evidence bags and the ER's digital camera in her hands.

"None of us know what to say," she told Leah.

Leah had no words, simply nodded, relieved that it was Rita. The charge nurse and Leah were a lot alike, both able to focus on the job at hand, no matter how difficult. Leah could depend on Rita; she wouldn't break down, and that would make what happened next as painless as possible.

"Just know, we're here for you," Rita continued as she sorted her evidence collection supplies. "Anything you need, you just ask."

Which would have been a comfort if Leah could find the energy to think far enough ahead to know what she needed. Right now, it took everything she had to remain calm for Emily. The last thing her daughter needed was to see her mother break. Leah swallowed her emotions like shards of broken glass. Emily. She had to keep it together for Emily.

It was what Ian would want. *Ian, oh God…* Leah closed her eyes, her face buried in Emily's hair, forcing the image of him from her mind. *Don't think, just do. Get through this. For Emily.*

Numbly, Leah followed Rita's instructions, posing Emily on her lap for photos, first with Emily's PJs on, then again once they stripped them off, documenting her lack of injuries. It became a macabre game of Twister as Emily screamed and fought Leah's attempts to move her. But finally, it was done. Now it was Leah's turn. Rita forced Emily's hands free from their white-knuckled grip on Leah and pulled her away to dress her in clean hospital pajamas while the police officer took over the camera.

As Emily left Leah's arms, she shrieked, shrill enough that the policeman jumped. But then the scream cut off, mid-breath, and Emily sagged limp in Rita's arms. Rita laid her on the exam bed, and she didn't move, her eyes wide open but not seeing, not responding. As if she'd surrendered, body and soul, to the horror of the night.

That's when Leah's heart crumbled. She'd thought seeing her daughter's pain was bad; this was so much worse. Anxious to get her daughter back in her arms, she quickly posed for the police officer, gave him her jacket, stripped free of her bloodstained scrubs, washed the blood from her hands and finally held them out for him to document. Once he'd finished, she only took long enough to dress in the fresh scrubs Rita brought, then she scooped Emily up off the bed, back into her arms.

The officer left, carrying his bags of evidence. Leah almost called out; those stained clothes represented her husband's final moments, but she reminded herself that they weren't him. Not really. All that was left of Ian was right here, on her lap. Emily. She had to protect Emily. Starting with: where to go from here?

Rita, with the instincts of every good charge nurse, anticipated Leah's needs. "I've put a call into psych."

It was a good idea—one Leah should have thought of herself. "Who's on call?"

"Dr. Kern. She's on her way in."

Leah sighed. Jessica Kern was the psychiatrist who ran the free clinic where Leah volunteered. She liked Jessica—everyone did—but her irrepressible eagerness wore Leah out at the best of times. "I didn't think Jessica took call."

"Not often. I have the nurses up on peds finding Emily a bed—they're short staffed, so it will take a little while. But she can't be discharged, not in her condition." Her words reverberated through Leah's mind. Not only was Emily virtually catatonic, but even if the ER did discharge them, they had nowhere to go. No home—not anymore. "In the meantime, can I get you anything? Call anyone for you?"

Leah was certain that by now her boss and all her friends at Good Sam had been alerted to her presence. She really couldn't start to imagine what she needed—except peace and quiet. She had no energy to talk to anyone, not even to thank them for their condolences or offers of help.

Rita gathered her paperwork and the camera, glancing across the room at the posters and brochures displayed for victims of violence. *Afraid to go home? Call this hotline; Victim of a crime? We're here to help; Feeling the shock and aftermath? Join our support group.* The posters featured artfully mussed-up models with blackened eyes and purple photoshopped bruises. Leah felt like she might vomit. How many times had she used all the same clichés? Had she actually ever been able to help anyone?

"Want me to call them?" Rita asked. "Victims' assistance?"

Victim. The label rankled. "No." Leah was surprised how normal her voice sounded. "Thank you."

"Okay, then." Rita hesitated, her hand on the door. "I can come back once I get this in the system. Stay with you. If you want."

Emily had her head buried between Leah's breasts, primal, guttural noises escaping her, otherwise unresponsive to the world.

"No," Leah said, stroking Emily's hair. "We're fine."

Rita pursed her lips, but left—propping the door open, presumably so the triage nurse across the hall could keep an eye on Leah and Emily. As if they were specimens on display. Leah shifted in her chair, putting her back to the door, hiding Emily from anyone who might pass.

Now, they waited. And Leah had never felt so alone.

Not even the time her mother had forgotten her at dance class when she was four and she'd had to spend the night with a classmate whose parents called the police when they still couldn't reach Ruby the next day. Of course, just as the cops arrived, Ruby came storming in flinging accusations, smelling of pot and booze and a strange man's cologne. One more friend gone forever, forbidden to play or speak with Leah.

Or the time Leah had chickenpox and Ruby couldn't take her feverish whimpering and left her for three days with a case of ramen noodles—the variety pack, she'd told Leah as if that made all the difference—and a box of Cap'n Crunch. She'd forgotten milk and Leah had scalded her hand getting the ramen from the microwave that she'd had to climb a chair to reach. She'd been seven.

And there were all the other times when Ruby would yank her out of bed or school and without warning drive her over to Leah's great aunt Nellie's. Over and over until one day when Leah was eleven Ruby simply never came back. Well, not for Leah. She'd still drop by Nellie's when she needed money—Nellie was a soft touch when it came to trying to fix Ruby's life.

Whenever Leah heard her mom's voice, she couldn't help herself. She'd think, *This time she's come for me.* And Leah would race to her room, grab anything she cared about, trying to cram seven tons of hope into a five-pound bag, wash her face, fix her hair, put on her best sunshine smile, anything so Ruby wouldn't think she was still too much work to love, and she'd dance downstairs to greet her mother, certain this was the day Ruby would take Leah back into her life.

That never happened. Most times Leah was lucky if Ruby even glanced in her direction. No matter how good her grades were or what special presents she'd made and kept safe for Ruby to make up for missed holidays, Ruby never said one word directly to her daughter, too focused on pursuing her transaction with Nellie.

Even now, in her best moments, Leah couldn't help but wonder, just for an instant, *Would she love me now?* and it galled her that decades later, that childish wish was still her knee-jerk reaction.

If Leah still wasn't over her own mother's abandonment, then how the hell was she going to help Emily get through what happened tonight? Not just seeing her father murdered, not only being terrified for her own life... but Leah hadn't been there for Emily. Her daughter had been alone in a house with her father's killer and she didn't even know how long for.

Several of the ER staff stopped by, offering condolences and help, but Leah couldn't avoid noticing the way no one touched her, as if violence was contagious, and how their eyes did a hit and skip every time they collided with Leah's gaze, glancing away faster than a car spinning out on black ice.

The sound of heels tapping echoed from the hallway. An older woman in her mid-fifties appeared in the doorway. Her blond hair was styled in an old-fashioned twist at the nape of her neck and she wore an equally vintage-style A-line dress with the kind of skirt that swirled with each step as she rushed to Leah.

"Leah. I heard." Jessica Kern bent down to envelop Leah and Emily in an awkward hug. Leah stiffened. Then she remembered: Jessica's own husband had died a few years ago, before Jessica moved to Cambria City. Leah felt guilty; she was certain there was a correct response to their shared grief, but right now she was too numb and exhausted to think of anything to say.

"You didn't have to come," Leah said. "It's three in the morning."

Jessica pursed her lips. "Of course I came. How could I stay away?" Her lipstick matched her shoes; she could have just stepped out of a Cary Grant movie. The one staring Grace Kelly or no, the one with the spies and Eva Marie Saint.

Leah's mind fogged for a moment, escaping her dismal present for a blissful past. Aunt Nellie had loved those old movies—she'd let Leah stay up late and they'd huddle on the couch, pop popcorn in the fireplace as they were transported to another time and place. Leah in turn had introduced Ian to them and he'd given her a box set of Cary Grant DVDs on their first Valentine's Day together. That and a tin of popcorn. They'd sat and watched movies all night long, not worrying about missing out on any fancy dinner or roses or other traditions, instead creating their own.

Jessica pulled the exam stool close to Leah's chair, sat, then laid a hand on Emily's head, stroking her hair. "It's a terrible thing. It's why I've come."

Leah's thoughts meandered to the charity gala where she'd first met Jessica and somehow allowed herself to be talked into volunteering at the free clinic. Andre Toussaint had bought a table for the ER and trauma attendings. It'd been right before Christmas. Ian had looked so handsome—different than Cary Grant, better in many ways, at least to Leah's eyes. Leah had splurged on a new dress—on sale at a discount outlet—and since they had no money to bid on any of the expensive silent auction items, she and Ian had danced the entire night. It felt magical, floating across the floor wrapped in his arms, as if they were alone in the universe, as if that night might never end.

"Leah?" Jessica asked. "What can I do to help?"

Leah had no answer. But that didn't stop Jessica.

"It might be too soon, everyone goes at their own pace, but I wanted to be here for you," Jessica said, her words coming in a rush. She seemed genuinely upset. It was a harsh contrast to the cold that enveloped Leah: solid, thick ice she wasn't sure she'd ever break through. It made the world around Leah feel blurry at the edges; all the noise and motion seemed very distant, nothing to do with her.

Jessica shifted her weight, reached a hand to Leah, then stopped and dropped it. "I never told you, but it happened to me as well. My husband. What you're going through. Back in Chicago. Home invasion. Gordie… gone."

Leah jerked her gaze away from Emily to focus on the other woman. Beneath the carefully applied makeup, dark circles smudged her pale skin—as if they'd been there too long to ever be erased. "You think it's the same man?"

Jessica's eyes went wide. "No, sorry. No, they caught the—a drug addict who thought the house was empty. It should have been, but I forgot my phone and Gordie went back…" Now she clutched at Leah's arm, keeping Leah's focus from straying. "I know as physicians we're taught to always feel in control, never admit weakness. And working in the ER, you probably don't want to confide in the victims' advocates you see every day. So, I came."

Leah simply stared, Jessica's words still not penetrating. Did she want to do a therapy session, here? Now? Some small, rational part of her brain knew that research showed that earlier intervention after trauma led to less PTSD and other long-term effects, but the rest of her shuddered at the thought of breaking down and sharing her feelings. Especially with someone she worked with. Not now, she had to stay focused—for Emily.

If Leah had her way, maybe not ever. Maybe she could bury these feelings so deep she'd never need to experience them.

Rita returned, carrying a small tray with medication. She held the tray out as if an offering.

"I ordered a dose of midazolam. Thought it might help," Jessica said, standing up and moving aside so Rita could reach Emily.

Midazolam. A powerful sedative with the welcome side effect of mild retrograde amnesia. Something else Leah should have thought of—would have thought of for any other patient, in any other circumstances. "Thank you."

Leah knew the sedative wouldn't be enough—not after what Emily had suffered—but it should get them through the night. Four hours and twenty-seven minutes until morning. She could do that. Four hours. Twenty-seven minutes.

After that, all she could imagine was an abyss. A future without Ian. The prospect felt dark, a black hole devoid of life. Impossible to fathom.

Emily didn't even flinch when Rita gave her the shot. Rita left once more, and the sedative kicked in. Emily finally relaxed, her entire body sighing in relief, leaving Leah's skin blanched bloodless where Emily had held her in a death grip.

"There we go," Jessica said, resuming her seat on the stool, her skirt swishing as she folded it around her legs. Leah still marveled at how put-together the psychiatrist looked at three in the morning. But that was Jessica, never a hair out of place or seen without her makeup. "Tomorrow I'd like to start therapy for Emily—we'll combine it with the forensic interview the police will no doubt insist upon."

Leah jerked, banging her elbow on the chair arm. "She's a witness," she said more to herself than Jessica, trying to drill down on what that implied for her daughter. How many children had she interviewed at the Crisis Intervention Center, documenting their own abuse or preparing them to testify? Had she done more harm than good, extracting their stories? How could she trust anyone to invade Emily's psyche that same way? Force her to re-live Ian's murder?

"Exactly. I'm assuming you'd prefer me, with my experience in dealing with traumatized patients, over one of your ER colleagues who usually man the CIC. I can safeguard Emily, help her to only need to go through this once while also giving the police everything they need."

Leah nodded, not because she was following, more because Jessica paused and seemed to expect it. Jessica reached around Emily to pat Leah's arm again. "And after Emily, we'll get started with you. Unless you'd like to talk tonight? Walk through what happened? It might be helpful."

"No." The single syllable was dragged out along with all of Leah's breath. She'd already spoken to the police officers, who said a detective would be coming to hear everything and she didn't have the strength to go through it more than she needed to. Jessica leaned back as if she took Leah's refusal personally. "No," Leah repeated, her tone modified. "Thank you, though."

"Okay then. But the sooner the better, you know that." Jessica's gaze moved past Leah to the victims' advocacy posters. "The one thing the victims' groups—don't you hate that word, victim? As if everything else you've accomplished in life is suddenly negated by that label?" Jessica took a breath before continuing, her tone now more clinical, as if she'd closed the doors on her own emotions, resuming her professional façade. "Anyway, the one thing they get right, is that talking helps. So, when you're ready, call me. Anytime." She handed Leah a business card with her private cell number and stood.

Jessica headed to the door, then pivoted on her heel. "Take care, Leah. I truly am sorry you're going through this. But please know, I'm here. You are never alone."

And yet, with Ian gone, Leah was alone.

She pulled Emily closer, the silence enveloping them both, an insulation against the world beyond.

Finally, a nursing assistant appeared with a wheelchair and the news that Emily's room was ready. Leah shifted Emily's dead weight onto her hip and, ignoring the wheelchair, followed him to the elevator.

Once the pediatric nurses had Emily settled, they left them alone in their room, closing the door on the muffled nighttime noises of the ward beyond. Leah stank of blood—her hair was sticky with it—but she didn't want to leave Emily's sight, so she kept the bathroom door open while she washed her hair in the sink. Then she filled a basin with soapy water and carefully gave Emily a sponge bath, taking extra care to keep the water soothing warm and to gently comb free the tangles in Emily's hair. She didn't do as good a job as Ian would have. The thought ambushed her, left her gasping for breath.

Emily was usually an active sleeper, flipping and flopping and mumbling the night away. Not now. But it was good she was sleeping, blissfully able to shut off her brain, if only for a few hours. Leah crawled into bed with her daughter and wished she could switch off as well.

Time seemed to move in fits and starts, even occasionally spiraling backward or stopping altogether. As she lay there, watching the luminescent hands on the clock creep forward, Leah fought against the images of Ian that battered her exhausted brain. A muffled knock came on the door and it opened before she could say anything.

She sat up, expecting the nurse. Instead, it was a man in his late thirties. "Mrs. Wright?" he said, meeting her gaze without flinching or looking away. "I'm Detective Luka Jericho from the Violent Crimes Unit. I'd like to ask you a few questions."

CHAPTER 5

Hospital rooms made for less than ideal conditions to interview a witness, but tonight Luka had no choice. EMS had whisked Leah and her daughter away before Harper had arrived on the scene, so all Luka had to go on was what little information Leah had given the responding officers.

The uniforms had come up with nothing solid during the door-to-door. The townhouse beside the Wrights' was for sale and empty. A few people reported hearing the sound of a car engine or maybe a motorcycle going too fast down the street. Some had video doorbells that would help to determine the traffic on the block around the time of the murder once the techs downloaded and reviewed the footage. As for the rest of the neighbors, despite the fact that Ian Wright must have shouted for help, no one had heard anything above the sounds of their TVs.

The CSU guys were as pessimistic as always and this scene had an overwhelming amount of evidence to process, but the sheer level of violent chaos had Luka hoping their actor left some trace of himself behind. Blood and DNA from where his hand had slipped against his weapon, a stray palm print or skin trapped under the victim's fingernails. There had to be something.

What worried him the most were the bloody footprints Maggie had found. The CSU supervisor had examined them more closely and found that they were made by shoe covers, hiding the real imprint. Which meant their actor was smart enough to arrive prepared to literally cover his tracks.

But now, walking down the hospital's labyrinth of hallways, Luka couldn't help but notice how ubiquitous boxes of gloves and shoe covers were. Could the killer be tied to Leah's work as a physician?

He was glad he'd arranged for security to watch over Emily Wright. Good Samaritan's administrators had insisted on using their own guards—for liability reasons, they claimed, although Luka was certain the hospital would find a way to make a profit on the arrangement—and Luka's commander had agreed, citing his own budget concerns over the cost of assigning an uniformed officer around the clock.

When Luka reached Emily's room on pediatrics he knocked and looked inside. The nurse said Emily was sedated, but he knew Leah wouldn't be asleep, might never have another good night's sleep again, not after tonight. It'd been seventeen years since Cherise died and still, more nights than not, he woke from night terrors, trying in vain to save her.

What made him hesitate was the girl. From what little he could see of her on the patrolman's video he'd thought she was a toddler. Had hoped she might be young enough to never remember, no matter how compromised that might leave his case—any decent person would wish that. But now, lying still on the bed, her mother holding her, he saw she was older, five or six. Old enough to remember. Old enough to be forced to relive it again and again if—*when*, he promised himself—they found the killer and the case went to trial. He paused long enough to whisper a prayer before stepping inside and introducing himself.

Leah raised her head to meet his eyes. The light spilling in from the hallway fell short of reaching her, leaving her in shadow. Luka had run a NCIC check on her as well as a Google search. He knew what she looked like, all her vital statistics: she was thirty-four years old, had brown eyes and brown hair, a clean record and three years left on her driver's license before it expired. She was a Penn State undergrad, went to Johns Hopkins med school, and had been an emergency medicine residency at Pitt before moving to Cambria City four years ago. He'd even found a few videos, interviews she'd done with local TV stations, public service announcements, and the like.

But nothing prepared him for the woman herself. Most victims' families would see him and immediately start asking questions, filling the silence with anything, whether tears, protestations, denials, prayers, demands… Not Leah. She moved slowly, sliding out of the bed, beckoning him to follow her, and he did. She wasn't tall, the five-five on her DL a bit of wistful thinking, and moved with the posture of a dancer. As she passed him, he smelled shampoo and saw that her hair was wet, masses of dark curls resting heavy on her shoulders.

She crossed the sliver of light escaping through the half-open hallway door, and he could see that her lips were pressed tight, as if it took every ounce of energy not to scream. Taut muscles corded her neck, and she probably didn't realize it, but both her hands were tightened into fists.

He closed the door to the hall behind him, softly, without a sound and she led him into the bathroom. There was a nightlight glowing above the nurse's call button between the sink and toilet. Leah positioned herself leaning against the sink, facing the open door and through it her daughter.

Luka hesitated, not wanting to stand between her and the girl—worse than getting between a mother bear and a cub; even a childless bachelor like him knew better than that—but it felt inappropriately intimate to sit on the toilet or crowd in beside the shower stall. Definitely not a conducive environment for an interview.

"There's a room down the hall," he started, already floundering and knowing it. His voice boomed against the tile walls, ricocheting back to him. He cleared his throat and tried again, softening his tone. "Or we could—"

All she did was move her eyes. Not her face. Only her eyes. A quick flick dismissing his suggestions before her gaze settled back on her daughter's sleeping form. "No. I'm not leaving her."

He gathered a breath, stepped past her to take up a position opposite, leaning against the towel rack. "I understand."

Luka was used to allowing witnesses to set their own pace—he'd long ago realized that everyone had a story to tell, if you had the patience to let them tell it their way. If this was how Leah needed to tell hers, so be it. But it wasn't often that a witness was able to unsettle him so thoroughly—and quickly.

"Did you catch him?" she asked. "Did he say why? Why us? Why—Ian?"

"No, ma'am. We're still investigating." He slid his phone free, reached across the space separating them, and set it on the small glass shelf above the sink. "I'll be recording this, if you don't mind."

She nodded. "I understand."

"Later, we'll do a formal interview down at the station." Probably more than one—new questions always arose in a case like this, new memories unveiled as shock receded. "I might also need to ask you to walk through the scene—your house." He wasn't at all certain about the last, in fact, he'd prefer to avoid it. Victims always underestimated the trauma of returning to the scene in the light of day. But right now he had so little to go on, it might be necessary, if only to see if anything had been taken by the killer.

"I'll go, but not Emily," she replied, obviously assuming he meant some sort of reconstruction.

"Is there anyone you want me to call for you? Family? Friends?"

She blinked as if surprised by his question, as if it had never occurred to her to ask for help. "Ian's parents, they're in Seattle. I need to call them…" Her words trailed off.

"The coroner's office can make arrangements for someone to go to their home, tell them in person."

"No, no." She was shaking her head even though her gaze never left her daughter, giving Luka only her profile. "I'll do it. I just need—" Now she closed her eyes for a long moment. "I'll do it."

He didn't push the point, allowing her the pretense of control over at least one small portion of her life. "Anyone I can call, for you? To help with your daughter?"

Another, longer pause. He'd been hoping for a list of family contacts—they were always good for background on the victim. But he'd made a mistake when he mentioned Emily. Leah's expression went stony; there was no way in hell she'd trust anyone with her daughter.

When she didn't answer, Luka pivoted. "Tell me about yesterday. Start in the morning and walk me through your day. Anything that stood out, anything you think I should know."

Her hands were braced against the edge of the sink, fingers gripping it tight as if that was the only thing keeping her on her feet. But she nodded again, even though she still wasn't making eye contact, staring past him out the door. Her chest rose as she took one breath, then another.

As he watched the emotions roil through her, barely perceptible, Luka realized how hard she was working to compartmentalize her feelings. It made sense; she was an ER doctor, used to dealing with blood and trauma in others—of course she'd take control, distance herself from feeling anything, especially with her daughter to care for. His job was to break through those barriers, extract the information he needed to find her husband's killer.

"Yesterday," she finally said, her voice low as if reading a bedtime story. Or, more likely, amazed to discover that yesterday still existed in her memory, on the other side of the crevasse that separated now from then. "Yesterday was a normal Monday. I'm working noon to midnight this week. No matter my schedule, we always try to have breakfast together. Ian got Emily ready for school, he was dressed for morning office hours and then he was off the rest of the day. I was still in my pajamas—" A ghost of a smile flitted across her face. "Emily got them for me for Christmas. Dancing hippos. And then..." Another breath. "Then they were gone. The house was quiet. A good kind of quiet. Peaceful."

He nodded—not that she was looking in his direction. Luka totally understood what she was describing; he enjoyed that sort of quiet too. It would explain the well-lived-in living room, truly a family room, the center of their days and nights. He had a feeling when they ran the credit cards and financials they weren't going to find many charges for nights out on the town. Groceries, clothes for a growing girl, Netflix or the Disney channel, maybe a few trips to the local museums—three tickets, two adults, one child.

Family like that, with a capital F—he'd had it, growing up. Hoped he might again with Cherise. Before that dream died. He'd thought he'd left those dreams behind, outgrown them. But something about Leah Wright's voice as she described a normal day with her family, it woke a long-ago-smothered pang of envy, a desire for what could have been.

He forced his focus back to the present. Reminded himself that the first suspects in any domestic homicide were the family. Despite her rock-solid alibi, Leah couldn't be ruled out. If there were fractures in Leah and Ian's marriage, she may have taken desperate measures. And given the extreme amount of violence at the scene, Ian Wright's murder felt personal. Very personal.

"Tell me about your finances." He kept his tone level, knowing this was often where witnesses balked. But Leah didn't flinch.

"We're doing okay," she replied after a moment's thought. "Had to replace the furnace duct work a few months ago, so that set us back. It's my fault we're not more ahead—we want to start saving for Emily's college, but I have six figures of student loans I'm still working on. And Cambria College doesn't pay near what Carnegie Mellon did."

"Why did you leave Pittsburgh?"

"My great aunt Nellie, she had cancer. All she wanted was to die at home—took her two years. Only way to save her house with all the medical bills was for us to pay them off." Her tone turned wistful—as if she didn't regret helping her great aunt or saving Nellie's home. He wondered if Ian had felt equally as charitable, mortgaging their family's financial future to help a dying woman.

"Your husband's work—what can you tell me about it?"

"Not much. This semester it's mainly advising grad students and his government work with CERT—the cyber emergency response team. He started with them while he was at CMU before we moved here. That's all classified, so Ian never talks about it."

"Any outside jobs?" He couldn't get the image of the footprints with the shoe covers out of his mind. Maybe Ian had been targeted for his government work—but if money was an issue, he could have also gone over to the dark side, perhaps working for an illegal hacking ring. At this stage Luka couldn't rule anything out. "Consulting, maybe?"

"No, I don't think so. At least nothing he's been paid for."

"What did you do, after Ian and Emily left?" Luka steered her back to yesterday.

Leah shook herself from her reverie. "I took my time getting ready for work, didn't really do much of anything—read a journal on the treadmill, ran a load of laundry, grabbed a shower…" Her shrug was tight and angry. Resenting those wasted moments that she could never reclaim. "Then I went to work."

He gave her a moment before prompting her, "Anything unusual at work? Did you speak to your husband during your shift?"

"Ian never calls during a shift, unless it's an emergency. Usually I try to break away around Emily's bedtime, at eight, to call home, say goodnight. We chatted about her day, I promised to make her a special breakfast this morning." She frowned in the direction of her sleeping daughter, regret filling her face.

"Was that the last time you heard from your husband?"

Her frown deepened but she turned to aim it at him. "He said he was going to wait up for me."

"Anything else?"

"I didn't speak to Ian again, but—" She stopped, thinking. "Right before I left the ER, a bouquet of roses came."

"From Ian?"

"No, yes—I mean, I thought so. Who else would send them? But Ian never sends flowers on holidays. And never roses. He knows I grow my own, so when he sends flowers it's always a surprise, out of the blue, and something unexpected and exotic. Besides, he already got me the perfect Valentine's gift."

"Something he gave you before he left yesterday morning?"

"No. He had my car serviced while I was at work. If you need to, you can see the receipt, I left it in the car. It might help you track his movements for the day. The parking garage should also have footage of him picking up my car and then returning it."

He added those to his mental list of assignments for his team. "Was there a card with the flowers? Anything to say who sent them?"

"I guess maybe they were from Ian after all. The card said to expect a surprise when I got home—he said almost that exact same thing yesterday morning before he left and again when we talked on the phone. Maybe after our call, he knew I was having a bad day, so he ordered them from the gift shop? Just to give me a smile before I came home?" Her gaze drifted away, not focused on anything. "That's definitely something Ian would do."

They stood in silence, the glow of the call button as soft as candlelight. Luka felt a knot forming beneath his breastbone. He'd done the same for Cherise, buying bunches of bright blooms on "ordinary days" just for the chance to make her smile. He wished now that he'd realized exactly how extraordinary those days had been, each a snapshot of memory to be cherished now that she was gone.

He cleared his throat, bringing them both back to the task at hand. "Do you know what time the flowers arrived?"

"No." Her gaze cleared as she focused on his question. "I didn't see them until I was leaving for the night at the end of my shift."

"When you spoke on the phone, did Ian mention anything about his day? Meetings he had, maybe a phone call or someone came to the house? Maybe he was expecting someone?"

Creases dug into her brow as she thought. "No, nothing. We'd never invite anyone over, not that late at night." Married life, Luka thought. Where anything after eight p.m. was considered late. "After putting Emily to bed, he usually cleans up, reads, maybe works up in his office—he tries to wait up for me, but since we never know when I'll be home, half the time he falls asleep, reading in bed."

She glanced at him, that hopeful expression witnesses always got, wanting approval, some indication that what they said was actually helpful. Problem was, Luka never knew what exactly would turn out to be helpful, especially at this early stage. Right now, he was collecting information, following facts to see where they led—more often than not, it would be right smack into a dead end, but then he'd grab another thread of the timeline and follow that. The key to closing cases, he'd found, wasn't any flashy shootout or chase scene like in the movies. It was more about getting people to talk and then paying attention to what they said.

"Mrs. Wright." He purposefully avoided her professional title, wanted her thinking of her husband, her home. "Do you have any idea who might have done this? Any inkling at all—maybe someone watching the house too closely or possibly taking photos? A strange hang-up on the phone? Anything unusual at all in your lives lately?"

Her jaw clenched even as she nodded her understanding. And kept on nodding, lost in the image he'd conjured, her gaze distant as she considered. "No. No. Nothing."

Two denials more than he needed. He pressed her to be certain. "Maybe not something strange or out of the ordinary. Maybe not an overt threat, just an uneasy feeling. Maybe about someone you or Ian knew? Someone who'd want him—"

"No." The word exploded from her before he could finish. She flinched at the hollow thud of her own voice as it struck the tiles surrounding them, then stepped toward the door, watching her daughter anxiously. The little girl didn't stir.

"No," she said firmly but quietly as if she hadn't already answered his questions. "There's no one who'd ever want to hurt Ian."

Luka stood silent, giving her time to fill the void, but she said nothing, didn't even glance in his direction. Her shoulders slumped as if she were surrendering and she hugged herself. Now came the hard part. Over the next few days Leah would be telling this story many times, but Luka needed to be the first to hear it, naked and unadorned by any outside influences.

"And then you finished work and drove home," he prompted her, breaking the spell, her gaze darting around the tiny room, avoiding his face, finally settling upon her daughter once more.

"And then I drove home," she echoed, her voice remote.

Luka held still as she walked him through the discovery of her husband's body, stifling his breathing so as not to distract her. She was a good narrator, able to distance herself from most of the emotional distress—although he saw it in her face, she didn't flinch away from painful details—and she was an excellent observer. He knew a few fellow police officers who could learn from Leah.

And then she finished. He went back to review a few points—more for the recording to document her lack of uncertainty and the accuracy of her recollection.

Finally, they were back where they began: silence.

Until she asked the question he had no real answer for—he had details, advice, phone numbers, a tentative timeline, but not the answer she really needed. And that lack troubled him because he wished more than anything that he could provide the solace she sought.

"What do we do now?" Leah asked, her gaze fixed on her daughter's sleeping form as if the rest of the universe had ceased to exist.

CHAPTER 6

Before he left Good Sam, Luka swung downstairs, hoping the news of Ian's murder might loosen some lips in the ER. The desk clerk confirmed Leah's time of departure as well as her story about the roses.

"No idea who sent them?" Luka asked the clerk, a man in his thirties whose arms were covered with tattoos—not jailhouse art, but sophisticated well-designed graphics that reminded Luka of Japanese anime.

"Nope. The gift shop closes at seven but there's an area with vending machines. Has flowers, balloons, other odds and ends." The timing fit with the roses being bought from the vending area, not a gift shop clerk he could interview. Luka made a note to check out any CCTV near the shop before leaving Good Sam.

"You work much with Dr. Wright?" Luka leaned against the counter, reflecting the clerk's own casual posture. "What's she like?"

"All the ER docs do nights," he answered. "Leah's the newest. Took her awhile to find her footing—she's used to big time trauma centers, teaching hospitals where you can always call for help when things get too crazy. Once she asked for a derm consult on a Saturday night." He shook his head at the outrageous idea.

"But you guys are a teaching center, you have residents here." Luka had suffered through the multiple interrogations of several interns when he'd brought Pops in when his diabetes was first diagnosed.

"Residents from the Penn State and Temple programs rotate through here to see what life's like in a real hospital, away from the academic centers. We're only a level three trauma center—but they brought Dr. Toussaint in to change that, move us up to level two. That way we can keep more patients here and get more referrals—more money for the hospital." He leaned forward conspiratorially. "That's why he was so pissed at Leah when we had to close to trauma because of one of her patients. Kid was DOA, but she brought him back, tying up our last ICU bed."

"Which means you have to turn potential patients away?" Luka translated.

The clerk nodded. "Plus, the kid Leah saved was one the cops brought in. Turns out he was trying to rape a girl. Seems to me, guy like that, maybe he got what he deserved, you know? And who knows who we could have saved if we weren't closed to trauma? Already my shift, they've had to send two car accidents to Hershey instead of keeping them here."

Luka made a mental note. Technically the assault case was one of Luka's, but not one he had to worry about since the DA wasn't going to press charges against the bystander who'd intervened, making it an easy close.

He thanked the clerk and moved through the ER, talking to Leah's other co-workers. Their opinions were divided. The nurses and medics seemed to admire her, respect her abilities. Her fellow ER physicians voiced support, deemed her above average in competence—given that they seemed a rather competitive lot and Leah was the youngest member of their ranks, Luka decided this was probably a compliment. But the trauma staff who'd handled her DOA case uniformly damned her as arrogant and overstepping her bounds. Interest piqued, Luka made a note to interview the surgeon involved later, after he'd cleared higher priority items from his burgeoning to-do list.

He did take time to swing by the gift shop, confirming what the clerk had told him about the vending area, and noting a camera that might possibly tell them who sent the roses. Leah had called her husband after eight o'clock and the gift shop closed at seven. If Ian Wright ordered the roses before his call with Leah, then the gift shop should have a record. If he decided to send them after their phone call, as Leah had suggested, he must have called someone to pick them up from the vending area for him. And, if Ian Wright hadn't sent the roses, who had?

The flowers kept niggling at him as he drove back to the crime scene. It was four-fifty, the night at its bleakest, but he smiled as he pulled up to the curb a house down from the Wright residence. Other than the CSU van, a lone patrol car, and Harper's unmarked, all the vehicles had departed as had the press and the other residents. There was a scattering of lights shining up and down the block—whether they reflected an inability to sleep or a newfound need for increased security, he wasn't sure. Probably both. A crime this extreme and violent would impact the entire neighborhood whether people knew Ian Wright or not.

What made him smile, though, was that his timing had been perfect—he'd missed Ahearn and the other brass along with the media circus. Ahearn loved to insert himself into high profile investigations, and Luka had learned with experience it was better to avoid the Commander altogether. Otherwise he'd find himself and his team following Ahearn's priorities—which somehow always seemed to focus on anything press-worthy—rather than their own leads.

His smile was cut short as soon as he crossed the yellow crime scene tape and climbed the steps to the Wrights' front porch. Leah Wright's shattered expression as she described crawling over her husband's body to save her daughter haunted him.

He found Harper in the attic where Ian had his office. "Anything?"

"CSU just cleared it, so only just got up here myself," she answered. "Geek squad took all the electronics, so there might not be much left to find."

Luka stood at the top of the stairs and observed the room. It was an interesting space with its exposed brick walls, beamed ceiling that followed the pitch of the roof, and two octagonal windows that in daylight would expose sweeping views of the city. One corner had a thick play mat and held a child-sized easel, desk, chair, and an assortment of wooden brain-teaser puzzles. Between the two windows sat a large workstation that must have been assembled inside the room given the steep and narrow steps leading up to the attic. Empty space and dangling cables on both desks made the father and daughter workstations appear abandoned.

On either side of the larger desk were similarly inexpensive, utilitarian bookcases overflowing with a hodgepodge of titles ranging from histories of Russia, China, and India to fat, heavy art books, to biographies of composers and World War Two codebreakers, to poetry and kids' books, including every Dr. Seuss book ever written.

"You can learn a lot about a person—and his family—even without access to their emails, texts, and files," he told Harper. He crouched before the bookcase, his fingers caressing the volumes of poetry. The classics, of course, Tennyson, Dickinson, Frost, Eliot among others, but also a few that mirrored Luka's own collection. Robert Hayden, Chinua Achebe, Rainer Maria Rilke, Rita Dove.

"Well, so far all I've learned from rummaging through their kitchen is that they like Thai carryout and delivery pizza and that they're out of eggs and fabric softener." She turned to the small child's desk, eyeing the tiny chair with mistrust, then lowered herself to sit on the floor. "There's not much of a paper trail at all—I think, given Wright's job, these guys lived their lives online. I couldn't even find a paper checkbook downstairs much less a bank statement." She paused. "If Ian Wright was targeted and this wasn't a random home invasion, what kind of person could do that? With a kid right there in the house? And why leave the kid alive?"

Her questions paralleled Luka's own. "What do you think?"

She fiddled with one of the puzzles, considering her answer. "I think the violence is all for show. This was carefully planned—no, that's not the word. Orchestrated. But what I can't figure out is why. I've come up with two things. Someone was after his government work. Except, then, why leave the computers behind and why leave a witness alive? If you're that cold-blooded, why not a quick, simple bullet to the head for both Wright and his daughter? Then trash the place, make it look like a robbery."

Luka agreed it was a possibility. "And your second idea?"

"You're not going to like it."

"Go ahead. This early on, no idea is out of bounds."

She carefully placed the toy back where she'd found it. "The only person who would care if the daughter lived is her mother."

Luka was a bit taken back. Of course Leah was on his list of suspects, but he hadn't really given her that much serious consideration. But Harper had a point—a good point. If they were looking for a reason why Emily had survived the attack on her father there really was none better.

Harper reached under the little girl's desk to retrieve a stylus. "The geek squad even took the girl's iPad." She twirled the stylus around her fingers. "If she's anything like my nieces and nephews, there's going to be hell to pay in the form of tears and tantrums."

"Emily Wright is sedated," he told her. "And I doubt her iPad is what she'll be crying about when she wakes up."

She winced, obviously chagrined by her callous words. "Sorry, boss."

"No apologies necessary. It's totally understandable—gallows humor, distancing yourself in the face of this kind of violence. It's a healthy protective mechanism." He almost rolled his eyes—not at Harper but himself. He of all people needed to learn to practice what he preached. But Harper was young, just starting her career. Maybe she could learn better than he had. "Just remember," he finished. "These are people. We serve them. They deserve our respect as well as our best efforts."

She made a tiny noise that she quickly swallowed. "You sound just like my dad. He's a preacher."

"Didn't mean to give you a sermon. Just a reminder." It was the first personal piece of information—other than her career ambitions—that she'd shared. "How'd the daughter of a preacher end up a cop?"

Her hesitation made him regret the question. It wasn't his job to pry, only to observe and evaluate her performance. Decide if she was ready for promotion to detective.

"I'm the only girl, but I've got four older brothers who followed him into the family business." A tone of wistful regret underscored her words. "Guess I'm just the black sheep of the family." She attempted a faltering smile. "Literally. I'm adopted. They're all white."

Luka nodded his understanding, imagining what it would have been like, growing up in a family like that. Always an outsider, the equivalent of an asterisk on the family's annual Christmas card.

"CSU found no evidence the killer came up here," she said, turning the topic away from her personal life.

Luka remembered the booties that had obscured the killer's footprints. The lack of other obvious evidence. "This actor doesn't leave any evidence besides what he wants us to find. And if he—or they—were after Wright's work, this is where they would have come. Maybe they did take something like a hard drive or copies of Wright's work."

"Then it's up to the cyber nerds." She caressed the collection of wooden puzzles—none of them cheap, a few obviously hand-crafted.

Luka glanced below the desk beside him, spying a colorful stuffed penguin hiding in the far recesses. Dropped while sitting on her father's lap as he worked? Loving father, husband willing to sacrifice his academic career to move here and help care for his wife's great aunt… why was Ian targeted?

He slid into the desk chair. It was positioned several inches lower than he'd expect for a man of Ian's height—low enough to accommodate a squirming six-year-old on his lap. He opened the first filing cabinet drawer and found the usual collection of detritus that any top desk drawer held: pencils, pens, markers, paperclips, tape, stapler, sticky notes, an assortment of paper pads of varying sizes, and, a tumble of crumpled receipts and notes. Harper joined him, spreading them onto the empty space left behind by Ian's computer and smoothed them flat, taking pictures of each. Dry cleaning tickets, a variety of restaurant receipts—all places within walking distance of the college campus and all timed around lunch—a few random shopping lists and grocery receipts, and one from an art supply store.

That caught Luka's interest. Supplies for Emily? Maybe a school project? Sketchpads, expensive pencils, high grade drawing paper, charcoals, and pastels—too sophisticated for any kid. He turned the receipt over—there was writing on the back, a dainty feminine hand: *Tues 1pm, can't wait, Trina.* An address and phone number accompanied the note.

"Trina? Trina who couldn't wait… Who the hell is she?" Harper said in an excited tone. "Maybe our victim was having an affair? Could that have been what got him killed?" As she craned forward to examine the receipt and the note, her foot hit the stuffed animal on the floor. She bent down to retrieve it.

When she straightened, she was holding a long cardboard tube, the kind used to carry architect drawings and blueprints. "This was in the back corner, behind the file cabinet."

Luka pushed the chair aside and they both stood over the desk as Harper popped the plastic end cap off of the tube. Inside was a roll of thick art paper.

She spread the papers out over the desktop, framed between her gloved hands. Slowly, she turned each, revealing images of a naked woman in a variety of poses. All labeled "Trina" with dates scrawled in the bottom corner. Going back months.

"What do you think? Our motive?" Harper asked. "Maybe Trina's a jilted lover? Except, sure as hell no woman killed Wright singlehandedly."

Luka didn't answer, still examining the artwork, noting the intimate details, the loving attention to the model's expressions.

"More likely," Harper continued her theorizing. "The wife discovered the affair. Had an accomplice." She nodded, liking the idea. "Gave herself a rock-solid alibi saving lives in the ER while her husband's being killed."

CHAPTER 7

He'd driven all night. First, over darkened, empty side streets, zig-zagging his way through the route he'd practiced so many times he could pilot the motorcycle without thinking. His body and mind numb, blank. He couldn't remember where he'd come from—or where he was going. He only knew he had to keep moving, not slow down, not look back. Never look back.

He crossed the river on one of the older, two-lane bridges, the concrete scarred and pitted, jostling him. More than that, it was a shift in his awareness, as abrupt as jumping from fourth gear to second, speeding around a tight curve too fast.

Like waking up and remembering a bad dream.

He paused at an intersection, the bike idling, a monster preparing to pounce. He was meant to go right, head down the service road beside the highway where there were no cameras. But every time he looked that way, something tugged him in the opposite direction. As he peered through the pre-dawn mist rolling down the mountain, he saw a golden glow inviting him to turn left instead of right, to follow his heart.

His body rebelled when he steered the bike to the left and accelerated, gears whining as he missed shifts, the entire bike wobbling as he struggled to control it. He focused on the golden glow; it flickered, a candle floating through velvet shadows. For a moment, only an instant, shorter than a firefly's light-span, he saw a grinning boy standing beyond the glow, calling to him, inviting him to play. His heart pounded but his breath came easier at the sight of his son. His heart. His home.

What had he done? His vision was stained red by blood smearing the visor of his helmet. Not his blood. He pushed the visor up, the icy air slapping him until tears welled, every breath bringing with it the scents of firewood burning and pine needles. What had he done?

A woman's face appeared, floating against the blood-red of his vision. She held a baby—their baby. His son. Was it her voice he heard, thundering down every nerve ending? It didn't matter. His son. His beautiful baby boy. All this was for him, to save him.

He sped toward the river. The valley was quiet—the kind of quiet you could only find this time of night. The dead hour. A light shone in the distance, off the road—the old Quinn place, the new owner a chronic insomniac. Past that lane, the church and graveyard where the white-washed walls and silver granite tombstones gave off a ghostly glow in the dim starlight. As always when he passed the graveyard at night, he crossed himself.

Then he spotted it, the welcome bright yellow of his porch light. He turned down the gravel lane, spun to a stop in front of the small house, and padded silently up the porch steps. He didn't go inside, not covered in another man's blood, but crept around the side of the house to his son's window.

He pressed his gloved hand against the glass. His angel. Still asleep, so peaceful, curled up in the race car bed he'd built for him. He'd used a crib mattress, sized the bed perfectly to fit a toddler. His beautiful boy.

Her words repeated in his mind. *Finish it. It's the only way to keep him safe. We need to do this—for him.*

Bowing his head, he turned and silently headed back to the bike. He knew she was right—he had to save his son. No matter the cost.

He drove out to the carwash at a strip mall near the interstate, his mind wandering like a creek during a drought, starved down to a path so thin and thready that it felt as if he'd vanished into the earth, never to be seen again. When he tried to remember his past, all he saw was the woman holding a baby. She was angry—at him. They sat at a steel table in some sort of cafeteria. She wore a pretty summer dress, her hair was shiny, let down to dance over her shoulders, just the way he liked it. He wore a cotton uniform—and so did all the other men gathered around other tables surrounded by other women and children. Prison. He'd been in prison.

A flicker of recognition almost came to life, but it died as he focused on his baby boy, while the woman, his son's mother, vanished. Just as she was gone in real life, he somehow knew. Now it was just him and his boy.

He had to keep his son safe. That was the only thing that mattered. More than his own life. More than anybody's.

CHAPTER 8

Being an ER physician meant making decisions quickly and Leah's intuition had always guided her. Until now.

Now she had dozens upon dozens of choices but she couldn't face any of them. She felt overwhelmed by the urge to crawl under the covers and imagine yesterday was all a dream.

She had the phone number of the victims' advocate she could call for support, but every time she opened the glossy brochure and saw the damaged souls depicted there, she felt trapped. How had she become a victim? That wasn't her. Leah was the one people called upon in their time of need.

How could she work with those people ever again if she gave them access to her private hell? Bad enough the police were burrowing through her dirty laundry—literally and figuratively. But to lay claim to the title of "victim" and invite strangers to hold her hand while she called Ian's parents? Or found a motel room or shuttled her Subaru from where it was still parked in her garage? Or ran to Walmart for clothing and underwear and supplies for her and Emily? She crinkled the brochure into a ball and tossed it into the trash.

A glance at Emily's sleeping form left Leah's stomach lurching as if she had tumbled down an endless abyss. She *would* do this. They would get through this. She just couldn't think too much about what "this" really was, that Ian was gone, that she was all Emily had left.

Leah picked up the breakfast menu the nurse had given her and tried to focus on the choices. She sat staring without seeing, the letters an inky blur floating over the page, when a soft knock came at the door.

Maggie Chen poked her head into the room. "Okay if I—"

Leah nodded. She was too tired to move from the chair to the relative privacy of the bathroom, but Emily hadn't stirred, not even when the nurses came and took her vitals, so Leah simply gestured to the empty chair beside her. Even that movement left her drained, her hand falling into her lap, surrendering the fight against gravity. It felt strange that Maggie was the investigator assigned to Ian's case by the medical examiner; although since Leah had met most of the death investigators, odds were they'd send someone she knew and Maggie was by far her favorite. She frowned, trying to remember—yes, Ian had actually met Maggie. A few months ago at the free clinic fundraiser. Was it weird for Maggie, working on someone she knew?

"How's Emily?" Maggie interrupted Leah's ping-ponging thoughts.

"Sedated." Leah didn't mean to sigh—it felt like wallowing in self-pity and she had no time for that, there was too much to do. "I have no idea how I'm going to tell her."

"There's no right or wrong words." Death investigators were charged with next of kin notifications, so Maggie spoke from experience.

"I can't even decide what to order for breakfast, much less—"

"Let me help with that." Maggie slid the menu and pencil from Leah's limp fingers. "Breakfast is actually the best meal they do, so you can't go wrong." She pursed her lips, checked a few boxes, then left to deliver the menu to the nurses' station. Leah barely noticed she was gone and didn't look up when she returned. "Lucky break, got it in just as the dietician was collecting."

Maggie settled back into the chair she'd vacated. They sat in silence, the sun rising outside the window, coloring the room in a bruised purple light. This was a different silence than the one that had haunted Leah during the night. That silence had been crowded with voices—and screams.

"This is probably the most difficult thing you'll ever go through," Maggie finally said. Leah agreed, but said nothing—what was there to say? "Can I tell you something my grandmother once told me?"

Leah shrugged, inwardly cringing at the thought of more empty words for her to accept and thank someone for—her gratitude was definitely running on empty, the same as every other emotion. Empty. Hollowed out. Unable to connect with reality. Maybe she was a ghost? Or dreaming? Maybe this never even happened. She could hope.

"My grandmother, she told me that grief is the price we pay for love. But love is what saves us from grief." Maggie's voice surprised Leah; she'd forgotten she was even still there, sitting beside Leah, close enough to touch.

A tiny noise emerged from Leah—she almost didn't realize it came from her. A cross between a sigh, a sob, and a gasp of recognition. Huddled in the unfamiliar, uncomfortable chair—her legs tucked under her just as they would have been if she were back home on her couch, Ian beside her—she suddenly felt a weight settle on her shoulders. Not an unpleasant weight, rather a familiar, comfortable one: Ian's arm. Wrapped around her, supporting her, not letting go.

Her throat choked with unshed tears; all she could do was nod. Maggie rested her hand on Leah's and their silence continued. Except in Leah's mind it was anything but silent. Instead, she heard Ian's voice. "I've got you," he whispered as the morning light stretched the shadows beside her, completing the illusion that he was actually there. "You can do this." And then, with a ghost of a sigh that raised the hairs on the back of her neck. "I love you."

"Is Ian... he's downstairs?" Leah finally asked.

"Yes. That's why I came up. I have a few questions. When you're up to it."

"Who's going to…" Leah trailed off once more. For some reason she couldn't find the words to finish her thoughts.

Thankfully Maggie filled in the blanks. "Ford Tierney. He's the best. Ian's in good hands."

"When?"

"Later this morning."

"I should be there."

Maggie laid her hand over Leah's. "No. You shouldn't. He wouldn't want you remembering him, not like that."

"It's no worse than finding him—"

"I know, but still. You know what an autopsy is like. Clinical, detached. Ian won't be Ian, not there and then."

"Just another piece of evidence."

Maggie didn't waste Leah's time with vague platitudes. "It has to be that way."

Against her will, Leah nodded. "But someone should be there—for him. To honor what he did, what he went through, protecting Emily."

"Letting us do what needs to be done to catch his killer is the best way to honor him. That and your being here for Emily. Right now she needs you more than Ian does."

Leah understood—at least the logical, clinical, physician part of her brain did. But the rest of her wanted to scream and kick against the idea of her husband being diced and sliced with no regard to the man he once was. And, shamefully, not a small part of her knew it was easier to act as witness for Ian downstairs in the morgue than to stay here and fumble her way through caring for Emily, worried that each step through the emotional minefield her daughter was stranded in might detonate, cause irreparable damage.

"You'll be there?" She was doing more than asking Maggie.

"I will. And Luka as well."

"Luka?" The name felt familiar, but Leah's mind couldn't hang onto it.

"Luka Jericho. The lead detective."

"Right. He was here earlier. Gave me his card. I just—I'm not remembering names, faces like I should right now."

"That's normal."

"Jericho. Where do I know that name from?"

"Luka's from across the river. Would've been a few years ahead of you in school. Growing up, did you ever go apple picking or do the hayride out at Jericho Fields? Or the history class field trip? Their farm was a stop on the Underground Railroad."

"Right. They used to stock Nellie's lavender chocolate and her honey in their store."

"Those are Luka's grandparents. Were. His grandmother passed last year."

"Jericho Fields. I loved going there when I was a kid. We should take Emily—" Leah stumbled. There was no more "we." Only her. As if she'd been torn in half and the half that was left behind was a pale shadow of what once was.

Maggie waited patiently as Leah turned her head and sniffed, swallowing brine and sorrow. "If you have any questions—even if you think you've asked them before, it's no problem—write them down. Or if you remember anything from—"

"I can't forget," Leah said bitterly. "It crowds out everything else. It's all I can think of—that and Emily."

"Would you mind? A few questions?"

"You found something during your preliminary exam?"

"Probably nothing. Did Ian maybe have a blood test or give blood in the past few days?"

Leah shook her head, puzzling over the question. "No. His last checkup was before Christmas and he's never sick. He would have told me if he donated blood—usually he'll only do it when we have the blood drive competition between the ER and the police and fire department. Even then I have to bribe him. He usually faints as soon as he sees the needle." She glanced at Maggie, the other woman's face coming into focus for the first time. "You found a puncture wound?"

"Left antecubital fossa. Was Ian right-handed?"

"No." Which meant he could not have injected himself. It had to be the killer. Why take the time to drug Ian if it was a simple robbery? "Tox screen?" The question was more reflex than considered.

Maggie hesitated and Leah knew she was holding back. Because she wasn't speaking to Dr. Wright, the ER physician. Or Leah Wright, the friend who showed up when Maggie and her husband performed at local bars' open mic nights. Maggie was gauging her words carefully, straddling the line between friend and a professional charged with keeping forensic details confidential until the coroner finished his investigation. Right now, she was speaking to Mrs. Wright, Ian's widow. "Prelim was inconclusive. And his initial chemistries were abnormal. Sky-high glucose, lactate."

"He wasn't diabetic. Stress reaction—he was fighting for his life and Emily's."

"Maybe." Maggie didn't sound convinced. "We'll see after the full tox panel returns." Which could take weeks to months, Leah knew.

A knock on the door came, followed by an aide entering with the breakfast tray. Leah had never been a patient before and was quickly realizing how irritating it was to lose your basic rights to privacy.

Maggie stood as the aide set the tray on the bedside table and left again. "I'd better get going."

Leah stood as well, somehow finding the energy to walk Maggie out the door. The ward was waking for the day. A flock of white-coated residents gathered a few doors down, heads bobbing in an eager buzz of conversation; a pharmacist assistant pushed a med cart in the opposite direction, its wheels click-clacking with irritating precision; ward clerks were in the process of shift change, their voices a low murmur as they huddled over the computer, while the nurses gathered in their glass-walled conference room giving report.

Leaving Emily's room, crossing the invisible line that separated patient from healthcare provider made Leah feel as if she were trespassing into a restricted area, one she no longer had the requisite permissions to enter. "Please. Maggie. Let me know if they find anything. This not knowing, not being able to do anything—it's driving me crazy."

"I will. And let me know if there's anything I can do to help. I could call Ian's family for you, if you want, have the local PD send someone out to their house."

"No." Leah blew out her breath. "No. I need to do that. They're in Seattle, so I have a few hours before they'll be awake."

"Leah." Maggie rested her hand on Leah's arm. "I know this feels like a nightmare that won't ever end. But I promise you, it will. In the meantime, please don't forget, you're not alone."

Everyone kept telling her that, Leah thought as Maggie walked away. She stood outside Emily's room, the early morning buzz of the ward coming to life surrounding her, and realized Maggie's words, however well intentioned, were a lie.

CHAPTER 9

After Harper found the drawings of the mysterious Trina, Luka let her run with tracking the young woman while he took his time going through the crime scene and following up on the canvass of the neighborhood. He strained to understand why Ian had been targeted. The why behind a crime almost invariably led to the who.

The CSU techs were still hard at work by the time he finally left, an hour before the February sun could be expected to rise—if it was seen at all today, given the clouds gathering, blocking out the moon. As he drove away, he noted the TV vans returning, lining up to get live footage for their morning shows. He saluted them in his rearview, once again thankful for his timing. He only wished he'd been able to leave a bit earlier so he could drive out to the farm and check on Pops before his day became as consumed by the Wright murder as his night had been. But that's how a homicide went—chasing leads as fast as possible while memories and crime scenes were fresh.

He hadn't realized how hard it would be, looking after an old man who didn't want to be looked after. All it took was one burner left forgotten on the stove or a fall down the steps or... As he pulled his car into the secure parking lot at the station house, Luka made a note to call Janine, the home health aide he'd hired to help out, ask her if she could stay at the farm a few nights until Luka got this case under control.

The Cambria City PD's building hadn't been updated for decades, still housed in a five-story post-war building that could have easily passed for a VA hospital with its utilitarian yellow brick design and lack of ornamentation. An anonymous box—not unlike the apartment he'd lived in before moving out to the farm a few months ago.

Living at the farm he'd been surprised by a sense of rediscovery, an almost childlike joy in simply watching out the window, observing how even under a leaden winter sky, the world was in constant animation. For the first time since Cherise died he'd been moved to poetry. Not to write it—that creative well had been bricked over after Cherise was gone. But to read it, examine it, use it to see the world. Preserved in boxes in the rafters of the cider house, he'd found his old books, his favorite poets being those who didn't simply pour their own emotions onto the page but who rather used their insight to reveal the world for what it really was, beyond what the people sleepwalking through it wanted it to be. Keen observers not only of their environment but of the human soul. He'd devoured their words, hoping to absorb their insight, their vision… their clarity.

Luka reached the station's personnel entrance, bathed in the glare of security lights. He glanced down and saw a flash of color against the mud and snow beside the pavement. Three small flowers. Irises, his gran's favorites—Cherise's as well, although the ones he bought her were much larger than these miniature rebels. Two were a deep, vibrant purple and one was a bold yellow that dared you to ignore it.

And yet, he'd bet that of the hundreds of people who traveled this path day after day, he was the only one who'd noticed these valiant harbingers of spring.

"Having a senior moment?" a familiar voice called from behind him. Ray Acevedo, his second in command. Despite the fact that, unlike Luka, he'd had a full night's sleep and the advantage of morning grooming, he appeared grizzled beyond his forty-two years. Ray always looked like that—back when he'd worked undercover, he did so to disappear into the background, watching and listening while feigning a drunken stupor.

Ray held the door open for Luka and together they strolled inside, waving to the officer manning the desk.

"Hear we have a red ball," Ray said. "Told Denise not to wait up for me tonight."

"Smart thinking." The team would be running full throttle on the Wright murder in addition to juggling their other open cases, plus Ray and their fourth member, Scott Krichek, would be taking any overnight calls tonight. It might be a few days before any of them made it home for more than a shower and change of clothes.

Luka and Ray avoided the ancient elevator that was prone to temper tantrums and together climbed the stairs to the third floor where the investigatory units were housed.

"How'd the kid handle it?" Ray meant Harper, although technically Luka was three years younger than Ray.

Harper puzzled Luka. She was next up on the promotion list but had already been passed over by the other investigatory units—something she was clearly unaware of, given her attitude. When her file reached Luka's desk, he'd had mixed feelings. Her test scores were superlative, after six years on the street her jacket was still clean of any red flags including civilian complaints or official reprimands; she even had two citations for valor.

But the reviews from her commanding officers painted her as over-zealous, arrogant, ambitious, and an "independent thinker." All traits that would have been seen as advantageous qualities in a man, Luka couldn't help but notice. So he'd taken a chance and requested she be assigned to his squad even though officially she kept only her patrol officer's rank. Best of all worlds. He got the extra manpower he needed along with a chance to evaluate her firsthand. It made Commander Ahearn happy as well—patrol officers cost less than detectives.

"Didn't hear anything from the fifth floor," Luka said, referencing the top of the building where supervisors like Ahearn had their offices. "Maggie said she did okay. Plus, Harper gave me cover so I could take my time with the widow."

"What's she like? The widow? She a POI?" Person of interest—the politically correct term for anyone who tipped past mere witness into the realm of suspect.

"Too early to tell. She's—" Luka paused at the landing, searching for the right word to describe Leah Wright. "Self-contained. Hard to get a read on."

"Because she was in shock? Or because she's a conniving sociopath?" Ray asked cheerfully as he opened the door leading into the bullpen. He wouldn't care which was the right answer, as long as they nailed their man—or woman—in the end.

They wove their way through the maze of desks—most empty since day shift for detectives didn't start for another hour—Ray dumping his navy peacoat and canvas messenger bag at his desk while Luka went into his closet-sized office to shed his own coat. The floor's layout always made Luka think of an industrial floorspace: the assembly line gathered in the center, then small offices, interview rooms, storage closets rimming the periphery, anchored at either end by larger conference rooms. The cubicles were meant to be randomly assigned, but like always found like: the drugs and vice guys had clustered at the far corner, shoving their desks together as if defending the Alamo, their sergeant's office opposite Luka's, while Luka's squad was spread out in a semicircle, marking their own territory: their coffee machine and the "good" interview room with the chairs that didn't squeak.

He checked his messages—nothing urgent that couldn't wait—then arranged his notes to share with the rest of the team. Finally, he headed back out to the bullpen, weaving through desks to the coffee station. Every member of his squad except Harper had their own personal mug and beverage supplies arranged in cubbyholes above the machines. It was a sacrosanct space that no one, not even the vice squad pranksters, dared to invade.

Luka's own mug was a nondescript indigo blue ceramic that was so old he hesitated every time he reached into the microwave to retrieve it. Cherise had bought it at Target when they'd moved in together senior year of college. Seventeen years ago and he refused to replace it. Once, it had a matching partner. He rubbed the tip of his middle finger. The scar couldn't be seen, not after all these years, but he remembered the blood swirling through the soapy water after the cup had shattered while he was doing dishes, waiting for Cherise to come home from her LSAT review.

The night she never came home. The night the knock on the door had come and when he'd opened it, it'd been the police. The cut on his finger had healed but no amount of time could dim the memory.

The microwave chimed and he opened the door. What would Leah Wright be haunted by after last night? The sight of her dead husband? The feeling of crawling through his blood to get to her child? The vacant look in her daughter's eyes?

The mug was hot, too hot, enough that he couldn't pick it up by its body, had to resort to holding it by the handle. Seventeen years. Past time to let go, he knew. But he couldn't. He just couldn't.

Luka headed to the conference room that functioned as the Violent Crime Unit's nerve center. Scott Krichek and Ray Acevedo already waited at the battered conference table, a strangely elongated ovoid, seventies style slab of faux hardwood. Ray had his trademark Steelers mug of coffee along with a laptop and his reading glasses, while Krichek had surrounded himself with a special self-warming cup of some noxious hipster butter-coffee-mushroom combo that he called his brain food, along with laptop, tablet, phone, notepad and pen. Luka set his own mug of herbal tea—he was saving caffeine for later when he hit his wall and needed it—beside a fresh notepad at the head of the table. He enjoyed handwriting his notes; something about the scratch of pen against paper allowed him to think better.

"Where's Harper?" he asked.

Before anyone could answer, the door sprang open and Harper rushed in, juggling her tablet and a stainless-steel travel mug. "Here, here," she said as if this were rollcall. "Was following up—"

"On the donut run?" Krichek asked, stretching lazily. "Cuz I don't see any, boot."

Harper stopped half in and half out of her chair, a chagrined expression on her face. Boot was what rookies were called when they began their patrol training. With one word, Krichek had firmly cemented Harper's lowly position in the squad's hierarchy—the position he'd vacated when she came on board.

"Relax. Krichek wants donuts so bad, he can get them himself," Luka assured her, aiming a quick scowl at Krichek, who immediately sat up straight. "Give them the bullet."

Harper fumbled a bit at first with the summary, but then hit her stride, providing a coherent and accurate picture of the crime scene, enhanced with photos projected onto one of the whiteboards lining the far wall. Luka highlighted major characteristics of their unknown killer by writing them on a second whiteboard along with a timeline.

By the time Harper finished, his whiteboard was still almost completely blank. Except for a short list: the killer wore booties and undoubtably had forensic knowledge, nothing obvious was missing from the house, and, despite the extreme brutality of the attack, the killer left a witness behind. The timeline itself was not all that helpful: the time stamp from when Ian picked up his wife's car followed by his wife's phone call ending around eight twenty and then nothing until twelve forty-one when the 911 call had come in.

Luka stood at the whiteboard, marker in hand, facing his team. Krichek and Harper both leaned forward, palms braced on the conference table as if eager to race out and chase down errant clues and suspects.

"Thoughts? Ideas? Impressions?" He liked to open a case up, especially this early on. Eventually, the facts would build the story of what happened, but too often Luka had seen detectives settle on their story first, then twist the facts to fit the narrative they'd committed to. He'd found that brainstorming as many avenues of investigation as possible helped to prevent that tunnel vision.

Ray scowled at the photo of Ian's body projected on the whiteboard. "That much violence takes a hell of a lot of passion."

"Right," Harper agreed, coming close to interrupting him. "Passion. Like maybe from a love triangle." She looked to Luka for permission and he gave her a small nod. Usually he would have waited until after they dissected the crime scene before beginning to build a profile of their victim, but she appeared ready to burst. "We found these." She tapped her tablet and photos of drawings of the naked woman in her twenties appeared. "They were hidden behind the victim's desk. And there was this note, dated last year—maybe when they first met?"

"Wright was having an affair?" Krichek joined in, sounding eager.

"That's why I was late—tracking down the girl in the pictures," Harper told them. "Full name is Katrina Balanchuk, twenty-four years old, here from Ukraine on a student visa, getting her MFA."

Ray glanced at the clock: not even seven thirty yet. "Who'd you wake to get that info?" Meaning, had she tipped Balanchuk to their interest, maybe spooked her or given her time to bolster an alibi.

"Instagram and Facebook," Harper retorted. "She's not on Twitter."

"Loving husband and father, giving his own life to defend his daughter—or older married professor involved with a much younger student?" Ray mused. "Scorned lover seeking revenge? Or the wife discovered the affair, went after the husband?"

"No way a woman did that," Krichek said, nodding to the crime scene photos of Ian's mutilated body. Then he paused. "Unless she wasn't alone. Had a partner."

Luka tapped the marker against the board, snagging their attention. "Harper, what else did you learn while you were on the scene?"

"Calendar crowded with their work schedules and activities for the kid—only social event I saw was a Superbowl party. Tons of pictures of the kid, seemed like she's the center of their world." A hint of wonder crept into her voice as if she couldn't imagine such an insular life.

Neither could Luka. Hard enough helping his grandfather out these past few months since his gran died; he marveled at people who worked fulltime and juggled kids. Funny, because when he was younger, still in school, when Cherise was still alive, he hadn't dreamed of anything but having a family.

"Wright did government consulting," Harper continued. "I couldn't find out much last night. Maybe today I can make some calls to the feds."

That earned her a grunt of skepticism from Ray; the feds were not likely to share and if Wright's killing had anything to do with his government work, they'd want in on the case in the name of national security.

"Point is, this isn't a routine home invasion." Harper sent a nod in Luka's direction, indicating that she'd been listening when he'd schooled her at the scene. "Not with our actor leaving no trace of himself. And no way was Wright some random target."

"Let's start there," Luka said, reining them in. "Why Ian Wright?"

"Three Ps," Ray said. Harper frowned, not yet knowing the team's shorthand.

"Three motives," Luka explained. "Power, profit, passion."

"Definitely not profit," Harper said before anyone else could comment. "Nothing obvious taken. Not much to take, in fact.

I found paperwork for student loans they're still paying off, not to mention the cost of a kid. These guys might both be working nice jobs, but they weren't getting rich, at least not that you could tell from the house."

"Once we get the financials, we'll learn more," Luka said.

"What about life insurance?" Krichek asked. "What's the wife get, now that hubby's kicked?"

"Might also be a reason for the bloody overkill," Ray added. "Some policies you get double the payout for homicide."

"Not to mention saving the cost of a divorce and custody fight," Harper put in.

"Krichek, you work the finances," Luka said. "Have your warrants ready to go as soon as the banks open."

"You really think the wife could have set this up? Put her daughter through that?" Krichek said, reminding Luka of how young he was. Maybe not in years, but in experience.

"Wife got to play the hero," Ray reminded him. "That video the uniforms took is pure gold in the hands of the right defense attorney. She's an ER doc, blood wouldn't bother her." He looked to Luka. "Any vibes from the interview?"

Luka shook his head. For some reason it was difficult for him to see Leah as more than a victim. He reluctantly wrote Leah's name on the whiteboard beside Balanchuk's, leaving a large space below it where they would fill in the gaps with actual facts.

"Canvass pop anything?" Ray asked.

Luka nodded to the stack of field interviews the uniformed officers had submitted from the scene. He'd already reviewed them and prioritized a select few for follow up. "Patrol found three neighbors with doorbell cameras. Only traffic the cameras caught during our window was a motorcycle speeding down the street at eleven fifty." He added the data to the timeline with a note: *Motorcycle near scene.* "Video's too blurry to make any ID, but the tech guys are trying to clean it up."

"Our actor leaving the scene?" Krichek asked. "Makes sense. If he knew the wife's work schedule, he'd want to be gone before she got home."

"Why?" Ray played devil's advocate. "He could kill her just as easy as the husband if she walked in on him."

"Except she didn't—she called 911 from the back door," Harper put in. "If he was still inside, he'd have the cops to deal with, not just the wife."

"Maybe the wife was in on it, setting up an alibi," Krichek interrupted. "I mean, her shift ended at midnight, right? But the call didn't come in until twelve forty-one. How long's it take to get from the ER to her house? Maybe she was there the whole time, watching her accomplice do in the cheating hubby and made the 911 call after the killer left and was in the clear. Just saying—"

"We don't know if this motorcycle guy is our actor," Luka reminded the younger detective, before he could spiral too far away from the facts. "But he is someone we need to talk to. He could just as easily be a witness."

"Here we go." Harper's excitement bled into her voice. She scrolled down on her tablet and selected the image, transferring it onto the whiteboard. "Traffic cam a block away on Second caught a motorcycle heading away from the area. Timing fits, gotta be the same one. There's not much traffic in that neighborhood that time of night. A few cars, SUVs, but that's the only bike on that camera half an hour either way."

"Great, there you are. Go get him."

Harper didn't surrender to Ray's needling. "Plate obscured; driver's face shielded by a full-face mask on his helmet. Tinted," she added before Ray could say anything.

"I already put in a request for the tech squad to check the other traffic cameras, see if we can track him," Luka told her. Her expression appeared deflated—she obviously hadn't realized exactly how much he'd gotten done after he'd left her at the house.

"Not too many traffic cameras in that part of the city," Krichek said. Luka remembered that he'd worked that patrol sector while still in uniform. "You might have better luck with private ones. There are a few ATMs that might have caught him. And a jewelry store on the other side of the park, if he turned down Maple, headed to the interstate."

Harper nodded and made a note as if she planned to knock on every door herself. "Thanks."

"We've Casper the Fucking Ghost on a motorcycle, maybe our actor, maybe not. And an actor smart enough to cover his tracks—" Ray glanced at Harper.

"So far nothing from forensics. But they have a shit ton to go through. We may still get lucky."

That drew a wry chuckle from Ray and Luka. They both knew how fickle luck could be.

"What else do we have to go on?" Luka asked.

"What about the roses the wife got in the ER?" Harper asked. "The card was typed, not signed. And having them sent to the ER's desk clerk? Seems like a good way to make sure she had witnesses when she left Good Sam, setting up an alibi."

"I checked when I was over there," Luka answered. "The ER clerk confirmed the time. And," he added as Harper opened her mouth to ask another question, "the gift shop closes at seven but has an automated vending area."

"Cameras?" Ray asked.

"One that might have caught it. But we'll need a court order—and the hospital will need to review the tape first, make sure there's no patient confidentiality issues."

Ray was too mature to roll his eyes but Krichek wasn't. Probably because he was their designated warrant writer, spinning the slightest probable cause into warrant-granting gold.

"We should also check phone and credit card records," Harper put in. "See if the victim called and placed the order. And when, maybe narrow our window."

Luka frowned. Something about those damn roses... but if Ian hadn't sent them, who had? "So we might have both profit and passion, what about power?" he asked. "Who would want Ian dead? Maybe a rival at work?"

"A bit of overkill for a battle over tenure or some other academic bullshit," Ray scoffed.

"Don't forget the government consulting," Luka said. "Ian had access to classified and proprietary information, could be worth a lot to someone."

Krichek was typing fast. "How about a hacker Wright helped catch? I found an article saying he was instrumental in stopping those guys who stole over a hundred million by hacking that bank last year. Hundred million? That's one hell of a motive for revenge."

"You think some nerd who lives in his parents' basement playing Minecraft did this?" Harper scoffed.

Ray glanced at Luka—asking permission, since they usually kept their personal lives out of the squad room. "You do know, Harper, that the boss lives in his parents' basement."

Harper looked stricken. "Sorry, I just meant—"

"And he's like a ninth level wizard elf mage—" Ray broke down laughing. "Shit, I can't."

Now they were all chuckling, Harper joining in last, a bit uncertain if they were laughing at her or Ray.

"Relax," Luka told her. "No idea is a bad idea, not this early on. This is the time to brainstorm every possibility, see where the facts might lead us."

"If we actually had any," Ray put in. Luka shushed him with a glance—both Harper and Krichek were too new to this to discourage them this early in a case, especially one where nothing was as it appeared to be. He couldn't get the image of the boot prints

Maggie had found out of his mind—so cold, calculating despite the chaotic frenzy of the murder itself. Was there anything about the crime scene that he could trust?

Luka capped the marker, eyeing the whiteboard. Then he shook his head and erased everything except the timeline. "We need facts. Verifiable facts. I want this board filled by end of day. Ray, build the timeline, victim's movements the past few days. Chat up his neighbors and colleagues. And find this Katrina Balanchuk, see what she has to say, what kind of relationship she had with Ian."

"I can do that," Harper interrupted, obviously nettled that he'd given her lead to Ray. But Ray was an experienced interviewer and Luka trusted his judgment, while Harper was technically still a patrol officer, plainclothes or not.

"No. You work the forensics. Follow up on Ian's computer, the lab stuff. Keep on them—they just bought that fancy new DNA machine, supposed to be so damn fast, let's make sure they're using it. And find me that damned motorcycle."

"When's the PM?" Ray asked.

"First thing this morning. Maggie pulled some strings, got us Tierney."

"Nice." Dr. Ford Tierney, the assistant medical examiner, was painstakingly meticulous when it came to parsing out information, but he was also brilliant at finding the truth, taking nothing for granted.

"I'll go," Harper volunteered.

"No." Luka softened his tone. She was eager to prove herself, he knew. But she needed to learn to pace herself. Especially with a case like this. "I've got the postmortem. And I'll follow up with the wife while I'm over at Good Sam."

"Maybe the kid will be talking by then," Krichek said hopefully.

"Maybe," Luka murmured. But he had little hope that Emily saw anything—or, as traumatized as she was, that she'd be able to communicate it in a way that would help the case.

His phone rang. The farm's landline. "Get going," he dismissed his team and waited until they left before answering. If something was wrong it would be Janine calling from her cell, unless something happened to her? "Pops, everything okay?"

"Hey there, big brother."

Luka's fingers clamped down on the phone as if wanting to strangle it. Or the woman on the other end of the line. "Tanya. What the hell are you doing at the farm?"

"Whoa, nice to hear from you, it's been too long. Jesus, Luka, you always gotta be judging folks before you even say hello?"

"When they're junkies who've already stolen everything they can from this family, broken every heart they could, damn right I judge. Now what do you want before I send a patrol car over to bust your ass?" He was bluffing, but he couldn't stand the thought of her rampaging through Pops' house, stealing what little was left after the last time she'd relapsed and had come home.

That was almost four years ago—she and her "friends" had converged upon the farmhouse, conning his grandparents into feeding them, taking over the whole damn place, until Luka came by for Sunday dinner and found the house in shambles, all the cash and anything pawnable gone, his grandparents in tears over "poor little Tanya." Who of course had vanished like a thief in the night. Tornado Tanya was more like it.

"Nothing they can bust me for. I'm clean. Have been for a while now. Long enough to take care of some unfinished business. Family business."

"You're not a part of this family, not anymore, not after what you've done." His parents had gone into bankruptcy, had to sell the house he'd grown up in to pay for one of her stints in rehab. Their church had raised the money for another—except Tanya had never made it to the hospital. Instead, she stole the money. Still, they'd given her another chance, somehow scraping up the money for one last rehab—and it had killed them. His folks had died almost ten years ago—a car accident one snowy night, rushing to make it to Tanya's rehab before visiting hours ended. Luka hadn't seen or spoken to Tanya since. She never came to the funeral, not their parents', not their grandmother's last year.

"I need your help, big brother. Can't do this alone."

"If you think this family has any more money—"

"Don't need money. Wouldn't take it if you offered." Her words shocked Luka—not the Tanya he knew, wheedling and begging and outright stealing when those didn't work.

The conference room door opened. Harper, trying to get his attention.

"I'm busy," Luka told Tanya. "Can't talk now." He envisioned his schedule, tried to think of a window when he could meet her—here, in the city, get her away from the farm and Pops.

"Sure," she said before he could offer a time and place. "Big brother, big-time homicide detective. No time for family. Nothing's changed." She hung up.

Luka stared at the phone in his grasp as if it were a snake. What the hell was going on… Who had let Tanya in—was Pops okay? He started to call Janine, the home health aide helping him with Pops. Then he realized Harper was still standing there. "What?"

She jumped at his tone. Then gathered herself, standing up straight. "Look, I know I'm the new guy brought in from patrol, but I want to do more than just babysitting details. I've passed the detective's exam, I'm ready for more."

"Babysitting?" What was she talking about?

"First, you have me babysitting the crime scene all night long, and now I get to babysit the lab geeks, watch over their shoulders. Boss, I want to get out there, do something."

He swallowed the rebuke her words generated. Took a breath. "You're part of a team now. If you want to stay part of a team instead of driving a patrol car—"

"Yes, sir, I understand." Her shoulders stiffened as if she stood before a drill sergeant. "Thank you. Sir." She pivoted to the door.

"Harper," he called her back. "I'll call you when I finish at Good Sam. We can tackle Katrina Balanchuk together, let Ray focus on the neighbors and coworkers."

"Together?" The hope that brightened her face was impossible to ignore.

"You and me. But first, I need to get to the PM." Tierney was doing them a favor, scheduling the postmortem exam so quickly. Last thing Luka wanted was to irritate the hyper-punctual assistant ME by being late.

"Thanks, boss." This time it sounded genuine. He wondered if someone, somewhere had tried to break her and not in the "build them back up again" way. Was it something that had happened on the job? Or in her personal life? Maybe it was what had driven her to become a cop in the first place.

Luka glanced out the open door to the bullpen, now filling with detectives. Did Harper have what it took to join their ranks?

CHAPTER 10

As Leah watched Maggie go, she realized that Ian's death must already be on the news. What if the media tried to ambush Emily? A vision of reporters sneaking onto the ward, desperate for a story filled her mind. She had to protect Emily from more than the trauma of Ian's death.

She needed to prepare for what came next.

Leah slid her phone free from the pocket of her scrubs. The battery was almost gone and she still had to call Ian's parents. Barely past five a.m., their time, but even if she woke them from a last good night's sleep, she had no choice. Now she couldn't put it off any longer, because as soon as the news hit the internet, there was a chance they might see it. Telling them would break their hearts and she couldn't risk Emily overhearing.

The clerks had finished their morning change of shift. The new one—his name tag said Arthur Nguyen—glanced up as she approached the desk. "Dr. Wright, what can I do for you?"

"Have you seen—did what happened to my husband… is it… do people know?" She faltered, not sure of the new vocabulary that now defined her existence. Widow, victim, witness, grief-stricken, murder, shock… so many words she never dreamed she'd need.

"It was on the morning news," he said, not meeting her gaze. "I heard it on my drive in. I'm so sorry for your loss."

Loss? As if Ian was a misplaced wallet instead of part of her life. Loss? No. Gone? Too small a word. Passed. No. Expired was the medical term but it sounded too much like a sigh, a misbegotten exhalation. A gallon of milk past its due date.

Was there a word large enough to encompass her entire future without Ian? She doubted it.

"Thanks," she replied automatically. "Is there a way we can make sure no one bothers my daughter?"

"Yes, of course. They already have extra security on the floor, just in case..." Now it was his turn to falter. "I'll also alert the staff," Arthur finished. "Anything else I can do for you?"

Leah blew out her breath. The list of what she needed was growing by the minute: a shower, fresh clothes, phone charger, cash, her car, a place to stay, her daughter to wake up and miraculously have forgotten everything about last night, someone to call Ian's parents and tell them their only son was dead...

She started with basics. There were spare clothes in her office. And a phone charger. Plus, a little cash. "I'm going to run down to the ER, grab a few things and call my husband's family—they don't know what happened yet. Is there someone—" She didn't know the staff here on Peds, not like she knew the ICU and surgical nurses who often rotated through the ER. She turned back to Emily's open door, torn, reluctant to trust any stranger.

"Cindy from child life just got in," Arthur said, anticipating her needs. "Want me to ask her to sit with your daughter?"

Cindy? Leah knew Cindy—the child life specialist worked miracles distracting anxious kids down in the ER. "Cindy's here?" He'd just said she was, but somehow Leah felt as if she might have misheard through the low, constant roaring consuming her brain.

"Calling her right now. Emily will be fine."

Leah waited until Cindy arrived. Cindy had an air of constant, playful energy that was infectious, but her usually sunny smile dimmed when she saw Leah. "Leah," she said, then without waiting for Leah's response pulled her into a tight hug. "How can I help?"

Leah blinked hard, her throat filling with tears. Arthur came to her rescue. "Dr. Wright needs to attend to a few things. Her daughter's sleeping, but she doesn't want to leave her alone."

"Of course, I'll watch her. Emily, right?"

Leah nodded, swallowing, fighting to regain her voice. "She probably won't even wake, but… Call me if she does. I won't be gone long."

"Of course. No problem."

She checked on Emily one last time. Still under the spell of the sedative, Emily's face was relaxed as she slept. Watching her, Leah wished for so many things: that when Emily woke, she'd have forgotten all her pain and terror; for a way to speed them both into the future, past this awful, gaping wound of a present; for the strength and ability to make everything better for her daughter. Bad enough she couldn't save Ian; she had to find some way to save Emily. But short of a magic fairy godmother appearing to grant all her wishes, Leah was left with nothing.

She grabbed a few sausage links from Emily's untouched breakfast tray and forced herself to eat them as she took the stairs down to the ER—she wasn't hungry, didn't even taste them as she chewed and swallowed, but knew she'd need the energy. The back hallway to the ER staff offices was quiet. They shared four to a room, but since all the physicians worked shifts and only used their offices to store possessions, prepare lectures, do chart reviews and research, there was seldom more than one person there at a time.

This morning Leah's office was empty, saving her from stuttering her way through a conversation no one wanted to have. Condolences had always been difficult for Leah to master. Stumbling, fumbling for the exact right words, daring to hope they might ease someone's pain and knowing, every single time, that she was doomed to fail. Now, being on the receiving end, she realized exactly how wrong she'd been, imagining her words might help. Because every "I'm so sorry" people offered her hit like a sledgehammer, with no way to dodge the blows.

Closing the door behind her, she stopped, stunned by the silence after a night spent on the ward. She took a few breaths, emptying and refilling her lungs as if she could hope to carry the peaceful quiet with her when she left. Then she moved to her desk, put her phone on the charger, and used the landline to call Ian's parents in Seattle. She felt guilty for not calling earlier.

She started the call standing, but as it progressed, she ended up crouched in her desk chair, her entire body curled into a ball, her forehead resting on her desk. They were crying, she was crying, but the worst part was what she couldn't tell them—not on the phone, maybe not ever. The sight of Ian's body, her crawling through his blood to reach Emily, their beautiful granddaughter turned into a cowering, feral creature.

"But Emily, she'll be all right?" Ian's mother, Tilda, asked, breaking through her sobs.

"They gave her a sedative." Leah used her clinical tone. It helped, pretending to be professional, distancing herself from the pain. "Once she wakes, we'll start counseling."

"Right, to prevent post-traumatic stress," Ian's father said. He was a Gulf War veteran, had been on the ground in Kuwait and Iraq.

"But they won't make her testify, will they?" Tilda put in. "I mean, she won't need to relive that, face this monster when they catch him? You won't let that happen, will you, Leah?"

Leah had no answer to that. Right now, it was taking everything she had to make it through this phone call, much less a theoretical trial that could be years away. "She'll be fine. I'd better go. Get back to her."

"Right," Bruce, Ian's father, said, his own tears breaking through his attempt to stay in control. "I'll text you when we have flights and a hotel sorted."

"Maybe I should call one of your neighbors," Leah suggested. "Someone to stay with you, help with the details?"

"No," he said, reminding her of why she'd always liked him so much. Bruce and Leah were a lot alike, handling their problems—and emotions—in private. "You just take care of Emily. And yourself."

"Tell her we love her." Tilda's voice carried through the line before it went dead.

Leah hung up. Her tears flowed so hard her entire body jerked and swayed in anguish. She pressed herself into the corner of the room and covered her mouth, crushing her eyes closed, and screamed into her fists. Her heart felt ripped to pieces. Agony seared her, and then noises in the hallway as staff bustled past her door reminded her she could not let go here. She bundled those feelings, folding them inside her heart. An origami of pain to be deconstructed and dealt with later.

Finally, she was composed enough to grab what she needed, and head down the back hallway to the women's locker room where she took a quick shower. Her clothing choices were limited: scrubs, workout clothes, or her all-purpose going-to-court, teaching, TV-interview outfit that she kept for emergencies. Since she imagined that today would be spent up on peds, in bed with Emily, she took the easy way out and went with the scrubs. Here in the hospital, they made her anonymous, as if there wasn't anything different about her now, as if she was still the same woman who'd just twelve hours ago held a boy's heart in her hand and started it beating again.

Sam Davidson, head of the ER and Leah's immediate boss, was working this morning and she wanted to thank him for arranging coverage for the shifts she'd be missing. She crossed through the main ER to find him, passing through a barrage of staff rushing up to her, taking her hands, hugging her, a few crying themselves.

When Sam saw her, he frowned and also hugged her, then walked her past the nurses' station to the empty staff room. Leah was pretty certain she said the right words because his face creased with concern as he nodded and mouthed more words back to her. The sounds were instantly consumed by the roaring in her brain and she honestly had no idea what she was saying—or what he had said.

Her face was a sheet of ice, ready to slip and expose the chaos behind her mask. She couldn't maintain her composure for much longer. Leah left her boss and drifted down the front hall, passing the room where she and Emily had been sequestered last night. She knew how to do this, knew how to lock away her emotions better than this. After all, she'd dealt with loss time and again, her whole life—how many times had Ruby left, forcing Leah to grieve and figure out what to do next and how to make sense of the world, only to return and repeat the cycle? By the time Ruby finally left Leah with Nellie, Leah had no idea what to believe. All she knew was it had to be her fault—she was the reason why Ruby couldn't stay, couldn't bear to live with Leah, not another day.

Her phone buzzed with missed calls and texts, most from neighbors, colleagues, acquaintances from Ian's church, all offering sympathy, food, help. She knew their hearts were in the right place, but no one could help her with what she really needed: Emily safe and whole. Warm thoughts and prayers and heart emojis weren't going to bring Ian back. They weren't going to stop this nightmare.

She shoved the phone back into her pocket. As she moved past the ER's triage desk and waiting area, someone shouted her name. Then more shouts came—a chorus yelling out.

She glanced up in surprise and saw a bunch of reporters crowded into the waiting room, surging past the lone security guard at the desk. Flashes filled the air as they shouted questions. Overwhelmed, she ducked her head, clutched her gym bag close to her, and spun around to flee.

Only to have her path blocked by a man who didn't look like a reporter. He wore a flannel shirt over a stained, once-white tee and torn jeans that sagged around his hips. He held a bloody towel around his left hand. "That's her! That's the doctor who killed my wife! How's it feel? To finally get what you deserve?"

CHAPTER 11

"You killed my wife!" the strange man screamed as he grabbed the bloody towel wrapped around his hand and flung it at Leah's face. Leah stumbled backwards, hitting the wall.

A second man came from across the hall and shoved the first man, propelling him into the waiting room. Reporters surged forward, shouting questions as the security guard struggled to fight his way through, chasing after Leah's attacker. Leah didn't move, couldn't move, the maelstrom of activity blurring as if she were very far away—except for the panic that kept her feet tethered, frozen to the ground. She couldn't speak if she tried, her throat closed tight, hands held up near her face as if warding off an attack.

Her anonymous rescuer guided her by the arm away from the waiting room, down to the secure doors leading to the hallway separating the ER from the main hospital. Leah felt better once the steel doors were between her and the commotion in the waiting area. She slumped against the wall, trying to remember how to breathe; her lungs felt on fire. Too deep a breath, too much oxygen, and she might spontaneously combust.

"You all right, doc?" The man wasn't cloaked in a lab coat, but instead wore a casual button-down, jeans, worn work boots and a tight-fitting knit cap over his head.

She nodded, unable to speak, her free hand rubbing at her face. None of the blood had gotten into her eyes or mouth, in fact there wasn't any trace of it, but still, just the idea...

"Sure, doc? You look kinda pale."

"I'm fine." The words sounded almost normal. As if being accused of murder and then assaulted by a strange man happened every day. Leah had had her fair share of verbal threats from patients. Usually they were intoxicated or suffered mental illness; nothing personal, just part of the job. But this felt very personal.

Suddenly being alone in an empty hallway with a total stranger didn't seem like such a good idea. The man must have picked up on her discomfort. He shuffled his feet and pulled open the door leading back into the ER. "Glad you're okay," he mumbled. "Sorry about what happened to your husband." And he left.

Leah's panic slowly subsided. Until another man appeared at the far end of the hall. Her heart raced, despite the fact that he wore hospital scrubs and was too far away to hurt her. She ran for the stairwell, swiped her ID—had to do it twice, her hand was shaking so badly—and pulled the door shut behind her.

Pediatrics was on three, but she stopped on the landing below it, her breath jagged, her mind spinning out of control. Who was that man who attacked her in the ER? She didn't know him. Who was his wife? Like every physician, Leah had lost patients, but she didn't remember the man—and Leah definitely remembered every family she had to give bad news to. Suddenly the face of the stabbing victim from last night danced in front of her.

Not *victim*. She forced herself to bend her thoughts to use Andre Toussaint's label for the boy: rapist. What had happened to his victim? Had she died? Was the man in the ER the victim's husband? What if Leah's act of compassion, her triumph of resuscitation, served only to create more pain, violence, and bloodshed?

That boy… that rapist… the man accusing her of murder… What if they were all connected? With shaking hands, she slid Luka Jericho's card from her pocket and dialed.

"Jericho," he answered, the sounds of traffic in the background.

"It's Leah Wright." She faltered, certain her imagination had spiraled out of control. He'd think her a fool.

"What can I do for you, Mrs. Wright?"

He never used her title—usually she didn't care, preferred people to call her by her first name, but somehow it felt as if Jericho made that choice on purpose, to manipulate her emotions. She reminded herself that was his job, but still it rankled. "There was a man in the ER. Accused me of killing his wife. And there was a kid last night. Stabbed. I saved him, but the cops said he attacked a woman—"

"Wait. Who was the man who attacked you?"

"I have no idea. He ran, maybe security—" God, she did sound insane. Rambling.

"But he's connected to your stabbing victim?"

"I don't know. Maybe. I just thought, if the woman last night died, maybe he blamed me for saving the kid—" Her logic unraveled and she realized she was making no sense—the whole thing made no sense. But the man's eyes, crazed with fury and grief... maybe his mind was as overwhelmed as her own.

"You're talking about Eric Winters, the sixteen-year-old who tried to rape a woman last night." His voice was calm, so rational compared to her own turmoil of careening emotions. "The woman lived, only a few bruises. So did the civilian who interceded. Only casualty was the rapist you saved."

Leah digested that. "Okay. Sorry for wasting your time."

"Not a waste. I'll call hospital security. Have them track down this guy from the ER. Is your daughter ready to talk? We have the forensic interview set for eleven with a Dr. Jessica Kern, but I could do it sooner—"

"No." The word shot out from her, sharp and final. She cringed at the loud sound echoing from the cement walls of the stairwell. "No," she said more softly. "Emily's still sedated. I'm not sure when she'll be ready." Leah had performed dozens of forensic interviews on victims; she knew when done well, they were meant to empower, aid in healing, preventing PTSD—as well as help the police and prosecutors. But the mother in her dreaded Emily having to tell her story to strangers, reliving it at all.

"I'll see you at eleven," he said and hung up.

She sank down to the floor, held her head in her hands.

She couldn't do this alone. She needed help.

Ian's parents would try, although they'd be more work than help, suffering through their own pain and loss.

No. She didn't so much need someone as she needed some*place*. Someplace to hide, where she could protect Emily. Someplace quiet, where they could both begin to heal. Someplace like home—except home wasn't home anymore and might never be again. Not without Ian.

A safe haven. Before she met Ian there was only one place where she'd ever felt that way. Nellie's house.

After Nellie died, Leah's mother had moved in. Leah hadn't spoken to Ruby in over six years. Not since Leah threw her out of the hospital's maternity ward when Ruby came to see Emily and brought one of her boyfriends. Both Ruby and the man had been drunk or high or some combination, pawing and grabbing at Leah's newborn as if Emily belonged to them. Making her vows and promises, creating grandiose plans of trips to Disney and pony rides, to the point where Leah, in her exhaustion, finally broke down and screamed at them to leave, to never come back. Told them Emily would never, ever be abandoned and betrayed by broken promises like Leah had been. That she'd rather Emily never know her grandmother than to have the kind of childhood Leah suffered through.

She'd never forget the look on Ruby's face. Stunned, finally realizing the truth of where they were and what they'd done and what was about to happen. If Leah had slapped Ruby she would not have looked as shocked.

Ruby had blinked, her gaze flitting around the room, taking in reality for the first time in probably decades, finally settling on her daughter who had baby Emily curled protectively in her arms, shielding her from Ruby.

"You're probably right," she'd said. Then she and her date left. It was the last time Leah had seen or spoken to her mother. Ruby hadn't even come to Nellie's funeral, had simply moved herself into Nellie's farmhouse a few weeks later without a word to Leah.

Leah swiped her tears—how was it possible that she had any left?—and stared at the phone's screen. She didn't have a number for Ruby, but she did have Nellie's old landline memorized from when she was a child. Without even thinking, feeling the same way as she had as a child, blowing out birthday candles and making her desperate wish, the same wish, year after year, she dialed it.

The phone rang. And kept ringing. The noise brought her to her senses, and she was just about to hang up when a woman's voice answered. "Hello."

Leah almost dropped the phone, the voice sounded so much like Nellie's.

"Hello?" the woman repeated.

She swallowed, no idea what to say. But deep within her brain, the part of her who was still that fearful child yearning to feel safe and cherished—the little girl who could never stop believing that her mother would finally, someday, come rescue her, actually want her, choose her—emerged. "Can I come home? Please, I need to come home."

Instantly ashamed of her weakness, she hung up before Ruby could answer.

Leah's frantic breathing echoed against the cinder block walls of the stairwell. How could she be so foolish, calling Ruby? She'd spent the first half of her life in a futile attempt to earn her mother's love and the second fleeing her. No way in hell did she need Ruby back in her life, not now. And Emily most especially did not need to be exposed to Ruby. Not now, not ever.

Except it wasn't really Ruby she'd been reaching out to. It was Nellie.

And, like Ian, Nellie was beyond Leah's reach.

CHAPTER 12

His breath heaved as he ran. *All that blood.* He slammed into the side of a pickup truck. Blinked. The world around him swam in a sea of red then steadied once more. *His* truck. He gasped, spun around, placing his back against the driver's door. Who was he running from? Why? Where was he?

All that blood…

He hauled in one breath, then another, his pulse slowing, adrenaline ebbing enough that the roaring in his brain subsided. Sweat dripped from his brow. His mouth was dry, tasted of metal. He looked around. Gray concrete with parking markings. The smell of gas and motor oil. He was in a parking garage. There, a sign. Good Sam—what was he doing at the hospital? His son—was he sick again?

Panic surged. Was he coming? Going? Where was his son? What happened?

All that blood… *Not* his blood.

A man and woman emerged from the hospital, strolling to their car, the woman obviously pregnant. Both talking very fast, heads turned to each other, shutting out the rest of the world, so excited, so happy. He watched them, trying to remember… The way her hand felt against his, her skin under his calloused palm as she pressed it just there, the baby kicking. They'd both laughed so hard…

Ambushed by grief, he turned, leaned his forehead against the truck's window to hide from the world. *Remember.* He needed to remember. What had happened? How did he get here?

Where had all that blood come from? His son, was he safe?

He closed his eyes. Took another deep breath to steady himself. His head throbbed. Blood filled his vision, surging, spraying, sluicing… not his blood. His throat tightened with terror. His son? No. No. His son was fine. He remembered now. Getting home last night—from where? What was so important that he'd left his son? He'd never do that—

Getting home. Watching his son sleep. Kissing his forehead, just like his mom used to do checking for fever. Showering and crawling into bed for a short nap until it was time to start the day. His dreams strange, filled with blood and fists, men scowling and, worse, grinning—memories of prison.

He'd woken screaming his son's name. He'd blinked, the room slowly coming into focus. Through the slivers of sunlight peeking through the cracks in the curtains, he saw that he wasn't in his bed, he was on the couch in the living room. Had he been sleepwalking again?

He'd leapt from the couch and raced to his son's room. His boy sat in his race car bed, a picture book on his lap.

"You okay?" he'd asked.

His son had nodded, never looking up from his book. The sunlight streamed through the windows, giving the boy a golden glow, yet also casting shadows on the floor, a black chasm. He inched his toe forward but dared not cross. Times like this when his son was happy, not sick or feverish, he always felt scared to touch him, get too close. Afraid his clumsy loving would trigger… something. Maybe he hadn't always been the best father, but now it was just the two of them and he vowed to do better.

"Need anything?" he asked, still from the doorway. He remembered wanting more than anything to run into the room, hug his son, plop down beside him, and hold him tight. But he couldn't. Not only because he was worried about hurting his little boy. It was the blood, staining his memory. As if it might contaminate, corrupt a child's innocence.

And now he was here, at the hospital. But how had he gotten here?

Before he could worry about it, a sharp pain exploded in his head, radiating through his skull to his jawbones, into his teeth, drilling deeper than any dentist. *You shouldn't be here.*

He collapsed against the truck, both hands flying up to cradle his head.

He needed to be watching her.

The widow.

"What did I do?" His shout emerged as a whimper, silenced by the pain thundering through his skull. A man screaming, the flash of a blade, the thud of flesh and bone breaking. He slid to the ground, rocked back and forth, his head caught in the vise of his two hands. "What did you make me do?"

CHAPTER 13

Luka steered through the streets, heading toward Good Sam and his appointment with the medical examiner. After hanging up from Leah, he'd called Good Sam's security—who had lost the man in the ER but promised to help identify him. He'd also confirmed that they had guards watching Leah and her daughter. The man who assaulted her didn't sound like the same person who had killed Ian—more opportunistic, less meticulous—but the incident did raise some interesting questions.

The weather guys on the radio were going nuts over a storm that was rolling in; it was expected to take today's spring-like temperatures and send them plummeting with high winds and blizzard conditions. Luka scoffed. Must be nice having a job that paid you to be wrong more than half the time. Last time they got excited about a storm—schools cancelled, stores depleted of bread and milk, the city ready to implement its Code White emergency plan—all they got was a measly three inches that melted before the snowplows even left their garage. He turned the radio off and called Janine. He had to warn her about Tanya.

"Where are you?" he asked when she answered, unable to restrain his anger at Tanya's sudden explosion into his life. "Is Pops okay?" He instantly regretted his tone—none of this was Janine's fault. Tanya always brought out the worst in him.

"Why wouldn't he be? What happened? I'm not at the farm yet. It's grocery day." Janine was in her mid-fifties, her four children out of the house, either in grad school or already working. She'd raised her kids as a single mother as well as taking care of her own ailing father—a Polish immigrant who'd given his life and lungs to the Cambria coal mines—and she didn't take attitude from anybody. Which made her the perfect companion to Pops.

"My sister happened. She called me from the farm." He hadn't told Janine anything about Tanya. It'd taken all his negotiation skills to convince Pops to allow a stranger into the house at all. The first four aides had quit before the end of their first day. Janine was the only one Pops had tolerated and the last thing Luka wanted was to risk scaring her off. "Tanya's an addict and she has a history of stealing from Pops. The case I'm working is—I can't make it over there, not for a while."

He hesitated—he paid Janine better than the other aides he'd tried but he was worried he was asking too much of her, asking her to deal with Tanya. "Look. I know this is above and beyond. But would you mind watching out for him? Just until I can get home. I told Tanya to leave so you probably won't even see her, but I need to make sure Pops is okay." He paused. "And then maybe stay a few nights?"

"I'm in the checkout now and headed over to the farm," Janine answered after a long pause. "But I don't do junkies and I don't do criminals. If she's high or has done anything against the law, I'm calling the cops. Don't care if she is your family, she's not mine and you can't pay me enough to deal with that crap. Clear?"

"Yes, ma'am. Thank you." Luka was used to giving orders and having them obeyed, but somehow the older woman intimidated the hell out of him. Maybe because she reminded him of his gran— she'd been a force of nature, impossible to resist. "I—we—very much appreciate it."

"As for staying the night, I can tonight and tomorrow. At my usual hourly." Ouch. That was going to eat into the budget—paying her for sleeping on the job? Was it worth it? "But we need to have a discussion about a more long-term solution. All three of us."

Luka was not looking forward to that. "That sounds like a plan," he said in a neutral tone. "Call me if you need anything."

"You're welcome." She hung up just as he pulled into the Good Sam parking garage.

He glanced at the clock—he had a few minutes before Tierney was expecting him. He could use it in a myriad of ways: interrogating the security guys about the man in the ER, following up on the hospital gift shop and the roses, interviewing more of Leah Wright's co-workers. Instead, he sighed and dialed the farm.

Tanya answered—as if she'd moved in, lock, stock, and barrel. "Hey there, big brother."

"What do you want?" He cut to the chase, no time or patience left to play her mind games.

"Like I said, just to talk." She sounded weary, her breath coming long and heavy.

Dealing with Tanya was like a trip to the dentist—best to get it over with as quickly as possible. "I'll be at Good Samaritan most of the morning, working. Text me when you get here and as soon as I have a free minute, we can meet in the cafeteria."

"My time ain't valuable? I gotta sit and wait on Mr. High and Mighty?"

"When Mr. High and Mighty is working a murder where a little girl is the only witness to her dad's decapitation, yeah, Tanya, you have to wait." He hated what he had to resort to in order to break through her narcissism and felt a tinge of regret dragging the Wrights into this at all. Not that the details of Ian Wright's death weren't already being broadcast over every media outlet.

"Okay," she relented. "I'll text." She hung up.

Luka stared at the phone, wishing he could be in two places at once—here, doing what needed to be done for Ian Wright, and at home, jettisoning Tanya from Pops' house, protecting him from whatever bullshit con she was very likely spinning in his ear. Pops was too susceptible, and Tanya was going to break his heart. Again.

He walked through the garage, the only person on this floor, his footsteps echoing off giant concrete pillars, feeling as if he was moving across a desolate moonscape. He took the elevator to the basement level and entered the morgue, signed in at the security desk, took his pass, and turned his phone to silent mode. As he passed through the doors to the ME's inner sanctum, he drew in a breath, returning his focus to the case, trying not to imagine the damage Tanya could do even in the short time it would take Janine to get there. When had Tanya gotten to the farm? Last night? This morning?

"Dressing in?" Maggie Chen greeted him at the hallway leading to the locker rooms. With routine cases Luka would observe from the viewing room, where he could watch through the window and also on the video screen if the ME needed him to see something up close. But this case was anything but routine.

"Yes," Luka answered, eying the clock. Seven 'til eight. Just enough time—punctuality was Ford Tierney's catechism. "Maggie—" He hesitated, knowing he was asking her to cross a line. "How well do you know the widow?"

Maggie hesitated, obviously uncomfortable with his question. He remembered the way she'd avoided answering when he'd asked her about Leah at the crime scene. "Luka, I'd tell you if I knew anything pertinent to your case. But I won't spy for you."

"No. Of course not. But, any insights? She's so composed, restrained—I can't get a good read on her."

Maggie twisted her lips, considering. "She's good. Good doctor, always goes the extra mile when she can, even follows up on patients after they've left the ER."

"She just called me. It was weird. She wasn't hysterical or upset." He struggled to describe Leah's tone. "More like her mind was moving faster than her words. It sounded as if she thought her husband was killed because she saved a kid in the ER last night."

"You mean the stabbing case? Eric Winters? I just reviewed his chart—he died a few hours ago, post-op blood clot. Andre

Toussaint, he's the chief of the trauma service, is livid because the death will be attributed to his care as a post-op complication. Says Leah should never have resuscitated the kid; he was down too long, it wasted precious resources."

Luka considered it from Leah's point of view. She would have had to make a split-second decision that could cost a life but without knowing the full story—barely knowing any of the story. "So. Did she do the right thing? Bringing the kid back? Or should she have just let him go, used all those resources to save someone else instead?"

"Andre Toussaint would say she made a mistake. The kid's family wouldn't agree."

"I'm asking you. What if it was you, what would you have done?"

She thought about it a long moment. "Honestly, everything I see around here? What's going to happen will happen. All you can do in the moment is the best you can."

They reached the locker rooms. "See you in there," Maggie said as Luka ducked into the men's locker room. He grabbed a pair of Tyvek coveralls, shoe coverings, and a scrub cap. When he emerged into the autopsy suite Ford Tierney and Maggie were huddled together at the oversized computer touchscreen, reviewing Ian Wright's X-rays.

The two made an interesting contrast. Maggie was petite, and despite standing still seemed to radiate movement and energy—*fey*, his gran would have labeled her even without her bright-dyed hair. The assistant medical examiner, though, was the opposite in almost every way. Although he was only in his late forties, his hair had already gone white in that way that redheads had; he was taller than Luka and weighed twice as much, a hulking figure with an over-ample belly barely contained by his scrub pants. Give him a beard and he might be mistaken for Santa—until his piercing scowl of constant disapproval burst that fairytale comparison.

Luka joined them. They were staring at an enlarged image of Ian's skull. Even Luka's untrained eye could make out the multitude of fractures, shards of bones crisscrossing in unnatural angles that had him cringing. Tierney enlarged one area, highlighting a small shard of metal.

"Is that a piece of the murder weapon?" Luka asked. "Broken off?"

"Maybe," Maggie said, obviously pleased with herself.

"We're not sure," Tierney hedged. He backed away from the monitor, glanced at the shrouded body on the autopsy table behind them. He sighed, his near-constant scowl deepening. "One way to find out."

Luka and Maggie exchanged a glance as they each placed protective masks over their faces. Tierney hated anything that messed with his prescribed routine, which would have usually left examination of the head and skull until later in the autopsy.

"Thanks," Luka told Tierney while Maggie removed the body from its sterile coverings. He cut his apology short at the sight of the naked man lying before them. Despite having seen Ian's body at the crime scene, Luka hadn't fully appreciated the extent of the man's injuries. Now, unclothed and with the blood washed clean, the damage was exposed. Luka exhaled, his mask creating a loud echo as his breath rasped against it.

Tierney made quick work of the preliminaries, mainly noting new bruises and contusions that had appeared since Maggie did her initial documentation at the scene. Including evidence of restraints around Ian's wrists and ankles and a needle track in his left arm.

"Tox screen show anything?" They all leaned over the small pinprick, examining it through the large magnifying lens that hung down on rails, easily positioned anywhere over the body.

"Prelim was inconclusive," Maggie answered. "We had weak presumptives for PCP, LSD, steroids, and methamphetamines."

"What's that mean? He was a user and they were already out of his system?" Luka doubted that—how could a computer guy at Ian's level function with a cocktail of hallucinogenic drugs poisoning his system?

"More likely that we're dealing with an unknown substance that shares similar toxicologic markers," Tierney answered. "We've sent samples for further analysis and I'll excise the needle track, send it as well."

"How long will that take?" Luka grumbled—he knew the answer, but still had to ask, hoping some miracle of technology had changed overnight.

"Weeks, maybe months. Depends." Maggie shrugged, her mask shifting on her face. "But whatever it was, it messed with his natural stress response. His biomarkers—adrenaline, cortisol, you name it—were off the charts."

"They restrained him then pumped him full of chemicals that would make him hallucinate and fight harder?" Luka asked. That made no sense. Especially as there was no evidence that the actor restrained the daughter—so whatever he'd done to Ian before the struggle that led to Emily's room, it couldn't have created too much noise if the kid had slept through it. "And then he broke free?"

"We don't know yet what drugs they gave him," Tierney corrected Luka. "All we know is how his body responded. And remember, his response was also exacerbated by extreme physical pain and mental stress."

"Fear for his own life and his daughter's, chemicals that heightened that response, the physical injuries." Tierney glared at Luka's assumptions—the ME preferred to deal in facts and findings, not speculation—but Luka stood his ground. "Any way to tell which injuries were inflicted while he was restrained versus during the struggle after he broke free?"

"We don't have evidence that he did break free." Tierney raised the less damaged wrist and moved the magnifying lens over it. "See how the hairs have been removed? And we found residue from adhesive, indicating he was restrained with tape. No patterned petechiae or bruising suggesting that he tore free. It appears to have been removed by someone else. Wrists and ankles the same."

"They restrained him, injected him with a hallucinogenic cocktail, then let him loose? And after all that, they chased him through the house, fought, and killed him? Why?" What the hell had gone on in that house? Luka had never had a crime scene where every piece of evidence they discovered seemed to contradict the others. It was like a puzzle with too many pieces.

"Your job, not mine. All I can do is document my findings."

Luka frowned. "It makes no sense, it's too risky and too much work. Why not just put a bullet in his head if you wanted him dead?" Unless the idea was to maximize pain and fear—best way to do that was to dangle hope as bait. "They knew he'd do anything to protect his daughter," he answered his own question. "Used her along with the drugs and the pain—it was the ultimate torture."

Someone had wanted Ian Wright to suffer greatly—that sounded personal, which usually translated to family. Could Leah Wright have arranged for her husband to be tortured and brutalized with their own child in the house? Then act the role of grief-stricken widow? He remembered the video of Leah extricating her daughter from beneath the bed. A defense attorney's dream and a prosecutor's nightmare—no jury would convict after seeing that display of maternal courage. Was Leah that cold and calculating?

He glanced at the clock—still too early to get anything from the banks. But he texted Krichek to make sure their warrants covered the wife's financials as well as the husband's. Just in case. Then he reached out to Harper, following up on the motorcycle and its rider—still no joy there, either.

"Are we talking more than one attacker?" Luka asked Tierney. Everything at the scene suggested one man, but everything at the scene had been staged, so…

Tierney's eyes tightened, but he relented. "I've found nothing to indicate multiple attackers."

Luka blew his breath out, desperate for a fact, some solid piece of evidence he could build a case on. "Can we see the remnant from the murder weapon?" That earned him another glare from the medical examiner.

Maggie intervened, "You mean the shard of metal found in the skull X-rays."

"I mean the one piece of evidence that might not be inconclusive," Luka snapped.

Tierney humored him and moved to the head of the table. Maggie had inserted a colored pipe cleaner to indicate where the tiny bit of metal lay beneath the flayed and bruised skin. It was between Ian's left eye and ear. Maggie adjusted the lights and repositioned the magnifier. This time she turned on the camera, directing the image to the large monitor.

"This is interesting," Tierney mumbled.

"What?" Luka said, focusing on the monitor where Tierney's gloved fingers glided over the dead man's skin, a maestro and his instrument. Luka tried to be patient, but this was what always killed him when he had to deal with the forensic guys—they'd go off on some fascinating scientific tangent, ignoring what was right in front of them.

"If that's part of the murder weapon, you can possibly match it," he said, unconsciously mirroring Tierney's formal tone. "Right?" he added, remembering that he was a mere supplicant in these hallowed halls of science. And Tierney was doing him a favor.

Maggie's eyes crinkled as she held back a grin. Tierney seemed oblivious. He carefully excised the entire area of skin in a deft move that could have been called graceful if not for the macabre circumstances. Now it was just bits of muscle and bone and other things Luka couldn't identify lying beneath the magnifier. At the center was a knot of thicker white tissue, glistening under the light. Embedded in it was the tiny metal sliver.

Instead of plucking the metal piece out, Tierney used the handle of his scalpel to lift the knot of tissue. "Trigeminal ganglion," he told Luka. "A collection of nerves."

"Trigeminal?" The word was vaguely familiar. "When I was a beat cop we had a lady who tore most of her face off. Thought it was PCP or something, but the docs said it was that. Trigeminal. Said it got inflamed, drove her mad with the pain."

Tierney nodded. "Trigeminal neuralgia or *tic douloureux*. There have been cases of suicide in the past—we had no effective long-term treatment until recently." He angled the clump of nerves and focused on the piece of metal. "Looks like the broken tip of a spinal needle."

"Excuse me?"

"They're extra-long needles used for spinal taps and other procedures," Maggie explained.

"What's it doing in my victim? Was it maybe there for a long time, left over from some surgery or something?"

"I reviewed the medical records," Maggie said. "There's no mention of any facial surgery or injuries."

Tierney ignored them, probing the area from the broken needle tip down to Ian's lower jaw. "There's a track," he said triumphantly.

"Meaning?" Luka asked, his patience at an end.

"Several things. First, this is a new injury. Most likely sustained in the perimortem period. Second, whoever inserted this had at least some limited medical or anatomic training. And third, you were right. Ian Wright was tortured before he was killed." He positioned the magnifier and zoomed in on a faint line of darkened tissue surrounded by yellow fat globules.

Maggie gasped.

"What?" Luka asked.

"Tissue damage," Tierney answered. "Faint, but there if you know where to look. Which we wouldn't have if the tip of the needle hadn't broken off. Charred tissue. Probably from an electrical current. I'll know more once we do the microscopic evaluation."

"You stick a needle in it and shock the nerve bundle with electricity, what happens?" Luka thought he knew the answer but needed to make certain.

Tierney cleared his throat. "Pain," he said as if confessing a sin. "Severe, extreme pain. Some have called trigeminal pain the worst torture imaginable."

"All those drugs—those would make the pain and terror even worse, right?"

Both Maggie and Tierney nodded.

"How difficult would it be for a layman to get to the trigeminal ganglion?"

"Usually it's done under CT scan guidance, although there is an older blind technique, using a spinal needle inserted up through the face," Tierney answered.

Exactly the path the needle used on Ian Wright took.

"It was a doctor?"

"Not necessarily. The technique used here was neither surgical nor precise."

"But a doctor would know how to get to that area?"

Tierney shrugged. "Anyone with a working knowledge of basic anatomy would."

"Or five minutes with Google," Maggie added. "There are YouTube videos of the technique."

Luka ignored them to stare at the mutilated man on the table. "Drugs and medical needles." An ER doctor would have access to both. "They torture him, drive him mad with pain. And then they let him loose, tell him they're going after his baby girl if he doesn't stop them… so the scene looks perfect for a home invasion. It wasn't simply staged—it was choreographed."

He stared at the tiny sliver of needle magnified on the screen. So small, yet the story it told was huge. Maggie finished her photographs and stood back as Tierney plucked it free and dropped it into a specimen cup.

"Any way to trace it?" Luka asked.

"No," Tierney said.

"Excuse me." A man's voice came from the viewing room's door. They all whirled. A medium-sized Caucasian man in a dark gray suit strode through the door, holding a set of credentials before him as if it was a shield. "George Radcliffe. Defense Intelligence Agency. I'm here for Ian Wright." He strode forward, eyeing the naked body on the table. "Guess I'm a bit late." He chuckled at his own inappropriate joke, drawing glares from Tierney and Maggie.

"Back!" Tierney ordered, pointing a bloody hand wielding a scalpel at the intruder. "Maggie—"

"On it." She rushed over to the man, guiding him to the far corner where she wrapped him in a scrub gown and corralled him until he had donned sterile booties and a scrub cap. Radcliffe didn't protest, instead he seemed bemused.

Luka couldn't help but wonder how long the man had been watching and listening from the observation room—it felt as if his appearance wasn't as sudden as it first appeared. Finally, Maggie released him, and he stepped toward the autopsy table.

"Behind the line," Tierney commanded. Radcliffe stopped obediently, toeing the red-taped line on the floor a few feet away from the table, giving him an adequate view but nowhere as up close and personal as what Luka had. "No touching, no taping, no talking unless necessary."

"It's necessary," Radcliffe told him. "Dr. Wright's work with us was quite sensitive."

Luka braced himself. Damn feds. They were taking over his case. His phone buzzed and he stepped back, slipping off his gloves to retrieve it from inside his Tyvek jumpsuit. Probably Ahearn calling to tell him to stand down, turn over everything.

He glanced at the screen. Not Ahearn. The farm's landline. Radcliffe was watching him, an eyebrow arched in challenge. Luka declined the call, let it go to voicemail. Then he texted Krichek, asked him to verify Radcliffe's credentials.

Radcliffe sidled over, toeing but not crossing the red line. "I'm not here to interfere, Detective Jericho. Nor to take your case. Merely to help, offer our resources. And to protect the interests of national security. I'm sure you'll agree that's a priority?"

Luka's only priority was catching the sonofabitch who did this before he had a chance to hurt anyone else. He ignored Radcliffe and turned back to Tierney. "Any ideas about the weapon or weapons?"

"My initial thoughts, based on the fracture patterns and skin damage, are a wedge-shaped blade along with a sharp awl-like instrument that could pierce."

Maggie touched the computer screen. "Something like this, maybe?" A sketch of a short-handled hatchet with a wide blade and narrow-tipped head appeared.

"Yes, they could be combined into one weapon," Tierney allowed.

"I drew it based on my preliminary exam. The configuration matches several types of survival axes. Technically not sold as weapons but there are a ton of videos with people using them that way."

What would would-be criminals do without YouTube? Luka thought. "Any chance you can narrow that down to a specific model?"

"Once I get the microscopic examination of the kerf marks, perhaps," Tierney said. "But more likely the best I'll be able to do is tell if any weapon you find is a match or not. And it will—"

"Take time. I know. Anything else?"

Tierney stared at him. "I've only just begun my examination."

Autopsies could take hours—and Tierney's meticulous evaluations of every anomaly could take all day. Luka didn't have that kind of luxury, especially not now with the feds on the scene.

"Call me if you find anything," he told Maggie as he headed out. To his surprise, Radcliffe followed him into the locker room.

"I'm not the bad guy here, Detective. Fill me in, tell me what you need. I can make it happen." He looked ridiculous standing there wrapped in the surgical gown, hair cap slipping halfway off. But he was right. The feds had resources Luka couldn't dream of accessing.

"How 'bout you fill me in on how you got here so quickly?"

"Your Commander Ahearn didn't tell you? He notified Homeland last night as soon as he realized Dr. Wright was working on sensitive material. And they called us—as did CERT and the university once they heard the news about Dr. Wright's passing. Of course, by then, I was already on my way." The DIA agent paused, scrutinizing Luka. "I'm rather surprised you didn't call us yourself, Detective."

"It was on my to-do list." Smack dab at the bottom, since Luka knew damn well the feds were more likely to hinder than help. "But since you're here, what was Ian Wright working on for the government?"

Radcliffe made a clicking noise with his tongue as if Luka had disappointed him. "You know I can't divulge—"

"Any classified material. I know." Luka's phone buzzed. Krichek texting back. Radcliffe checked out—Krichek even included a photo as verification, along with Ahearn's instructions to give the DIA their full cooperation. Guess they were stuck with the man. "Don't suppose you could narrow that down or help us with a direction?"

"Why don't we start with what you've got already," Radcliffe said.

Weighing each fact before parsing it out to the fed, Luka gave him a quick summary of what his team had already found. Radcliffe fished his phone from his suit pocket and tapped on the screen, making notes.

"Sounds like you've got most of the bases covered. Of course, we'll need all electronics from Dr. Wright's home and office. My team will examine them, let you know if we find anything."

Luka hoped the cyber techs had already got what they needed from Ian's phone and laptop, because once the DIA grabbed them, they'd never be seen again. "That would be very helpful," he said in an overly gracious tone.

"Consider it done." Radcliffe's tone was filled with bonhomie, ignoring Luka's obvious sarcasm. "I need to review the crime scene, of course."

"We should be done processing it later today. I'll call you and we can arrange a walk-through." Luka was stalling for time and they both knew it, but to his surprise Radcliffe acquiesced with a nod. Luka pushed things further. "Can you tell me anything about Ian's work that might help me?"

Radcliffe took his time as he unknotted his surgical gown and unwound it, balled it up, and threw it into the laundry bin. "I can't." He shrugged. "But I have no indication it's the motivation for his murder. In which case, my work here is done as soon as I retrieve Dr. Wright's computers and all his research."

Could the man be any less helpful? Luka thought. This case was complicated enough and he didn't want the feds on his territory, bringing with them their own unique brand of chaos. Especially since the autopsy seemed to indicate a personal motive, someone who'd wanted Ian Wright to suffer beyond human endurance.

Radcliffe turned as if to leave, then turned back. "I should also tell you that Dr. Wright's consulting contracts were under review. He was scheduled to face a disciplinary board."

"Think maybe you should have led with that?" Once again, Luka fought and failed to keep the sarcasm from his voice, but it didn't matter—Radcliffe appeared immune, infuriating Luka more. He despised being patronized, especially coming from an empty suit like Radcliffe. "Why the review? What did Ian do wrong?"

Radcliffe reached the door and pulled it open. "I don't think you need to worry about any of that," he told Luka in a dismissive tone. "After all, aren't most homicides tied to the loved ones? I were you, I'd focus on the wife."

CHAPTER 14

Leah sat in the empty stairwell, trying to find the energy to climb the final flight to the pediatric floor, her phone still clutched in her hand. Despite the fact that Nellie had died two years ago, not a day went past without Leah thinking of her, especially when the chaos grew too terrifying. Nellie had taught her how to ride a bike and play games, she'd coaxed her to join soccer and Girl Scouts, eased her out of her isolation. Leah still had an aversion to crowds and was desperately phobic about attempting small talk, but the few social graces she had, she'd learned from Nellie.

Her phone buzzed, making her jump. "Dr. Wright?" It was Arthur. "The nurses are asking that you come back." He made it sound like a request but behind his words Leah heard a sound that flooded her system with adrenaline: Emily screaming.

Before he'd finished speaking, Leah was sprinting up the last flight to pediatrics, berating herself all the way. *Never should have left Emily…* her thoughts echoed the pounding of her feet. She pushed through the door and headed toward the clutch of nurses and the sound of a child's cries.

"I'm here." She flung herself into the room. Two nurses were trying to hold Emily down. Cindy stroked Emily's hair while also pinning Emily's head to her pillow so she wouldn't hurt herself. Leah edged one nurse and Cindy out of the way, taking Emily into her arms and receiving an elbow in the ribs from Emily as her reward. "I'm here, baby. Mommy's here."

"I called for another dose of Versed," one nurse said.

"No." Leah snarled the word as she fought to contain her daughter's flailing limbs. As tempting as the idea of sedating Emily for the next few days was, she knew that was no way for her daughter to move past her trauma. "No, thank you." She amended her tone.

Emily slowly responded to Leah's caresses, curling up into her chest. She was still sobbing, hard enough that hiccups rocked her body, and Leah tightened her arms wrapped around her.

"We'll be okay." She stroked Emily's hair, glanced up at the nurse. "Is Dr. Kern in?"

The nurses exchanged glances at each other and then the clock on the wall. "Not yet."

Of course not. Psychiatrists didn't follow normal hospital rhythms. Plus, Jessica also had her duties running the free clinic and she'd only left the hospital a few hours ago after seeing Leah and Emily in the ER. Still, Leah couldn't help but vent her frustration in Jessica's direction—although, the true blame lay with herself. She should have been here when Emily woke and needed her.

"I'll call Dr. Kern," the nurse said. "Let her know Emily's awake."

"Thank you." Leah hesitated, but after the man in the ER… "And the guard for Emily? I didn't see one when I came in."

"He's right across the hall at the nurses' station. We didn't want him at the door where the other children or Emily could see him and get scared. He can see Emily's room and the hallway from there." Of course. That's exactly why the nurses' station was positioned there to begin with, so patients were under constant observation. Leah knew it wasn't like the movies with two armed guards standing at attention outside a door—but that might have made her feel safer. She hugged Emily tighter.

The nurses drifted away, each with a lingering glance back at Emily. The last closed the door behind her and once again Leah and Emily were alone.

Leah shifted her weight to a more comfortable position, nudging the bag of clothing she'd brought from the ER to the floor. Her phone kept buzzing with missed calls and texts—the last four from Ruby, she saw with chagrin. She turned the volume off and placed it beside her on the nightstand. Emily's body was a dead weight—but unlike last night, her eyes were alive, scanning Leah's every move with suspicion. "It's okay, pumpkin. I'm here, I'm not going anywhere."

Over and over she repeated the words until finally Emily pulled her thumb from her mouth and the tears slowed. Emily yawned and stretched her arms around Leah's neck, laying her head on Leah's shoulder. Leah kept stroking her hair, rubbing the spot between her shoulder blades, humming loudly enough that she felt the vibrations go through her chest into Emily's. Slowly, slowly, Emily's body responded, shedding some of its panic. Finally, Emily fell back asleep.

Emily's breathing an irresistible metronome, Leah couldn't keep her eyes open any longer. *Just a few seconds*, she promised herself. *I just need a few seconds...*

Then Ian was there, and she wondered why she'd fought to stay awake. They were on the couch, both reading, Leah sitting sideways, her legs over the armrest, her back leaning against Ian's left shoulder.

"Do you ever think what life would be like, where we'd be, if we never met?" Ian asked. "I wish I'd known you when you were young. Then I could have been your first best friend, first love, first guy to step on your toes when we danced—"

"You were all of those," Leah answered. "First and last and only." She rested her head on his shoulder. In the ER the law of survival was to trust no one, assume nothing; be the ultimate cynic. And yet, somehow, despite his logical mind, the man she'd fallen in love with was a hopeless romantic at heart.

Exactly why she loved him so much. But a tiny part of her—the voice of that little girl left behind so many times—could never quit wondering why he loved her...

Her own sobs startled her awake. Emily was still curled up on Leah's chest, watching her with an impatient feline stare. Leah glanced at the clock—they'd slept for over an hour. She shifted Emily's weight so she could sit up. "You okay, pumpkin?"

"Daddy—" Emily's voice was hoarse. "Daddy, he's hurt."

Leah tensed. She wasn't ready for this, not at all. Part of her tried to hide behind the knowledge that she shouldn't contaminate the forensic interview the police would need. Most of her screamed that part down—hell with interview protocols. If her baby needed to talk, Leah wasn't about to stop her. But she was terrified of saying the wrong thing, of making the pain worse or retriggering Emily's panic. No amount of training could erase her instinctual maternal fear. She rubbed Emily's back with one hand and with the other reached for her phone, tapping the recording app.

"Yes," she finally answered. "Daddy was hurt really bad. But you did good, hiding, staying safe. That was very smart of you. You're a good girl, Emily. I'm so proud of you, being so brave." It felt strange giving her daughter the words she'd always craved from her own mother. And yet, they were so easy to give. Why couldn't Ruby have done this?

Leah measured her next words, terrified she was going to get this wrong. She kissed Emily's head. "I love you. And so does Daddy. With all his heart."

"Is he here?" The words Leah had been dreading.

"No, baby. He's gone. The bad man hurt him very badly."

"Gone away?" Leah didn't answer, fighting her own tears. "Mommy?" Emily pushed up to face Leah, her entire weight pressed against Leah's rib cage, but Leah couldn't feel the pain. "I think maybe, maybe Daddy's not coming back. I think the man killed him dead."

Leah lost it, crushing Emily to her, sobs draining from her.

She kissed Emily on both cheeks. "It's you and me now, pumpkin. I'll take care of you. No matter what."

"The blackspaceman, he was scary. I don't want him to come back."

Leah wondered at the weird phrasing, as if black spaceman was all one word. But now was not the time to question—Emily needed her to listen, to comfort. "He won't. I promise. Your daddy scared him away."

"Daddy told me to hide and not come out."

"And you did. You were a very brave girl. Daddy would have been so proud of you—and I'm proud of you. You did a good job." Leah took a breath, hovering on the edge of hysterics as her imagination filled in the blanks. No, she couldn't go there, not now, not with Emily near.

Emily frowned, still upset, but somehow was treating what happened with more objectivity than Leah could muster. Not dissociating, thank God, more like dissecting, trying to understand the chaos that had forever changed their world. Her expression, with that furrowed brow, lips pursed in dissatisfaction because things didn't quite make sense—how many thousands of times had she seen that exact same expression linger on Ian's face as he puzzled out a problem?

"Daddy was crying. And saying bad words," Emily said slowly, her gaze on Leah's face, gauging Leah's response. "Then…" Her sigh rustled the fine hairs on Leah's cheeks. "Then he was quiet."

Leah blinked, trying to decide if she should ask. But clearly Emily wanted to process what happened and she didn't want her silence to be misconstrued as disapproval. "Honey, did you see anything?"

Emily sighed again, her expression making her look much older than she was. "I heard Daddy shouting at someone—out in the hall. And loud noises. He kept shouting for me to hide and not come out. *Emily, don't come out.* So I did what he said."

"That's right, you did. Good girl."

"But I peeked." Emily said it as if an admission of guilt. "When the door banged open, I saw Daddy fall down. And I peeked."

"That's okay, Emily. You didn't do anything wrong." Leah wanted to ask what she saw, but knew it was best to let Emily tell the story her own way.

Emily placed both her palms against Leah's cheeks and brought her face close until they were nose to nose. Staring into Leah's eyes, she said in a whisper that could probably be heard out in the hallway, "Daddy was hurt. Real bad. I couldn't see his face, all I saw was blood. Why did the man hurt Daddy? Why, Mommy?"

Leah had no answer other than to hug her daughter as tight as humanly possible.

CHAPTER 15

Luka left the medical examiner's offices and prowled the halls of Good Samaritan, debating his new evidence. It was the paradox of good detective work: you had to simultaneously chase down every lead—otherwise a defense attorney could rip your case to shreds—but also learn to listen to your instincts when they urged you to follow a specific avenue of investigation.

The fact that Ian Wright was tortured before he was killed implied two motives: the killer either wanted his secrets or he wanted his pain and suffering. Which meant the murder was tied either to Ian's work—Ray and Radcliffe were already covering that territory—or his home life: his widow or the presumed mistress, Katrina Balanchuk.

Despite the complicated and obviously pre-meditated instruments of Ian's torture, Luka's gut was telling him this case had nothing to do with Ian's work. It was all too damned personal—intimate, even. And where did this new player, the man who'd assaulted Leah in the ER, fit in? That attack definitely sounded personal—was the entire Wright family being targeted?

Radcliffe wandered off to pursue his own "national security" leads, leaving Luka free to focus on Leah Wright. After stopping in at the security office—they were reluctant to help identify the ER attacker, quoted privacy regs, until Luka threatened to call the DA's office. Not that the DA would have done much—although technically throwing a bloody rag at a person was a form of assault—but invoking prosecution was always a surefire motivation. Suddenly, they promised results within an hour.

Next he tracked down the trauma surgeon Maggie had mentioned from Leah's case last night. He was curious about his take, not only on Leah's medical skills, but her decision making. Anything to gain more insight into the widow.

"Leah Wright?" Andre Toussaint scoffed. "Thinks she can save the world when really she's just wasting time and resources."

Luka had caught up with the man between surgeries while he and his team were making their rounds. Despite the fact that Toussaint was considerably shorter than Luka—and considerably older—he could barely keep up with the surgeon as he swept from one doorway to the next while his white-coated team danced after him, presenting him with patient updates or cleaning up dressings and surgical paraphernalia left in his wake.

"And the kid from last night?" The nurses in the ICU had told him that despite her own trauma, Leah had still found time to call and check on her patient this morning.

"She got his heart beating again, yes," Toussaint admitted grudgingly. "But I wouldn't call that saving anyone's life. Kid was down too damned long, his brain would've been mush. Of course, now I'm the one the family blames for his death. Leah gave them false hope, let them expect miracles. Too bad, really. The kid would've made a damned fine organ donor, could have saved lives."

Luka blinked at the surgeon's detached assessment. Toussaint noticed. "You think I'm heartless. I grew up in the South Bronx, did most of my training there. I've been doing this for going on thirty-seven years. So, no, Detective Jericho, I'm no longer young and idealistic like Dr. Wright. I'm a realist and I'm not afraid of the hard choices—not like she is. That's what I was trying to explain to her last night. I was trying to help her learn from my own early mistakes. Sooner or later she'll learn. We all do, if we stay in this business long enough."

"Learn what?"

Toussaint's shoulders sagged as he sighed, no longer the cocky surgeon but appearing world-weary and worn-out. "The truth is, not everyone can be saved. Not everyone is worth fighting for."

With that, Toussaint turned away, squared his shoulders, and whisked his team through the doors to the ICU, leaving Luka to return to the ER for Emily Wright's interview.

As Luka traversed the labyrinth of Good Sam's hallways, one hand scrolled through his phone. Ray had already uploaded summaries of his initial interviews and Krichek had come through on the warrants and court orders they needed.

He called Krichek first.

"Anything on the money trail?" Luka asked.

"Only weird thing so far is ten thousand cash withdrawn from their joint account last week."

"Ten thousand?" Seemed too little to pay an accomplice. "Withdrawn by whom?"

"That's the thing. It was the husband who took it out. I was thinking maybe blackmail?"

Luka made a mental note to prioritize the Katrina Balanchuk interview. He'd hoped to make it to the cafeteria to talk with Tanya, get that out of the way so he could focus on work, but it might need to wait. He ducked into an alcove leading to a pair of restrooms, out of the path of the busy hospital corridor. There was a janitor's closet beside the restrooms; fumes of bleach and ammonia overpowered every breath. "Anything else?"

"Did you see the video from the ER this morning?" Krichek asked.

"What video?"

"Some guy throws a bloody rag at Leah Wright, accuses her of killing his wife."

"She called me after. Security is working on getting me a name. I also arranged for a guard for her and her daughter."

"It's gone viral. Anyway, Good Sam just sent over a copy of their incident report. Guy's name is Jefferson Cochrane. Got a conviction for domestic battery. No motorcycle registered to him."

Of course not, it couldn't be that easy. Only an amateur would show up in his victim's wife's ER hours after the killing and threaten her. And the cold calculation of Ian Wright's murder seemed anything but amateurish. More like lovingly planned and executed. But they had to rule out everything. He was almost tempted to assign Krichek and Harper to the Cochrane interview but then he glanced at the info Krichek texted him—Cochrane's address was less than ten minutes from the farm. Two birds…

"Call me if anything else pops," he told Krichek. When he hung up, he saw that Janine had left a voicemail.

"You might want to see about getting home," she said, not sounding particularly excited, more like resigned. "Your sister is gone. No idea where. All she took was some cash your grandfather gave her. Said she'll be back later tonight. And she left your grandfather in tears."

He glanced at his watch: almost eleven. Tanya was no doubt already here, waiting for him. Emily Wright's interview was scheduled to begin in a few minutes. After it, he'd deal with Tanya. And then Cochrane, hopefully combined with a quick run out to the farm to check on Pops. If he was lucky, somewhere in there he'd be able to grab a bite to eat and follow up with Balanchuk.

As he headed down the ER's back hallway to the Crisis Intervention Center's interview rooms, Luka texted Harper, who replied that they still had no luck with their mystery motorcycle, then he called Ray Acevedo, hoping for better news. "What did you find at the college?"

"Forget getting a vicious killer off the street or avenging the death of their colleague," Ray said, his tone filled with scorn. "Idiots are more concerned about a bunch of computer code—as if I'd know enough to even give a shit. And Wright's boss said Wright's office and work computers are off limits to us, that we'd need to go through the DIA. Said they're sending a government jabberwonky up from DC."

"Your government jabberwonky is here already." He explained about Radcliffe and his so-called cooperation. "Turns out the DOD stopped working with Wright a few weeks ago—Radcliffe wasn't saying why."

"They'll be digging diamonds from coal mines before the DIA will share anything useful they find," Ray scoffed. "Tierney find anything helpful?"

Luka told him about the abnormal tox screen and the possibility that Wright had been tortured and the killing staged.

"Tortured?" Ray's whistle echoed through the phone.

"Any complaints from students or other faculty?"

"Dr. Ian Wright. Great guy, everyone loved him, adored by all near and far." Ray's tone was a mocking singsong. "Usual shit. Got the same from the neighbors about both Mr. and Mrs."

Typical. No one ever wanted to speak ill of the dead—especially not a murder victim. Not at first, anyway. Eventually they'd ferret out Wright's dirty little secrets, then folks would be lining up to say, "I had a feeling…"

"Anyone talk about him losing his DOD consulting gig?"

"Nope, no one would say anything about his work other than he was some kind of genius at it. Except, there's this one guy, grad student, gave his prof the stink eye while the guy was talking up Wright. I want to chase him down, see what's up."

"Good. After that, wanna play bad cop?" It was a rhetorical question; Ray lived to play bad cop. "Did you see the video from the ER this morning?"

"Guy who threw the bloody bandage at the widow? Yeah. Hospital hiding behind privacy laws?"

"Gave him up, after a bit of persuasion. Krichek ran him. He's got a history of domestic assault charges—only one ever made it to trial. Name of Jefferson Cochrane."

"Doesn't ring a bell." Ray had an encyclopedic memory when it came to actors he'd encountered. "You bringing the guy into the house or are we ambushing him at work?"

"Neither. Uniforms tracked him to his home. I'll text, meet you there soon as I wrap up here." Luka gave Cochrane's address to Ray and hung up. Interviewing subjects in the comfort of their home tended to relax them, give them a false sense of confidence and security. Which he readily used against them—while also gaining the advantage of a casual look around. Anything in plain sight was fair game and sometimes enough to get a warrant for a more thorough search.

He shook his head—his simple home invasion had become much too complicated, but he'd suspected that it might from the beginning. One time he wished his gut instinct was wrong.

CHAPTER 16

Emily was still yawning as Leah helped her through a quick shower and change into clean pajamas. Exhausted, she'd probably sleep on and off all day. As a survival mechanism, Emily's ability to sleep while her brain processed her trauma was an excellent one. Ian was the same way, could sleep through anything while Leah would toss and turn, enviously watching him slumber.

She'd just finished combing Emily's hair when Jessica arrived to escort them downstairs to the ER's Crisis Intervention Center. "You didn't have to come yourself," Leah told Jessica as the elevator whisked them away from the pediatric floor. Emily said nothing, merely held Leah's hand tight while squinting at Jessica with suspicion.

"I thought a familiar face—although, I'm sure you already know the social workers from the CIC. And…" Jessica crouched down to Emily's level. "I wanted to make sure Emily didn't have any questions."

The elevator came to a stop and they emerged into the main floor hallway that ran behind the ER, leading from the hospital entrance to the cafeteria. Emily glanced in the direction of the cafeteria—home to her favorite hamburgers and all the frozen yogurt with toppings she could eat.

"Hungry?" Leah asked, happy to grasp any excuse to postpone the interview.

Emily frowned and shook her head, then turned and followed Jessica through the secure doors. They reached the children's interview room, which was designed like a playroom, filled with interactive games, dolls, stuffed animals, and a variety of art supplies. The decor was soft edges, pastels, intended to allow kids to relax even as they disclosed their painful secrets.

Jessica opened the door and waited for Emily to step inside. "You can play with anything you want," she told Emily. "But I thought first we could show your mom a magic trick. Want to help?"

Emily stood inside the door, her gaze circling the room, taking in every detail as she twisted a length of hair and chewed on it. Leah regretted not having the time to braid it—Emily's hair was like Leah's, had a mind of its own if not tamed. She gently removed Emily's hand from her mouth. Emily stared at the wet hair clenched in her fist as if she hadn't even realized what she'd done.

"Pumpkin, how about if you explore for a minute while Jessica and I talk?"

Emily nodded and moved to methodically dissect the contents of the room. Leah and Jessica watched from the doorway. "You'll be using a trauma-informed interview format?" Leah asked.

"Combined with Palouse mindfulness-based stress reduction," Jessica answered. "I know you're worried about any adverse impact on Emily, which is why I thought we might use one of my research projects." She bent over the child-height table and opened a box that sat on it, revealing a small EEG cap. "Gordie, my husband, and I were working on this when he died. It's an enhanced, wireless EEG. I can monitor Emily's responses in real time, slow down or stop if anything is too disturbing."

Emily, drawn to the adult discussion, had drifted near to the table. "Is that the magic trick?"

"It's a special hat you use to make it work. Want to try?"

Emily nodded. Jessica slid the cap onto her, snugging it tight and aligning the electrodes over her skull. Then Jessica donned a similar cap and turned on the video game console. "Okay. This is easy. Kinda like T-ball. You hold the joystick to control the bat—the idea is to hit the ball and dunk the clown. But you won't be doing any of the work, you won't even see the pitch or anything except the clown in the dunking booth."

"How can I hit the ball if I can't see it?" Emily asked.

Jessica set her tablet onto the table and sat on the floor, her skirts flouncing around her. "We do it together. I see the ball coming and—here's the magic part—I'll guide your hand to swing at just the right time to hit it."

"You'll hold my hand?" Emily seemed deflated. "Daddy lets me play games myself—I even beat him. Lots of times."

"Just try it." Jessica motioned for Emily to sit at the video games. "Hold on tight but don't move the controls. Ready?"

Emily nodded, focused on the clown mocking her from its perch on the dunking stool. Jessica flicked a screen on her tablet, revealing Emily's brain waves, watching them for a moment.

"Imagine moving your hand on the joystick but don't actually do it," she told Emily. A spike blipped across the screen. "Perfect," Jessica said. "All right, here comes the magic—watch the clown." Jessica gripped an imaginary joystick and as the pitch soared across her tablet's screen she flicked her hand with a definitive motion.

The sound of a bat smacking a ball sounded from Emily's screen followed by the splash of the clown being dunked. Emily jumped up. "Mommy! I dunked the clown by magic. My hand moved the stick without me even thinking about it." She turned to Jessica. "Do it again! Show me how it works. Please?"

Jessica repeated the feat. This time Leah kept her gaze on Emily's hand on the controls. Sure enough, Jessica's motion was mirrored by Emily's own hand, even though Emily couldn't see Jessica.

"You're stimulating her motor cortex?" There was an edge to Leah's voice that drew Emily's attention. There was no way for Emily to know that Jessica had basically just taken over Emily's hand—without even asking Leah's permission.

"What's a cortex?" Emily asked, joining them as if she were an equal.

"It's part of your brain," Jessica explained before Leah could say anything. She lowered herself to Emily's eye level and drew a quick sketch on the tablet. "If I'm thinking of moving my hand and I know where in your brain your hand muscles live, then I can send a tiny spark of electricity and make your hand move."

"Electricity?" Emily considered. "From your brain to mine?"

"Exactly. That's all our thoughts are, really. Electricity."

Emily nodded, satisfied. "Mommy, I need to learn more about electricity. Can we try some more experiments?"

"Maybe when we're done talking," Jessica promised. "If your mom says it's okay. And I can show you other stuff, too. Like building a special place in your head where you can go if you get scared or sad or anything. Your own private, magic world where you can make anything happen." She stood, smoothed her skirt, then removed her own EEG cap and patted her hair into place. "I'm going to send Veronica, our social worker, in. She'll show you the other toys and then I'll be back, okay?"

Leah hesitated. She stepped over to Emily, knelt on the cushioned padding that covered the floor. "Did it hurt? When she did that?"

"No," Emily said. "Just a tingle." She pointed to the side of her head. "I watched my hand but I wasn't telling it to do anything. I want to learn how to do it—the kids at school will think I'm so cool." Then her expression turned sad once more. "I wish Daddy was here. He'd know how it works, we could build our own."

"You're okay talking to Dr. Jessica? You know if you need to stop or want me, just tell her. I'll be right behind that mirror, watching."

Emily focused on her reflection. "I can't see through the mirror but you can? Can I see how?" It seemed that while Leah's defenses centered on avoidance—putting off until tomorrow what she couldn't deal with today—Emily's involved curiosity, keeping her mind active and engaged.

"Sure. Follow me." Leah led Emily out the door and then into the observation room situated between the children's interview room on one side and the adult one—currently empty—on the other. It was a narrow space kept dark so as to not impede with observation, even though now all their interviews were filmed and a social worker watched them live, ready to intervene if necessary. Emily pressed her face against the glass, then nodded, magic secret revealed. Jessica introduced her to the social worker, who led Emily back to the playroom while they waited for Luka Jericho to arrive.

"You should have asked my permission before you did that, taking control of her hand to play that game," Leah told Jessica.

Jessica shrugged. "Just a harmless parlor trick, but it impresses donors when I apply for grants. Then I let them fly a drone remotely, using only their minds to control it. Their wallets open every time."

"Does it work like the new artificial limbs that can be controlled by the wearer's thoughts?"

Jessica's smile flashed bright. "My Gordie created the tech for those, I simply adapted it to the enhanced EEG unit. Saving the world, one limb at a time, Gordie used to say." Then her smile faltered, turning to sorrow. Leah remembered that Jessica's husband had also been murdered. She regretted bringing him up.

Jessica seemed to understand. She laid a hand on Leah's arm. "You'll feel the same. It's a gut-kick, every time. Nothing to do but keep on living for those who can't."

They stood silent for a moment, watching Emily decide on a set of Legos to play with.

"How are you?" Jessica asked.

"Fine," Leah answered reflexively.

"Seriously. How are you?"

"I'm fine, really." Leah tried to steer the conversation away from her emotions. She'd have a lifetime to deal with them later, after making certain Emily was all right.

Jessica's expression grew skeptical. "Right. *Fine.* You aren't one of those people trying to tick off the stages of grief like a Chinese menu, are you? Because that's what we professionals call denial."

"I don't have time for any Kübler-Ross timeline. Emily needs me. Once I'm sure she's safe, then maybe..."

"You really think grief is something you can schedule later like a dentist appointment? It's not a timeline or appointment or even measurable stages. It's a damn monster, a Hydra. And as soon as you chop one head off, two more attack you from behind. It will smother you, strangle you, if you don't pay attention—and where would Emily be then?"

Leah's shoulders collapsed with her sigh. She was too damned tired to stand up straight, much less think clearly. "What can I do? I'm all she has left."

"My point exactly." Jessica glanced out the window to Emily, who was on her knees chasing a robot toy. "We have a few minutes before Detective Jericho arrives. Let me try to help you."

"How?"

"Sit down, close your eyes."

Leah was uncertain—she'd always failed miserably at meditation or any relaxation exercises. But Emily was safe... for now. And she could use any help she could get. She slumped into the chair the social worker had vacated and did as Jessica instructed, taking several deep breaths.

"Now, picture Ian. He's standing right in front of you. What would you say to him?"

As if Jessica had woven a magical spell, Ian appeared before Leah—shaking his head as if disappointed in her, no trace of blood over his bright yellow Curious George pajamas, his body unharmed, his face whole. She sucked her breath in so fast her chest burned.

"Go on," Jessica urged, her tone low and hypnotic. "Tell him how you feel. It's okay, you're in a safe space. Nothing can hurt you or Ian, not here."

Suddenly that burning in Leah's chest roared to life. "What the hell were you thinking?" She wanted to shout the words but instead they came out strangled, barely audible. "Fighting back? Getting yourself killed! What am I going to do now? I'm all alone. It's so like you, leaving me to pick up the pieces!"

She fell back in the chair, chest heaving as she gasped for air, hands curled into numb, frozen, useless fists. Her eyes popped open, banishing Ian's ghost. "No, no, that's not right. I don't blame him—how can I? He saved Emily."

"But he left you. Abandoned you. And you don't understand why," Jessica said. "It's perfectly normal. Anger, rage—at him, at yourself, at God. Terror at what comes next. It's what everyone goes through." She was silent a moment, giving Leah a chance to slow her breathing.

Feeling eased back into her cramped hands and she stretched her fingers, grabbing hold of the chair's arms as if they were lifelines.

"So, you were unhappy?" Jessica asked.

"No. God, no. Sure, I was always the practical one while he had his head in his work, but he was definitely the better parent. We have—had—a wonderful life, Ian and I." Leah hesitated, but Jessica said nothing, simply stared at her with a piercing gaze that demanded honesty—the whole truth. "Sometimes… I worried our life was so good, it was more because of him than me. I gave him everything I could, but I think I always still held some part of me back. Tried to control things, protect myself by being who I thought he wanted me to be."

"I think that's every intimate relationship, don't you? We either lose ourselves in the other person or we hold back a bit to prevent that."

"Selfish, letting him do the heavy lifting—" She stopped; it was just too painful to put into words.

"Leah, Ian loved you. He died to protect your family. So whatever you gave him in return, it was enough."

"No. No it wasn't. He poured his heart and soul into our family, into Emily, while I—"

"While you what? What do you pour your heart and soul into, Leah?"

Leah swallowed hard. "Work. Not for the thrill of it, the adrenaline rush. Not because I don't love my family just as much. I can't explain it. It's like I'm paying penance, trying to make up for something or prove myself. Like if I can help enough people, save enough lives, then maybe…" She knotted her hands together. This all sounded so stupid. She couldn't believe she was even here talking about this when there was so much more she needed to do. Starting with getting Emily through her interview.

"Maybe you'd be worthy of love? A good enough person to deserve Ian's love?" Jessica suggested in a quiet tone. Leah nodded, her lips pressed tight as she blinked back tears. "Where do you think that comes from, Leah? Who taught you that you weren't worthy of love?"

Leah couldn't meet Jessica's eyes. Thankfully a knock on the door prevented Jessica from probing further into Leah's psyche. Luka Jericho arriving for Emily's interview.

As Jessica greeted the detective, Leah stood, facing the observation window, hands fisted by her sides. She knew damn well where she'd learned that lesson—a lifetime of being abandoned. No matter how good she was, it was never enough to earn the love of the person who mattered most. Her own mother. Ruby.

CHAPTER 17

After introducing himself to everyone, Luka settled in beside Leah at the window looking into the children's interview room.

The narrow, dark observation room had a few folding chairs leaning against the wall, but with the video equipment and desk where the social worker sat, headphones on as she monitored the interview, and two more adult-sized humans crammed into the tiny space, it was too crowded to make use of them. Besides, it felt wrong for Luka to sit in comfort while Leah stood.

Parents usually weren't allowed to observe—last thing you wanted was for a kid to disclose something and have the parent right there working on a rebuttal or worse, a plan to silence the kid—but it wasn't as if anyone had consulted Luka on the matter. Leah Wright was allowing her daughter to be interviewed voluntarily, and Luka needed to hear what his only witness had to say. He resigned himself to make the best of the situation, using it as an opportunity to study her more closely.

She was holding up well, he thought. Better than most. Exhaustion would set in soon, though, and her defenses would crumble. As a detective he needed to remain objective, but Luka couldn't help feeling sorry for her.

His phone pinged with a text. Krichek alerting him to more videos popping up on social media. All accusing Leah Wright of malpractice, racism, even sexual impropriety. Serious charges. Except that the videos Luka clicked through, leaving the audio off so Leah wouldn't hear, were obviously fakes, edited clips of random people interspersed with text skewing their words, directing their accusations at Leah. He even recognized one shot from a recent police shooting across the country in Oakland. Damn trolls, already mobilized and out in force, feeding off the latest tragedy they could exploit.

He glanced at Leah, who had one palm and her nose pressed against the glass as Dr. Kern began by leading her daughter through her day yesterday. Maybe Harper could act as family liaison—she'd hate the idea, think it was because she was a woman, and it was, but that didn't change the fact that the family needed watching over and you never knew what they might let slip once they grew comfortable.

He texted Harper, checking again on her progress in tracing their mystery motorcycle. *No joy*, she sent back.

"Mrs. Wright," he said in a low tone. With her headphones on, the social worker couldn't hear him, but standing in the dark like this, at such close quarters, it felt appropriate to whisper. Like hushing your voice in church. "The man in the ER earlier. What can you tell me about him?"

She said nothing, her gaze on her daughter, her entire body now leaning against the glass as if she wanted to claw her way through it.

"Mrs. Wright?" He purposefully avoided her medical title, wanted her to answer as a wife and mother, not with the clinical detachment of a physician. "The man in the ER?"

"What?" She frowned as she finally turned her face to him. "I have no idea. I don't remember ever seeing him before. Why?"

"His name is Jefferson Cochrane. He seemed rather… volatile. Said you were responsible for his wife's death." He let his words linger, waited as she refocused her full attention on the implications.

"I don't remember him." The words emerged slow and heavy, as if she didn't realize she was repeating herself.

"Maybe you never met him in person before? Do you ever make death notifications over the phone? Or to other family members if the husband isn't available?"

Her frown deepened. "I had a long-distance trucker die in a crash on the interstate. He was from Oklahoma, so I had to call his wife, tell her—after Maggie talked to the local authorities, made sure they sent someone out to be with her. Guess I didn't even have to really do that, but I wanted to give her the chance to ask any questions. People, they always have questions and you don't want them to feel like you're ignoring them. It's important to give them any answers you can."

"Do you have any malpractice suits brought against you? Maybe the wife didn't die right away?"

She shook her head vigorously. "No. Only case I've been party to was when I was a resident and it was dismissed. And that patient was a man."

"Anyone else make complaints against your care here in the ER? Someone who might not take their grievance to a lawyer, might make it personal?"

Her gaze drifted past him to where Emily was talking about the dinner she and her father had cooked. Trees—broccoli, Luka interpreted—mac and cheese and ham. Classic. When he was a kid his mom used to set the broccoli upright in the mac and cheese, create a little forest. He wondered if Ian had done the same. Or maybe Emily was a picky eater, liked all her food separated and not touching. And the way she spoke, her vocabulary and grammar—definitely advanced for a six-year-old.

Not that Luka knew much about kids. They made him nervous. When they finally deemed to glance up from their ubiquitous screens, they peered at him as if he were a specimen of some long extinct species. Give him old folks like Pops to deal with any day.

Luka slid his hand into his pocket where his phone was, half-tempted to text Janine, see if Pops was okay. But the psychiatrist had gotten to the heart of the night, and Emily was describing waking to the sound of shouting and thuds that made the house shake. Luka listened to the little girl as he watched her mother.

Kern had Emily so relaxed. At first. Then her voice drew tight, her words coming in halting gasps, barely above a whisper.

Kern glanced at her tablet, then gave Leah a nod. Through the glass he could see that Kern was monitoring Emily's brainwaves, which explained the weird cap she wore. Despite the psychiatrist's reassurance, Leah's palms against the window drew into fists. The muscles around her jaw clenched and her shoulders were rigid.

Not for the first time, he was glad he'd never had any kids. His phone buzzed—Tanya waiting in the cafeteria, threatening to leave if he didn't get there soon. As if whatever her problem was, it was somehow his fault. As if he was the one who'd chosen drugs over her family. He'd never understand that—would maybe never forgive either. Was meeting her now, losing traction in a homicide case, even for the few minutes it would take to read her the riot act, worth it?

As Emily began describing crawling under her bed and how scared she'd been, Leah startled Luka by suddenly leaving, banging through the door leading to the hall. Luka started to follow but stopped when he saw her enter the second soundproofed interview room—the one designed for adults with its intimate arrangement of comfortable chairs. He couldn't hear her, but through the glass that separated them he watched her slam the wall with her palm and throw her head back as she screamed so hard every muscle along her neck tightened into thin, taut ribbons.

Luka couldn't begin to imagine the mother's pain of being forced to watch her daughter relive the trauma of seeing her father killed, helpless to erase Emily's memories, powerless to intervene. He was torn between Leah's pain and his duties—which did not include playing trauma counselor. In fact, Ray would argue that catching a suspect during an emotionally vulnerable time was a good way to get the truth from them.

His phone buzzed again. Tanya. Again. He ignored it, glancing through the window. Emily finished telling her story—what the hell was a blackspaceman?

The social worker looked up, gesturing to the computer screen where she had a close-up of what Emily was drawing. It was a human figure, not fat but with its torso and limbs bulked out like a comic book astronaut, drawn all in black. And where its head should have been was a circle, larger than life, out of proportion to the figure's body. As he watched, Emily carefully filled the circle in until it was a solid, menacing chunk of black.

Then she added a slash of yellow along the top of where the figure's face should be. Curved. Like a reflection.

Not a spaceman, Luka realized. A man in padded leathers, gloves, and a black tinted motorcycle helmet with its shield down.

It made sense. If you didn't want to contaminate a crime scene with your own DNA or fingerprints there was nothing better. Want to avoid easily observable victim's blood? Check. Expecting your victim to fight back? Thick leather designed to protect against road rash after a spill was just as effective in protecting against someone's efforts to defend themselves.

Whoever their actor was, he knew exactly what he was doing.

CHAPTER 18

Watching Emily fighting so hard to be brave, Leah wanted to hit something, someone, wanted to shout, yell, anything to unleash her rage.

She fled to the other interview room, thankful for its sound-proofing, and gave voice to her grief and madness. Keeping the light off, she pounded the wall, screams of frustration tearing out of her, feeling like a tortured animal. The man she wanted to hurt wasn't here and she didn't know what to do with the awful awareness that he was out there somewhere. Her breath came in jagged gasps, until she collapsed against the wall, her weight pressed against her fists, her forehead bowed in surrender.

She couldn't do this. Not without Ian.

The door opened behind her. She turned her face to look at the intruder silhouetted in the light coming from the hallway. Luka Jericho.

"I have to go but thought maybe..." He left his sentence hanging. He did that a lot, leaving people to fill his silences with their own stories. It was the same technique she used in the ER when interviewing a patient. Except this time as the silence lengthened, he was the one who yielded. "I know you have resources, know the people to call, but if you want me to—I mean, I understand in our professions, it's not easy. I can recommend someone to talk to. If you want."

"I'm fine, thanks," she lied.

"Dr. Kern, she seems pretty good, the way she's working with your daughter. Maybe she could—"

"What did the autopsy show?" she asked. "Were there defensive wounds? Did Ian fight back? Was that what set him off, the killer, why he got so violent?" Her voice rose. She didn't blame Ian, of course not, but she'd seen his body, knew he'd not given in to the intruder, and could not help the anger churning through her, a fire in her veins even as her face and fingers grew numb and cold at the thought of him leaving her. Abandoning her.

How could he do that to her? To Emily? By fighting back, he kept the killer in the house longer, putting Emily's life in danger. Why would Ian do that, risk that? She spun away from Jericho, slapping the wall once again, her breaths coming so fast that she realized she was in danger of hyperventilating. *Ian, what the hell were you thinking?* "Why didn't he give him what he wanted? Get him out of the house before he could get anywhere near—"

"It wasn't your husband's fault." Jericho's voice was calm, the voice of reason. Yet these emotions scorching through Leah felt anything but reasonable.

Through sheer force of will, Leah slowed her breathing, feeling pinpricks spread across her numb lips and fingers as life returned to them. "How long?"

"Time of death was right before midnight. While you were still in the ER. You couldn't have saved him if you had gotten home sooner—and might have ended up a victim yourself."

She hated how he knew exactly what she was asking and why. Hated that he'd done this so many times that it was second nature, these ugly, desperate questions that had no place in anyone's life. Hated that he could be so calm. Most of all, she hated that he was holding back, not telling her the truth. At least not all of it.

"Don't lie to me, Detective. No autopsy can put the time of death that accurately. And don't you dare tell me he went quickly in the end—I saw his body, saw the damage. He suffered, damn it!

He was in pain and he was fighting for his life and Emily's and I wasn't there for them. So don't you dare tell me, don't you dare—" Her logic unraveled and she clamped her lips tight.

"You're right," he said, which infuriated her more. Maybe that was the idea—give her a target to vent her rage on? A victim, he was treating her like a victim. Helpless, emotional, malleable. "We didn't narrow time of death from the PM—it came from witness statements."

She jerked her chin up at that. "Witness? What did they see? Did they recognize him? Do you know who he is?"

"No. Not yet. We have surveillance video of a man in a black motorcycle helmet, his face covered, wearing black leathers. Just like your daughter saw." He held out a sheet of drawing paper for her to see.

She sagged against the wall in relief. "Emily never saw his face. And he must know that, know she can't identify him." Which meant the killer wouldn't be coming after Emily; she was safe. "Why? Why us? Why pick a house where people were awake, lights on?"

Jericho carefully folded Emily's drawing and slid it into the inside pocket of his coat. "We're working on that. Mrs. Wright, did your husband ever use drugs? Of any kind? Recreational? Prescribed?"

Leah frowned at the abrupt change in topic. Drugs? Ian? Never. "Ian was a health nut—had to be, with a job staring at the computer all day. Exercise was his drug of choice. He hated taking medicine of any—" She stopped, staring at him, realization finally breaking through the fog smothering her brain. "Wait. Maggie said she found something. On the tox screen. What? What did you find?"

"We're not sure," he said slowly, choosing his words carefully. Treating her like a victim—or a suspect? The thought rekindled her anger, but she'd exhausted all her adrenaline, had no strength left for outrage. "The preliminary tox screen showed possible hallucinogens. But nothing common. Dr. Tierney is sending for special tests, thinks they might have been designer drugs."

"You think my husband was doing some kind of designer drug?" PCP could account for the level of violence—but Ian had not done that to himself. "You're crazy. He'd never. Never would he take anything that would cloud his mind. Ian's mind, it's special, like a Bach composition; works on several levels at once, absorbing what he sees and hears and translates it into beautiful, glorious ideas and solutions to problems people haven't even imagined." It was what had made her fall in love with Ian. "Poetry. That's Ian's mind. He'd never use drugs—never."

Jericho watched her with a clinical expression. Leah couldn't help but wonder if that was also how she appeared to her patients? Aloof, observing without feeling?

"Have you thought of anyone who might have targeted your husband or your family?" he asked.

"No. I already told you—" She stopped. Thought about the crazed look on the man who'd assaulted her in the ER earlier. "Ask my boss for the crank files. People who make up crazy accusations about their care in the ER. I don't remember anyone specific directing them at me, but a lot of times they don't even remember who they saw when they were here. It's easy to latch onto any name, a face."

"And right now yours is definitely out there." He hesitated. "You'd mentioned money was an issue."

"Not an issue. We're just needing to watch carefully, stick to our budget."

"What was the ten thousand dollars for?"

Leah stared at him, certain she'd misheard. "Ten thousand dollars? What ten thousand dollars?"

"The ten grand your husband withdrew from your checking account last week. In cash."

She fought to keep the surprise from her face. Ten thousand dollars cash? That was their emergency fund. What the hell had Ian needed ten thousand dollars for? Why hadn't he told her? And cash—carrying that much money around with him, maybe somebody saw, followed him back to the house. Maybe that was what started all this. It would explain why nothing obvious had been taken from the house.

"Mrs. Wright?" Jericho persisted.

"Sorry. I don't know anything about that." She sounded guilty as hell—saw it reflected in his expression, the way it closed down.

"Okay." He seemed disappointed. "Do you know anyone named Katrina Balanchuk? Or maybe Trina?"

"No. Sorry." She shook her head, the strange syllables of the woman's name echoing in her mind.

"You're certain? No Trina in your or Ian's lives?" He held his phone up to her. "Recognize this woman?"

It was a photo of a blond in her twenties, eyes wide as the camera flashed, obviously taken for a driver's license or other ID photo. "No. Who is she?"

"We're not sure. Maybe nobody."

Jericho shifted his weight, the first time she'd seen him uncomfortable about a topic. He was evading the truth. She wasn't entirely certain that she wanted to know the truth—what had Ian been involved in?

She kept her voice steady, calm, inviting him to trust her with the truth. "Is this about Ian's work? Is Trina one of Ian's students?"

"No." He paused, the weight of the silence bearing down on her as her mind leapt to a myriad of suspicions—none that she wanted to acknowledge as being even remotely possible. "She and your husband began meeting several months ago. Two to three times a week from the dates."

Stunned, she turned to the wall, anywhere to avoid seeing his face, hearing his words and what they implied. "You think… Ian… No. No. You're wrong." Her words felt weak, defenseless against his accusations. Could Ian have betrayed her? Never.

He cleared his throat. "We found some drawings. Made by your husband. She was nude."

His words hit like a gut punch, staggering her. Drawings? She and Ian had met at an art class—but he hadn't done anything more than doodle since they were married. At least not that she'd seen. Or that he'd shown her. Her mouth went dry at the thought of Ian meeting another woman the same way he'd entered Leah's life. No. Impossible… But people didn't change, history repeated itself, and Lord knew she wasn't the perfect wife.

Had he fallen in love with someone else?

"I need to leave," she choked out, fighting the bile burning her throat.

For a moment Jericho looked like he was going to stop her, ask her more questions that she had no answers to. But he relented, standing aside so that the doorway was clear. "Do you know where you're going? After Emily is discharged?"

"No. I guess a hotel. Ian's parents are flying in from Seattle, so wherever they've booked a room." She hated to leave the protection of Good Sam. She felt safe here. Out there, in the world that let Ian die, where her husband might not be the man she'd loved and trusted more than anyone else in her life, that world felt anything but safe.

"I could arrange for an officer to accompany you. Protect you from the press."

"Protect me? You don't actually mean from the press, do you? Are you saying we're in danger? Why would the killer target us when he made sure that Emily didn't see anything?" She didn't like the way his frown spoke louder than any words might. He *was* worried. "Is it because of that guy in the ER earlier? I told you, that has nothing to do with me. He was confused, upset, that's all."

Or maybe it was because of this Katrina woman? Or the missing money? But asking those questions made Ian's betrayal seem too possible, too real.

"Just tell me before you leave the hospital. I've already asked security to place a man on Emily's ward."

"So now we're prisoners?" she flared. But they both knew it wasn't the idea of being sequestered here at Good Sam that had her upset. It was the thought that this wasn't some random home invasion. That Ian had been targeted. That she and her daughter might still be in danger.

Ian, what did you do? The words screamed through her brain.

Leah straightened her posture, using all her energy to stay in control. She couldn't lose it, not in front of Jericho. Couldn't let him see her vulnerable. "Thank you." The words almost strangled her. Not with lack of gratitude but with fear as the enormity of the situation overwhelmed her. "You'll let me know—"

"Of course. We'll need to discuss this further, take a formal statement. After you get your daughter settled."

She had the feeling he meant something very different. Like maybe after he finished dissecting Leah and Ian's lives. Dug up more of their secrets. God, if he found Ruby—she hated to even think of the tales her mother would spin, basking in the limelight of a police investigation.

"In the meantime," he finished, "call me if you need anything."

As he left, Leah couldn't help but wonder if Jericho still saw her as a victim... or as a suspect.

CHAPTER 19

After leaving Leah, Luka's first move was to call Harper to let her know that their motorcycle rider had just moved from potential witness to possible armed and dangerous suspect. She sounded frustrated by her lack of progress and promised to update him as soon as she found either the bike or rider.

He decided to meet Tanya and grab a sandwich from the hospital cafeteria before he left for Cochrane's interview. Lord only knew when he'd get a chance to eat again. Tanya—his stomach roiled with anger at the thought of seeing her again after all these years. Nine years since she'd dared show her face to him. Not even coming to their parents' funerals. He debated stopping by the hospital's ATM to grab some cash as an incentive for her to leave and never return, but it would only go straight into her arm, so what was the use?

As he waited in line to check out, a turkey and avocado wrap and a milk in hand, he realized a large part of his anger and frustration had nothing to do with Tanya. Usually Luka loved the whirlwind rush when an investigation heated up and he found himself juggling multiple leads, each a thread weaving through the background noise to form a tapestry revealing the truth. More than multi-tasking, it was as if his mind switched focus so quickly from one idea to the next that he could almost glimpse the whole. Not quite knowing the answers to every question, but enough that he'd feel optimistic that he and his team could actually control the chaos, find the answers they needed. But Ian

Wright's murder was not giving him that satisfying rush. Instead, Luka felt overwhelmed. Everything about Leah was confusing him. She'd honestly seemed stunned when Luka asked her about the money and Katrina Balanchuk. Yet, she didn't demand to see any proof, instead had turned the tables, interrogating Luka with an unnerving calm.

He remembered how he'd felt after Cherise's death. The more he bottled his emotions in, the more they escaped, lava surging through cracks. Leah seemed even more self-contained. Was her breakdown in the interview room a symptom of the same grief-stricken pain he'd suffered—or was she simply a very good actress who'd chosen then and there to display emotion because she knew Luka was watching?

Luka paid for his food. He'd already spotted Tanya when he'd arrived, sitting at a table in the farthest corner of the cafeteria. Although the cafeteria was warm, she wore a wool coat that hung off her shoulders, was several sizes too large. She'd lost weight, her hair was cropped short—an abrupt change from the long, long tresses she'd been so proud of when she was young.

"What, nothing for your long-lost little sister?" Tanya greeted him as he approached. A half-empty cup of tea and a pile of empty sugar packets sat before her. "Kept me waiting long enough."

Luka took the seat opposite, the chair's metal feet squeaking against the linoleum. He removed the lid from his milk, unwrapped his food, took a bite and washed it down before answering. "I'm here. What do you want, Tanya?"

"Hi, Tanya. How ya doing, Tanya? What's been going on in your life, past nine years?" Her voice was singsong, taunting him.

"I don't need to ask, I already know the answers," he retorted. Was she high now? No. Her face was gaunt with need and although her eyelids sagged, her pupils were normal in size.

"Right. Mr. Detective, all-seeing, all-knowing. You know nothing."

Luka's phone buzzed. Ray asking on an ETA for the Cochrane interview. As Luka typed he replied to Tanya, "Cut to the chase. What's it going to take to get rid of you this time? Pops doesn't have any money, but you already know that, don't you?" Long-buried rage boiled over. "I don't have a house to mortgage for you like Mom and Dad. And you're never getting the farm—"

"Not my fault Mom and Dad lost the house—"

"What do you think happens when your junkie daughter eats up all your savings and you can't make your mortgage payments?"

"You still blame me, don't you? You think I'm the reason they're dead."

Luka couldn't push words past the fury tightening his throat. Of course he blamed her. Who else was there to blame except Tanya? Their deaths had crushed Luka. Not Tanya. After they'd died, she'd left rehab and vanished.

"Must be nice never to feel guilt or remorse or face the consequences of your actions. Take a look in the mirror sometime, Tanya. Then ask yourself why they're dead. Maybe you'll finally hear the truth. I doubt it, though. Doubt you hear anything except your own damn lies."

"Talk about lies—where were you the day they died? They said you were coming, so excited you were actually for the first time coming to see your little sister, finally give me a chance at forgiveness. But no. You put work over your own family. Like always."

His grip tightened on his sandwich, squashing the avocado until it ran out the end. He threw it down, his appetite vanished. "What do you want?"

"Told you, I need help." She glanced past him as if the hospital visitors and staff were more interesting than their awkward family reunion. "I talked to Pops. He said he'd—"

"I told you. He's got nothing left for you." So typical, trying to take advantage of an old man. A decade's worth of ire churned through him. "None of us do. There's nothing left, Tanya. Nothing for you here."

"Maybe it's not for me," she retorted. "Ever think of that, big brother? Ever think of anyone but yourself?"

"Let me guess. One of your friends got arrested and suddenly you think your big brother cop can bail them out." He remembered too damned many times, her dragging her friends to their parents' house. "If you think I'm helping any of your addict friends, you've lost your mind."

She held her cup with both hands but still it shook, clattering against the tabletop. "This was a mistake. Asking you for help." She scoffed. "Should've known better. You've got no heart at all, never have."

As if Luka was the bad guy here. His phone buzzed again, reminding him that he didn't have time for Tanya's BS. He scraped back his chair, standing so fast it almost toppled over. "You're right, Tanya. There's nothing left for me to give—Pops either. You've already taken everything. Go away. Leave us in peace."

"Don't worry, big brother." Her tone was filled with venom, yet he could swear she blinked back tears. "You'll never see me again. You've got my word on that."

Luka shook his head. She was as hopeless as ever. He stalked away without looking back, a sharp prickling behind his eyes.

He left the cafeteria and headed to the ER's admin office where he asked the secretary to get him a copy of the crank file Leah had mentioned. After Cochrane's assault in the ER earlier, he was curious to see how many other patient families might hold Leah responsible for their loved ones' deaths.

"You've seen Leah, then?" the departmental secretary asked Luka while she waited for her boss to call her back with permission to release the information. "Is she doing okay?"

Luka noticed the way she used Leah's first name—the other ER staff members, even the clerks and nursing assistants had as well.

Was Leah someone uncomfortable with her position of authority? Or someone trying hard to fit in with everyone else?

"She's as well as can be expected," he replied.

The secretary's phone rang—it was her boss, telling her she had to go through the legal department. She hung up and then spoke to someone there before returning her attention to Luka. "It will be a few minutes. They need to print them out so they can redact any patient information."

"No problem. I really appreciate your help—it's so important, especially this early in the case."

Her eyes widened. "Of course. Anything I can do. We're putting together a gift basket—a few basic necessities for Leah and Emily. And one of the charge nurses is setting up a meal calendar."

"I love how you guys come together—like a family." He couldn't help but think of Tanya. To her, family was an ATM, something you hit up over and over whenever you needed it, but never paid anything back. Hell, never even tried to give anything back. He hoped she was as good as her word about leaving for good this time, but knew she wasn't. He needed to find a way to protect Pops for when she did inevitably return.

"Exactly," the clerk said, making Luka blink and return his focus to her. And his case. This was no time to let Tanya distract him. "That's what we are—family. Just like you police officers and the firemen and paramedics. We know what it's like on the front lines, you know?"

He leaned his hip against her desk. "Don't suppose you could do me a quick favor? One more, I mean? I need to verify if someone was ever a patient of Leah's—and if he was, then I can go to a judge and get a court order for his records, but…"

"Why spend all that time to get the court order unless you know he actually was ever here in the first place?" she supplied eagerly.

"Exactly."

She edged a glance past him out the open door leading to the hallway. No one was there—in fact, no one had passed the entire time Luka had been standing there. It seemed that ER doctors rarely used their offices. He glanced at the name plate in front of her desk.

"I'd really appreciate it, Sara."

She turned to her computer, holding her body to block Luka's view. "What's the name?"

"Cochrane. Jefferson Cochrane." Luka gave her Cochrane's vital statistics.

"He's been seen in the ER, several times, but never by Dr. Wright. Oh, last time he was here was this morning." She blanked the computer screen and turned back to him. "Does that help?"

"It does. You just saved me hours of time." His phone buzzed. Harper. "Sorry, I need to take this."

"Checked in with the CSU guys," Harper started. "They found finger and palm prints not belonging to the victim, but all that came up were seams and patterns consistent with leather driving gloves. And that stuff the ME sent over, the scrapings from under the victim's nails?"

"Black leather."

"Bingo. So I left them to keep working—they promise they'll call if they find anything at all," she rushed to add, sounding a bit like a kid caught playing hooky, "while I kept working the motorcycle angle."

"Anything on the traffic cams?"

"Nothing so far," Harper said. "So, I tried a different approach—"

Luka waited, hoping she hadn't been distracted—that seemed like Harper's flaw, going after the bright and shiny instead of digging deeper. That and an overwhelming need to impress. Which meant she hadn't called him simply to give him bad news.

"I figured out what kind of bike it was," she continued, rewarding his faith in her. "Turns out it's kinda rare, at least compared to

Hondas or Kawasakis or Harleys. A 2012 Polaris Victory Hammer 8-Ball. I'm running local owners."

"Anything?"

"Narrowed it down to twenty-seven with addresses in the county. But," she added in a triumphant tone, "only eight of those have records. So I'm starting with them."

He frowned, disappointed. Reminded himself she was new at this. "You're on your way to interview them?"

"Thought I'd start with the ones in the city, work my way out." She sounded excited. Until he let the silence lengthen, waiting for her to see the error of her ways. "I should have told you first."

"But you didn't because you knew I'd say going to interview a potentially violent subject alone is a bonehead idea. And then you'd accuse me of treating you like a girl instead of a cop or some other baloney. Let's just cut to the chase. You pull over at the first restaurant you see, call Krichek and invite him to join you, buy him lunch for being such an idiot. Then together you work your way through the list. Forward it to me and make sure you keep dispatch informed every step of the way. Is that clear, Officer?" He stressed her rank, knowing that it would rankle.

"Yes, but—"

He wasn't sure whether to be impressed that she was actually standing her ground or irritated. "Look, even I'm stopping what I'm doing to join Ray on an interview. You seriously think he whined or complained about not being allowed to go alone? Two pairs of eyes are better than one and you want someone who has your back, just in case."

"Yes, sir, I understand." Harper sounded contrite. "But have you ever eaten with Krichek? Or ridden with him after? The man has some serious digestive issues, is all I'm saying."

"And that, Harper, is your cross to bear. Next time you'll think twice before going off alone."

"Yes, sir." She sighed.

An elderly man wearing a pink volunteer coat entered with a large manila envelope, handing it to Sara. There was a note attached to the top.

"Harper?" he added before he hung up. "Good work."

"Thanks, boss." He could feel the smile in her tone. "We still going after Balanchuk? Or are you waiting to see what we come up with on motorcycle guy?"

Luka was torn. He needed to check out Cochrane first. With his assault on Leah this morning, he had already proven himself to be a volatile subject, making him a higher priority.

"For now, focus on the motorcycle." He hung up.

Sara handed Luka the envelope. "All identifying information has been redacted, the lawyer said to tell you," she said, reading the note. "They say if you need more, you need a court order and to go through their office not ours." The lawyers sounded offended, as if Luka had been trying an end run around the law. But how could he know he needed a court order before knowing if there was anything to look for? Besides he really didn't have the time or manpower to waste if this didn't pan out.

He gave her a kind smile. "Thanks. I'm hoping I won't even need these, but I really appreciate the help."

She didn't smile in return. Instead, she looked worried. "Do you really think—I mean, could someone Leah took care of have done that to her husband?"

Luka could only shrug in reply.

"But if someone is that obsessed," she continued, "is Leah... is she safe?"

CHAPTER 20

After Jericho was out of sight, Leah paced the short hallway, feeling like a caged animal. She'd spent these past twelve hours locked into small prison cells: the ER exam room, Emily's room on peds, and now this forty-foot corridor. At least her cages were getting bigger. Thank God, because she needed to move, to think.

But no matter how fast she strode, counting floor tiles, forcing her breathing deep from the belly, she couldn't escape the face of the woman Luka had shown her. Ian had betrayed her. He didn't love her. He'd found someone else, younger, prettier, someone who could give him everything Leah couldn't.

Ian was going to leave her.

Hours spent together, Ian drawing the pretty, much younger woman—what else had they done? Jericho said she was naked in the drawings…

Touch the wall, pivot, twenty-three steps back, one, two, three, four…

She pulled up abruptly, a flash of red stealing her attention in the otherwise featureless wall. A tiny plastic box at eye level. Inside, no toy prize but the fire alarm. *Pull in case of emergency.*

Leah stood, frozen, entranced by the simple yet bold instructions. Emergency? She was the one who came to life when there was an emergency. She was the one everyone looked to to take charge, wade through the chaos and do what had to be done to save lives.

Ian was going to leave her… Ian already had left her. Ian was gone. Forever.

The emergency was long over—she'd missed it, clueless, oblivious. She remembered last night, how she'd smiled, cradling his roses, practically skipping down the garden path he'd shoveled and salted for her return home. How she couldn't wait to see what his surprise was—or to climb into bed, press their bodies together in a way that no one could ever, ever divide.

Was Jericho trying to force her off-balance? Was it some kind of police technique? Except... Jericho had seemed almost reluctant, sorry to show her the picture of—what was her name? Katrina. Trina. Pretty name, pretty girl.

Leah slid her fingers over the transparent fire alarm cover. It was secured only by a flimsy latch, designed to avoid accidental alarms. She toyed with the latch; the cover popped open. She could pull the alarm. Empty the building, create chaos for the entire hospital, patients and staff and visitors rushing into the freezing streets, their robes and white coats too thin for the February wind, milling around waiting for someone to tell them everything was safe, everything was all right, their lives could go on...

The thought made her want to smile, but she didn't. All her life she'd defined herself by being left behind. First, the little girl trying so hard to be good, to be no bother at all, to even be the caregiver, waiting for her mother to finally, for once, stay. Then the eleven-year-old who had no idea how to be a child being raised by a childless woman, always playing catch-up, pretending how to act like a kid like all the others who had real mothers and never quite succeeding.

College and med school, no time to figure out who she was, she was so determined to prove to the world that she belonged there, that she was worthy. And then, Ian. Who never cared how awkward and out of step with the rest of the world she was, who'd loved that about her instead of loving her despite it, who let her take control when she needed and who let her cling to him when life overwhelmed her.

Had he betrayed her?

She felt guilty even thinking the question—as if she were the one betraying Ian by questioning his loyalty, their love. She touched her fingers to her wedding band. The gold felt cold, as if his absence had drained it of life.

If she couldn't believe in Ian, who could she believe in? Ian had taught her how to love; he'd taught her how to be loved. Was it all a lie?

No.

Leah's fingers were on the fire alarm's lever, poised to pull it. Carefully, avoiding touching the alarm again, she pushed its plastic cage back into place, secured it. Then stood back. Who was she? She didn't need to even ask the question; she knew the answer: she was Emily's mother.

She pivoted, marched back to the observation room, lips clamped tight, voices in her head locked away in a cell as tiny as she could imagine, ready to get to work.

When she entered the narrow, dark space, it was empty. On the other side of the glass Jessica was leading Emily through some basic cognitive behavioral therapy. Emily, always one to enjoy the attention of an adult, talked a lot—but without actually revealing her true emotions, Leah noted. Too much like her mother that way, guarded. From Jessica's gentle prodding, it was clear she saw it as well.

As she waited, Leah scrolled through the missed messages on her phone. Well over a hundred now—so many people whose lives Ian had touched, pouring out their love and sympathy. Her chest tightened as she read, thinking of Jericho's accusations.

Emily's voice drifted to Leah from beyond the glass. She was describing her "happy place" to Jessica as she taught Emily a relaxation exercise. It sounded exactly like Nellie's lavender gardens. They'd lived at Nellie's house a short time before Nellie died. Emily had only been a toddler at the time. Did she still remember Nellie's old farmhouse, the fields of lavender surrounding it, the large rose garden that perfumed the air?

Her phone buzzed. The hospital operator. Leah answered. "This is Dr. Wright."

"Why won't you answer my calls?" came Ruby's voice. "I'm here, but they won't let me upstairs."

Leah froze. Her finger hovered over the phone, ready to disconnect.

"I was glad you called me," Ruby said, her tone tentative as if she, like Leah, had no real idea what to say.

"I wasn't calling you," Leah snapped, her anger pushing her beyond social niceties. It'd been a long time coming—twenty-three years to be exact. "Do you remember what you told me when you left me at Nellie's that last time?"

"You were blubbering, wouldn't let me go. I pushed you away, just so I could get out the door. You started shouting that you hated me."

"And what did you say, Ruby? What piece of worldly advice did you give that sobbing little girl who wanted her mommy?"

Ruby was silent. Leah could almost imagine the faraway look that would overcome her mother, eyes looking up and to one side, gazing into the heavens, searching for a convenient lie.

"What did you say, Ruby?" Leah's voice rose. Something she usually never let happen. Anger pushed people away. But she'd already lost Ruby long ago, so who cared?

"I told you to get used to it, that everybody leaves. But they leave faster if you're a snotty-nosed brat instead of being—" Ruby's voice broke. "Being a good girl."

And there it was. Leah blew out her breath, her fist closing, nails digging into her palm. The moment that had shaped Leah's life.

Maybe Ruby meant to teach her how to lose people. Maybe it was some warped kind of blessing, preparing Leah for this moment, this terrible, awful moment that was now redefining her entire life.

But what eleven-year-old Leah had learned was that it was only if she was good enough, only if she swallowed her anger, never showed fear, played the part of the "good girl," only then could she maybe, *maybe* hope that the people she loved would stay.

A hysterical laugh itched the back of her throat, begging to be set free. Everything Leah had learned her entire life, how to swallow her emotions, play the role others wanted, it was all a lie. Because no one stayed. Not Ruby, not Nellie, not Ian.

"I was never good enough," she said. "Not for you." She emptied her clenched fist. "Not for anyone."

"Leah, honey, no. I was wrong. Please, Leah, I heard what happened." Ruby's voice came over the phone as if from a distance. "Let me help."

"No."

"You never let anyone into your heart, never can be big enough to forgive…" Ruby's words faded into static as Leah gazed through the glass at Emily.

Her touchstone. Just like Ian. And Nellie. The three people she'd loved who'd loved her back… now down to one. Emily.

"Don't call again." Leah hung up. What had ever possessed her, calling Nellie's house? A moment of weakness she already regretted. The last thing she needed was Ruby back in her life.

No. What she needed was answers, beyond the vague reassurances the police gave her. She needed somewhere safe for herself and Emily. Blinking, she glanced around the empty observation room that had witnessed so much tragedy over the years. What was keeping her here? Nellie was gone, Ian was gone, Ruby no longer had any claim to Leah or her life.

Her phone was filled with friends and neighbors offering to help, offering shelter, but she couldn't allow anyone to take the risk. Even though the killer knew Emily couldn't identify him, there were still men like Cochrane out there. No. It was up to Leah to protect her daughter. She'd need money. Could she use their credit cards and access their bank accounts or had the police frozen them? Her credit cards and debit card were at the house, so she couldn't even try with the hospital ATM.

She began making a list. Get the car, get any cash and cards from the house. Checkbook, that too. Withdraw all the cash she could, cash was invisible. And then... go. Take Emily and just go, far away from here, far from the feeling of someone always watching her, away from the pain and the memories and everyone's expectations of how Leah should act, what she should say.

But where?

The door opened and Leah startled, almost made a noise but stifled it. Jessica. Leah glanced through the glass. Emily was playing with the doll house, her hair flattened from the EEG cap Jessica had removed.

"She did great," Jessica reassured Leah. She glanced at the clock—over an hour had passed. "Natural resiliency—she's still going to have some rough patches, especially at night."

"But no more drugs?" Leah asked. Sedatives had their place but came with the risk of side effects.

"No. I think it's best if we let nature take its course. Why don't you take her back upstairs? I'll stop by this afternoon and we'll do a session in her room."

"Thanks, Jessica. I know how disruptive this was for your schedule and I really appreciate your taking the time."

"Leah. Please know that everyone wants to help in any way they can. Seriously, call me. Anytime. For Emily—or if you need to talk."

Tears stung as Leah blinked them away. She nodded her thanks and dragged herself through the door to retrieve Emily.

Leah paused outside the interview room, staring at the door handle as if puzzling out how to open it. She slumped against the tile wall, the too-bright overhead lights making her brain buzz. No child should ever have to face what Emily was going through. And yet, she was also so very proud of how brave Emily had been as she answered Jessica's questions. Finally, she gathered the strength to open the door and face her daughter.

Emily ran up to her, her expression filled with concern beyond her age. "Did I get it right, Mommy? Did I do okay? Are they going to catch the bad man now?"

Leah crouched low and gathered Emily's body into hers. "You did great. I am so proud of you. Daddy would be, too." God, it was so damn hard to remember to use the past tense—nothing about Ian felt like it was past. Nothing. "You were a huge help."

Emily hugged her back, but it was a half-hearted, distracted hug. Leah stood and took her daughter's hand. Together they walked through the security doors leading out of the CIC and back into the main corridor of the hospital. The ubiquitous hospital smell of vanilla air freshener competed with the hunger-pang-inducing perfume of French fries wafting from the cafeteria. The hall was filled with busy people intent on important, life-saving errands; visitors wandering, their gazes blank with overwhelm; gossiping staff heading toward the cafeteria and their breaks. They all wove their way around Leah and Emily seemingly without noticing them, a river of humanity parting around a tiny island of desolation.

"Ready for that ice cream?" Leah asked Emily. It was past time for lunch and hey, ice cream had calcium and protein, right? Besides, Leah wasn't shooting for mother of the year here, she just wanted to see Emily smile—a real smile—if only for a few minutes.

Emily shook her head, looking over her shoulder as if searching for someone. "No, thanks. Not without Daddy. He knows how to get the sprinkles just right."

They walked toward the elevators. Emily was dragging, obviously exhausted by her session with the Jessica. Leah picked her up, balancing her on her hip, despite the fact that Emily's legs were getting long enough to tangle with her own. Rate she was growing, Leah wouldn't be able to hold her like this much longer. The thought made her hold on tighter.

"Want to watch more cartoons?" she asked.

Emily shook her head again.

"There's a ton of toys in the playroom," Leah suggested as they climbed into the elevator.

Emily shook her head. Leah hit the button for the pediatric floor.

"Hungry? We can get lunch." Leah hated the hint of desperation that crept into her voice. Five minutes out from therapy and she felt like Emily was drifting away again, lost to her fears and the memories of last night. Despite her own instinct to run, Leah realized she couldn't. Emily's needs came first.

Emily shook her head. Then she laid it on Leah's shoulder.

"What do you want, then? You can tell me, honey. It's okay."

"Didn't I do good enough for Daddy to come back?" Emily's breath echoed in Leah's ear like distant thunder. "Where is he? I want Daddy."

So did Leah. Except... had either of them ever truly known the real Ian?

CHAPTER 21

Luka made his way to Jefferson Cochrane's address across the river. Once he drove over the bridge, he was in rural farmland with thick forests that climbed up and over the mountains. The founding fathers' dream of a sprawling metropolis had never quite come to life, so almost a third of the city's population lived across the water, still inside Cambria City boundaries, despite the fact that all semblance of urban life ended at the river.

The farm was less than three miles from Cochrane's place. If Ray wasn't at Cochrane's when Luka arrived, he promised himself he'd head over to Jericho Fields and check on Pops, if only to relieve the nagging anxiety and allow himself to better focus on his case. Until he moved in with Pops, Luka had never appreciated how much freedom he'd enjoyed, never worrying about family matters encroaching on his attention or interfering with his work. How did people with families do it? He made a note to ask Ray, who on wife number three had finally seemed to get it right, raising two kids.

Luka had no idea why or how but here he was staring down forty and somehow his job was all he had. After Cherise, women had come and gone, but none of them stuck around long, tired of his inability to commit to coming home on time for dinner, much less a long-term relationship. But now there was Pops and suddenly instead of his only worry being late for Sunday dinner and withstanding the withering wrath of his grandmother, Luka found himself responsible for another man's health and wellbeing.

He wasn't ashamed to admit it, it was damned hard work, caring for an old man set in his ways, suffering from grief, depression, high blood pressure, and diabetes. Chasing criminals was much easier.

He arrived at Cochrane's address, a dilapidated bungalow that sported roofing shingles for siding. Luka drove past, noting a surprisingly new Mustang that sat in the carport, with no sign of any motorcycle. A quick double check of the list Harper had emailed confirmed that there was no Polaris Victory Hammer 8-Ball registered under Cochrane's name. Although, of course, that didn't mean Cochrane didn't have access to one. Borrowed or maybe paid for in cash, unregistered. Luka spotted Ray parked in the gravel driveway of the trailer court opposite.

As he pulled off the road, parking about twenty yards down from Cochrane's address, an old Ford F-150 with more rust than paint pulled into Cochrane's drive behind the Mustang. The man who emerged matched Cochrane's description.

Luka waited for the man to go inside then got out of his car. Ray met him at the side of the road. As they walked toward the dilapidated bungalow, Ray told him about the lead at the college. "Grad assistant or assistant professor, not sure, he talked so damn fast, but young, eager, and pissed off because Ian Wright insulted his research. Anyway, got a bone to pick, but dangled an interesting rumor. Seems Wright refused to contribute to a project Cyber Command wanted him in on. He didn't think it was ethical and the government suspended his consulting contract."

They stopped, supposedly admiring the view—despite the fact that it consisted of the trailer park, a vacant lot filled with weeds and trash, and Cochrane's house. Ray's hand rested on his weapon as they approached the house. "You want point?"

Luka nodded and they split up, Ray moving to cover both the carport entrance and the front door from the driveway while Luka rang the bell. He stood to the far side of the door and listened. It wasn't difficult, the walls were that thin. If he needed to, he could probably kick through the exterior layer of roofing shingles and the interior drywall faster than he could break down the door. He would prefer not to do either.

"Mr. Cochrane? It's Detective Sergeant Jericho, Cambria City Police. We'd like your assistance on a case. If you could open the door."

He heard the sounds of cabinets and drawers being closed.

"Mr. Cochrane? Are you all right, sir? Do you need assistance?"

"No!" came the rapid shout back. "I'm fine. Hold on. Let me—er, let me get some pants on."

As if Luka hadn't seen the man not two minutes ago fully dressed. He waited for a short ten count. "Sir, we really need—"

The door popped open and Cochrane stood, blocking Luka's view inside. He made a show of buttoning his jeans—the same pair he'd been wearing when he left the Mustang. A bulky dressing was wrapped around his left wrist and hand. "What'cha want?"

"Sir, are you alone?"

"Yeah, what business is it of yours?"

"We'd like to discuss a private matter. Seeking your cooperation, you understand. Sensitive case, we wouldn't want word to get out…" Luka let it dangle like catnip. It was amazing how often people—even hardened criminals—jumped at the chance to get the inside scoop on a case if you worded your request correctly, made it clear you weren't asking them to snitch.

"Really? You need my help? What for? There's a reward? I'm not talking to no cops unless there's a reward." He eyed Ray, who approached from the driveway. "Who's he?"

"This is Detective Acevedo." Luka held his ID up for Cochrane to see. He glanced over his shoulder at the cluster of single-wide trailers across the street. "Maybe we should talk inside?"

Cochrane narrowed his eyes at the photo ID, pursed his lips, then blew his breath out. "Not sure what I can help with, but if there's a reward… Yeah, c'mon in."

He stood aside and ushered the detectives in as if he was a butler at Buckingham Palace. Luka went first, comfortable with the knowledge that Ray watched his back, and scrutinized Cochrane's home. Palace wasn't as far off as he'd imagined, despite the humble exterior. The combination living room/dining room had no formal tables or chairs but did sport a massage recliner along with two fancy leather gaming chairs in front of a TV as wide as Cochrane was tall, complete with the latest Xbox system and surround sound. An old sofa was pushed back against the corner to make room for sparkling stainless steel workout equipment that would have been at home in any upscale gym.

"What'cha do, win the lottery?" Ray joked.

"Yep. Fifty grand." Cochrane pointed to a small framed photo near the window that showed him accepting an oversized check from an official. He turned to them. "But that's not why you came, is it? You said you need my help. Before I tell you anything, what's the reward?"

Luka glanced at Ray, saw him squaring his shoulders, ready to wind up for his version of bad cop, but then he spotted a makeshift shrine set up in the far corner of the dining area, complete with candles and a framed photo draped in a black silk scarf. The woman in the photo was laughing, sun dancing off her sunglasses. Beside it was a framed photo of Cochrane along with the woman and a young boy, maybe two or three years old.

He gave Ray a slight shake of his head and edged toward the shrine, Cochrane following. "Is this your wife?"

"Was. Well, technically, common-law." Cochrane sidled between Luka and the shrine as if protecting the photo—and his memories—from the detectives. "She was killed."

"Actually, Mr. Cochrane." Luka colored his tone with respect. "That's why we're here. We think you can help us—"

"Put the bitch behind bars? The one who killed my Nikki?" Cochrane's voice raised, reverberating through the space, fueled by fury. "If it's Leah Wright you're going after, damn right, I'm in."

Luka motioned to Cochrane to sit. The man plopped himself into the recliner. Luka wasn't about to lower himself into one of the gaming chairs—both of which still had their plastic coverings on, as if Cochrane thought buying them would somehow magically also bring him friends to occupy them. Instead, Luka leaned back against the wall while Ray moved to the side, out of Cochrane's sightline, casually wandering toward the hall to take a look around.

Luka held out his phone. "All right to record?" Technically he didn't need permission, but he liked to get it when possible.

"Damn right, record. I want all this on the record."

"Thank you, Mr. Cochrane. First of all, just a formality—where were you last night?"

"Last night?" Cochrane narrowed his eyes. "Oh right. When her husband got himself killed. You want my alibi. No problem. I was at work until eleven—my PO just got me a new gig driving a delivery truck evenings. You can check my timesheet and they've got cameras all around. Takes me about forty-five minutes to get back home after my shift, but I'm always too wound up by then, so I stopped at Roadie's for a few beers. They can vouch for me, too. Finally made it home around one."

"Okay. Thanks. Now, tell me about your wife, Nikki."

Cochrane's entire body slumped as he sighed. "She was everything. Beautiful and smart—too damn smart for her own good half the time. It'd get her in trouble, mouthing off at me." His voice grew sharp and Luka remembered the domestic violence beefs on Cochrane's record—the ones that had resulted in police intervention. Probably the tip of the iceberg. "We had our ups and downs like any couple," Cochrane added, his tone softened with regret, "but we always came back together, stronger than ever. Until Leah Wright, that was."

"When did Nikki first see Dr. Wright?"

"Nikki, she's clumsy, you see. Always walking into walls and falling downstairs." He gestured toward the hallway. "So she was in the ER a lot. Dr. Wright, she saw her a few times when she got banged up—somehow twisted Nikki's mind around that I was the problem, got her to leave me, take our kid, too, and press charges."

"So that's why you blame Dr. Wright for Nikki's death?"

Cochrane frowned. "Hell, no. I blame her for being a busybody, sticking her nose in people's business where it don't belong. Our love was too strong for her meddling, Nikki always came back. She couldn't live without me."

"How did Nikki die?"

"We'd been apart for a while—I had to do a few days in lockup," he admitted sheepishly. "I'll never forgive myself for being gone when she needed me. But she was here, waiting for me when I got out and she looked awful. Pale, too skinny, bruises under her eyes. I was furious, thought someone had done something to her, but she said no, it was all from worry about me. But then she got a nosebleed while making dinner and it wouldn't stop bleeding, so that night I took her to the ER." He stopped, his right hand bunched into a fist, drumming against the arm of the chair. "Should've known better, should've kept her here with me."

Luka allowed the silence to grow, but Cochrane said nothing, just kept staring past Luka at Nikki's shrine. "Dr. Wright, she was the doctor Nikki saw that night?"

Cochrane nodded, obviously straining to hold back tears. "Before she went in, I told the doctor that I was in lockup, I didn't have nothing to do with what was wrong with Nikki. I told her Nikki was scared and if it was anything bad, that doctor had to tell me first. I'd decide how to tell Nikki. But that damn bitch, she didn't listen."

"What was wrong?"

"Cancer. Bad. So bad that they wanted to keep Nikki in the hospital, start treatment right away." He knuckled both fists against his eyes and sniffed. "They told Nikki—that doctor, she knew I was just out getting coffee, but she didn't wait, she marched in and gave Nikki a death sentence like some Gestapo killer. I didn't even find out, not until it was too late. If I'd known, I would have never told Nikki, would have taken her away from that hellhole. We could've gone to Niagara Falls, or maybe down to the beach, seen the ocean, gone anywhere, made good use of the time we had left. But that doctor, she stole it all. Took everything from me."

"Was she wrong? Did Dr. Wright get the diagnosis wrong?"

Cochrane shook his head. "No. Bitch was right."

"Then help me understand—"

Cochrane sat up—not an easy feat given the recliner's zero gravity position—and glared at Luka. "She *told* Nikki. I told her not to. I told her to tell me first, let me handle things. Didn't matter that Nikki and me weren't married on paper. She was mine, it's my job to take care of her. Not some meddling doctor."

As if any physician would have followed Cochrane's orders. Not only was it patronizing and unethical, Luka wasn't even sure if it was legal to withhold a diagnosis from a patient. Ray reappeared at the hallway, jerked his head toward the front door. Luka gave him a small nod. "When was all this, Mr. Cochrane?"

"Few months ago, right before I won the lottery. She missed that—Nikki would've loved it, getting her picture taken and all. She'd still be here if it wasn't for that doctor."

"How many times have you seen Dr. Wright since Nikki's death?" Luka wondered exactly how Nikki died—suicide brought on by her diagnosis, maybe? Or had the cancer gotten her? But that could wait.

"I've been there, to Good Sam a few times since. My kid's sick a lot, so we're there all the time. Sometimes it's me. I always ask for her, the bitch, but they never give her to me. Keep thinking maybe I'll finally be able to give her a piece of my mind, let her know what she stole from me, make her see what she's done to us."

"And today—"

"Today I finally see her. Told her how she killed Nikki, right to her face." Cochrane's hand fisted, his bandage tightening over his knuckles. "Would've done more if that guy hadn't pulled me away. What do I care? With Nikki gone, what does anything matter? Who'd care if I went to jail? At least that bitch would've gotten what she deserved."

"And what exactly is that?"

Cochrane's gaze was cemented to Nikki's shrine. "You know the way to hurt someone real bad, make them suffer the most? You don't go after them. You take away everything they love. That's what Leah Wright did to me. That's what I feel every day. When she killed Nikki, she as good as killed me, too. Only reason I got to live is my boy. I almost lost him, too—all because of Leah Wright getting me thrown in jail. But he's mine and no one's ever going to take him from me. No matter what." He glanced up at Luka. "You'll see to it that they do something, right? Make her pay for what she did."

"Thank you, Mr. Cochrane. You've been very helpful." Luka pocketed his phone as Ray joined him. "I don't suppose you'd like to join us down at the station, go ahead and make your statement formal? It'd be a big help."

Ray raised his eyebrow at that, but Luka had a feeling about Cochrane. Man was unstable to say the least. He made a note to call Children's Services, make sure Cochrane's son was all right and that all those ER trips hadn't been the result of any abuse. A little boy made for an easy target now that his mother was no longer around to protect him.

Cochrane twisted his lips, considering it. "Can't today. Gotta pick up my kid. But tomorrow—his grandparents have him."

Luka handed Cochrane his card. The man was on parole, so he had other ways to get Cochrane off the street. "That will be perfect. Thanks."

They were already at the front door before Cochrane hauled himself free of the recliner. "Wait, what about the reward?" He jogged after them.

"We'll call you if you qualify," Ray told him. Cochrane slammed the door so hard the entire house shuddered.

"What'd you find?" Luka asked as they walked to the cars.

"Weed, a few oxys, handgun on the back of the toilet, shotgun beside the back door. Everything in plain sight. Can't believe they let a kid live there, but Children's Services doesn't have any complaints on him. Called his parole officer, he's coming over for a surprise visit. Ready to revoke. Next time we see Cochrane, he'll be back behind bars."

"Good. We don't need him running free, going after Leah Wright or her family."

"You really think a guy like him could've pulled this off? There was no sign of any designer drugs. And let's face it, he's not exactly the brightest bulb on the Christmas tree."

"He's got the passion and anger, that's for sure. Maybe he thought using medicine to torture her husband was the ultimate way of getting revenge?" It felt weak, but they had no other viable suspects—other than the widow herself. Luka buttoned his coat; the wind was picking up, smelled like snow coming sooner than what the weatherman had predicted. "We need to check out his alibi before we talk to him again. And see if he has any access to a Polaris motorcycle or the designer drugs used to torture Ian Wright."

Ray shrugged one shoulder—his version of an eye roll, but Luka didn't disagree with the sentiment. Cochrane wasn't an ideal suspect, but neither could they ignore him.

"While I was at it," Ray gestured with his phone, "I also pulled up the report on his wife's death. She bled to death. Nosebleed. Two days after the ER visit with Wright. Maggie was on the case, said it looked like she'd been hit a few times, had multiple contusions and such, but with the cancer her platelets were so low she couldn't clot her blood, so a slap across the face and a nosebleed—"

"Became a death sentence." Luka glanced back at the lonely bungalow. "They didn't press charges because of the underlying cancer diagnosis?"

"Exactly. DA couldn't make a case that Cochrane touched her—she could've gotten those bruises doing almost anything, bad as her cancer was. Maggie said without treatment she wouldn't have had more than a few weeks at best. Said even with it, the odds were against her, the cancer was too advanced." Ray focused on his phone. "Cochrane's company does hauling for pharmaceutical companies. Who knows what could have fallen off one of their trucks while he was loading it."

"Follow up on his work and alibi." Luka glanced at the house where Cochrane glared at them from a grimy front window. "Have patrol sit on him until his PO can make the surprise visit and revoke his ass, do a more thorough search of the house. Then we can question him more. But, you're right, if he's our guy, he's a lot smarter than he acts."

"Could've learned forensics and how to cover his tracks while doing time. Cons love to share helpful little tips like that."

"Maybe," Luka allowed, glad he'd insisted on a guard to watch over Leah and Emily Wright.

"What's your next move?"

Luka was scrolling through the messages he'd missed while interviewing Cochrane. "Katrina Balanchuk, the possible love interest. Then, CSU has cleared the scene for us to go through. I want to get there before those damn feds."

"I'm surprised they haven't snatched the body yet."

"Radcliffe's not the type to get his hands dirty."

"You know," Ray said. "Screwy case like this, if Cochrane's not our actor, it might not be so bad, letting the feds take it all. Get it off our balance sheet, you know?"

Luka didn't answer. Instead, he got into his car and slammed the door. He remembered Ian Wright's body, propped up against his daughter's bed, fighting to the end to save her. The same way Leah Wright was fighting still, despite her own pain. No way in hell was anyone taking this case, burying it, stealing justice from that family.

Not if Luka had anything to do about it.

~

CHAPTER 22

By the time Leah and Emily arrived back on pediatrics, Emily was asleep on Leah's shoulder, drained by Jessica's lengthy interview. The clerk, Arthur, flagged her down as she carried Emily past the nurses' station.

"Dr. Wright. Dr. Kern just called. Said she needs to speak to you as soon as possible."

"I just left her." Why would Jessica be calling her? She'd said their next session wouldn't be until this afternoon.

"She asked that you call her back right away. She's in the clinic but said you can have her paged."

"Okay. Let me just get Emily into bed. If you could go ahead and call the clinic?" It would probably take several minutes before Jessica could disengage herself from patients to take Leah's call.

She carried Emily into her room and tucked her into the sprawling field of crisp white linen, not a wrinkle in sight, inviting slumber. Her eyelids sagged at the mere thought of sleep.

By the time she returned to the nurses' station Arthur was on hold with the clinic. "Where's the security guard?" she asked him. "Detective Jericho said he'd be here?"

"I think since you were gone, they went to lunch. I'll call them back." Arthur turned his attention to the phone. "She's right here," he told the person on the line. He handed her the receiver. "Dr. Kern."

"Hey, Jessica. Did I forget something?"

"No, I did. I forgot what idiots the Utilization Review people were along with the insurance companies. They called. They'll only approve Emily's admission as a twenty-three-hour observation. And with it being peak RSV and flu season, they need her bed."

"You're kicking us out? But Emily—" Leah twisted around, hiding her face from Arthur, who was listening to every word. "What if something happens? How can I—"

"No one expects you to go it alone." Jessica was using her reassuring shrink tone—the one for patients, not colleagues. "You have my number. Call me anytime. And I still want to set up outpatient sessions for both of you—and any other family members."

Leah was silent, waiting for her to offer some magic fix. But as the silence lengthened, she realized there was no fix. Despite Jessica's reassurances, she was alone.

"You can't do it all yourself, Leah," Jessica said, using her shrink spidey-senses to read Leah's mind. Not that it wasn't pretty obvious what she was frightened of. "I can give you the names of some good grief counselors and you already know the victim advocates. Maybe also arrange for someone to provide respite care so you can leave Emily in good hands while you deal with—" Now she hesitated. "With the police and all that."

"All that" being the myriad of details Leah hadn't begun to process, much less plan for. Funeral. Transport from the morgue to the funeral home. Service or viewing? Given the extent of Ian's injuries, could they even consider an open casket? Church or graveside or both? A wake at home was out of the question, of course.

Home. Forget about where to call home in the foreseeable future or her fantasy about grabbing Emily and driving off into the sunset, leaving all this behind—they needed a place to sleep. Tonight.

"Thanks, Jessica." She handed the phone back to Arthur, ignoring the fact that Jessica was still speaking. She didn't have time or energy for niceties.

Arthur hung up the phone. "Lunch trays came up while you were gone. I put one aside for you and Emily." He nodded to the other side of the hall where a small kitchen served the ward and the staff. So many parents ended up camping out for the duration that it saw a lot of use.

"Thanks." Leah walked down to the kitchen to heat up their lunches. While the microwave was zapping Emily's pizza, she grabbed a few cartons of milk and then called Ian's father's cell, hoping to catch them before they were in the air. He hadn't sent her an itinerary and if she and Emily were going to a hotel, she wanted to book the same one. Although the idea of leaving Cambria City behind still tempted her. She sighed. One conversation with Ruby and she was starting to think like her, dreaming that running away would magically erase all her problems. No. The answers she needed were here.

"Leah," Bruce answered. "I was just getting ready to call you. You saw the weather? We tried. But no luck. They're cancelling flights, wouldn't book us. Said to call back tomorrow."

"The weather?"

"Yeah, the storm. Hit here this morning and is heading your way. Supposed to meet up with the system you guys already have brewing, form an even bigger storm. Even if we were able to get a flight out, we'd be stranded in Chicago or Denver. I'm so sorry."

In a way it was a relief. Ian's parents would be a help as far as babysitting, but they'd also be two more wounded, grieving people for Leah to try to ease their pain. And honestly, she was having enough trouble with her own feelings.

"No," she said. "I totally understand. Don't feel bad. Things here are still crazy. Maybe it's for the best."

"Does that mean the police have the guy?"

"No. But they're working on several leads." She knew it sounded vague, but it was more definite than Jericho had been with her. No way in hell was she going to ask Ian's parents if he was having an affair. The ache behind her breastbone at the thought of Ian betraying her felt like molten lead, hardening her heart. "If I hear anything, I'll let you know."

"Still, we want to help. I don't want to intrude, so please tell me if I'm crossing a line, but we thought maybe we could handle some of the arrangements? After all, nowadays everything's done online or over the phone and it would save you—"

"Yes," she interrupted, leaping at his offer. "That would be so helpful. Thank you."

"Was there anything in particular? Anything you and Ian discussed that we should—"

Ian and Leah both agreed that the body was a vessel, meaningless after death. But now that it was time to decide what to do with his body, she knew he'd want whatever would bring his family comfort. "Whatever you decide is fine. Thanks again." The microwave dinged and she said goodbye.

Balancing a tray with two plates of food and drinks, she crossed past the nurses' station to Emily's hallway. Arthur was nowhere to be seen, probably running labs or the like.

She pushed open the door to Emily's room and stepped inside. Someone had drawn the privacy curtain around Emily's bed. She continued into the room, past the curtain with its bright cartoon characters. Then she stopped.

Emily was still asleep. On the pillow beside her was a bouquet of red roses.

Leah clutched the tray, wondering at the sudden rush of fear that overcame her. People sent flowers when someone died—but to a child's hospital room? And who would have put them on Emily's pillow instead of in a vase? She set the tray on the bedside table.

They were only flowers, nothing to be afraid of. But they looked exactly like the bouquet from last night, the one with Ian's final message to her. They probably came from the hospital gift shop like the ones last night, that was all. But… She shot her hand out and snatched the bouquet away from the pillow. For some reason she did not want these roses anywhere near her daughter.

With trembling fingers, she sought out the card nestled between the cloying blossoms. She tossed the flowers into the garbage can, then opened the card.

Did you enjoy the surprise I left you last night?

CHAPTER 23

As he drove back to the city, Luka couldn't help but feel that Ian Wright's death had a strange duality to it: technically complex but also intimate. The devastation inflicted felt very personal. And yet, the extremely well-planned and organized initial attack, lack of forensics at the scene, creating and bringing a designer cocktail of drugs—that felt cool, remote. Psychologically the two parts of the crime were disconnected. Two actors, not one? One the brains, one the brawn.

If so, then Ray was right: Cochrane was definitely not the brains. Although Luka could imagine Cochrane working himself into a lather, pushing harder and harder on that shiny new exercise equipment, eager to get his revenge on the woman who, in his mind, had taken his wife from him, threatened his son.

He glanced at the crank files sitting on the passenger seat. How many more Cochranes were out there? What had Cochrane said? Best way to torture someone is to go after their family? Which would make Leah Wright the true target, not her husband.

He was glad he'd followed his instincts and put the extra security on Leah and Emily. He only wished he'd been able to get real cops into Good Sam instead of relying on their private security. Luka decided to send Harper over as soon as she finished interviewing motorcycle owners—the administrators didn't need to know, and he'd feel better with extra protection for Ian's family.

Where to next? If the killer was targeting Leah, then Cochrane's sentiment also fit with a spurned lover, perhaps someone obsessed with Ian Wright, someone who, after Ian rejected her advances, was driven to punish the wife Ian loved more than her. Which made interviewing Katrina Balanchuk essential. Could she possibly be the brains behind the brawn?

He needed to find the damn motorcycle. It could be the key to tying everything together. So far Harper and Krichek had come up empty with their interviews of registered local owners. Time to let the feds do what they did best: search through reams of data. As he drove over the bridge leading back into the heart of the city, he called Radcliffe.

"Detective Jericho," the DIA man answered in a jovial tone, getting Luka's rank wrong. On purpose, he was certain, putting him in his place. "Did you crack the case already?"

"No," Luka admitted through gritted teeth. "I actually need your help."

"Really? I mean, it all seems so clear to me. Philandering husband, nice chunk of life insurance, not to mention no custody battle—all kind of makes you wonder about the widow, doesn't it? Given the way Wright was drugged and tortured, fact that she's a doctor and all."

Luka actually felt the opposite—the more he learned about the details of Ian Wright's torture, the less he suspected Leah. Was that because he sympathized with her? After all, he understood sudden, violent loss better than most. Or because he respected her strength, the way she'd do anything to protect her daughter—which also argued against her being the mastermind behind her husband's brutal murder.

"We narrowed down the make and model of the motorcycle seen leaving the scene. Can you run all the registered owners, follow up on anyone suspicious?"

"No problem. My guys can run a national search, correlate it with any known associates of the Wrights—both husband and wife." Meaning a much, much more thorough job than what Luka and his team were able to do with their limited, local resources. Whatever worked, Luka told himself. And bonus points if it kept the feds off his back for a while.

"Thanks, I appreciate it. I'll text you the details and the list we're working from." Luka hung up before the fed could ask for more details of Luka's side of the investigation.

He parked half a block from Balanchuk's address. The Ukrainian grad student lived near the river in the Wharf District, a collection of old warehouses that were being converted into loft apartments and condos in an effort to attract new money to a broken city. The red-brick building that Balanchuk lived in offered stunning views of the river and mountains beyond—if you could get past the gang graffiti, the rusted-out cranes tilting like drunks ready to fall into the water, and the homeless who had done their own gentrification, converting the abandoned building next door into a makeshift encampment.

Before he left the car, his phone rang again. Maggie.

"Give me some good news."

"Not sure if it's good or bad," she said. "Definitely interesting. They re-ran Ian Wright's tox screen and in addition to our designer stimulant drug compound, they found another drug: scopolamine."

"Wait. Isn't that for motion sickness?" Ray had used it when he'd taken wife number two on a cruise.

"And it's been used by criminals to facilitate sexual assaults and robberies. Known on the street as Devil's Breath. Supposedly you blow it into someone's face or mix it in a drink and they turn into walking, talking zombies, obeying any command. And then after? Total amnesia. I pulled up a bunch of case reports. This stuff is crazy wicked." She sounded excited.

"Cases from around here?" He frowned; he hadn't heard of any street drugs that could do all that. What had the killer wanted Ian Wright to do for him?

"No," she admitted. "They're from Europe and South America. And the compound in Ian's blood, it wasn't what you'd find on the street. This stuff is pharmaceutical grade."

"Where would someone get that?" Maybe at last a tangible lead.

"Not sure. Maybe a research lab? Scopolamine is definitely not approved for human use at these levels."

Luka sighed. There went his lead. "Could you ask around? It had to come from somewhere."

"Definitely. I'll call if I find anything."

"Thanks, Maggie." He hung up and was heading toward Balanchuk's building when she appeared from the opposite direction, dressed in jeans and a parka, a large portfolio slung over her shoulder. She didn't appear particularly furtive, not rushed or even the slightest bit apprehensive as he approached and identified himself.

"I wanted to speak with you about Ian Wright," he told her. "I believe you knew him?"

"Yes, come, come." Her tone was almost business-like. She led the way inside the building and up to the loft apartment. Luka took a moment to admire the space with its exposed brick and expansive views. The walls were naked, the only artwork visible a series of charcoal sketches arranged on easels surrounding a modeling couch. He wondered how a foreign grad student newly arrived in the country could afford such a luxurious apartment—maybe the ten grand Ian Wright withdrew wasn't Balanchuk's only payment from him? Or she had other benefactors?

"Coming from a class?" he nodded to her portfolio, which she carefully laid flat on a large dining table before removing her coat and tossing it over the back of a chair.

"Yes." She didn't elaborate. "I heard the news. Ian's dead. Awful. Terrible."

"When was the last time you saw him?"

"Tea?" she asked as she moved into the kitchen area.

"No thanks." He gave her a moment as she filled an electric kettle with water. "The last time you saw Ian Wright?"

"Last session for work was two, three weeks ago."

"Session?" He was intrigued. "Exactly what was your relationship with him? How did you meet?"

"Class. Live drawing—beginners," she explained. "I was teaching assistant. He wanted practice, private lessons. So we meet." She gestured to the couch surrounded by easels.

"That's all you two did? Art lessons?" He thought of the receipt with the note from Trina. It'd been dated October. "Four months of drawing lessons?"

"He was good student. Learned fast."

"And that was the full extent of the relationship?"

"Of course."

He wondered at that, but her expression gave nothing away. "I don't suppose you could give me the exact date?"

She frowned, her lips pouting, then pulled out her phone, swiped, and showed him the results. "Yes, here. See, he paid, last payment."

Forty-five dollars for a modeling session. Nowhere near the ten grand Ian had withdrawn a few days ago. "And he never paid you any money beyond these classes?" His skepticism put finger quotes around the word "classes" but she didn't rise to the bait.

"No."

"Did you see him yesterday?"

"No."

"Could you tell me where you were last night?"

She gestured, a broad sweeping motion. "Here. With my partner. Olivia Karmody."

Luka took down Karmody's contact information. "You never met Ian outside of your classes?"

"No." Now it was her turn to scrutinize him. "You think we sleep together. Not true. Only art. Ian, he love wife. Very much.

Love family." She seemed somehow both annoyed and wistful, as if maybe she'd wished for more from Ian. Or again, Luka reminded himself, she could simply be a skilled actress.

"So you haven't seen him at all since that last drawing class three weeks ago?"

"No," she said but she nodded her head. Then frowned and paused. "Friday, I see him on campus. Walking."

Nothing remarkable there. So why deny it? "And?"

Her frown deepened. She glanced toward the windows then the door as if realizing how vulnerable the wide-open space left her. "He was being followed. By a man in black."

"A man in black? Like a black suit? Or coat?"

"No. Special clothes. Like for road."

Luka showed her the grainy traffic cam photo of the man on the motorcycle. "Clothes like these? Like you'd wear on a motorcycle?"

"Yes, yes."

"Katrina, did you see his face?"

"No. Just his back. He was very far away."

"Was he tall? What was his skin color? Anything else—any details, distinguishing marks?"

She kept shaking her head as if wanting to deny everything. "Tall. Yes. But not too tall. Skin. Light, pale."

"Hair color?"

"No. He wore hat. I saw nothing else. But when Ian saw me and wave hello, the man, he—" She moved her hand very fast in a shooing motion. "He turn, other direction, back the way he came, and then he just gone." She snapped her fingers. "Vanish."

"Tell me exactly where and when." Maybe they'd get lucky with security cameras. But Luka doubted it. So far, this actor had remained almost invisible.

How long had this man been stalking Ian Wright?

CHAPTER 24

Her stomach churning as she fought a wave of nausea, Leah's pulse roared through her temples. Was the person who left the roses still here? She opened the closet door, looked in the bathroom. No one. She stepped to the still open door and glanced up and down the hallway. No one appeared suspicious.

Whoever left the roses was long gone. As much as the panic roiling her belly left her wanting to find the man and tear him apart with her own two hands, that wasn't an option.

Leah froze as she read the card one more time. Not from fright but because there were about eight hundred and eleven things she needed to be doing. Run after the bastard who'd left the roses, gather Emily in her arms and flee, call the police…

She carefully lowered the card and set it on the nightstand, trying not to touch it more than she already had. She took a breath and centered herself as if facing a mass casualty alert in the ER. Triage. What was her priority?

Emily's safety.

Leah grabbed the bag that contained what little they had—she still hadn't gotten any clothing for Emily so the hospital PJs would have to do—slung it over her shoulder, and with practiced hands scooped Emily's limp body from the bed without waking her. Then she backed out of the room, scanning for hidden dangers, spun around in the doorway, and left.

Had whoever left the roses stayed to watch her reaction? Maybe he'd follow her, knowing she'd never risk Emily by staying?

Was she playing right into his hands? The low murmur of Arthur and a nurse discussing something with a patient's mother was the only activity coming from the nurses' station. A little girl looking wan and scared was in a red transport wagon, bundled with blankets, an IV pole hanging above her, the transport attendant and her parents trundling her toward the elevator, and a white-coated doctor whom Leah didn't recognize from the back following them.

No sign of Jericho's promised extra security. But also no sign of anyone out of place. Leah waited for the elevator doors to close behind the group of people, then started toward the stairwell, heading toward the safest and most private space left to her: her office down in the ER. If she had a free hand, she'd be calling Jericho, giving him an earful about his so-called protection, but that would have to wait.

Emily woke as Leah strode down the hall. "Mommy? I smell pizza. Is Daddy back?" She rubbed the sleep away against Leah's neck. "Did he bring me my pepper-ronny?"

A family joke from when Emily was first starting to talk. She'd been late to speech—would have had both Ian and Leah worried except that all her other developmental milestones had been fine. When she finally did decide to speak, her first words had been, "I want pizza, please." The memory of Ian wiping smeared tomato sauce from her chubby toddler cheeks made Leah blink. It felt like yesterday. *Worse.* It felt like tomorrow. As if she could glance over her shoulder and see Ian following behind her, a carryout box from Tonio's balanced in his hands.

Then Emily jerked fully awake, straining to climb down from Leah's arms. "Where's Daddy? Where are we going? How's he going to find us?"

Emily clawed at Leah as if her mother were the enemy—Leah felt like one as she lowered Emily to the ground, wrapped her fingers around Emily's arms, and crouched down to meet her gaze.

"Emily, Daddy's gone." Leah understood from Emily's expression that she knew that, hadn't forgotten—it was simply a child's desperate hope that sleep had magically erased an unpleasant reality. "We're going down to my office." Leah searched for a way to explain things so that Emily wouldn't be frightened. "For a special lunch. Okay?"

Emily didn't like the idea. She balled up one fist and rubbed her eyes. Then she nodded, blew her breath out in a long-suffering sigh, and took Leah's hand as if she were the parent, not the child.

Leah had originally intended to take Emily down the stairs but Emily tugged her to the elevator. She was still young enough to see them as amazing conveyances rather than the too-small, too-smelly, too-slow deathtraps that Leah did. Emily never let go of her hand the entire trip down. Which was fine with Leah, who was focused on her next steps: call Jericho, find food for her daughter, then a place to stay, clothing, she still needed her car...

By the time the elevator stopped on the ground floor, Leah realized Jessica was right: she couldn't do this alone. She needed help. Another adult. Someone who understood. Who wouldn't ask too many questions or try to coax Leah into sharing her feelings—feelings that were too sharp, too explosive to be let loose, not yet.

Remembering the man who'd accosted her earlier, Leah steered Emily down the back hallway, avoiding the chaos of the ER and its waiting area, and took the long way around to her office. Once they were safely inside, she felt as if she could finally breathe.

Emily tugged her arm. "Mommy, I'm hungry."

Leah dumped her bag beside her desk and crossed over to the desk across from hers and rummaged in the side drawer. Andi always had a stash of protein bars and other, less healthy treats. She grabbed a bag of pretzels and a protein bar and handed them to Emily along with a bottle of water. It made for a poor lunch but would stave off any hangry meltdowns until she could get Emily something more nutritious.

"Here you go." She lifted Emily onto her desk chair and set a hospital notepad and several colored dry erase markers and an assortment of highlighters beside her. "When you're done, you can draw me some pictures."

Emily bit into the protein bar but eyed Leah warily as Leah edged toward the door. "You're not leaving?"

"No. I just need to make a few calls. Can you be quiet for just a minute?"

"Then can we go home? I want Huggybear."

Leah stared at her daughter, no idea how to explain why they couldn't go home—might never go home again—much less the fact that Emily's beloved teddy bear was now part of a crime scene. "I'm working on it," was the best she came up with.

Emily pursed her lips—an expression she'd stolen from Leah, Ian always insisted. But the calculation in her gaze was pure Ian. Finally, she nodded. "Okay." Then she turned back to hunch over her makeshift coloring tools.

Leah sighed and dialed Jericho's number. "Dr. Wright, I'm a bit busy right now," he answered, the distant sounds of a car's engine echoing his words.

"What happened to the protection you promised us?" She allowed her anger to color her voice until she saw Emily's head snap up, alert to Leah's mood. She lowered her tone and chose her words with care. "Someone left a bouquet of roses in my daughter's bed. While she was sleeping. With a note. Like last night."

"Where? At the hospital?"

"Yes."

"Are you secure? Where are you now?"

"In my office, with Emily."

"Stay there. I'm on my way."

"But—" Too late, he was gone.

Leah returned to Emily, caressing her hair. She'd drawn her blackspaceman again, almost filling the page with his oversized head, only now she'd added color: elongated drips of red extending from his fingers, a river of color at his feet, splashes against his helmet. So much red that there was barely any white left on the sheet of paper. But Emily wasn't done, her hand slashing with the red marker against the black figure over and over as if she was trying to do to him what he'd done to Ian.

Leah pressed her knuckles to her lips as she watched in horror. Jessica said to let Emily express her emotions. Emily's movements became more frenzied although her expression remained calm—as if she didn't even realize what she was drawing. Surely Jessica hadn't meant this? It couldn't be healthy. Could it?

She needed help. Maggie had just worked a night shift, was probably home sleeping. Her friends in the ER—yes, friends, but also colleagues—she couldn't ask them, it would alter the dynamics too much, create invisible friction. Neighbors? Most of them were elderly and because of Leah's strange work schedule with its always changing shifts, Ian knew them better than Leah. When they'd first moved here Leah had been so focused on taking care of Nellie and on her new job, she'd somehow missed having a life outside of work and home. Not that she regretted it—she loved her life.

But now that life was destroyed, and she was racing around like a rat in a maze, dragging Emily with her.

Time. She just needed to buy herself time to think. She fumbled Jessica's card from the pocket of her scrubs. The words on it were so sharp and clear, a beacon of hope—or if not hope, at least relief.

Leah took out her phone. As she hesitated, she could hear Ian's voice, heckling her for being a control freak, too damn proud and independent. In their relationship, she was the one who never asked for directions, always knew where she was going and how to get there. He was the wanderer, content to amble and chat with people, no shame about asking for directions or help or even where to head next. Letting fate and chance and random strangers decide their next adventure.

She drew in a breath and dialed.

"Good Samaritan Free Clinic, Dr. Kern speaking."

"Jessica? It's Leah Wright. Would it be okay if I took you up on your offer? I think maybe… I need help." Leah explained the situation in a whispered tone, her cell pressed against her cheek.

"I saw it on the news," Jessica said. "That man who attacked you in the ER. Horrible. Why didn't you mention it earlier?"

"It's on the news?" That explained why her phone was blowing up with texts and voicemails. She'd turned it off while Jessica was interviewing Emily and now regretted turning it back on.

"Come to the clinic. You'll be safe here," Jessica promised. "I'll send someone over to get you. His name is Brody. You can take the tunnel over. There's no way any reporters could be down there to ambush you—or see where you're going."

Which also meant no one would be able to track her to the clinic building across the street from the main hospital. "Thanks."

Leah hung up, texted Jericho with the change of plans, then turned to Emily, who had stopped her drawing to watch, her eyes hooded. The novelty of the day had clearly worn off, replaced by worry. "Dr. Jessica is over at the clinic and we can get lunch there. Are you still hungry?"

Emily's face was smeared with chocolate and pretzel crumbles, but Leah wasn't surprised when she nodded.

"Okay. Let's clean up your drawing stuff."

A few minutes later there was a knock on the door. Leah opened it cautiously. A man in his twenties appeared. He smiled when he saw her, even gave her a jaunty wave. "Hi, again."

She stepped back in surprise. "You're the man from the ER this morning. The one who helped me."

"I'm Brody. Dr. Kern sent me to escort you and your daughter. She wanted to make sure you didn't run into any trouble." He tapped a volunteer's ID badge hanging from the collar of his shirt.

The photo matched his face, Leah saw. Emily ran up beside her, half-hiding behind her legs, half-poking her head out, unable to resist her curiosity.

Brody squatted down to meet Emily's gaze. "You must be Emily. My son, Charlie, he's not quite your age. He's with the doctor now at the clinic. But he said to tell you that the playroom is super dooper." He glanced up at Leah. "If it's okay with your mom, of course." He rose back to his feet. "Oh, and there's banana pudding for dessert today."

There was no way Brody could know, but he'd just spoken the magic words Emily needed. She gave a tiny squee and tugged at Leah's hand. "Mom, Mom, did you hear?" Then she scowled at Brody in suspicion. "Banana pudding and... Nilla wafers?"

It was a test. But Brody passed with flying colors. "Well, of course. You can't have one without the other. But it's dessert—I'll bet your mom will want you to eat your veggies first. There's broccoli and carrots and the main course is chili mac." He shrugged at Leah. "Nothing fancy, but good comfort food."

Leah couldn't help but smile as Emily's expression finally approached one she was familiar with—bright, unguarded, no shadow of fear or worry. She knew it wouldn't last long, but it was a relief to know it was still there. "Comfort food is perfect. Thank you, Brody."

"Yes ma'am."

Brody led them down the seldom-used rear staircase to the basement floor where the entrance to the tunnels lay. The oldest tunnels, including this one, had been built as part of Good Samaritan over a hundred years ago, designed to give nursing students safe passage from their dormitory—the building that now housed the free clinic—to the main hospital. The path was well marked and, in keeping with its original purpose, well lit.

As they walked through the white-washed brick-walled tunnel, a bevy of hospital workers crossed their paths. Busy with their own work, no one did more than glance at Leah.

Brody walked on Emily's free side, matching his stride to hers despite his longer legs.

"So, you volunteer here at the hospital?"

"Lots of us clinic parents do—Dr. Kern calls it community service in return for all the stuff she helps us with. My boy, Charlie, he's got cystic fibrosis, so he's here at Good Sam all the time. Used to be, at least. But Dr. Kern, she's a miracle worker, has him on new medicine that's finally helping. He's getting some testing done now but maybe when he's done he can play with Emily—he's a wiz at Candyland."

"That's my favorite," Emily said.

"Dr. Kern is your son's physician?" Leah asked. "She's a neuropsychiatrist, not a pediatrician."

"When she took over as clinic director, she saw how all the specialists kept making things worse for Charlie—the GI guy would start a medicine that messed up the lung doc's treatment, stuff like that. So when Charlie got really sick, she stepped in to coordinate his care, get everyone talking to each other, on the same page. He was so bad off, they told me he might die. But, thanks to Dr. Kern, now he's doing great." He sighed and touched the knit cap he wore. "I owe her everything."

Leah frowned. She would remember a kid that sick if he'd been in her ER. But Brody looked so familiar—she remembered also thinking that this morning when she'd first met him. Maybe she'd seen him in passing in the cafeteria or waiting room? "I didn't get a chance, this morning, to thank you."

"I'm just glad you're all right. Sorry he got away."

"He did?" Leah's gait faltered. Could the man from the ER have brought the flowers to Emily's room? He would have had plenty of time, but how could he have known where to find Emily?

"Ran out before the guards could grab him. Don't worry, though. We'll keep you two safe." Brody's tone was confident.

It felt like suddenly Leah had more than Jessica on her side— Brody spoke as if the entire clinic, staff and families, were sworn to protect her and Emily. She knew that wasn't what he really meant, but still, it felt good knowing there were others far less exhausted and brain-muddied keeping an eye on Emily. Right now she was so sluggish she didn't trust her own judgment.

"Guess it was karma I was there," Brody said. "I mean, I owe you a lot more than that." Leah frowned, her pace slowing. He flushed and looked away. "You don't remember me. No reason you would—I was a lot younger then and you probably saw tons of kids like me."

"I treated you?"

He ducked his head as if embarrassed. "Yes, ma'am. Back in Pittsburgh. I was dead, but you brought me back."

She squinted once more at his name tag, this time he stopped and held it steady so she could actually read his name. Allan Broderick. Realization flooded over her. It was over four years ago, just before she left Pittsburgh to come to Cambria City. Sixteen-year-old kid caught in a drive-by shooting. Brought in no vitals, down an unknown length of time before Leah got to him, multiple gunshot wounds.

She remembered the blood, his shirt shredded into his wounds along with street gravel and chips of brick that had ricocheted from the building behind him. Remembered how young he'd looked when she'd finally glanced up from cracking his chest, her hands plunged wrist deep into his body, and she'd caught a glimpse of his face. Just a baby, she'd thought at the time. All those kids coming in during that summer of some gang's bloody turf war, they'd all been so young, mere babies. "Allan Broderick."

"Brody's what everyone calls me now." He finally raised his head, almost but not quite meeting her eyes. "You weren't there anymore when they let me out of the hospital—took most of a year before I could go home. My brain was so messed up I had to learn everything again. Still have some memory glitches, but anyway, I always wanted to say thanks. Now I finally can."

"You're welcome," she stuttered, still taken aback. "You are so very welcome. I'm just glad—wait, you have a kid? How old?" Brody himself couldn't be more than twenty, twenty-one.

He beamed. "Charlie's three. He only just came into my life—his mom's out of the picture, I guess you could say." They arrived at the doors leading into the clinic building. "He's my everything. I live to see him smile, know what I mean?" He glanced down at Emily, who was unabashedly soaking in their every word. "Yeah. You do."

Brody stood aside, waiting a beat, catching Leah's gaze as if making sure she was ready, before he swiped his ID to open the door and hold it for her and Emily. "I know you're scared," he said in a low voice. "But don't worry. The doc will take good care of you. Just like she has me and Charlie. Dr. Jessica saved us."

Leah held Emily's hand as they passed through the security doors into the clinic building's lowest floor. Brody followed behind.

"Dr. Jessica's office and the playroom are on the fourth floor," Brody said, playing the role of tour guide. He nodded to Emily as they reached the elevator bank. "Want to push the button? Charlie always likes to push the buttons."

Emily tapped the call button. A waiting car opened its doors and they entered. "Can you find four?" he asked.

Emily pushed the correct button and turned to Brody. "I can count to infinity."

"You can?"

"Sure. Once you make it past the first hundred, it's easy."

"She gets it from her dad," Leah said. "The genius gene. But Emily, remember, it's not nice to boast."

Her face fell and Leah regretted her words. This was no time to be nagging—but somehow that had become her side of the parental seesaw. Ian and Emily flew free while Leah was the anchor constantly pulling them back to earth.

"I don't think it's bragging if you're telling the truth," Brody said. "Especially not if you share what you know with your friends.

Maybe when Charlie's done with his treatment you can teach him how to count real high like that."

Emily beamed and nodded. "Sure. I can do that. Then we can both count to infinity and beyond!" She zipped her hands like Buzz Lightyear.

Such a big brain in such a little girl, who, no matter how smart she was, was still only six, Leah reminded herself. Would that make it harder for Emily to cope with what happened? Leah was a grown woman and was having a difficult time—she'd barely stopped herself from blocking the elevator doors from shutting, half expecting Ian to rush through them and take his place at their side. Every time she spotted movement out the corner of her eye, the constant tightness in her chest uncoiled, relaxing, knowing it was Ian—until it wasn't, and Leah's world came crashing down all over again.

But what scared her most was the knowledge that soon this feeling would vanish, erased by time—and she wouldn't instinctively expect Ian to be there at all. She'd need to make an effort to remember him because he'd no longer be a constant in their life.

Then she'd truly be alone, she and Emily.

CHAPTER 25

As soon as Luka hung up from Leah, he called Good Sam's security. Last night when he'd offered to post a uniformed officer outside Emily's room the hospital administrators had refused, something about liability issues, and had insisted on using their own people. Probably so they could triple-bill Leah's insurance company, he'd thought at the time.

Which left the poor slob who answered the phone now on the receiving end of a tirade where Luka vented all his frustrations about this case. After a few choice comments about incompetence, possible civil action, and even hinting at criminal negligence, "After all, your department's actions—or inaction—led to the endangerment of a child," he felt no better. It'd been his job to secure his witnesses' safety and he'd failed. "I want a man at her room preserving the crime scene—tell him not to go in or touch anything. Pull all the video from the pediatric floor as well as outside the gift shop. I'll be there in ten."

His next call was to Harper. "How far out from Good Sam are you?"

"We're over the bridge, up the mountain coming from the Smith compound." A sprawling family of neo-Nazis who dabbled in the manufacture of meth to finance their political endeavors. "About fifteen, twenty minutes. What happened?"

"Did you find the motorcycle and the rider?"

"We thought we had a lead when two of the Victories came back registered to the Smiths." Krichek's voice sounded through the speaker phone. "Both with records. Should've seen their faces when Harper came knocking."

"Yeah, but then Krichek did some bonding over dog breeding—"

"Anyway, they both have solid alibis. So that's it for our list of offenders, guess we're back to square one."

"I need you both at Good Sam. Leah Wright just called. Someone left a bouquet of roses with a threatening note in her daughter's room. I'm on my way there now. Krichek, you go over the security video—they're pulling it for you. Harper, collect the evidence from the room, get it to forensics, then call me. I've got another job for you."

"Any chance Wright sent the flowers to herself?" Harper asked. "And what about the mistress, Balanchuk?"

"I just came from interviewing her."

"You did?"

Luka had forgotten that he'd told Harper they could tackle the Balanchuk interview together. But she needed to learn, a case like this, you had to go where the evidence sent you and prioritize your time. Right now finding the motorcycle was their top priority—along with protecting their victims. "Balanchuk said she saw a man in black motorcycle leathers following Ian Wright on campus four days ago. She was too far away to see his face, but I have campus security pulling any video footage from the time frame."

"Let's hope they're more competent than Good Sam's security," Krichek said.

"Balanchuk could have said that to throw us off," Harper put in. "If she and motorcycle guy were working together—"

"I'm here," Luka told them as he pulled into the hospital's garage. He hung up. Harper made a good point, but right now his main concern was Leah and Emily's safety. A text pinged his phone: Leah saying there was a change of plans, she and Emily were now in the clinic administrator's office.

Cursing the ER doctor's inability to follow orders, but relieved they were somewhere safe and out of the main hospital building, so hopefully beyond the killer's ability to surveil, Luka decided to take two minutes to check with the staff on peds. Harper and Krichek would follow up, but Harper's comment about Leah potentially smuggling the roses into Emily's room herself rankled—he hadn't even thought of that. Could he really trust Leah? He wanted to, his gut instinct told him he could, but his job was to explore facts not feelings.

When he arrived on the pediatrics floor there was a hospital security guard conspicuously posted outside the room.

"Anyone been inside?" he asked.

"No. I was told not to disturb any potential evidence."

Luka went inside the room. There was a patient bed, covers pulled aside, pillow still dented from a child-size head. Beside it stood a table with a lunch tray, the food undisturbed. And a trash can with a bouquet of roses wrapped in green florist paper. Given the boxes of gloves scattered throughout the hospital, the actor would have to be a fool to have left any fingerprints. The card was on the nightstand, exactly as Leah had described.

Blowing his breath out in frustration, he didn't touch anything, but left the room and went to the nursing station. The clerk's desk had an unobstructed view of Emily's room.

"Did you see any floral deliveries for Emily Wright?" Luka asked the clerk after explaining the situation.

The man, Arthur Nguyen, shook his head. Luka waited. Nguyen swallowed hard, then found his voice. "No. I didn't see anyone go into Emily's room—but it was right after lunch, a busy time for meds and labs and patient transport. I might have missed something."

Luka glanced at the ceiling. "You have cameras monitoring the floor?"

"No—no, sir. Only at the elevators and stairs. Because of protecting the kids' privacy. There was a guard here, but he left for lunch when Dr. Wright took her daughter down for her interview. She and Emily got back before the guard did."

Of course they did. "Okay. My people are on their way. They'll want to talk to everyone who was on the floor and who might have seen anything. Make a list and try to help them coordinate that, okay?"

"I'll ask the charge nurse to help."

The security guard at Emily's door got a phone call and nodded to Luka. "There's some woman downstairs, keeps trying to come up. Insists she's Dr. Wright's mother. You want to talk to her? Apparently she's been at it all morning, even tried sneaking up with another family."

"I'm on my way." Luka traveled back down to the security office where the man at the front desk cringed when he appeared. Good to know someone was taking Luka seriously. If this woman was Leah's mother, why hadn't she called Leah directly? If they were estranged, it might be interesting to see Leah's response. Anything to force her to drop her mask of composure, expose what was really going on behind it.

The guard at the front desk hit a button and a moment later a door in the back opened and another guard, this one older with sergeant stripes on his uniform, appeared along with a middle-aged redhead dressed in swaths of color and layers of jangly jewelry. She looked like a flower child, but her tone of voice as she protested her treatment was anything but floral. Lashing, harsh as a whip, was more like it.

"Are you the officer in charge?" She strode forward to stand toe-to-toe with Luka. "I demand to see my daughter and granddaughter. Right now."

The security guy shrugged, with the hint of a smirk, gesturing with his hands to say, "She's all yours."

"Ma'am, I need to see some identification." Luka kept his voice steady despite his urge to rush over to the clinic where Leah and

Emily waited. If this woman was Leah's mother, he had to play this carefully. "Please," he added, and was rewarded by a softening of her glare.

"Already showed it to these bozos." She handed him a driver's license along with a collection of photos of Leah Wright as a little girl. None past Leah at around age twelve, no high school graduation or college photos. "And here." She held up her phone, scrolling through a variety of snapshots of her with Emily, along with Emily and Ian. Interestingly, Leah was not in any of these more recent photos.

"Ruby Quinn Jackson," he read from the license. The address was just across the river, only a few miles from the farm. It was a gamble, but one with little downside. And he needed something in this case to break—even if he had to force a confrontation between Leah and her mother. "Come with me."

CHAPTER 26

They arrived at the clinic's administrative floor. Leah had never been up here. When she volunteered, she saw patients down in the urgent care center on the first floor. Brody waved at the volunteer on the front desk with casual familiarity then led them past the waiting area to Jessica Kern's office. Emily lagged behind, eyes focused on the glass-walled playroom across from it. One of Jessica's first projects when she took over the clinic had been to provide a play area—in fact, the play area was the reason behind the fundraiser where Leah had first met Jessica last year.

"Mommy, look," Emily whispered loudly. "Can I go play? Please?"

The playroom was empty apart from staff, and easily visible from Jessica' office, the reception desk, and the waiting area—designed that way to allay parents' fears, no doubt.

"I can watch her while I wait for Charlie," Brody volunteered.

Leah didn't want to let Emily go, wanted to hold onto her so tight that no force of nature could tear them apart. What would Ian do? Finally, Leah nodded her assent. As Emily excitedly entered the playroom, Leah turned around to see Jessica standing in her office doorway, smiling fondly as she watched Emily explore.

"Brody, would you mind asking Mary to call down for lunch for our guests?"

"No problem, doc." He ambled across the waiting area back to the reception desk, the volunteer, a woman in her late sixties, beaming as he approached.

"He seems to know everyone," Leah said. "Said his son's here a lot. Cystic fibrosis?"

Jessica sighed. "Poor Charlie. What that child's been through. But you and Emily—I'm so sorry to hear things are getting worse. Please, come in, enjoy some peace and quiet."

Leah followed Jessica into her office. It was small, but quiet. The walls held bookcases and a variety of artwork obviously done by patients. There were no diplomas or certificates, although there were several photos: Jessica and a man receiving an award, each holding a prosthetic arm raised victoriously and surrounded by men in military uniforms; a candid shot of Jessica in a well-equipped, high tech lab with an Air Force pilot, a drone flying beyond them and no controls in sight; and one of a young soldier in a military uniform, a black ribbon across the upper corner. A flag framed in a triangular wooden case stood on the shelf beside it.

Leah stepped back from the memorial, feeling as if she'd intruded. Jessica said she'd lost her husband, but her son as well? She glanced at the older woman, who was sliding an armchair away from the wall to join the one already sitting in front of the desk, angling them so that they faced each other but also provided a clear view out the door to the playroom. Jessica smiled at Leah, sat down in the chair she'd moved into more intimate proximity and gestured for Leah to take the other.

"Thanks," Leah said as she sank down, the vinyl upholstery sighing. Her phone vibrated—it had been going off nonstop. She slid it from her pocket, frowned at the Facebook message, hoping it was Ian's parents, miraculously able to make it past the storm. It wasn't. She held it out for Jessica to read.

"It won't stop," Leah said. "Not only reporters or people who know Ian, but strangers texting, commenting. The things they say, about me, about Ian, about Emily. Go ahead, scroll down. It's awful."

"Trolls."

"This is more than heckling—some of these are so… perverted. And the details. It's terrifying. Now people are sending me links to videos accusing me of mistreating patients, racism, horrible things." Leah glanced across the hall to the playroom. Emily was eating with Brody, out of earshot. "Jessica, she was there, asleep, right there in the room. They laid the flowers beside her on the pillow. Anything could have—" Fear throttled her words.

"You called the police?"

"As soon as I got Emily out of there, yes. They're sending someone." Frustration bled into her tone—she no longer trusted Luka Jericho and the police to protect Emily. Which meant it all fell to Leah.

"Maybe the flowers weren't sent by the killer? But by someone else wanting to take advantage of your vulnerability?"

"No," Leah said without thinking. "How would they know to write that on the card?"

"You said Ian bought his bouquet from the gift shop. If someone worked at Good Sam—"

"They'd know how to find Emily's room." Leah glanced around the office, her gaze ricocheting from Jessica's artwork to the variety of textbooks lined up on her bookshelves to the flag in its memorial case and back again. "That would mean… someone I know, maybe someone I work with…" She couldn't bring herself to finish the thought.

Jessica rested a hand on Leah's arm. "It doesn't mean they hurt Ian. Could be as simple as someone you pissed off taking advantage of a chance to elicit pain. So many of these trolls are like that—they don't actually want to hurt anyone, they just want to be heard, their emotions, pain acknowledged."

Leah shook her head as if the movement might erase the idea that she'd hurt someone so badly that they chose this moment to punish her. To twist the knife while she was already reeling from Ian's death. "No. They threatened Emily. They can say anything they want to me, about me—but they cannot threaten Emily. Not while she's already been through so much."

"With more to come, I'm afraid." Jessica squeezed Leah's arm before releasing it. She gestured with Leah's phone. "A lot of victims of domestic violence come through here. I have a stash of prepaid phones—we can give the police yours, let them deal with the trolls." She slid her chair back behind the desk and pulled a phone from a drawer. "They're not fancy, not many apps or anything, just a basic phone, but—"

Leah took the new phone like it was a lifeline. It would only take a minute to transfer her contacts and her photos were saved in their cloud storage—she didn't really care about anything else. Ian had drilled a distrust of apps that required personal info like banking details, so abandoning her phone was no great loss—not compared to being able to escape the media and the strangers who now demanded access to her life, as if her suffering was some warped form of entertainment.

"When you don't need it anymore, return it and we'll pass it on to the next person who needs it."

"Jessica, thank you. Seriously, this is so thoughtful."

Jessica shook away the praise. "I'm just sorry you need it at all."

Leah turned the phone on and quickly set it up, her first text to Ian's parents so they would have her new temporary number. Then she followed Jessica's eyes out through the open door. Emily sat at the playroom's large drawing table with Brody, who'd somehow managed to fold himself into the small chair opposite. He still wore his knit cap, reminding Leah of that old comic book character, Jughead.

As the silence lengthened, Leah's gaze drifted back to Jessica's bookshelf with its photos. "You and your husband worked together?" she asked, anxious to change the topic to anything that didn't involve killers or stalkers. "With injured veterans?"

"A new form of prosthetics," Jessica said proudly. "Artificial limbs controlled entirely with the patient's thoughts." She paused and the bright look in her eyes faded. "Our work. Mine and Gordie's. Back when I still worked in research. No time for that now. Ever since Gordie… research seems so unimportant compared to patients I can see, feel, touch, help. Know what I mean?"

Leah nodded. "What was it like, working with your husband?"

"We had our ups and downs, like any partnership. What kept us going was Jonathan—our son." Her gaze traveled past Leah to the photo of the young man in dress uniform. "His unit was training Afghan police in counterterrorism tactics. One day someone tossed an IED inside his classroom, locked the door, walked away. Killed them all, men trying to help him and his people. No one ever suspected they had a traitor right there beside them." She closed her eyes, a sigh escaping her. Leah sat still, not sure what to say. *Sorry* was such a small empty word, she'd learned already.

"Anyway," Jessica opened her eyes and continued, "Gordie and I, we switched gears from civilians to working with soldiers. Gordie was an engineering genius but couldn't always see the bigger picture like I could as far as real-world applications. Maybe if he had, we could have saved Jonathan—"

"How?"

"Our enhanced EEG—the one I used with Emily. It's better than even functional MRI as far as detecting lies, deception, intent. With it, I can tell exactly what areas of the brain are being activated. It's lightweight, portable, perfect for field interrogations. Or will be, once I get the prototype perfected. Gordie didn't want to pursue that line of research, said it could be abused too easily."

Her gaze morphed from wistful to sorrowful. "That last day, right before he… we were fighting about it… and then he was gone and I was all alone. My whole world shattered into nothing." Jessica shook herself as if waking from a daydream. "I'm so sorry. You don't want to hear all that, not when your own loss is so fresh. How can I help?"

Leah squirmed in her chair. She appreciated Jessica trying to help, but she'd had more than enough of shrinks and counseling for the day. Before she could make an excuse to leave and join Emily in the playroom, a man appeared in the open doorway. He wore a conservative gray suit, white shirt, black tie, and held a leather credential folder up before him.

"Dr. Wright, you're a difficult woman to track down," he said as Leah scanned his ID. Defense Intelligence Agency. "George Radcliffe, DIA. Your husband consulted for us." He snapped the thin leather wallet closed and slid it into his breast pocket. "Sorry for your loss."

Radcliffe's expression never changed as he uttered the empty platitude. Leah pushed out of her chair, feeling vulnerable with the government agent standing over her, his posture not aggressive but also not relaxed.

"Did you find something? Do you know who killed Ian? Was it something to do with his government work?" Once she began, the questions came so fast and furious that she could barely restrain herself long enough to allow Radcliffe to answer. "Do you know why? Why Ian?"

Beside her, Jessica also rose, moving to stand behind her desk as if presiding over an impromptu staff meeting. Radcliffe ignored both women, strolling around the perimeter of the room, admiring Jessica's photos and awards, tracing a finger over the spines of her textbooks. "Dr. Kern—you use your maiden name now?"

"Professionally, yes. Have we met before?"

"Your work with DARPA, I'm very familiar."

"What does any of that have to do with my husband's murder?" Leah snapped, her patience long since exhausted.

Radcliffe let a research abstract drift from his fingers back onto the shelf. "I don't have any answers about your husband," he told Leah, dashing her hopes. "But I do have questions." He glanced at Jessica. "Perhaps we should speak in private?"

The last thing Leah wanted was to be left alone with this man who seemed as devoid of emotion as he was of personality. She had the uncomfortable feeling that he already knew all the answers to any questions he might ask, just as she was certain that he already knew all about Jessica's background, previous research, and life before coming here two years ago.

"No," Leah said as Jessica joined her, the two women standing together, side by side. "Jessica can stay."

"Very well, then. What work did your husband bring home with him?"

"Never anything classified—he used a special computer on campus, some kind of dedicated connection? And he never discussed any of his work," she added, anticipating his next question. "Not beyond generalities. I could learn more about cyber security reading a newspaper than from Ian."

He didn't look at Leah, continuing his perusal of Jessica's photos and books. "Ever own a motorcycle? Specifically, a Victory Hammer 8-Ball?"

"No. But if you know what kind of motorcycle the killer rode you can track him, right?"

Radcliffe ignored her question as he slid out a small framed photo that was partially hidden by the larger photo of Jessica's son and scrutinized it. Leah couldn't see what the photo was, but she felt Jessica stiffen beside her, obviously not liking the federal agent's manhandling of her personal memories.

"*Know* anyone who has a motorcycle?" he asked Leah, oblivious to Jessica's discomfort, casually tucking the photo back behind the larger frame, out of sight. "Specifically, a Victory Hammer 8-Ball?"

"No." Leah stepped forward, trying to snag his attention. "Please look at me when you speak. This is my husband's life we're talking about. I'd like to know you're taking it seriously."

Radcliffe stopped, his back to her, then slowly, as if it was his idea, he turned to face her. "Actually, Dr. Wright, this is your husband's death we're talking about. And I take that very seriously. In fact, I have a team poring through vehicle registrations, searching for the owner of that bike. I have another team tracing your husband's movements for the past week, to see if anyone was following him. While a third team is digging into your own life, here and back in Pittsburgh—you moved here from there, correct?"

"Yes. But Pittsburgh? That was years ago, why would you—" She paused, digesting his words. "Do you think the killer was targeting me, not Ian? Is that why they sent the flowers?"

His shrug barely creased his well-tailored suit. "We're examining every possibility." He glanced at an expensive-looking watch. "I have appointments, but perhaps we could speak more later." For some reason he looked past Leah as if asking Jessica permission.

Before Leah could ask any of her own questions, a commotion coming from the reception area had her whirling away from Radcliffe, crossing into the hallway.

A woman shouted Leah's name and Leah froze. She knew that voice. Slowly, fighting every instinct screaming at her to grab Emily and run, she turned toward the reception desk.

Jericho stood at the desk, one hand holding an older woman's arm, restraining her. The older woman was in her late fifties, with rich auburn hair streaked with gray, and blue eyes so bright they burned. She shook off Jericho's hand and strode toward Leah, reminding Leah of Nellie. Yet this woman was the opposite of her great aunt in every way.

"Did you think I wouldn't come?" she demanded. Leah stared at her bright tie-dyed wrap skirt, bohemian fringed tunic, dangling peacock feather earrings, wrist bangles, and rings adorning every finger. Anything to avoid looking her in the eyes.

Leah trembled. She positioned her body against the glass wall of the playroom, hoping to block Emily's view. Her muscles clenched. She wanted to flee but the eleven-year-old trapped inside kept her frozen. That little girl wanted to fly. Fly straight into the arms of her mother.

CHAPTER 27

"Ruby." Leah's voice emerged as a childish, shrill gasp.

Before Leah could move, Jericho stepped forward. "Mrs. Wright, I found this woman trying to get to your daughter's hospital room. She claims to be your mother."

Leah stood silent, trying to decide whether to get Emily and run or… what? Let Ruby into their lives, now when they were most vulnerable? "No."

"Honey," Ruby pleaded. "Please—"

"Maybe we should move this into my office?" Jessica suggested.

Leah glanced around, searching for an escape, and saw Radcliffe stepping into an elevator, the family drama of no interest to him. She wished she could go with him; even his abrasive dissection of her life would be better than dealing with Ruby. Instead, she nodded to Jessica, who briskly gestured to Jericho and Ruby, leading the way back to her office.

A few moments later they surrounded Jessica's desk, crowding the tiny office. Leah remained standing and kept herself closest to the door, which she edged most of the way shut, not risking Emily seeing Ruby. Ruby took the chair Leah had sat in earlier. Jessica moved behind her desk while Jericho stood, his back to the bookshelves where he could keep the others in view.

"Mrs. Jackson, care to explain yourself?" Jericho began.

"Jackson?" Leah blurted out. Damn it, just walk away, she told herself. But she couldn't help it. "What happened to Mrs.

Franklin?" He'd been the husband, Ruby's second, before the boyfriend who'd accompanied Ruby to the hospital after Emily was born, and after the man Ruby had dated when Leah was eleven and she left her at Nellie's for good.

"It's Jackson now," Ruby said without a trace of apology. "Kept it after the divorce."

"Time flies," Leah snapped. Ruby had been living in Nellie's house across the river, not fifteen minutes away from her daughter and granddaughter, for almost two years and she couldn't even be bothered to tell them she'd changed her name? Again.

"Mrs. Jackson is known to you?" Jericho asked, motioning Ruby to silence.

"She's my mother." Leah felt like she was on the witness stand admitting her own guilt. "We haven't seen each other since my daughter was born, six years ago."

"I did what you asked," Ruby protested. "I stayed away. You knew where to find me." Then the words that twisted Leah's heart with both hope and fury. Words she'd waited her entire life to hear, but now it was too late. "And I'm not going anywhere."

Leah had no energy to deal with Ruby or her false promises, so she focused on Jericho. "Did you find who sent the flowers? What about the man from the ER? Cochrane? What's going on? I need to know my daughter is safe."

Before he could answer, Jericho's phone rang. "I need to get this." He left the room, talking to someone named Harper.

Ruby left her chair and turned to Leah. "I was glad you called me."

"I told you, I wasn't calling you," Leah snapped. She sighed. "Jessica, could you excuse us for a moment?"

It was Jessica's office, but she didn't argue. Instead she rose from her chair and smiled graciously. "Of course. I'll be right outside if you need anything." She left, closing the door behind her.

"I want to help," Ruby said once they were alone—Leah couldn't even remember the last time she'd been alone with her mother.

"Please, I know I can. I've been there, I've felt what you feel right now." She took a step toward Leah.

Leah raised her outstretched hand, palm flat like a stop sign and Ruby froze, her arms half lifted as if she'd actually thought a hug would revive two decades of a withered relationship.

"How could you possibly understand what I'm feeling?" Leah raged. "You'd need to be able to love someone other than yourself for that to happen."

Ruby's face drained of color. She sank back into the chair, her chest heaving. "How can you say that? You know what I went through. Everything I did, I did for you."

"Leaving me any chance you got? Dumping me on Nellie so you could run off with your flavor of the week boyfriend? Please."

Ruby's entire body twanged, a violin string tightened too far. "She never told you where I was, why I left? All these years, I thought you knew—"

"Knew what?" Leah demanded. What lie would Ruby spin, trying to justify her narcissism?

"Did you ever stop to ask yourself why I showed up drunk after Emily was born?"

Sad to say, Leah never even wondered. Ruby often turned to drugs and alcohol for recreational purposes, but her true cravings were constant praise, bigger better thrills, and lavish affection. If a man bored or disappointed, she'd move on to the next loser, often without bothering with a goodbye or explanation.

"I wasn't always like that, you know," Ruby continued. "When I was young, I was just like you. Smart—enough that Nellie gave me money to go to college." She shook her head as if amazed she'd ever been so young. "And then, then your father came along."

Even now, all these years later, Ruby refused to use his name. When Leah was little she used to ask Ruby about her father. All the other kids had dads, why didn't she? Where was he? What was his name? What did he look like? Every time, Ruby would not only not answer, she'd spiral out of control.

Leah learned not to ask anymore.

So now, she kept her breath shallow, not daring to interrupt, not even to breathe. Her father was a gaping black hole in her life, a void that until now Ruby had refused to fill with any answers. Leah sank into a chair, knotting her hands together, holding as still as possible. It might be her first and last chance to ever learn the truth—if she could trust or believe anything Ruby told her.

"Your father," Ruby sighed. "Nellie hated him, you know. Forbade me to follow him when he left to join the Army, said I'd regret it the rest of my life, sacrificing my education, my future for trailer trash like him. But I had no choice. You know that old saying about falling in love at first sight? We didn't just fall. We grabbed each other and ran off a cliff, plummeting down, down. We were everything to each other, sun, moon, stars; the rest of the universe could go to hell, and as long as we were together, we wouldn't even notice."

She stopped, the distant hum of the heat vent the only sound as she stared unseeing at Jessica's bookshelves, her gaze filled with longing and sorrow. "And then the Army sends us to Texas. I'm seven months gone with you but already filled to bursting. God, it was so damn hot, I've never felt heat like that. Like being roasted on the surface of the sun. And I didn't know anyone out there, was all alone, waddling around trying to set up a proper home for him—and you. We were only there a week, he'd just started with his unit, when it was someone's birthday—I don't even know who—and they all went to some strip club."

Ruby grimaced. "Nellie was right about him. He was wild. Marriage couldn't tame him; guess I was hoping having a kid might. Make him want to come home at night without smelling of whiskey and some other woman's perfume. I still remember that night. Falling asleep with ice cubes melting on my chest and belly and the fan buzzing as high as it could go. The doorbell startled me, but it was you who woke me up. You were kicking and squirming like you were ready to bust your way out even though it was way too early. I thought he'd lost his keys again but then I open the door and—" Her breath rattled through the air between them. "They said he was gone. Bar fight. Hit his head. Dead before the ambulance made it there."

She rocked forward, hugging her arms around her chest. "They have big, fancy words to describe how I felt," Ruby continued. "Traumatic grief. Reactive depression. They're not the right words, though. Try devastated, shattered, consumed. Got so bad I went into preterm labor, almost lost you, too. Docs put me on bedrest—wouldn't even let me go to his funeral. Army wanted to move me out, but the docs got me an extension, and there I was all alone, stuck in bed, not remembering to eat or bathe and, most of all, not caring if I lived or died. But then, out of nowhere, because Lord knew I hadn't called her, Nellie showed up. She took care of me, saved me—saved you. After you were born, she brought us back here, thinking I'd heal, that I'd get over him, get my life back… but I never did."

Ruby huffed out a breath, almost as if she were back in labor. "So, I know how you feel now. I don't want you and Emily to end up like me. When he died, your father, he took the best part of me with him. And that meant I didn't have it in me to share with you like a mother should."

Leah jerked her chin up at that—it was the most maternal thing Ruby had ever said to her. Also the most insulting, implying that she'd ever abandon Emily the same way Ruby had abandoned her, over and over again. "Did you even try? There's meds, counseling—"

"Of course I tried," Ruby snapped. "I'm not some monster, to give up on my baby girl without a fight. Everything the doctors gave me made it worse. Didn't help that you look just like him. Every time I look at you, he's all I see, it hurts so damned much."

She tapped her fist against her chest as if her pain was physical. "They put me in the hospital a few times when things got bad—the longest was when you were eleven and I left you at Nellie's. Did shock treatments. New drugs. Nothing took, not for long. So I figured out my own therapy. Never staying too long in one place, always on the move so the pain couldn't catch up, couldn't find me. But it always does.

"You paid the price for that, but I didn't know any other way. Not until the day you said I couldn't ever see my own grand-daughter." Ruby glanced at Leah, her expression filled with regret. "I knew, I just knew, that even if I'd lost you, I couldn't lose Emily, too. So, I cleaned up my act, met and married Joe. He's a good man, church going, sober, but even he couldn't give me what I needed most, so we split up. Then Nellie died and I came back here. And the real work began." She managed a weak smile. "But it was worth it. Because I finally got what I'd been looking for, for so long. My family back."

Leah simply stared. All those years Ruby treated her as if she was nothing more than a mouth to feed, and it took Ian's murder for Ruby to suddenly feel whole again, feel like she was now a part of a family?

"Point is," Ruby continued, oblivious to Leah's seething desire to slap her, "I got over my grief, working through the pain. You will, too. Us Quinn women, we're strong like that. You and Emily will be just fine, you'll see. And you have me to help you—not like me, I had no one, had to go it alone." She raised her face, clearly expecting Leah to thank her for inviting Leah into Ruby's world of delusion.

"No," Leah said, surprising herself by how firm her tone was. "I can't. No." She'd run out of words to express her feelings, felt drained beyond exhaustion. Ruby's attempt to wash away decades of neglect by creating an instant family bond was one step too far, too much to ask. "No."

The door opened after a tentative knock. Jessica stood there holding Emily's hand. Beyond them, Luka Jericho leaned against the glass walls of the playroom, still on the phone, obviously eavesdropping on Leah and Ruby. Leah spun to face Emily, quickly composing her face—she hoped.

"See, Emily," Jessica said. "I told you she was all right." To Leah she said, "Emily was worried when she couldn't see you from the playroom."

Emily slid free of Jessica's hand and stepped inside. She frowned at Leah, a silent scold for making her worry, but then turned and smiled at Ruby. "Miss Ruby, what are you doing here? Mom, look, it's Miss Ruby, Daddy's friend."

As Leah watched in horror, Ruby crouched down and Emily stepped into her waiting arms for a hug. "I'm so sorry about your daddy." As she held Leah's daughter, Ruby glanced up at Leah. "I can explain. Later. Please don't blame Ian."

But who else was there to blame? Leah gagged back her fury. *Ian, what did you do?* This was a far greater betrayal than having an affair—to expose Emily to Ruby's toxicity? Behind Leah's back? What the hell had he been thinking? She stepped forward to take Emily's hand, not so gently untangling her from Ruby's arms. "We're leaving."

"Where will you go?" Jessica asked. "If you'd like, you could—"

"Come home with me," Ruby interjected. "Or without me, I don't care. Nellie's house is more yours than mine anyway. I can leave if you want. But I know that's what Nellie would want. You and Emily safe at home."

Emily squirmed as Leah squeezed her hand too tight. Leah grabbed her bag, slung it over her free arm, and marched Emily out to the reception area where Brody stood watching. He gave Emily a small wave of his hand as they walked past him to the waiting area, Ruby and Jessica trailing behind. Before she could reach the elevator, Jericho caught up to her, gestured her to wait as he spoke on his phone.

Finally, he hung up. "No luck with any witnesses seeing the roses delivered. I'd like to assign one of my team to you. Make sure nothing like this happens again. Where are you headed?"

The question Leah hadn't dared to ask herself. She still yearned to take Emily and flee, head in any direction, away from this madness that her life had become. But she didn't even have her car, much less a roof to sleep under tonight.

"Can we go home?" She knew the answer, but the question was more exhausted reflex than driven by logic. Wishful thinking, Ian would call it.

"No." His expression of pity shattered what little hope Leah had conjured. "We'll be holding it for several days, maybe weeks— follow-up tests, the DA might want a video reconstruction for when we go to trial. And then the cleaning—"

"Mommy, I want to go home!" Emily's scream sliced through the large open space, startling a mom who sat rocking her baby.

"I'm sorry." Leah dropped to her knees before Emily. "We can't go home, not yet." Maybe not ever, but now wasn't the time to broach that possibility. She yearned to be close to Ian, smell his scent, see his somehow-organized clutter… but Jericho was right. She might never have the strength to return to their home. And she couldn't risk Emily reliving the horrors of last night.

The elevator doors opened and a black woman with thick bleached braids gathered into a ponytail appeared, strode over to ask Brody and the receptionist something, then spotted Jericho and joined them.

"This is Officer Harper." He made introductions. "She'll be acting as your family liaison." Emily crinkled her nose in a question and Jericho surprised Leah by addressing Emily directly. "That means she'll go home with you, watch over you, keep you safe."

From the sour expression on Harper's face she didn't like the idea. Neither did Leah. She glanced at Ruby, the lesser evil compared to a hotel room. "Emily, we're going to visit Miss Ruby, stay with her."

That got Emily's attention. "Really? Miss Ruby says she lives in a big house across the river." Then she frowned. "But I need Huggybear. And my PJs. And," she whispered loud enough to be heard on the moon, "clean undies."

"I'll take Emily," Ruby volunteered. "We can stop at the store."

"No," Leah snapped, standing up. Spending the night in the same house as Ruby was one thing—trusting her with Emily? Never.

CHAPTER 28

Leah huddled beside Emily in the back seat of Jericho's car while Harper followed behind them. Ruby had gone ahead to get things ready and Jessica had been kind enough to give them the use of one of the clinic's loaner car seats.

Emily sensed her frustration and patted Leah's arm. "It's okay, Mommy. Dr. Jessica says Daddy is a hero. Do you think they'll name stars after him, like Orion?"

Leah smiled weakly, half tempted to steal Ruby's truck once they got to her house, keep driving until she was certain they'd outrun all pain and danger and that Emily would be past all this, safe and sound. But there was nowhere far enough to run to.

"Are you mad Daddy asked me to keep secrets?" Emily asked after they'd traveled several blocks in silence. "He said it wasn't because it's a bad thing, me meeting Miss Ruby, but because it's a sad thing and sometimes it's okay to keep secrets if it helps people not be sad."

"He was worried your mother would be sad if she knew you met Miss Ruby?" Jericho asked from the front seat, not giving Leah a chance to answer for herself. She met his gaze in the rearview, gave him a warning shake of her head.

Emily nodded, her curls bouncing against her shoulders, and spoke directly to Jericho as if Leah wasn't sitting right beside her. As if this was some kind of philosophical discussion or a game like the ones Ian and Emily designed together on the computer. But it was Ian's betrayal they were dissecting, and it took everything Leah had to not break wide open at the thought of it. She pressed her face against the window, hiding from Emily's recitation of the facts.

"Daddy said a long, long time ago they had a fight that made Mommy really, really sad. But that maybe I could help that." Leah could see Emily's frown reflected in the glass. "That part I don't know about. But Miss Ruby's really nice. I'm sure the fight was a big mistake. Like when I took Caleb's computer game apart to see how it worked and he was mad because I should've asked first but then he would've said no because it was his favorite and I had to do chores until I paid him back and got him a new one and then we were friends all over again." She sighed, her shoulders rising to her ears. "Mommy says don't get mad, it's bad. She says better to smile and walk away."

They stopped at the red light on Park. Jericho swiveled in his seat. "Did your daddy ever take you to meet anyone else?" he asked. "Like this woman?" He held his phone up, showing Emily the photo of Katrina Balanchuk.

That jerked Leah back to reality. She turned back to face Jericho. "Stop."

Emily considered the photo, tilting her head one way and then another. "She's pretty."

"Have you seen her before?" he asked, pocketing his phone as the light changed.

"Nope. But I like her hair. How do I get hair like that?"

"Can we talk about something else, please?" Leah said, hoping to regain control of the conversation. She understood Jericho was only trying to get answers he needed but she didn't want Emily to feel responsible if she couldn't help. And she definitely didn't want Emily exposed to the idea that her father might have betrayed them both.

"I saw your toys up in the attic," Jericho said. "Nice your dad let you play up there while he worked."

"Daddy let me work, too. He says I'm a prodigy." Emily sat up straight, her chest puffed with pride. "That means someone very special and very smart." Then she deflated. "But I guess Daddy's never gonna work with me again." Tears threatened to spill from her eyes.

Leah reached across the space between them, hugging Emily. "She and Ian used to create games together," she explained to Jericho. "He taught her computer coding."

"Coding?" he asked. "At her age?"

"Yeah. Her mind works like his." They'd discussed this, had meetings with the school after Emily tested as gifted, had tried to give her opportunities to explore her talents while also letting her enjoy her childhood.

Emily sat up, Leah's arms falling away from her, obviously upset at being excluded from the conversation. "Did you know there's no Santa really? Mommy says I need to keep that a secret from the kids at school. That's when Daddy told me it's okay to keep secrets, sometimes. Because Tricia cried last year when I told her, but it's the truth. I figured it out a long, long time ago. He's not real. But maybe a long time ago he was, but not now. That's called being a myth. Like King Arthur or Robin Hood."

She frowned. Paused for a long moment. "Daddy was real but now he's gone, so is he a myth? Does that mean we need to keep him a secret and not talk about him? I don't like that. He's real and he's my daddy and he's brave like the myth people—more brave because he fought the blackspaceman—and I want to talk about him, not make him a secret and hide him like Christmas presents."

Her voice grew until it filled the car with anger and fear and pain. Leah tried to hug her again, but Emily flailed her arms, pushing her away, as if afraid to trust her own mother.

"You can talk about your daddy all you want," she assured Emily. "Dr. Jessica was right. He's a hero and heroes are good to talk about."

"Right," Jericho chimed in, annoying Leah that he felt the need to insert himself in her and Emily's relationship. "Heroes help to inspire people—do you know what that means?"

Emily shook her head.

"It means that you want to be like them when you grow up because they're brave or strong or smart or—"

"Daddy's brave and strong and smart." Now she was bobbing her head, Jericho somehow able to provide comfort that Leah couldn't, making her feel even worse. "He was super smart. And everyone wants to be like him. I want to grow up to be just like him. He's better than Santa, even. Because he's real and he's my daddy."

Emily squinched her nose and mouth, delighted at being the center of attention once again. "My dad is a policeman like you, only he doesn't need a gun to stop bad guys. He uses his brain. That's why it's important to never stop learning new things. You have to keep exercising your brain." She said the last as if giving Jericho a performance evaluation, which he barely passed.

"Detective Jericho is helping us, Emily. It's not polite to tell someone how to do their job."

"No, it's okay," Jericho said with a smile. "And just for the record, I've never had to use my gun. Because your dad was right, Emily. Using your brain is a much better way of solving problems."

Leah shivered and hugged herself, then twisted in her seat to look out the rear window. Harper's car was directly behind them, hovering at a reassuring distance.

"Emily, when we get to Nellie's house," Leah could not bring herself to call it Ruby's house, "no going online. Offline games only. Do you understand?"

"Did I do something bad?"

"No, sweetheart. This isn't a punishment. It's more like we need to play hide and seek. And it's our turn to hide from anyone looking for us—in the real world and on the computer."

"Because the blackspaceman came from the computer? He's one of the bad guys Daddy catches?" Emily blinked and curled into Leah, stretching her arms past her safety harness to wrap around Leah's neck. "Only he caught Daddy first."

Leah met Jericho's gaze in the rearview mirror. His tight lips and creased brow mirrored her own concern—but none of her fear.

"It's okay, sweetheart," she tried to soothe Emily. "The bad guys aren't going to find us. Because we're very good at hiding and because Detective Jericho is going to find them first. And stop them."

It wasn't a promise she could keep—and not hers to make in the first place. But Jericho's jaw clenched and his chin jerked, accepting her challenge.

They turned onto the four-lane highway leading across the river. As Jericho drove them over the bridge, a motorcycle swerved into the passing lane, keeping pace directly alongside them. Leah tried desperately to think of something to distract Emily, but it was too late: she'd already spotted the motorcyclist wearing a black jacket and helmet.

"Mommy," she cried out.

Leah unbuckled her seatbelt and crawled over to Emily's side of the car, hugging Emily to her, turning her away from the window.

"Jericho. The motorcycle." Leah's voice emerged shrill, near hysterical. But with Emily sobbing in fear, fingers clutching Leah's hair, and the rider mere feet away, only a thin pane of glass separating them, she wasn't about to apologize.

The bridge was old and had no shoulder wide enough to pull off. Jericho slowed the car, but the rush hour traffic ahead was also slowing, enough that the motorcycle didn't pull ahead of them.

Leah heard him talking to Harper on his phone, but his words eluded her as she tried to calm Emily, who was having a full-blown meltdown. And then she clamped her lips tight, her entire body sagging into the booster seat. "Mommy, I'm sorry," she whimpered as a dribble of urine seeped down her pants. "Please. I'm sorry."

Leah ignored the wetness as she unbuckled Emily and scooped her onto her lap, scooting over to the far side of the car, using her own seatbelt to strap them both in. "It's okay, pumpkin. It's nothing to be sorry about. It wasn't your fault. We'll get you all cleaned up once we get to Nellie's."

Emily, exhausted, curled into Leah, fists gathered in Leah's hair like she used to do when she was a baby. Beyond her Leah saw Harper flash her police lights as she pulled into the lane behind the motorcycle. The motorcyclist pulled as far off the road as they could, Harper's car stopping behind them, blocking traffic. Finally, their lane began to move forward. Leah twisted and looked out the back window as Harper emerged from her car, and the motorcyclist removed their helmet. It was an Asian woman, early twenties, long black hair.

"Wrong make and model for the bike," Jericho said in the sudden silence as Emily quietened and they drove off the bridge and turned onto Route 15. "But better safe than sorry."

Leah sank back in her seat, Emily's weight anchoring her. What if it had been the killer? She would have been helpless to protect Emily. She squeezed her arms around Emily, who twisted her face against Leah's shoulder, leaving a trail of snot behind. Never in her life had Leah felt so vulnerable.

Emily stilled. Not asleep. Leah felt her tense with every turn or change in speed. More like resigned to her fate; a prisoner accepting that they were powerless against the shackles that bound them.

As the tires hummed over the pavement, Leah leaned her head against the window, staring at the landscape of her childhood. What had Ian been thinking, introducing Emily to Ruby? She heard his voice, almost as if he were sitting right beside her.

"She's old enough," he'd argue, totally side-stepping the fact that he'd lied to her, betrayed her. "They had that school project about ancestors and she didn't understand why your side of the family tree was naked. Bad enough your mother never told you who your own father was, but to have a grandmother so near, just across the river, and deprive her of that relationship? I couldn't do it."

"You had no right, going behind my back like that," she'd tell him. "You have no idea what Ruby's like, the damage she could—"

"I met her first. Several times. Laid out ground rules. Didn't even tell Emily that Ruby is your mother, just a friend of the family. That way if things went south, we had a way out. And I was there, every moment." His logic would be faultless. And then he'd take both of her hands and caress his thumbs against her palms until she began to relax. "She's changed, Leah. She really has. Maybe you should think about forgiving her? At least talk to her? Let go of some of the pain—for your sake, for Emily's."

As usual, he'd win the argument. Which was maybe why he never brought it up in the first place—he was waiting until she was ready, until his logic and persuasion weren't even really necessary other than to allow her to save face.

Still, it hurt, knowing he'd kept such a huge secret from her. She understood keeping his work secret, that was different, that had nothing to do with them—except, given Radcliffe's questions and insinuations, maybe now it had.

They bumped off Route 15 to turn down the lane that led to Nellie's and Leah found herself leaning sideways, nose pressed against the window. The original Quinn farm had had over a hundred acres, but it had been whittled down over generations, until now there were seven acres containing the farmhouse, barn, and a few outbuildings, surrounded on two sides by thick forest preserved from development as State Game Lands. The lane leading to the house wove between hemlocks, mountain laurel, and white pines until the final turn revealed the snow-mounded fields of lavender and rose bushes that Nellie had cultivated for decades.

Leah was relieved to see that the plants appeared well tended—the less hardy tea roses sheltered beneath burlap, the rows of lavender clear of obvious weeds. Much of her youth had been spent helping Nellie make her artisanal soaps, candles, and candy using the fruits of her garden. She half expected to see Nellie, clad in her uniform of jeans and flannel shirt with a wide-brimmed sunhat worn year-round, rise up from inspecting the plants, turn and wave at them.

But instead, it was another redhead who bounded through the emerald green front door. Ruby. Despite the cold, she pranced across the wide-planked porch barefoot, waving gleefully as if they might miss her in the gathering twilight. How typical. Leah and Emily were fleeing the man who murdered Ian and Ruby's response was to act as if they were having a girls' night out.

Jericho parked the car and came around to open their door. Leah unfastened the seatbelt. Emily climbed off her lap, tugging at her pajama top, pulling it down over her wet bottoms.

"Harper's staying the night. Tomorrow I'll send uniforms to relieve her. In the meantime, the only phone that's on is Harper's and that burner phone Dr. Kern lent you. The only number you call is mine." He paused. "Dr. Kern gave me your phone. Do I have your permission to search it? It will help us trace the people harassing you."

"Of course."

He jotted a receipt on his pocket notebook, had her sign it.

"If you make a list, I'll have someone go to the store for you in the morning."

Leah barely heard his words as she watched Ruby grab Emily's hand and practically dance her inside. One more betrayal to lay at Ian's feet. "This woman, Katrina, the one you think—" She couldn't even find the words. "You think she killed Ian? Or got him killed?"

"As soon as we learn anything, I'll let you know."

Her anger shattered her restraint. "I don't need any more lies, Detective. I need to know if my little girl is in danger. I need to know how to keep her safe. And I need to know who the hell my husband really was."

CHAPTER 29

Luka wished he had answers for Leah—if he did, he'd be that much closer to finding her husband's killer. His phone vibrated with another text and he shoved his hand deep into his pocket to smother it. Stray snowflakes filled the air, harbingers of more to come, and Leah's lips trembled with the cold as she waited for his response.

They stood in silence for a long moment—Luka searching for words adequate to the task, words that wouldn't sound trite or dismissive; Leah staring at him as if he had the key to understanding her husband's secrets. Until finally, a departmental Taurus sped down the drive, skidding to a stop behind Luka's car. Harper barged out of the driver's seat at her usual breakneck pace.

"Glad I caught you," she said to Luka, eying Leah as she spoke. "I didn't get a chance to update you on a few items Krichek just sent me." She joined them at Luka's car. "Mrs. Wright, perhaps you could clear up something for us."

Leah frowned. "What?" She stamped her feet and glanced to the house, her frown deepening. She didn't trust her mother with her daughter, Luka realized and wondered at that. Something Harper might untangle during the night, perhaps.

Harper's smile was as fake as her suddenly saccharine tone. She held her phone up to Leah. "I don't suppose you recognize this woman? Or this one?"

Luka glanced over Harper's elbow. Two grainy black and white photos of a woman in scrubs and a doctor's white coat, holding a bouquet of roses, long dark hair pulled forward to hide her face. Despite the fact that the time stamps on the photos were hours apart, it was definitely the same woman.

"A woman bought both bouquets of roses you received," Harper continued as Leah stared at the photos, her face tightening into a blank mask. "Any idea who she could be? Someone about your height and build, hair the same?"

Leah shook her head mutely, her feet shifting to point toward the house as if ready to bolt. She pushed the phone away and looked up to stare not at Harper but at Luka. "You think I bought them, sent them to myself? Why would I do that? Unless you think I—" She spun away, turning her back on them, heading up the porch steps. When she reached the top she whirled, staring down at them. "No. I don't care what you think. I didn't have anything to do with my husband's death." She ran inside, slamming the door behind her.

Harper rocked back on her heels, a smug smile crossing her face as she pocketed her phone. "That went well."

"You think?" Luka said, his gaze on the empty porch with its lonely swing shuddering as the wind gusted. He checked his phone—Harper was one of his missed texts. At least she'd tried to reach Luka before pouncing on Leah like a hawk swooping in on its prey. "Not sure alienating our primary witness is the best tactic."

"Primary suspect, you mean. C'mon, boss, look at the photos. It's her. Gotta be. Who else would send the flowers? They don't make any sense otherwise—sure as hell isn't your guy Cochrane dressing up in drag."

"Exactly why would she send the roses? Especially the second ones? We had nothing to tie her to anything, she had a solid alibi—"

"Partially established by the first set of roses," Harper reminded him. "That whole conversation with the desk clerk, making sure someone saw her leave the ER and noted the time. C'mon, that doesn't feel like a setup to you?"

"Maybe," he allowed, leaning against the Taurus as the upstairs lights turned on in the house. They cast a warm yellow glow that fell short of him and Harper, leaving them in shadow. Boundaries, he thought. Police crossed over them all the time, invading sacrosanct, private territory. So did ER doctors—patients stripped naked, turned into injured bits of flesh to be mended. It would take a degree of detachment to do that job. He remembered how calm Leah had been when he interviewed her in her daughter's hospital room last night. "But those second roses…"

"Attention," Harper guessed. "Excitement. Drama. Maybe she's seen too many movies, wants to play the suffering victim longer, who knows?"

He shook his head. "No. That's not it. She's not like that."

Harper crossed her arms over her chest, her glare at the house filled with contempt. "I'll give you one thing, she's a damn fine actress. Maybe the second roses were to set up an imaginary threat, give her an excuse to run away with her daughter."

"If so, it backfired, because now she's stuck with you."

Her smile bared her teeth. "Yep. And I'm not about to let her get away with shit."

Luka swallowed his sigh—Harper had to learn her own lessons, especially the one about not getting so wrapped up in a theory that you twisted the facts to fit it. But at least he wouldn't have to worry about Leah or her family tonight. No way in hell was Harper going to let them out of her sight.

"We got a warrant for the widow's phone yet?" Harper asked.

"Krichek's working on it." Convincing a judge to allow them to invade a grieving widow's privacy required both probable cause and finesse. "But, it's just to cover our bases. Leah gave me her phone voluntarily."

Luka's own phone kept buzzing. He slid it free and glanced at his missed messages: Janine, asking when he'd make it back to the farm. No time soon, but he wasn't about to upset her further by texting her back. At least she hadn't mentioned Tanya; that was progress. He pocketed the phone, his mind still on Harper's argument.

"She gave you her phone?" Harper scoffed. "It will be wiped clean—she probably already had a burner we know nothing about. But we should also get on the new phone, see who she calls from it. She'll think she's safe using it."

He understood Harper's eagerness—her first homicide, first major case. Of course she wanted to be the one to crack it. He remembered that feeling. But she was missing something—they were missing something. He studied the house where Leah Wright had spent most of her youth. He had a vague recollection of coming here when he was a kid, riding in Pops' truck, Nellie Quinn greeting them with lemonade that she'd garnished with fresh peppermint plucked straight from her kitchen garden.

Must've been before Leah moved in with Nellie. Had she enjoyed growing up here as much as he'd enjoyed his grandparents' farm? For him, the farm had meant freedom; some of his most joyful memories had taken place there. From the outside this house appeared to be a similar safe haven. Appeared. Maybe it was a trick of the light, the same way it gave the snow a nostalgic glow of wonder, masking its actual threat.

He reminded himself that Leah had left this home as soon as she was able. Instead of her safe haven, perhaps this house was an anchor forged by guilt. Weighing her down, forcing her back after her great aunt had become ill.

"Her colleagues all say she's a good doctor, dedicated. Maybe too dedicated," he added in the interest of full disclosure. "The head of trauma surgery thinks she has a God complex. Likes to pull people back from the dead, no matter the consequences."

"Control freak. Used to getting things her way," Harper said. "You said she moved here from Pittsburgh when her aunt got sick, took care of her until she died?"

"Great aunt. You thinking there's something there?" The snow was falling steadier now, to the point where if he stood still for too long it gathered in the folds of his coat.

Her shrug was much too casual. "Her kid would've been a toddler, right? Couldn't have been much fun taking care of a sick old lady, juggling a kid and husband while starting out at a new job in the ER here. And Good Sam isn't any prestigious big-time trauma center—not like Johns Hopkins or Pitt. I'll bet she missed the action, maybe helped the old lady along—she inherited this place, right?"

"You think Leah Wright killed her great aunt?"

"I think Leah Wright is a woman who isn't afraid to go after what she wants," Harper answered him. "She likes control. And when she loses it? That's when she's dangerous."

Luka didn't agree with Harper's theory about Leah's involvement in her great aunt's death, but he couldn't argue with her. After all, their only other potential suspects, Cochrane and Katrina Balanchuk, both had alibis. He couldn't ignore his gut—this killing was personal—but that left only the widow.

He wanted to trust Leah—but he had to examine every angle. He made a note to call the ME's office, have Maggie dig into Nellie Quinn's medical records. Which meant prepping yet another warrant. He eyed the snow collecting on the Taurus's windshield. He had to get back to the station house, shouldn't take time for personal business at the farm. But then Janine texted again, this one only three characters: *911*.

Harper stepped toward the porch, her gear bag slung over her shoulder, then turned back, smiling at Luka. "You know it, boss. There's something there."

"What makes you say that?"

"Because you stopped calling her Leah." With that, she gave him a wave and sprinted up the steps, into the house.

Luka's sigh was part exhaustion, part exasperation and quickly swallowed by the wind. He fingered his phone. Time to face the music.

He climbed into the Taurus and steered down the drive, heading towards home. Harper's words echoed in his mind. Could he have been wrong about Leah Wright? Was this all some kind of elaborate game she'd orchestrated to get rid of a cheating husband, create an unimpeachable persona as a grieving widow, and then collect the insurance and her daughter, escape to live the life she wanted, free of family obligations? She could have sent the flowers to herself, the motorcyclist could be her accomplice, and the ten thousand dollars Ian withdrew could have been for her.

Which was the real Leah Wright? Would they ever know?

CHAPTER 30

Leah stood inside the open front door, watching Harper and Jericho talk. She felt like a child again, hiding and trying to eavesdrop as the grownups talked about her. After Ruby would leave, she'd dissect every half-heard conversation, trying to figure out what she'd done wrong.

Not now. Now she was an adult with a child of her own to care for. She closed the front door and turned her back on the conversation outside. The foyer opened up onto a staircase, beside it a narrow hall leading back to the kitchen, and on either side, archways leading to the formal dining room and the living room with its large river rock fireplace.

She turned to the living room. Nothing had changed. Same ancient leather sofa and tapestry chair with its curved back and wide rolled arms, just the right size for a young girl to curl up and doze beside the fire. Same braid rug, same singed spots near the hearth, same photos lining the mantle: Nellie and her sister—Leah's grandmother; their parents and grandparents; a sepia wedding photo of the great-grandparents; some anonymous ancestor's christening photo; and all of Leah's school pictures lined up in a row documenting her evolution from gangly, crooked-toothed child to shy and awkward teen and finally to beaming med school graduate, radiant bride, and even more exhilarated mother, giving way to photos of Emily as a baby and then a toddler. Until Emily seemingly stopped growing, frozen in time at twenty-eight months when Nellie had gotten sick.

And yet, everything had changed. Gone were Nellie's personal touches—her never finished knitting projects, Leah's clumsy elementary school art class clay pots, esoteric seed catalogues and the medical paraphernalia that had cluttered the space during Nellie's final days. Gone also was her special smell, raw earth perfumed by lavender and roses. Vanished was the feeling of peace.

"I put you and Emily in Nellie's room," Ruby said from the top of the stairs.

Leah clutched her bag tighter and nodded, starting up the steps, instinctively avoiding the creaky third one.

"Emily's just out of the tub. Don't worry. I had a clean nightgown ready for her."

That made Leah pause, glancing up at Ruby with narrowed eyes.

Ruby didn't flinch, merely shrugged. "You can't blame me for hoping that someday… and now, here you are," she finished brightly as if oblivious to the reasons behind their unscheduled family reunion. "She's asking if you can braid her hair before bed."

Leah reached the top of the steps and after a long, silent moment Ruby stood aside so that she could pass without their touching. Leah walked down the hall, her steps echoing into the past as she retraced the path she'd taken a thousand times. The guest room was the first she passed, followed by her old room at the rear of the house. It faced north with a glimpse of the river beyond the woods in the winter. The door was open and Leah couldn't help but glance inside—the bed was the same as was the faded oriental rug that once upon a time Leah had pretended was a flying carpet, but all other traces of her childhood had vanished, replaced by Ruby's flea market clutter. Why hadn't Ruby taken Nellie's room, which was larger? Surely not out of guilt?

No, Leah thought as she noted the blackout curtains Ruby had hung. Nellie's room got the morning sun and Ruby was never a morning person. Just that simple.

Leah turned to retrace her steps back down the hall to the front of the house, passing the bathroom with its old-fashioned claw tub, steam still fogging the mirror over the sink. Then she reached Nellie's room with its wide bay window stretching out over the front porch roof. The antique spool bed still faced the window, a dressing table on the far side. A rocking chair was positioned in front of the window and Leah could swear that it moved—as if its owner had just stepped away. She inhaled deeply, not sure if she imagined Nellie's scent; but real or not, it still relaxed her.

"Mommy, look, Miss Ruby gave me a fairy princess dress." Emily bounced on the bed, spreading the ruffled skirt of the nightgown with its brightly sparkled neon pink picture of a fairy with a tiny waist and voluminous hair. The image was everything she never wanted Emily to aspire to, but she said nothing. Emily turned so that her back was to Leah and said, "Braids, please."

She'd inherited Leah's unruly hair, which required some form of restraint before a night of Emily's tossing and turning—otherwise it would be a knotted mess in the morning. Emily handed Leah a wide-toothed comb that, like the nightgown, appeared to be brand new. Leah ran it through Emily's curls. "Sure you're ready for bed, not hungry or anything?"

"No. I just want to be away from people. And scary stuff." She glanced over her shoulder. "It's nice here. But I'd like it better if I had Huggybear to keep me safe."

"I'm afraid you'll have to do with me for tonight. We can go to the store, find a new Huggybear tomorrow."

"There's only one Huggybear! He's special-extra!" Emily wiggled and squirmed, making Leah tug harder than she'd intended. "Ow, that hurts."

"Sorry, pumpkin, I hit a tangle. Hold still for a second." Leah teased the comb through the knot of hair—or at least she tried to until Emily jerked forward, whipping her head away, the comb slipping from Leah's hand still caught in the snarled hair.

"Mommy, stop! It hurts! That's not how Daddy does it. I want Daddy to do it."

Daddy had a magic spray can of detangler, but Leah was too exhausted to try to explain. Instead she reached for Emily and pulled her back onto her lap, wrapping her arms around her. "I wish Daddy were here. I would give anything. But we're just going to have to muddle through this together, you and me."

Emily's body was rigid, not yielding to Leah's hug, but finally she ducked her head and held her hair out to Leah. "Careful," she warned as if Leah was preparing to defuse a nuclear warhead.

"I'll go slow," Leah promised. She slid the comb free and instead used her fingers, slowly, gently, weaving them through Emily's curls. She massaged Emily's scalp like she had when Emily was a baby—she even took a sniff, missing the scent of the no-tears baby shampoo. Slowly, Emily relaxed. Leah began working her hair into a braid, her fingers mindlessly finding their rhythm in time with Emily's breathing. Emily's shoulders relaxed, giving Leah hope. A few hours of sleep, time for the brain to re-set, help to bury some of the day's trauma—they both needed that.

"No, Mommy," Emily murmured as she reached a hand to trace Leah's work. "Princess braids. Like Daddy does."

Princess braids? That was new. Leah searched her memory, trying to remember any special princess hairstyle she'd seen Ian replicate. Unfortunately, every time Ian did Emily's hair for dress-up, it never looked the same way twice. At least not to Leah's eyes. "I'm sorry, sweetie. Tell me what princess braids are?"

Emily flounced in Leah's lap, her head knocking against Leah's chin. "You know. Princess braids. Like Daddy does."

Leah took a settling breath and unwound her braid. "Princess braids? So two of them?" She began to divide Emily's hair but hit another tangled area.

Emily cried out and lunged off the bed.

"Daddy knows. You don't. I want Daddy," she screamed, yanking at her hair until it was a knotted mess once more. "Why isn't Daddy here?" Now came the tears, gushing down her cheeks as her hands fisted and her chest heaved. "Why didn't you fix him? Doctors fix people. Brody said you saved him. Why didn't you save Daddy?"

Leah reached for Emily, who dodged her. She backed away until she hit the bed, standing there, face flushed and furious, fists flailing as if Leah were the enemy.

"It's all your fault!"

The words broke Leah. She had no reply, no answers, no idea how to ease her daughter's pain. Before she could even try, the door opened and Ruby was there holding a large purple stuffed bear.

"Look what I found!" she said as if the bear were ancient treasure instead of still attached to its price tag. "Emily, sweetheart," she crooned in a honey-flavored tone Leah had never heard come from her before, "let's crawl under the covers and read a story."

Ruby moved to stand between Emily and Leah, crouching to Emily's level and bundling her into her arms, practically rolling her and the bear beneath the quilt. Emily aimed one last condemning scowl at Leah, then turned away, focusing on Ruby, who edged onto the bed beside her.

Leah stood speechless for a long moment. When she swallowed it felt like broken glass, her earlier tears had left her so parched. Ruby chose a book from the stack on the nightstand. She and Emily huddled together, head to head, the book open like a shield between them and the rest of the coldhearted world. Between them and Leah.

Leah fled to the bathroom, closing the door. With quick, jerking motions she shed her now-filthy scrubs and changed into clean underwear, yoga pants and a sweatshirt from her gym bag. When she finally raised her face to the mirror she stared at the red-eyed empty husk that was her reflection. Hell, she couldn't even keep her own hair combed, much less master princess braids. Had she been fooling herself all these years, pretending she and Ian were equal partners in raising Emily?

Because Emily was right. Leah hadn't always been there for every bedtime kiss, every dress-up princess party. She'd missed so much.

The woman in the mirror blinked, her forehead creasing. How the hell was Leah going to do this without Ian? What if Emily grew up hating Leah for not being there—for not saving Ian? For always finding the time to go to work and save someone else.

Finally, she turned the water off, patted her face dry, and went back down the hall to stand outside Emily's partly open door. Soft golden light spilled out, warm against the oak floorboards. Ruby's voice, a lullaby singsong as she read about an animals' pajama party, was hypnotic, so seductive that Leah felt her own body slump against the wall, desperate for sleep.

Then she heard the words that stole away all thought of sleep. "Read it again, Ruby. You tell it almost as good as Daddy. Can I stay here with you until he comes home?"

Choking back fresh tears, Leah pushed away from the wall and ran down the stairs, past the dining room where Harper had settled herself, and out the door.

CHAPTER 31

The thought that Leah might have been involved in her great aunt's death haunted Luka the entire drive to Jericho Fields. Could he have been that wrong about the woman? And then there were the images from the gift shop security camera. They sure as hell looked a lot like Leah Wright.

As he drove he used the time to call Krichek for an update on the myriad of details swirling beyond the drama that was Leah Wright. "CSU's almost finished with the scene," Krichek reported. "They want one last pass tomorrow. No helpful results on anything yet."

Which explained why they were headed back to the scene for another run. Given the extent of the scene, Luka was sure the forensic guys were just as frustrated as he was about the lack of actual usable evidence. "Radcliffe come up with anything on the motorcycle?"

"Just got off the phone with him. Bottom line was don't call him, he'll call us. I did follow up on Trina's alibi, still waiting to hear back from her roommate. Ray's checking on Cochrane's."

More nothing. Luka yearned for a single solid lead to follow up on—other than the ones that seemed to lead to the widow. Despite everything, he still couldn't fathom a scenario that included Leah Wright participating in her husband's torture and killing, not with her daughter there in the house. "Anything on the gift shop video? Confirmation that it was Leah Wright who bought the roses?" Or not, he hoped.

"Only thing new is that I got Ian Wright's credit cards and phone records: it definitely wasn't him. Can't prove it was the wife, not yet, but also can't rule her out."

"Thanks. Have Ray call me as soon as Cochrane's ready to talk. His parole officer should have him in custody by now." Luka blew his breath out, fogging the windshield. He had no choice but to keep focus on their most viable suspect. "Keep working the widow—we know she didn't do the actual murder, so there must be a trail leading to whoever she was working with."

By the time he reached the farm the temperature had fallen enough that the snow was sticking, clinging to the apple trees like sugar on lollipops. All the lights were on in the house—including on the second floor that Pops no longer visited, the stairs too steep for him to climb, which told him that at least Janine hadn't fled, abandoning Pops to the Jericho family craziness. Other than Janine's Explorer there were no other cars in sight, so hopefully that meant Tanya had kept her word and stayed away. For good this time, if there was a God.

He climbed out of the Taurus. He wouldn't be here long, too much to do, but he could at least grab a bite to eat, a change of clothing, and smooth Janine's ruffled feathers and Pops' anxiety over his wayward granddaughter. Luka strode up the back steps—only company used the front door—and entered.

He stood in the alcove inside the door, the mud room his gran called it. The smell of sizzling beef greeted him before he could stomp the snow from his shoes. Inhaling, he hung up his coat and stepped into the kitchen. Pops was at the table, Janine stood at the stove, but what stole his attention was the boy seated across from Pops in Luka's chair. He was maybe seven or eight with dark, wiry hair and pale hazel eyes. As Luka stopped and stared, the boy looked up at him with a fearful expression.

"Who—" Luka started.

Pops sprang up from his chair, more energetic than Luka had seen him in months. "Luka, you just missed Tanya. This is Nate. Tanya's son."

Son? Tanya had a son?

"Where the hell is she?"

"Language," Janine chided.

"She's gone. Dropped Nate and left." Pops' face clouded even as he laid his palm on Nate's head, rubbing the boy's hair and pressing him to his seat. "You need to find her."

"I do?" So damned typical. Tanya blowing into Pops' life and dumping her kid on him. "Why?"

That earned him a glare. Janine brought a pan of roast beef to the table and replenished Nate's plate. "Why don't you two talk outside?" she said pointedly.

"It's okay, I knows already," Nate mumbled as he chewed, his mouth open. "Mom's not coming back. Says I live here now. Says she'll never be back. I'm on my own now."

His delivery was so straightforward, so devoid of any sentiment, that Luka felt moved. Knowing Tanya, he could only imagine what the kid had been through.

"No," he surprised himself by saying. He took the seat beside the boy, waited until the kid managed to make some slight semblance of eye contact. "You're not alone. You're here with family."

"You're the cop," the kid said with suspicion. "You gonna call family services? I don't want to go to another foster. Better off by myself." His jaw tightened even as hope pushed past his anger for a fleeting moment. "Unless… you can find Moms? Bring her back, get her help? Before it's too late?"

"What do you mean, before it's too late?" Luka asked despite himself. For the past decade he'd assumed it was already too late for Tanya—if his parents would have only seen that, they'd still be alive. But he remembered how gaunt she'd looked at lunch today.

And how he'd stalked off without giving her a chance to explain. After all these years, was he wrong about his little sister?

Pops lowered both hands to Nate's shoulders, squeezing them in encouragement. "Tanya got herself clean, son. Worked hard—got custody back, took good care of Nate. All on her own."

"It was nice," Nate said wistfully. "I had my own room, got to stay at the same school for a whole year. But then…"

"She's sick," Pops said in a choked whisper. "Dying even. And she's out there, all alone."

Nate dropped his fork, clattering against his plate. He swiped at his eyes, then glanced up at Luka, his stare filled with longing. "You're the cop. You gotta save her. That's what family does, she said. Family helps each other, no matter what."

The last came out as a challenge—pure Tanya. A challenge Luka had no idea if he could meet.

Luka waited a few moments while Nate finished eating and retired to the den. Last thing he wanted was to traumatize the kid more.

"Tanya came alone first, this morning," Pops started. "You all were gone. I couldn't believe my eyes when I opened the door—she looked good, real good. Clean, right? Polished up, makeup, nice outfit, not too showy, more like professional. I did what you told me, didn't let her in, sat her down on the porch. At first. Then we got to talking and I saw she might look good on the outside but there was something bad going on inside. Like your gran before she passed. Huffing after every few words, lips pale, that hacky cough. I asked but she waved me off. Told me about being in jail for a few months down in Baltimore year before last. Getting clean—more, getting right. Job, halfway house, an apartment. Then she told me about Nate."

"You said she got her rights back, took him from foster care— you're sure she did that legit? Didn't just take him?" Luka would've loved to run a NCIC check on his sister but that would raise a ton of red flags, maybe even get him fired. But if he suspected the boy was at risk, he could bend the rules.

Both Pops and Janine shook their heads.

"I grilled her when she came back tonight with the boy," Janine said. "Wasn't about to be part of something illegal. She has court papers and all. But—" She glanced at Pops, who nodded. "She's sick. Said it's a heart infection, got it from shooting up. Chronic. They've tried all the meds but the bacteria just get resistant and now there's no hope left. She came here to find a home for her boy before…" Her voice caught. Luka was surprised. Hard-as-nails Janine actually bought Tanya's sob story?

"Before it's too late," Pops finished.

"How much?" Luka asked. "How much is she asking for? What's it going to cost us to get her back on her feet? Help out with the boy? Pay the doctor bills, whatever?" Both Pops and Janine stared at him as if he was the con trying to take advantage of them and not Tanya. "Don't you see? It's just another one of her lies, dressed up in a nice outfit and a sob story that, thanks to patient confidentiality, we can't ever check. Nice touch bringing the kid along to tug on our heart strings."

Pops sank into his seat. "Luka Jericho." His tone was mournful. "When did you grow such a stone-cold heart? Your gran is surely rolling in her grave, hearing you talk like that."

"Pops, don't you see? It's a scam. It's always a scam with Tanya. If Mom and Dad hadn't bought her lies, they'd still be alive. Do you seriously believe a single word from that girl's mouth?"

"You didn't see her—" Pops started, then stopped, one hand covering his mouth as if holding something bitter back.

But he had, Luka thought. He was thankful he hadn't told Pops about meeting Tanya at Good Sam. She'd looked okay for a life-long junkie. At least he'd thought so at the time.

"He's right," Janine said. "I've taken care of a lot of people in their end stages. She wasn't faking. Your sister, she's not got long, sad to say."

"Only thing she asked me for was to keep Nate safe," Pops said. His voice cracked. "How could I say no?"

Luka swallowed, torn between sympathy and anger.

Janine cleared her throat, rearranged the bowls Luka had just put into the dishwasher, then looked up. "Honestly," her voice dropped to a whisper as she glanced down the hall to the den, "I'm not sure she's even coming back to say goodbye. I think maybe she went to end things, go out on her own terms."

"You don't know Tanya," Luka protested.

Janine pressed her lips together, shaking her head. "You're right. I don't know her and I'm not family. But if you want to say goodbye or give that boy in there a chance to make his peace with his mother, then you'd better start looking for her. Now. Tonight."

Pops nodded his agreement. "I begged her to stay, wait for you, but she wouldn't. Said you'd never understand, would start a fight about all the bad things she'd done that you never let her forget. Said you'd never forgive, either. Have to say, she had a point."

He pushed his chair back, stood, and walked to the cubbyhole desk in the corner that had been where Gran ran the household. Pops opened one of the many drawers and pulled out a wad of papers. "Left these. Boy's birth certificate, school record, Tanya's custody papers, and this…" He shuffled through the sheaf until he found the document he wanted. "Signed over custody and guardianship to you, Luka. That boy's your responsibility now. You have to do right by him."

Luka took the paper, scanning it. It seemed legit. What the hell did he know about kids? He was shaking his head even as his mind spun with the ramifications. Money. Kids took lots of money and he was already spread thin keeping up with Pops' medical bills and the upkeep on the farm. Clothing, shoes, school—and what about after school, who would watch him? Couldn't saddle Pops with that—or the kid with taking care of Pops. And no way Janine would go for it—she had her own family to deal with.

Luka read the papers once more. This was happening. Whether he liked it or not. That kid in there, that boy who'd already been through more than his fair share, seen too much, too young—he was now Luka's responsibility.

And Luka had no idea what to do.

Before his mind could begin to process the idea of fatherhood, his phone rang. Ray.

"Bad news," he said without preamble. "All those videos slamming Leah Wright? We traced them back to Cochrane. This guy has even more of a hard-on for her than we thought. And just heard from his PO. Cochrane ran, he's in the wind."

"What about his alibi for last night?"

"No one saw Cochrane at the bar. And he clocked off work in plenty of time to make it to the Wrights' place." Ray cleared his throat. "And maybe even worse news. That apartment where Katrina Balanchuk lives? It's not hers. It's owned by her partner, a professor. Doctor Olivia Karmody. And guess what? She teaches chemistry."

"As in—"

"As in the lady has done a bunch of papers about street drugs, including PCP and meth."

Both found in Ian Wright's preliminary tox screen. "I'm on my way," Luka said as he grabbed his coat.

Pops blocked his path to the door as Janine looked on, frowning in disapproval. "Luka, no. You can't leave. You need to find Tanya. She's family."

Luka sighed. "I'll put out a missing person's report on Tanya. Did she say anything about where she was headed?" Both Pops and Janine shook their heads. "What kind of car was she driving?"

Janine answered. "Silver. Or gray. Small. Maybe a Honda, like a Civic? Or a Toyota. I'm not sure."

"Maybe I can trace her cell. How much cash did she have?"

"First time she was here I gave her forty dollars," Pops said. "Enough for gas for her to fetch Nate, bring him up from Baltimore."

Which meant she probably had enough left over for a bag of heroin. If she truly was clean, would that be enough to OD on? If she actually was looking to kill herself. For nine years Luka had imagined Tanya dying in an anonymous dark alley, nodding off and never waking up. He'd always hoped she had the decency to make sure anyone who found her had his number to call, spare his grandparents that burden. But now that the prospect seemed imminent, he hoped he was wrong. That Tanya herself would call him, let him help. Maybe Leah would know a doctor who could save his little sister—

His focus snapped back. Cochrane was on the loose, Leah and Emily might still be in danger. "I'll do what I can," he promised Pops. "But right now, I have to go."

CHAPTER 32

Leah fled to the back garden where she was relieved to find that Ruby hadn't destroyed her favorite childhood sanctuary, a miniature plywood pagoda so thickly overgrown with flowering vines that even as a child she had to crawl on her hands and knees to enter its quiet, perfumed embrace. Now it was surrounded by muddy patches where snow had drifted off the peaked roof and melted in the day's warmth, the puddles already frosted with new ice forming. The stars were obscured by thickening clouds promising more snow to come.

The wind sang through the forest, drowning out Leah's heavy, choked breaths. Vines twisted across the sagging wood structure like something out of a nightmare. Or one of Nellie's fairy tales. It seemed the only time Nellie put aside her pragmatic, practical, pilgrim-like austerity was after the lights were out, the chores and homework finished, and bed was beckoning.

"Once upon a time," she'd start, and Leah learned to love those four magic words because anything could happen afterward. Nellie taught her the value of hard work, self-reliance, facing harsh realities… but with those four words, she also taught Leah the wonder of possibilities, to dream, to imagine the impossible.

She sank to her heels, examining a tangle of uprooted roses, their canes black and brittle, snapping between her fingers. The wind howled in pain, deep and throaty as a man fighting for his life. A flash of blood filled her vision, the horror that she'd found last night when she'd returned home.

Home. She had no home, not without Ian. He was the one who made it all work, made them work. What was she going to do without him? She couldn't go back to her job, not with the hours the ER demanded, yet the ER was her life. Even if she worked shorter hours, she'd still need help with Emily. But how could she invite a stranger into Emily's life, after what Emily had been through? She crumbled the dead rose bark between her fingers. No way in hell could she trust Ruby with Emily. Sooner or later, Ruby would be Ruby, abandon Emily, betray her trust, or worse, make her feel worthless, discarded.

No. Leah was not about to let Emily be exposed to Ruby's unique brand of poison.

She stood, staring at the tiny pagoda, half-tempted to crawl inside, curl up, and let the night chill take her, numb her to reality. The soft glow of the lights from the house seemed as ethereal as Nellie's fairy tales. Maybe it wasn't real. For a second she wished she had the power of denial that Ruby wielded so effortlessly.

Denying Ian? That was no answer. Like the princesses in Nellie's stories, Leah was trapped in a labyrinth and would have to fight to find her own way free.

Her phone rang. It was Jessica—the psychiatrist's timing was uncanny. Just as Leah was feeling lost, here was a reminder that she wasn't alone.

"Thought I'd call, see how you were doing," Jessica said.

"Honestly, I'm spiraling." The confession felt good—as if Leah no longer needed to pretend that she was in control of anything, including herself.

"What's going on?"

"Emily had a panic attack on the way here—she saw someone on a motorcycle she thought was the killer, actually turned out it was a woman, but she just lost it, complete meltdown. Now she seems fine, even let Ruby put her to bed, said she never wants to leave."

"Kids her age—"

"I know, I know, resilient. And that's great, really. But me, all night, I'm barely hanging on. My chest is pounding, I can't sit still, and I keep seeing Ian—imagining Ian—and I'm all over the place. I'm sad and pitiful then I try to focus on the good times but then I get angry, so, so angry…" She turned away from the house with its warm glow and faced the dark woods, the treetops rustling in the wind as if some unseen force ran across them, desperate to escape the coming storm.

"It's normal to be angry, to even blame the victim for what you're experiencing. That doesn't negate your and Ian's love. Not at all. Try closing your eyes. Slow, deep breaths. Think of Ian. Of when you knew you loved him. Maybe when he proposed? Or when you first met?"

Leah did as Jessica instructed, allowing the other woman's soft words to hypnotize her. The images spinning through her mind morphed: Ian at the far end of the aisle, fidgeting with his tux, looking pale and ready to bolt from the church—the only time she'd ever seen him nervous, except during Emily's delivery. Him holding Emily as a newborn, her barely filling his hands, and the look on his face. Fierce, protective, true bliss.

"Tell me how you and Ian met," Jessica coaxed Leah.

"At Phipps Conservatory in Pittsburgh. We were both taking an adult ed art class. Drawing and painting the flowers and plants. I was a resident, working weird hours, but that month I was doing a derm rotation so had my nights free and needed something relaxing, something that got me out of myself, connected me to the real world, you know?"

"And Ian, why did he take the class?"

"It's what he did when he was lost in a problem at work—he'd pick a random class that fit his schedule."

"So you both, in some way, were searching for connection. Escape. And you found each other."

"Right." Leah chuckled. "I told him that first night he was full of it. That the real reason he took those classes was to pick up girls."

"A physical connection is still a connection," Jessica said in a serious tone. "You mentioned earlier that you felt distant from Ian—is that something new in your relationship?"

Now Leah hesitated. "No. It's a pattern—my pattern. It's not easy for me to trust, to rely on someone else. I mean, you met Ruby, can guess about where I'm coming from. But Ian was patient, he never tried to change me, he just waited. He was always there when I needed him most, without me even needing to ask." Her eyes stung with the wind and the cold, moisture freezing against her eyelashes. "Until now."

They were both silent. Leah swallowed. The knot in her throat began to ease, allowing her to breathe again. She tried to hold onto the image of Ian, that first night they met, his earnest expression as he attempted to sketch an orchid, stepping back to get the right perspective, toppling the woman behind him into a lily pond. Oh, the look on his face as he helped Leah out, her clothes clinging, revealing, her face on fire with embarrassment, the other students gawking. And Ian, like some gallant from ancient times—or one of Nellie's stories, which always had twists and laughs—promptly jumped in the water as well, so that now people were laughing and staring at him, allowing Leah to escape.

The image was clear in her mind, so clear she wanted to reach out and grab it, hold it in her palms to savor it.

"Less angry?" Jessica asked. "Any other feelings? Fear? Guilt?"

It was as if the other woman read Leah's mind. "All of the above. When Emily lost it, she screamed at me, told me it was my fault Ian was dead, that I should have been able to save him."

"Kids her age, the concept of death—they struggle with permanence, causality."

Leah spun in a tight circle, her shoes sinking deeper into the muddy ground. "Or she's right. If I'd gotten there sooner—"

"You might be dead, too. Then where would Emily be?" Jessica paused. "What made her think you could save Ian? She's a little old to expect her parents to be all-powerful gods."

"She knows what doctors do. And Brody told her that I saved his life when he was young—back when I was a chief resident in Pittsburgh. Guess he must have made an impression on her, because now she both blames me for not bringing Ian back from the dead and she talks like she expects him to walk back through the door any minute."

"Brody told her that?" Jessica's tone was sharp with disapproval. "I need to talk to him about what's appropriate—"

A noise came from the house. It sounded like a scream. Leah took off, running, the phone forgotten in her hand.

CHAPTER 33

The scream propelled Leah forward—Emily! Her feet slipped in the mud and newly fallen snow. As she rounded the corner, a man plowed through the front door, the screen door banging in protest. He leapt from the porch, flying past all seven steps, racing out of sight into the trees beside the drive.

"Leah, Leah! What's happening?" Jessica's voice reminded her that she still held the phone.

"Call 911," Leah shouted as she pounded up the porch steps.

Leah waited a moment, huddled to the far side of the open front door. No one followed the man, there was no sign of him returning, and no sounds coming from inside. Cautiously, she stepped over the threshold.

"It's me," she called out in case Harper was pursuing the intruder, poised to shoot. Her voice stuttered and tripped over the silence.

The first floor was completely dark, no lights on at the landing above either. Leah was desperate to rush up the steps to get to Emily, but images of last night filled the shadows, leaving her terrified of what she might find. What if her daughter was lying beside her bed in a pool of blood?

Her entire body trembled with urgency. But panic held her in its merciless grip, frozen, barely able to swallow air. Then a muffled moan came from in front of her and her training took over, breaking her free. She snapped on the lights, blinking at the scene they illuminated. The upper half of the banister was splintered, and Harper lay face up on the floor, motionless. Her gun was across the foyer, halfway down the hall to the kitchen.

Leah rushed to the detective, kneeling at her head to immobilize her neck. "Harper, open your eyes. Can you hear me?" No response. Airway clear, breathing normal, obvious hematoma already forming at the temporal parietal region. As Leah palpated the detective's cervical spine and skull, Harper moaned again, her eyes fluttering open. She flailed, trying to get up, but Leah held her still. "Stop. Look at me. What's your name?"

She'd been hoping for one of the detective's signature disdainful glares, but instead the younger woman blinked in confusion, then whispered, "Naomi."

"Naomi what?"

"Harper." This more certain, stronger. But then Harper tried to raise her left hand to her face and cried out in pain, unable to move it above her chest.

"Hold still," Leah commanded. "You might have a neck injury. I need you to hold still while I check on—" She swallowed, unable to say Emily's name. "Just hold still. Help's on the way."

At least she hoped it was. She grabbed her phone and stood, dialing 911 as she approached the staircase. The sense of déjà vu as she told the operator what was happening was overwhelming. It didn't help that there were dents in the plaster wall of the staircase and that a vase of Nellie's dried roses had toppled over from the table on the landing, their petals spewed down the oak steps like drops of blood.

She had to get to Emily. She wanted to vault up the steps, to fly down the hall, but it was as if part of her was trapped in the nightmare of last night.

Focus, she told herself. *Emily needs you*. Despite the evidence of a struggle on the steps there was no actual blood, and the level of violence was nowhere near what had happened at her home.

One step up, holding her breath, listening. The house was silent, no sounds of another intruder. Another step, her hand pressed against the wall. And another until she reached the top of the stairs, flicked the landing light on, and finally breathed deep.

"Emily," she called out, her voice choked. Unable to restrain herself any longer, she raced down the hall to the closed door of Nellie's bedroom. "Emily!" She hesitated with her hand on the doorknob, only a split second, a mere moment, but one that damned her as a coward. Bracing herself for what she might find inside, the image of Ian's body filling her vision, she opened the door. "Emily, it's Mommy."

She turned on the lights. Nothing seemed disturbed—except the bed was empty, covers thrown back. "Emily, it's okay. It's just me." Leah crouched down, looked under the bed. Nothing but dust, old shoe boxes, and a stray hair band. She stood, a strange fluttering filling her chest. Where was she? "Emily, come out. It's okay, everything's okay."

She threw open the closet door. Empty except for naked wire hangers rattling as if indignant at her intrusion. She whirled around. There was nowhere else to hide. But she'd heard Emily scream when she was outside—hadn't she? Could there have been a second man, one who'd taken her?

Sprinting down the hall, she opened every door. The linen closet: no Emily. The bathroom and guest room. Both empty. The door leading to the attic stairs—Emily would have never climbed those alone in the dark, but still Leah opened it and turned on the light. "Emily?" Her voice echoed through the cavernous rafters overhead. No answer.

The only room left was her old room, the one Ruby now used. She opened the door, nose wrinkling at the stench of marijuana. Turned on the light. Ruby was sleeping, oblivious to the world. And beside her, snoring lightly, was Emily, one of Nellie's old quilts covering her. Leah rushed to her, pulling her free from the quilt and into her arms.

"Emily!" She shook her and Emily's eyes opened halfway.

"Huh?" She blinked. "Go 'way, Mommy, I'm sleeping." Her eyelids drooped shut and her head sagged.

Leah reached over Emily to pull at Ruby's arm. "Wake up," she commanded. "Wake the hell up!" Ruby had always slept like the dead—the combination of alcohol, marijuana or whatever pills she could get her hands on, along with an absolute lack of a conscience. "Ruby!"

Ruby groaned, attempting to swat Leah away. Leah slapped her hand down. "What did you give her?" she demanded as Ruby's eyes slitted open. "What did you give Emily?"

"What?" Ruby yawned and sat halfway up. "What's the matter?"

"What did you give my daughter?"

"She had a nightmare. Couldn't find you. So I gave her the same as worked for you when you were a kid and I needed you to sleep. Mixed Benadryl in with juice. Works a charm."

Yeah, until you woke up in the backseat of some stranger's car parked out in front of a bar, not knowing when your mother would return. Leah said nothing, fearful that if she did, she might scream, wake Emily and scare her. Not that anything she said would do any good. She took a few deep breaths, swallowing her anger as she carefully smoothed the covers back around Emily. No need to wake her, the sleep would do her good.

Once she was calm again, she turned to Ruby. "Get rid of that pot, along with anything else you might have stashed. I'll not have Emily in a house with that garbage." Not that she and Emily were staying. She glanced at her sleeping daughter and sighed. Every decision Leah had made to keep her safe, to take control of this nightmare, they'd all somehow backfired. And she had no idea where to go next. "You might want to get dressed," she told Ruby as she headed out the door. "The police are on their way."

"Police? Aren't they already here? That girl, Harper?"

Leah didn't bother with an answer. She jogged down the hall and back down the stairs to check on Harper. Nellie's house was just outside city limits in the unincorporated area covered by the state police and a volunteer fire/ambulance service, so response times were slower than in the city. When she got to the foyer Harper had vanished, leaving behind a smear of blood where she'd hit her head. Her gun was gone as well.

"Harper," Leah called as she glanced into the living room. Nothing. She retreated and followed the narrow hallway back to the dark kitchen.

Harper was slumped over the sink, pistol clutched in one hand, the other holding her hair back as she vomited. Leah clicked the light on. Harper wobbled as she spun around, raising her gun halfway, her hand shaking.

"It's me, Leah." Leah stood stock still until Harper nodded and lowered the weapon. She carefully approached the detective, keeping her hands visible. "You hit your head. Blacked out. Have a concussion at the very least. Why don't you sit down, let me check you."

Harper allowed Leah to lead her to the kitchen table and help her into a chair. At least there were no signs of a cervical injury, but Leah noticed that Harper hadn't raised her left arm, the one she held her gun with, all the way. Probably a clavicle fracture. She was more worried about the detective's head injury. If it had been Harper's yell that she'd heard, then the detective hadn't been unconscious for more than a few moments before Leah found her, but that still didn't rule out a bleed.

"Do you remember what happened?" she asked as she checked Harper's pupils. A little sluggish, but equal.

"Have to call it in, clear the house." The words came slowly as if Harper had to search for each one. "I saw him."

"He's gone. Emily and Ruby are safe upstairs. Slept through everything. The police and an ambulance are on the way."

"Jericho—"

"You want me to call him?" It was a good idea, would save time explaining everything to the state police. And, given the large territory the local barracks patrolled, Jericho might get here first. She was glad she'd left Ruby and Emily upstairs. She remembered the chaos the police had left behind at her house.

And now here she was, in the middle of another crime scene.

If she and Emily weren't safe here, if the police couldn't protect them, then where could Leah run to next?

Then another thought struck her. The killer's notes had targeted Leah. What if Leah hadn't been keeping Emily safe by insisting they remain together? What if Emily was in danger because of Leah?

Who could Leah trust to protect her daughter?

CHAPTER 34

After Leah hung up from Jericho, she went upstairs to Ruby's room. Emily was still fast asleep, drooling onto her pillowcase, her arms wrapped around the outrageous purple bear Ruby had given her. Ruby hadn't dressed but she had put a robe on over her pajamas and was standing in the closet, reaching up from her tiptoes to the ledge above the door.

"There, happy now?" she asked Leah. She lowered her arms. "No one will find them there."

Leah thought Ruby severely underestimated the capabilities of the police, but as long as any drugs were far out of Emily's reach, she didn't care. Not like she and Emily would be here for very long. As soon as she figured out a safe place for Emily, they were gone.

"The police should be here soon. Will you keep an eye on Emily?"

"Of course. While you do—what?" Somehow Ruby made it sound like she'd gotten the raw end of the deal, watching a sleeping child from the comfort of her own bed.

"Detective Harper is hurt. If you'd prefer to—"

"Go, go. We'll be fine," Ruby said, sounding like a martyr. As Leah went out the door, she whispered, "That man. He had a gun?"

"I don't know."

"Why didn't Harper just shoot him?" She made killing a man sound so cavalier.

Leah closed the door. By the time she returned downstairs Harper was over the sink, vomiting again. Leah had just gotten the detective back to the kitchen table, a ceramic mixing bowl serving as a makeshift emesis basin, when the front door banged open.

"Harper?" Jericho's voice called.

"In here," Leah shouted back.

He strode in, coat open, hand on his weapon, gaze searching the space before finally focusing on Harper. "I looked around outside, no signs except a few boot prints in the snow. He's gone. How is she?"

"At minimum a broken collarbone and a concussion. But she needs observation and a CT scan to rule out a bleed," Leah answered.

Harper raised her head, hugging the bowl close. "I'm fine, boss."

"Good. Tell me everything."

"He—I—" Harper started, then stopped again, her mouth working silently, brow creased in confusion. "I saw him, I know I did."

"And?"

"I—I—" She stuttered to a stop. Gave her head a small shake then grimaced in pain.

"It's not uncommon to sustain a period of amnesia after a head injury," Leah told her.

Jericho sighed and laid a hand on Harper's shoulder. "Give it time."

The ambulance's siren echoed through the night. Leah gave the paramedics the rundown then stood aside as they packaged their patient for transport. Jericho secured Harper's weapons—her duty pistol, another strapped to her ankle, and a knife. As he deposited them on the dining room table alongside the detective's other gear, he beckoned Leah to him.

"What did you see?"

She told him everything, finishing in time to repeat her story for the state trooper who arrived just as the ambulance was leaving. While she was talking to the state trooper, Jericho was busy on his phone—calling in reinforcements, no doubt. They kept her away from the foyer and stairs, sequestered in the kitchen just as Ruby and Emily were upstairs.

The state police and Jericho were in the living room trading notes when a knock came at the kitchen door. Leah glanced up in surprise, then stood and unlocked it. "Jessica, what are you doing here?"

"Did you really think you could tell me to call 911 and I wouldn't come? I'm only sorry it took me so long. The snow's starting to come down hard." The older woman bustled in past Leah, brushing snow from her lambskin coat, then turning to gather Leah into her arms. "How are you? And Emily? Was anyone hurt?"

And there, in the comfort of Nellie's kitchen, wrapped in memories that smelled like lavender and chocolate, Leah fell apart. She told Jessica everything—several things more than once, she was certain, as she wasn't bothering to keep track or order anything in a logical fashion.

By the time she finished, they were sitting side by side at the kitchen table sipping cinnamon tea Jessica had brewed. How many problems had Leah and Nellie conquered sitting exactly here, drinking tea? But this, this was no ordinary problem—losing Ian. Leah closed her eyes against the pain, ducking her face into the mug to hide her feelings. "I just want it all to go away, to be able to forget it—to make sure Emily can forget it. Every time I imagine what she may have seen…"

"I could make that happen, you know," Jessica said in a half-joking way. She leaned forward and whispered conspiratorially, "Just don't ever tell the defense department. They'd lock me up, throw away the key."

"Your research has gone that far?"

Jessica nodded. "I'm this close." She held her thumb and forefinger up. "Imagine a world without PTSD, depression, phobias."

No wonder the DOD was interested. Maybe that was why Radcliffe had seemed more interested in snooping around Jessica's office than anything Leah had to say.

"It's early days," Jessica continued, taking another sip of tea, "but my initial trials at Western Psych were very promising."

"Western Psych in Pittsburgh? I thought you were from Chicago?"

Jessica waved her hand dismissively. "No, I never said that. You must have misheard." She sighed, a sound of sorrow mixed with satisfaction. "I'm so close to bringing Gordie's dream to life. Imagine a world where we could end so much suffering? A world in harmony." She laid her hand over Leah's. "Where good people like you and Ian would never need to be afraid. Where your daughter could grow up in peace, safe from harm."

Leah wanted to believe in Jessica's fairytale but was too mired in her own painful reality. "I should go check on Emily," she said, taking both empty mugs to the sink to rinse out. "I need to figure out where to take her, but I'm afraid." She turned back to Jessica. "What if the killer comes after us again? Worse, what if he's after me and I'm putting Emily in danger by keeping her close?"

Together they walked down the hallway to the front foyer. The broken bits of banister were gone and fingerprint powder littered what was left of the railing. The state police had left, and Jericho now had two other men huddled with him in the living room, standing by the fire even though it wasn't lit. He spotted Leah and Jessica and held a hand up to the men.

"I'm going up to check on Emily," Leah told him.

"That's fine, forensics is finished." Jericho turned back to the two men.

One of them, older, dressed in an expensive suit, stared at Leah with a frown. He stepped forward, joining them in the foyer. "This is her? You're Mrs. Wright?" he thundered, his words echoing through the high space.

Leah cringed—he'd wake Emily. Before she could tell him to quiet down, Jericho intervened.

"Commander Ahearn, Dr. Leah Wright." He made introductions.

"Why isn't she down at the station?" Ahearn asked as if Leah wasn't standing right there. "We need a formal statement. Now. Tonight."

"We're trying to determine a safe place for Mrs. Wright to take her daughter."

Leah bristled—no one had consulted her. Besides, the police were the only ones who knew she and Emily were here. Yet, still the killer had found them. Why should she trust the police at all? "I can take care of my daughter without your help."

"I really think—" Jericho started, but Ahearn interrupted.

"A police officer has been injured. That takes priority. Detective Sergeant Jericho will escort you to the station for a formal interview. We can call social services to deal with the child."

Leah opened her mouth to protest but Jericho's pleading look stopped her. He ushered the commander back into the living room. "Sir, I think we can make better use of our manpower. Have you considered—"

As Jericho distracted Ahearn, Leah and Jessica climbed the steps single file, sticking to the middle of the treads, away from the empty gap left behind by the broken banister and the silver fingerprint powder dusting the wall on the other side. Leah opened the door to Ruby's room. Emily was sprawled across the center of the bed, still asleep, while Ruby sat at the window seat puffing on an e-cig.

"What's she doing here?" Ruby rose up at the sight of Jessica.

"She came to make sure we were all okay," Leah explained. She sank onto the bed, stroking Emily's hair. Emily was right—Leah's braids had fallen hopelessly short of the task of keeping her hair in check. "You didn't dose her again, did you?"

"No. She's just exhausted is all. Best she sleep through all this anyway, right?"

"Could you please get some clothes together for her? And I'm borrowing your truck." Worst case scenario, she'd bring Emily with her to the police station, give them her statement, and take off from there. Although she hated to do that—last thing she wanted was her daughter exposed to more strangers.

"Why? You're not leaving. Not with that maniac on the loose out there."

"Safer out there than here with you," Leah snapped.

"Now it's my fault he came here? Why am I not surprised? Is there anything wrong that ever happened in your entire life that isn't my fault?"

They stared at each other in silence.

Jessica made a polite noise. "Emily can stay with me. You both can. No one would think to look for you there. And with the snow, the clinic will be closed anyway."

Ruby glared at Jessica, then at Leah. "You'd trust a stranger before you'd trust your own mother?"

Leah ignored her. "Thank you, Jessica. It'd only be for a day— two at most. Just until Ian's parents can make it in from Seattle."

Ruby made a scoffing noise, clamped the e-cig between her lips, tossed Leah a set of car keys, then stomped around the room, throwing clothing into a hamper. "If Emily's going, then I'm going, too."

A soft knock came on the door and Jericho appeared. "Mrs. Wright, Commander Ahearn is insisting on an interview. Tonight." His tone was apologetic, his frown deepening as he glanced at Emily's sleeping form. "Will you come with me down to the station?"

"Is she under arrest?" Ruby demanded. "If so, she's got rights."

"Call me when she wakes up." Leah pressed her lips to Emily's forehead, stood up from the bed, and walked past Jericho into the hallway, closing the door behind her. Emily was in good hands with Jessica—she only hoped that Jessica's psychiatric training prepared her for dealing with Ruby without bloodshed.

"Am I under arrest?" she asked Jericho, enjoying the way the question made him uncomfortable. They both knew she had nothing to do with Ian's death—hadn't tonight proven that?

"No." The syllable was clipped and his expression was devoid of his previous aura of concern.

"Then I'll follow you there. I'll need a car when we're done." Leah had no intention of getting stuck at the police station. It was almost midnight now. If the storm was getting as bad as Jessica had said, she'd need a car in order to get out of town, hole up somewhere as far from Emily as possible. The thought made her gag. Maybe she could still join them? After all, no one would ever think to look for her at Jessica's home.

She hated this buzz of uncertainty that spun through her brain. But it seemed as if every decision Leah had made, every action she'd chosen in order to protect Emily, had only ended up putting her daughter in danger.

Maybe, she thought as she followed Jericho down the steps, she should stay visible. Maybe go to work in the ER or back to her home if the police let her? Lure the killer out so the cops could catch him before he could hurt anyone else.

No. Too risky. The cops would never go for it. There had to be some way to keep her daughter safe. But how?

CHAPTER 35

Once he reached the station house, Luka stopped by his office. Leah Wright was waiting in the interview room, but he was in no rush to confront her. Not until he had a better handle on exactly what he needed to learn from her. Now that Ahearn had forced his hand with an official interview, Luka had to tread lightly. If she lawyered up, he'd get nothing. But he was also frustrated as hell by the little she'd told him—and shown him, other than her ability to control her emotions.

Maybe it was time to take a different approach. More confrontational. Ray could help with that—would enjoy it, no doubt.

He had one item of personal business to deal with first. Pops had forwarded all the info on Tanya he'd gotten from Nate and Luka used it to file a missing person's report with the Baltimore PD. The detective he spoke to sounded harried but sympathetic, right until the point where Luka told him about Tanya's history of drug use.

"We'll give it our best shot," was all he'd commit to before hanging up. Luka knew it translated to *Don't hold your breath.*

Then Luka called the one person he knew who would take it as seriously as he did: Maggie Chen. "I'm on it," she assured Luka, the warmth in her voice a sharp contrast to the Baltimore detective's tone. "I can reach out to the coroner offices in the tri-state region, go wider if need be. Alert the ERs, AA and NA groups, shelters—I'll make up an e-flyer, start it circulating."

"Thanks, Maggie. I really appreciate it."

"It's family, Luka. No need for thanks."

He'd hung up from her feeling marginally less guilty about not being able to devote his full energy to Tanya, then gathered what was left of his team in the conference room where they'd begun the day.

"Do we have Cochrane?" was Luka's first question. He fit the description of the man in black running from the house. Both Ray and Krichek shook their heads. "How about tracking his car and phone?" Fancy new Mustang had to have GPS.

"Waiting for the court orders," Krichek told him. "The ADA said she'd give us an arrest warrant for the online threats and the assault in the ER, just to get him off the street. And if Harper can ID him as her attacker—"

Luka shook his head. "She can't. Not yet, anyway. She saw the guy, but her head's messed up with the concussion."

"But she's gonna be okay?"

"All the doctor would tell me was that they were sending her for a CAT scan and it would be a while before they knew anything." His jaw clenched at the not knowing. "And what about this chemistry professor, Olivia Karmody?"

"Left this morning for a conference in Amsterdam," Krichek answered. "She and Katrina Balanchuk have been living together for a year—since Trina isn't a student in Karmody's department, the college was okay with it."

"So they disclosed their relationship?"

"Yep. I even called the college head of human resources to make sure Trina wasn't lying. Trina's parked over in Interview Two, if you want to talk with her some more. But so far everything she's told me has checked out. Their apartment building has electronic locks. The logs match with both Trina and Dr. Karmody being home together at the time of the murder." He paused. "Not sure about her sighting of the man in black on campus—still going through the red tape with campus security, trying to get any footage they might have."

Luka considered. Like Krichek, he hadn't gotten the sense that Balanchuk had lied during their conversation. He mentally searched for stray threads he could tug at, trace back to an actual clue. He'd started the day with no suspects and now it seemed he had four—Cochrane, Balanchuk, Karmody, and Leah Wright—but no actual proof. "How did they find Leah at her aunt's house? I'm certain we weren't followed—and Harper didn't see anyone on our tail either."

"Maybe they were tracking her phone?" Krichek suggested. "You had it with you on the drive to the farmhouse, right?"

Luka had already dropped Leah's phone off with Sanchez, the tech guy who'd been helping Ray weed through Cochrane's postings. He still wasn't sure if Cochrane was working with Leah Wright or against her—maybe both? What if she'd used Cochrane, somehow manipulated him into killing for her? Or maybe he was simply a random nutjob complicating things and Luka needed to focus on the women: the widow, the art student, and the chemistry professor. At this point anything was possible. He needed more evidence. "What would it take to do that? Track her phone?"

Krichek answered. "Feds can turn just about any phone into an omnidirectional microphone, activate the GPS and video. Supposed to have a warrant, of course, but I'll bet your DIA friend has ways around that."

"You think the Defense Intelligence Agency sent an operative to attack two unarmed women, a child, and Harper? Got a reason?"

Luka had already spoken with Radcliffe. As usual the DIA man had been less than helpful even while promising any government resources Luka needed. Luka had added Cochrane and his Mustang to Radcliffe's list of subjects to locate, which still included the man in black's motorcycle. After he'd hung up, he'd felt as if it was all a waste of time. But one of Ahearn's first questions when he'd arrived on scene was if Luka was cooperating with the DIA as ordered, so at least he didn't have to lie.

"Okay, okay, so not the DIA," Krichek conceded. "Maybe Cochrane was spying on Wright? Could he have planted some malware in her phone?"

"Doubt it," Ray answered. "Sanchez says Cochrane's cyber skills are amateur."

"Balanchuk?" Luka asked. "Any evidence that she's got hacking skills?"

"Not exactly what they teach in art classes," Ray answered. "Maybe her chemistry professor friend? The one who conveniently fled the country the day after the murder?"

And who was now out of their reach, Luka thought. "Have Sanchez check Cochrane and Balanchuk's electronics for evidence of spying software they could have used on Leah Wright."

Ray grabbed his phone and texted the cyber tech.

"I know you're going to tell me I'm paranoid," Krichek said. "But could Leah Wright have done it to herself? All along she's been playing the victim card—the video at the crime scene with her daughter, the roses and vague threats, Cochrane's postings trolling her. Then an attack at her mom's house, while she's conveniently safe outside, and the only person hurt is Harper? She's acting the sweet, sympathetic widow—but is she really?"

"If she's been playing us, we'll never convict," Ray argued. "Not without a confession or some hard evidence. Maybe not even then."

Luka paced the length of the conference room. "Do we have a love triangle? An obsessed stalker? A wife tired of her cheating husband? What the hell is really going on here?" He scrutinized the whiteboard. Krichek had been diligent in filling in Ian Wright's timeline going back twenty-four hours but there were still some definite gaps. "Let's start from the beginning. We have the time of the murder."

"We know the killer is a man and has access to a motorcycle," Krichek said.

"We know the killer wasn't working alone," Ray added. "If the roses the doc got are part of the mix, that is. Then he's working with a woman."

"It's not the chemistry professor. She couldn't have bought the roses today," Krichek said. "I verified it, she's definitely in Amsterdam."

"Helluva alibi," Ray said. "Maybe she orchestrated the killing and has Balanchuk doing the cleanup?"

"Krichek, put up the photos from the hospital cameras of the woman. Could that be Katrina Balanchuk in a wig?" They all leaned forward, staring at the enlarged CCTV images. The hospital's system was hopelessly outdated, the images lo-res and grainy.

"Could be my mother for all I can tell," Ray finally said. "But add to your list that the killer or someone working with him knew how to torture Ian Wright."

"And had access to a designer drug cocktail and knew how to administer it." Luka began jotting notes on the whiteboard, the squeak of the marker making his teeth itch.

"We need to consider that Ian Wright wasn't the primary target." Luka frowned. He needed to find a motive that made sense. He considered the board for a long moment before he turned back to the others. "I can't stop thinking about what Cochrane said. About if you really want to hurt someone you don't go after them, you go after their family."

Ray jerked his chin up at that. "You think the widow *is* the target?"

"I thought you said she was clean, no malpractice, no serious complaints," Krichek said.

"Let's dig into her patients, best we can."

Ray scoffed. "No way in hell are we going to get access to what, four years of patient records? You have any idea how busy that ER is?"

"Actually, it's more like eight years. We need to go back to when she worked in Pittsburgh as well."

Krichek began tapping at his laptop. "Eight years? Heck of a long time to hold a grudge."

"Not if you're serious about it," Ray told him. "I've known cons sent away longer, spent their entire sentence planning their revenge. Savoring it—some said it was what got them through."

"That's an idea. Any way to cross-reference ER patients and convicted felons?"

Both men glanced at Luka as if he was crazy. More like exhausted and grasping at straws. "Sure, if this was an episode of *Criminal Minds*," Ray scoffed. "Want a Gulfstream, too, while you're at it?"

"Unless we ask the DIA to help?" Krichek offered, earning glares from both Luka and Ray.

"Still, Harper might have been right all along," Ray said. "Oldest crime in the book: guy steps out on wife, wife hires a thug, teaches him how to torture the husband before chopping him to bits."

"There was a half million life insurance policy," Krichek put in. "Pays double for homicide."

"And she'd get to keep the kid without a messy custody battle," Ray added.

Luka jerked his head up at that. "While we were in the car, Emily said something about keeping secrets. Made it sound as if her father was hiding things from Leah."

"Besides a possible affair, missing cash?" Ray said. "We need to find a way to talk to Emily Wright without the wife watching our every move."

Easier said than done—if Leah Wright got a lawyer, they might never be able to interview Emily, not unless Luka got Children and Youth involved. Which would take a hell of a lot more evidence than he had now.

Ray sensed his reluctance. "Three attacks. Emily's life is in danger. Sounds like child endangerment to me. Possible grounds for removal? For the kid's own safety?"

Luka heaved out his breath. He still couldn't see Leah Wright traumatizing her daughter like that. "Keep it in our back pocket. Krichek, you keep working the patient angle. Get Sanchez up here to help. Ray, you're with me."

"Face it, Luka," Ray said as he scraped back his chair and stood. "Leah Wright checks all three Ps: passion, profit, and power."

CHAPTER 36

The thing about being an ER physician was that in addition to working with police and other first responders, Leah also often worked with prosecutors. Unfortunately, it was almost always involving sexual assaults or child abuse cases, but she'd learned a lot watching them interact with hostile witnesses, twisting their own words against them.

"That's why you always get a lawyer on your side," the Assistant District Attorney working Crimes Against Children had once told her over drinks while they celebrated a conviction. "People think that if they're innocent, they don't need a lawyer. Or even that it's their responsibility to help the police."

"Of course it is," Leah had argued.

"Not to help the police build a case against you." The ADA had tapped her beer glass against Leah's. "What's the big deal? Call a lawyer. Then tell the police whatever."

"If I was going to talk to the police anyway, why would I need a lawyer?"

"If a lawyer's there, the police are going to be more careful which questions they ask and how hard they push. Because a lawyer will tell you to shut up and yank your ass out of there long before you even realize you've wandered into quicksand and are drowning."

Now, as Leah waited in the barren interview room at the police station, she remembered that advice. Except that, other than prosecutors, she didn't actually know any lawyers. At least not criminal ones. She doubted the guy who'd drawn up their wills and family trust would appreciate a late-night call for a referral.

Besides, not only was she clearly innocent—she was the victim here. Why would she need a lawyer?

Exhaustion bobbed her chin to her chest. It was the first time she'd been truly alone since she left for work yesterday. Time had slowed to an excruciating grind. Leah folded her arms on the small table—it was cheap particle board, bolted to the floor, and scarred with a variety of graffiti. She lowered her head to her arms and tried not to think, not to remember.

For a moment she felt as if she were having an out of body experience, floating above herself, looking down, a totally separate person. Was there another Leah somewhere out there in the universe? Along with another Ian who was blessedly whole, who hadn't died? She knew it was only a dream, but still, it gave her comfort. She imagined Ian's fingers smoothing her hair, whispering that he was safe, Emily was safe, everything was going to be all right.

The door opened—the room was so narrow that it scraped along the edge of the table. Leah jerked up, swiped stray drool from her chin, and blinked. It was Jericho along with another man, a bit older and definitely more grizzled.

"Dr. Wright, this is Detective Acevedo. He's going to walk us through some preliminaries while I take notes."

She nodded, scraping her lightweight vinyl chair back to make more room as the second detective moved another chair beside her at the table. Jericho eased into the third chair in the far corner. Suddenly the room felt claustrophobic, her throat tightening as if there wasn't enough air. When she did manage a breath the sour reek of fear filled her nostrils. She hoped the men couldn't sense that it came from her—it made her feel ashamed, embarrassed, as if she was somehow guilty.

"How's Detective Harper?" she asked, breaking the silence. "What did her CT show?"

Jericho frowned at that. "The doctors say there's no sign of bleeding, but she has a pretty bad concussion. They're going to watch her overnight in the ER."

"Good. I'm glad she's going to be okay."

Another lengthy silence as the second detective, Acevedo, set a small digital recorder on the table between them, turned it on, and then shuffled papers from a large stack of file folders he carried. Finally, he selected one sheet of paper and slid it over to Leah along with a felt tip pen. "This is just a formality. If you can read and initial, then sign at the bottom. It explains that we record all interviews, video and audio, and also goes over your Miranda rights," he explained. "Most people only know Miranda from what TV gets wrong, so we want to make sure you understand that you aren't under arrest and can leave at any time. We can also take a break anytime you want one."

"In fact," Jericho put in, "do you need anything now? Something to drink, a snack?"

"I have a right to an attorney," Leah read out loud, shaking her head at his questions. She glanced up from the paper. Neither man made eye contact, their attention suddenly focused elsewhere as if wishing she'd skip over that part. "Do I need one?"

"That's entirely up to you, Mrs. Wright."

She noticed that once again, they'd dropped her title. Reminding her not-so-subtly that her being a doctor no longer held any power. "Harper, she said she saw the man? Do you know who he is? Have you found him?"

Acevedo made a grunting noise. "You saw him as well. Almost as close as Harper."

His tone was accusatory, as if she could have stopped the man or intervened. She understood that. A police officer was seriously injured, after all. "I only saw his back. Running away. It was dark."

Acevedo nudged the paper closer to Leah. "Any questions before we begin?"

All she had to offer them was the truth—surely there was no harm in that? Except… there were ways to use the truth against even an innocent person. Maybe she should ask for a lawyer? What could it hurt?

How much would it cost? Without Ian's salary money would be tight, even without the costs of crime scene clean up—two crime scenes now, she reminded herself. Not to mention she wouldn't be able to go back to work right away. When she did, she'd probably need daycare—she hated the thought of it. She was already regretting sending Emily with Jessica and that had only been a few hours ago.

"Mrs. Wright?" Acevedo gave her a verbal nudge. "Are you ready to begin telling us your side of things?"

There was something about his expression—it was like he knew something she didn't. Leah remembered what her friend had told her: a good attorney never asks a question she doesn't already know the answer to. Leah bet good detectives were the same way.

"I understand my rights," she said, signing the sheet and marking the box requesting an attorney to be present during questioning. "And I'd like an attorney."

Acevedo blew out his breath and leaned back in his seat, eyeing Jericho and giving the other detective a slight nod. As if Leah had done exactly what he'd expected.

That's when she realized her instincts had been spot on. The police hadn't brought her here as a victim or a witness. They'd torn her away from her daughter because they thought she was a suspect. That she'd been involved in Ian's murder.

Her stomach clenched as she pushed back in her chair and stood. The police couldn't help her protect Emily. Not if they were thinking she was working with the killer.

CHAPTER 37

After leaving the police station, the one thing Leah was certain of was that the only way to protect Emily was to stay as far away from her as possible. So she headed to the one place where she'd always felt safe and in control: Good Sam's ER.

She found Naomi Harper in the observation area, fumbling her way upright in her bed, obviously confused. Leah rushed to her side and gently helped the police officer back against her pillows. "Do you know where you are?"

Harper's eyes fluttered, then opened wide. "Gotta go. I saw—"

"You're at Good Samaritan ER. Do you remember what happened?" Harper wore a clavicle strap and Leah saw from the films displayed on the bedside computer that her head CT was normal, no bleeding or swelling. Good news. Both for the police officer and for the case. If Harper could remember what her assailant looked like.

"Flying?" Harper's words came slowly. "Face. I saw his face." She struggled to sit up again. "Jericho. Where's Jericho? I saw him."

"It's okay," Leah reassured her. "You fell and broke your collarbone as well as sustaining a concussion. Your CAT scan was normal, no signs of bleeding, but we need to monitor you for a while longer." Leah frowned. Was she still one of the "we" of Good Sam's ER staff? Or was she just fooling herself that she wasn't already exiled as an outsider?

"Can't stay," Harper muttered, trying to sit up again. Leah pushed the button to raise the head of the bed so she wouldn't strain her shoulder. "Have to get back to work." She slumped into the pillows, eyes drifting shut. "Tell Jericho I saw him." Then she lurched upright, her face contorting in pain as she moved her left arm. "Phone. I need to call—" The name was lost. "Phone. Please."

Leah regarded her with skepticism. "Sure you don't want me to call for you? You're still a bit out of it, you know."

"I can do it." Harper backed her words up with a glare. "Why are you here?"

Leah rummaged through the plastic patient belonging bag hanging from the foot of the bed. "I was worried about you." She slid a phone out, then maneuvered a tray-table over the bed so Harper could work the phone one handed.

Harper instinctively reached for the phone with her left hand but winced in pain. She closed her eyes, breathing through clenched teeth until the pain subsided.

"You can still move your hand a bit even with the clavicle fracture, but trust me, the more you do with your other hand, the better."

"What are you doing here?" The words emerged relatively slur-free. "Really?"

"I needed to thank you. For stopping him." Leah drew in her breath. "I can't believe I wasn't there. If he'd gotten to Emily—" She grimaced. "Anyway. Thank you. I'm sorry you were hurt."

"Doing my job."

"Back at the house, you said you saw him before? Did you remember where?"

Harper frowned. She clutched at the phone without actually calling anyone as if it was a security blanket. Her eyes drifted shut again. Leah took a seat at the computer. Least she could do was to sit with Harper—she'd probably wake up disoriented again. And maybe there was someone else she could help. She pulled the bedside computer closer and began to type.

"What's wrong?" Harper asked a few minutes later as she jerked awake once more. Her voice was steadier.

"You're fine," Leah assured her again. "What do you remember?"

"Doctor—other doctor, a man. He said my brain was okay, but my collarbone was broken." She squinted at the computer screen. "Right? Did they find something else wrong? They took a ton of blood."

"No. You're fine, all your labs are normal. I'm just searching for another patient's files. But he's not here."

"Who?"

"There's a little boy with CF—cystic fibrosis. His dad said he's been really sick, but I can't find any record of him." Leah tapped her fingers against the monitor. "He said he just got custody, maybe the kid has a different last name. I'll try the CF registry; it lists all the patients in the region."

"What business is it of yours? I mean, privacy, right?" Leah almost smiled—Harper sounded like her old, pugnacious, cop-self.

"Brody said something about complications. I want to make sure we didn't mess up in the ER, and maybe flag the kid's chart for the future, but—" Leah blinked at the screen. "There's no one named Charlie in that age range on the registry. That's weird."

Harper was fumbling for the bed controls, straining to drop the side rail. "Brody. That's what the receptionist called the guy in the free clinic. The one talking with your daughter. I saw him watching both of you."

"Yeah, that's him. Jessica Kern is his son's doctor."

"She's a shrink."

"She's coordinating Charlie's care because he's had so many problems. But there's no medical record for him, nothing. Brody said Charlie had some tests today—" Leah thought hard. "Maybe Jessica's treating him without a medical record? Save them money?

No, that would leave Good Sam at risk; not to mention, it might cause unnecessary delays in care—"

Harper raised her good hand to reach for her phone but Leah had moved it to the bedside table while she slept. She missed, the phone skidding past her fingers and flying off the table, practically into Leah's lap.

"What's wrong?"

"Brody." Harper's voice was loud, not a shout, a command. "Call Jericho." She slapped her good hand against the bed rail, beckoning to Leah.

"Brody?" Leah gasped. "Brody was the one who— No. I mean, why would he? No." But she gave Harper her phone.

Harper wrapped her fingers around the phone as if it were a lifeline. She pressed the speed dial for Jericho. He answered on the second ring. "Harper? Something wrong?"

"The guy. I know who he is, boss." The words tumbled out machine-gun fast.

"Hold on, slow down."

"He was here. At the hospital."

"A patient? They won't divulge—"

"Don't ask the docs. Ask the security guys. He was in the free clinic. He had a hospital ID. Name of Brody."

"Allan Broderick," Leah interjected loud enough for Jericho to hear. "He volunteers at the clinic. His little boy, Charlie, is a patient. Has cystic fibrosis."

"Broderick, Allan," Harper repeated. "They'll have him on camera. Maybe the parking garage?"

Brody killed Ian? As it finally sank in, Leah stood up from the stool so quickly that it sped across the floor, crashing into the wall.

"Wait," Harper told her.

But it was Jericho who answered Harper. "On it. I'll need you to point him out. You okay to do that if I send Ray or Krichek over to get video from security at Good Sam?"

"I'll be here," she promised. "We got him. Boss, we got him now."

Harper ended the call. Leah grabbed her coat, already had Ruby's car keys in her hand. Brody? How? Why?

"You can't go," Harper told her, her words slurring again as if she'd used up all her energy. "You need to tell Jericho—"

"No. I sent Emily home with Jessica. Thought she'd be safer there, away from me." God, how could she have been so wrong? Brody worked with Jessica, could know where she lived, might be heading there right now.

"Wait for Jericho."

"I need to get to my daughter. You and Jericho take care of Brody, call me when you have him locked up."

"But—" The word emerged in a whisper, Harper's eyes drifting shut again.

Leah didn't wait. She had to get to Emily. Now.

CHAPTER 38

Luka let Leah go after setting an appointment for the morning—with her and her attorney. He was more than a little disappointed when she'd asked for one. It was the smart thing to do, of course. But it was also the guilty thing to do.

Harper's call from the ER was the one bright spot in the night. Luka found several dozen Alan, Allan, and Allen Brodericks in the statewide DMV database, so he sent Ray over to Good Sam to see if Harper was coherent enough to ID the guy. She'd sounded pretty out of it on the phone. Even if her Brody wasn't in their database, if Harper confirmed the ID, the hospital should have a record of contact info—if he'd used his real address.

"I still think Leah Wright might be behind this," Krichek said after Luka dispatched Ray over to Good Sam. "Do I need to bother searching for her patients? If she killed her husband, it was because of something the husband did, not a patient from her past. And if this Brody character did it—"

"Still needs to be done," Luka said, glancing over the younger detective's shoulder. "There must be a connection between Leah Wright and Broderick—if he was a patient of hers, then it's another piece of circumstantial evidence to help build our probable cause."

A knock on the door interrupted them. "Marco Sanchez from the tech squad," the man identified himself. "You called for an expert consultation?" His smile was wide as he didn't wait for an invitation but moved to join them. "Where's Naomi? I found something—she owes me a drink."

"Harper was injured, is at the ER," Krichek told Sanchez, his voice frosty. Luka glanced between the two men—both about the same age, but there the similarity ended, with Krichek on the losing side of any comparison.

"I'm Sergeant Jericho," he said, interrupting the silent testosterone contest. "What do you have for us?"

"Finished with Leah Wright's phone. Turned up something interesting." Sanchez held up a tablet and a photo appeared on the whiteboard. "Everything was wiped clean—she used an encrypted text service that deletes everything—except she must have forgotten she downloaded this to the internal memory card."

Luka and Krichek stared at the photo. It was a man, dressed in black motorcycle leathers, holding a gleaming silver hatchet in one hand and his helmet in the other. Behind him, duct taped to a chair was Ian Wright.

"Jesus," Krichek whispered. "Boss, we got her."

Felt way too easy. Luka asked, "Any way to trace where the photo came from? ID the man?"

"Way ahead of you. Ran him through our facial recognition—guy has a record. Served time at Rockview for vehicular manslaughter. Name's Allan Broderick." The photo was replaced by Broderick's pertinent information. "Sorry, no current address. Nothing after he was released, not sure what the deal is there."

"Brody." Luka felt a surge of energy revitalize him. "Sanchez, you're drafted. Help Krichek find me everything on Broderick, any ties to Leah Wright. And a current location."

Both Krichek and Sanchez sat down at the table and got to work. Luka paced the length of the room, detailing items to take to the DA for an arrest warrant. He carried Cherise's cobalt blue mug, remembering how she'd laugh whenever he'd been faced with a problem in school and needed to walk it out, the rhythm and movement helping his thoughts to flow. Once Harper ID'd Broderick as her attacker, he'd have more than enough to arrest him on a multitude of felonies.

But Leah Wright? Despite the fact that his coffee was long gone cold and bitter, he raised the mug to his lips, envisioning Cherise. She had nothing in common with Leah, not really, and yet, ever since he'd seen Leah in the crime scene video last night, that stubborn set of her jaw, the determined look in her eyes as she cradled her child, protecting her from the carnage surrounding them… it was the same look Cherise got when she talked about why she wanted to become a lawyer. "Too many people don't have anyone willing to stand up for them," she'd say. "I want to fight for them. Protect them from a system that doesn't give a damn. Show them someone cares."

That was why he hadn't been able to see Leah Wright as a viable suspect. His own personal blind spot. Luka came to a stop in front of the whiteboard, the photo of Broderick standing over his helpless victim filling his vision. He forced himself to look beyond Broderick, to focus on Ian Wright. Reminding himself that he served the victims who couldn't speak for themselves. Victims like Ian. Then he turned away and set his mug down, abandoning it on the table.

"As soon as we have Broderick's location, we'll need ERT for the arrest," he said, thinking aloud. The Emergency Response Team went in heavy and hard, ready for armed resistance. Given Broderick's capacity for violence, it was the best way to keep Luka's people safe during the arrest.

"What about Leah Wright?" Krichek asked. "Do we have enough for a warrant for her?"

Luka shook his head. "No. An attorney could argue that anyone could have sent the photo to her phone as a threat like with the roses. And we still have no proof that she bought the roses. We need more. But first, we need to find Broderick, see if he'll roll over, give us the widow."

Lucky for Luka, there was a federal agent who might be interested in helping. He called Radcliffe, filled him in on the events of the night.

"Where's this Broderick now?" Radcliffe asked.

"We're trying to locate him—if you have any info, it'd be appreciated." According to the records, for some strange reason, Broderick had been released from prison after only serving sixteen months despite being sentenced to three to five years. He wasn't on parole, a judge had reduced his sentence to time served, so they had no current address. "We're trying to figure out if there's any personal connection between him and Ian or Leah Wright."

"We'll get right on it," Radcliffe promised. "Keep me informed."

As soon as Luka hung up, his phone rang. Ray. "Harper confirms, Allan Broderick is the man who attacked her. Address he gave the hospital is a phony, though."

"Great. I'm calling the ADA, getting an arrest warrant started. Tell Harper good job and come on back home." Luka dialed the Assistant District Attorney. After he filled her in, he called Commander Ahearn to update him as well. He was on hold with Ahearn, waiting for permission to mobilize the emergency response team when Ray arrived back in the conference room, shaking snow off his jacket, eager to help.

"I still need a location," Luka told him. It was just after three in the morning. Which hopefully meant Broderick was sound asleep in his bed at home. *Not for long,* he thought with a smile. "And floor plans, photos. For ERT. As soon as Ahearn signs off. Can you call McKinley, make sure his team is good to go?"

Ray nodded, grabbed a landline and called the ERT commander. "McKinley? Want to have some fun? Yeah, I know it's snowing—jeezit, you guys are wimps." He paused, made a quacking motion with his hands.

Ahearn came back on the line. "It's a go," he told Luka. "Keep me informed." Then he hung up.

Luka tapped Ray on the shoulder, took the phone from him. It took a bit of convincing but he finally got McKinley on board to take action tonight. If they got a location on Broderick.

Krichek looked up after Luka hung up. "Let me guess, McKinley doesn't want to get his shiny boots all muddy."

"Not until I told him who we were after. Chance to make the news? He's all in."

Sanchez rapped the table, calling for their attention. "Found an address. He's renting a place out past the old church on River Road. No floor plan, but got some pictures."

Ray joined Luka as they peered at photos of an ancient stone farmhouse. "Walls are solid," Ray said. "Think thermal will even work?"

"House that old, there'll be a cellar as well. McKinley is going to have his hands full."

"Harper mentioned he had a kid."

Sanchez frowned, his fingers typing furiously. "No mention anywhere of a kid. Not that that means much if the mother didn't list him on the birth certificate."

"Prison record is clean. Looks like he cut a deal to get out early," Krichek said. "Must've ratted on someone."

"What was the original crime?" Luka asked. He knew how violent Brody was now—the image of Ian Wright's body still haunted him—but had he always been that way?

"Broderick was seventeen at the time. Ran with a Pittsburgh gang, they were out at a movie theatre, getting payback for an earlier drive-by done by a rival gang," Krichek answered as he scanned the court files. "An innocent couple got caught in the crossfire. No, wait. They were in the parking lot. Broderick claimed he had no idea his buddies were planning the hit, so when the guns came out, he jumped in a car and took off, didn't want to have anything to do with it. But in his panic, dodging bullets, he ended up running over the husband. Killed him. Wife right there watching the whole damn thing."

"Right," Ray scoffed. "Poor baby, didn't want anyone to get hurt. Jesus, these guys and their phony sob stories just slay me."

There was a rap on the door and McKinley gestured for Luka. But then, Sanchez jerked his head up, muttering, "Got it, I've got it!"

Luka turned to his second in command. "Ray, can you fill them in on the tactical details? Tell them I'll be right there." Ray left with McKinley.

"I know how Leah Wright and Allan Broderick met up," Sanchez said, sounding triumphant. He patted his computer. "It's all right here. Four years ago, in Pittsburgh, she saved his life." A newspaper clipping appeared on the whiteboard. "She literally brought him back from the dead."

"Just in time for him to go out and kill someone else a year later?" Luka said.

"Talk about your bad karma," Krichek added.

Luka skimmed the article. Allan Broderick, sixteen, shot in a drive-by shooting in Pittsburgh's South Side, victim of gang-related violence, dead for over ten minutes before being resuscitated by Dr. Leah Wright. It was dated June, just a month before Leah moved from Pittsburgh to Cambria City to care for her great aunt.

"She might not have even known about Broderick going back to his gang, killing that guy," he said. "It was almost a year later."

"Yeah," Krichek said, bent over his own keyboard as if in competition with Sanchez. "There's an article about the trial that says Broderick was just getting out of the rehab hospital and his friends were throwing him a welcome home party. His lawyer said he knew nothing about the planned violence, yada yada. Guy pled down from felony homicide to vehicular manslaughter." He looked up, first to Luka then to Sanchez. "But still, it's a connection. She saves the guy's frickin' life, he gets out of jail, comes here just in time for her to ask for payback, convince him to kill her husband."

He turned to stare at Luka. "We gotta bring her in, boss. Even if she lawyers up. Think of her kid."

It made sense—except Luka still had doubts. Nothing logical, nothing he could express in words, just a niggling feeling deep down in his gut. But cases weren't built on gut feelings, they were built on facts.

And right now, Leah Wright had a lot of facts to explain.

"She's staying with that other doctor, the psychiatrist, Jessica Kern. Ray and I will fill in the ADA, head out with ERT to Broderick's. You start prepping warrants. We'll probably need Children and Youth involved as well."

"Sure you don't want me to come with?" Krichek asked, looking like a puppy dog left behind while his family went on holiday.

"Get me those warrants and you can go after the widow. But run them past me and the ADA first—we can't risk her slipping out on a technicality." Luka thought. "Oh, and don't forget about the search for Cochrane—he might still be involved."

"Yes, boss." He slumped in his chair.

"Need anything more from me?" Sanchez asked.

"Can you get more info from that photo on Wright's cell? Seems weird that there's nothing else on it—she mentioned getting texts and DMs all day, it's one of the reasons why she swapped it out for a burner."

"Sure, no problem."

Luka grabbed his coat and opened the door. "Call me if you find anything."

"Be careful, boss," Krichek called after him. "Lord only knows what a nutjob like Broderick might do when he's cornered."

CHAPTER 39

Leah rushed from Good Sam's ER, dialing Jessica as she strode past friendly faces trying to stop her with their gushes of sympathy.

"Leah?" Jessica answered. "Are you done with the police already?"

"It's Brody," Leah said, entering the parking garage. Her heart stuttered at the memory of Ian's final present to her. Then she steadied herself, focusing on the fact that no one was near Ruby's truck, peering through all the windows before opening the driver's door. "Did you know?"

"Know what? What does Brody have to do with anything? Leah, slow down, you're not making sense."

Leah got into the truck and locked the doors. She sat there, torn between a desire to make sense of everything and her need to get to Emily. "Brody. He attacked Officer Harper. He killed Ian. He might have followed you home, might be after Emily—" Her words tumbled over each other and she forced herself to breathe. "Is she, is Emily—"

"She's fine. Sound asleep, exhausted. Ruby and I were just having a drink by the fire. Everyone's fine, Leah. Calm down, you don't want to get into a wreck. I have a ton of security—honestly, this place is like a fortress. You'll all be safe here. Did you tell the police? Are they coming?"

"Harper told Jericho. They're hunting for Brody—" She started the truck, her hands trembling as they gripped the steering wheel.

"I'm on my way. Could you do me a favor? Double-check your security? I know I sound paranoid, but—"

"After everything you've been through, it's not paranoid. It's common sense," Jessica assured her. "But why would Brody target you? I thought you said you saved his life?"

Leah pulled out of the garage. The snow was coming down hard, a blustery wind whipping it into a fury. This early in the morning there was little traffic, but the snowplows and salt trucks also hadn't been out yet to clear the streets. Grateful for the truck's all-wheel drive, she steered toward the bridge.

"I don't know," she finally answered Jessica. "He's also somehow erased all records of Charlie—do you think he's planning to kidnap him? Or maybe he already has? Maybe Charlie isn't even his to start with?" The thought of what a monster like Brody could do to a sick child had her stomping harder on the accelerator until the truck's wheels slipped on a patch of black ice. She didn't brake, instead eased off the gas and regained control.

"One problem at a time. You concentrate on getting here safely—the roads are hell, and up here cell service is almost non-existent, so let me handle the police. I'll call them, tell them everything I know about Brody and Charlie in case it helps them find them faster."

"Okay. Okay." Making sure Emily was safe was Leah's one and only priority. Jessica could deal with the rest. "Thanks. See you soon."

Fear banished her exhaustion as she gripped the steering wheel. Suddenly, she felt Ian's presence beside her in the car, also urging her to hurry. Her stomach clenched. She'd made a mistake, an awful mistake, leaving Emily, letting her out of her sight. It didn't matter that Ruby and Jessica were with her, every fiber of Leah's being screamed with the need to have her daughter by her side where she could protect her.

She crossed the bridge and turned onto Route 15. A sudden gust of wind slammed into the truck and Leah fought to control it as the tires slid on the ice-covered road. She slowed down, leaning over the steering wheel as if that would help the road appear in the near white-out conditions. She inched along, frustrated by her slow progress. Finally, she reached the even more narrow road leading up the mountain to where Jessica's house was—no, not house, a mansion, built in the 1850s by a coal baron. She'd once visited it with Nellie, delivering hand-crafted chocolates for a wedding.

Jessica had joked about her work with the DOD, but clearly it paid well. Better than working in the ER, Leah thought as she steered the truck over the icy roads. She remembered the mansion from when she was a kid—rumors said it was haunted, cursed. The coal baron who'd built it had been driven mad by delusions that his workers, his staff, even his wife and children were trying to kill him. In the end, he'd hidden alone, barricaded behind an iron fence topped with sharp pikes, perched on top of his mountain with a view of everything he owned but could not visit for fear of being assassinated.

Leah made a mental note not to share the house's history with Jessica. She rounded a switchback, the truck trying to spin out on the steep curve, bringing her attention back to the here and now. The snow wasn't too heavy except when the wind picked up. Maybe four or five inches fallen since Leah had left Nellie's house a few hours ago—but with more promised by morning.

As she crept up the mountain, Leah searched for the entrance to Jessica's property. About two thirds of the way to the top of the mountain, the road began to descend along the other side. She must have missed the turn in the snow and fog. Leah cursed, searched for somewhere to turn around, and made a three-point turn. She kept her speed to a crawl, scanning the night.

Finally, her headlights spotted the steel gates guarding the entrance to Jessica's estate. She pulled the truck up to them, rolled down her window, and clicked the intercom. No one answered but the gates swung open, allowing her to pass. She glanced at the clock—three twelve.

She wasn't going to wait for morning, she decided. She'd use the storm to cover their departure, make it harder for Brody to track her and Emily.

Finally, she reached the top of the winding drive and parked in front of the mansion's doors. Leah stepped out of the truck, shuddering in the wind gusting around the side of the mansion, fighting to reach the shelter of the veranda. The front doors were huge, at least twelve feet of solid oak towering over her. She pressed the bell but couldn't hear it ring beyond the doors.

All she could think about was Emily. She raised a fist and pounded on the door not caring who she might disturb inside. This was her one last chance to protect her daughter.

CHAPTER 40

The tactical briefing was mercifully short, interrupted only by the ADA delivering warrants for both Allan Broderick's arrest and a search of his house. Luka stood at the rear of the room and listened as McKinley outlined his plan. Ray sat at the school-like tables with the operators, taking notes and listening intently—he loved tactical operations, had tried out for the ERT twice when he was younger, before joining the investigatory side of the department.

Luka worried that McKinley might use the bad weather to stall, merely setting up surveillance until it cleared, but the ERT commander had surprised him. Instead, his plan used the poor visibility to their advantage. The plan was simple and elegant: deploy his men in a cordon surrounding Brody's house, using the snow as cover, converge, then kick in the door. The presence of a child in the house was the only complication, which McKinley addressed by having his strike team leaders deploying nonlethal weapons until their subject was isolated.

The ERT team had their own pool of vehicles, marked and unmarked, so while they drove off in their armored vehicle, Luka commandeered an unmarked black Suburban for himself and Ray. Ray seemed more than a bit disappointed that he wasn't riding on the armored vehicle as he climbed into the Suburban's passenger seat.

Luka wasn't sure if it was the SUV's height, its fitted leather seat that made him feel like a pilot in a cockpit, or the way the all-wheel drive shredded the snow beneath the wheels, but for the first time since he'd walked into Leah Wright's house last night, he felt in control. He felt as if he understood what was going on.

"You guys were right all along," he told Ray. "About the widow." This was a primal crime of passion, nothing more. The window dressing—the extreme overkill, the torture, the drugs, the possible national security connection, the widow's rescue of the daughter—all distraction. Smoke and mirrors designed to keep them off balance.

"She had us all fooled." Ray paused. "Well, maybe not Harper."

They pulled in behind the other vehicles at their secluded staging area behind the old church down the road from Broderick's place. From where they were positioned, they could see the house without being seen in return. They watched as McKinley gathered his men for a final briefing.

Because of the weather and road conditions, their caravan had arrived a little later than they'd hoped. Luka noticed that Broderick's house was less than two miles from Nellie Quinn's house where Harper had been attacked earlier tonight. Luka's vision filled with a memory of the first time he saw Leah. How could he have been so wrong about her?

The tedium of waiting set his mind adrift. He imagined Tanya out in the cold, lying in some frozen Baltimore alley, oblivious. He blinked, opened his window, the frigid air shocking him back. There was nothing more he could do for Tanya, he told himself. He had to save his energy for this case. Because as soon as he had both Broderick and Leah Wright in custody his job would be to break them.

Finally, the ERT team deployed. He and Ray waited inside the comfort of the SUV, watching the video feeds from the body cams on Ray's laptop as McKinley and his men did their jobs. The team deployed swiftly and silently, surrounding and converging on the house.

"Thermal isn't giving us good readings," one of the ERT whispered over the radio. "Visual shows a motorcycle matching your actor's in the carport, no visible presence in living room or kitchen, a child's bed in the southeast corner bedroom, and blackout curtains in the room on the northeast corner. Proceeding with caution in case the child is in the room with subject. Do I have a green light?"

"Green light, proceed," McKinley ordered.

A moment later the team surged toward the house. The plan was for the first group to provide a diversion by taking down the front door, while the second entered through the window into the bedroom where Brody was presumed to be. Luka felt a thrill of adrenaline surge through him as the first group with their battering ram approached the front door.

Three loud thuds sounded, echoing through the SUV like thunder.

CHAPTER 41

As Leah waited on the mansion's porch, she realized that Andre Toussaint was right: she did live in a small world. What the trauma chief had been wrong about was that she didn't want or need a larger world—not a big house, not a job at a more prestigious trauma center, not more money. All she needed was her family, safe. Just that one small thing that she could guard and hold steady in her heart.

Except, she'd failed them. She wasn't strong like Ian, who'd given everything to protect their daughter; she wasn't as resilient as Emily, able to both cope with the horror she'd lived through and still find joy in the world. Leah felt as if she were drowning beneath the weight of her pain. She had to regain control of her life—for Emily. Starting here and now.

She pounded the side of her fist against the thick door one more time. This time it opened.

"Leah," Jessica Kern said with a smile. She wore silk slacks, a tunic with deep pockets, and a long silk robe. With the foyer's chandelier scattering light from above and behind her, the older woman practically shimmered as if wearing a halo. "Please, come inside."

Leah stood her ground, knowing that she needed to get going. "No, thank you. I'm just here to pick up Emily. Thank you for watching her, but we'll be going now."

Jessica frowned—even that slight creasing of her forehead seemed drawn from Doris Day pique rather than expressing true consternation. "Now? It's the middle of the night and there's a snowstorm. I've already made up a room for you. Plus, Emily's sleeping—I'm sure you don't want to disturb her, not after everything she's been through. Come in, we'll talk, wait for the weather to clear."

Everything Jessica said was perfectly rational. But Leah did not feel rational; she felt as if her world was ready to explode and she had one chance to escape. "I appreciate everything you've done for us, Jessica. But we need to leave. Now." The last emerged clipped and so loud it startled both of the women.

Jessica blinked and nodded. "All right, if you insist. At least come inside where it's warm while I go get her."

Leah walked forward as Jessica closed the door behind her. The marble-floored foyer was larger than her living room with not one but two grand staircases gracefully curving up to the second floor. Leah started toward one staircase, her shoes dripping melted snow onto the marble, but Jessica stopped her.

"No, this way." She led Leah through an arch at the side of the foyer into a traditional living room, then through it down a narrow hallway to a smaller den with comfortable recliners, plaid wallpaper, and one large wall dominated by a flat screen TV.

"Are you there, yet?" Jessica asked, turning to face Leah. Below the façade of carefully applied makeup, her eyes were shadowed and lines creased the corners of her mouth, making her appear brittle. "The pain. The feeling like you've been catapulted into a world where nothing makes sense? Your insides torn apart every time you think of him? Every time you remember his face, his touch, his smell? It's a pain like no other. Nothing dulls it, nothing can make it stop. Or silence the voices in your head, tormenting you. You're all alone, nowhere to turn, no one to trust, and you can't help blame yourself."

Leah jerked her chin up. She knew Jessica was describing the pain that had tormented her after her own husband's death, and it rang true. "Yes," she whispered, not trusting her voice beyond that single syllable that emerged strained, shredded with grief.

"Good." Jessica grabbed a remote, whirled to face the TV, and turned it on. "Because that's what I've lived with for the past three years."

There was no sound coming from the TV, but Leah didn't need any. She stood, shocked and confused, staring at the image: Emily lying in Ruby's lap, sleeping, both sitting on a concrete floor, Ruby stroking Emily's hair even as she glanced wide-eyed around the room, obviously terrified. The walls behind them were stone, appeared old, very old, and to one side of the frame was a shelf with curved racks designed to fit bottles.

"Jessica." Leah whirled on the other woman. "Where are they? What have you done with my daughter?"

Jessica smiled as if Leah had just given her a happy surprise. She touched a small earpiece concealed by her blonde tendrils. "Do it," she whispered, her tone urgent.

A shadow edged into the frame, looming over Ruby and Emily. Ruby's fear turned to panic, and she slid Emily off her lap, standing to place herself between her granddaughter and the new threat.

A hunting knife was visible in the man's fist.

"No, wait!" Leah shouted. "Stop! Don't hurt them."

Jessica gazed at the screen, pupils dilated.

Leah grabbed her by the shoulder and spun her around. "What do you want? Why are you doing this?"

"Get your hands off of me," Jessica snarled.

The man took another step toward Ruby; now Leah could see the length of his arm, his face still out of frame.

"Please," Leah pleaded, dropping her hands to her sides and backing away. "Stop."

Jessica whispered something Leah couldn't hear, and the man retreated. Then the screen went blank. Somehow that was worse. Leah pulled both fists into her belly, trying to quash her need to vomit, to run to Emily—except she had no idea where to run to—to strike out at Jessica. Instead, she pressed one hand against the other, deeper, harder, the pain forcing her to focus.

"Please. I just want my daughter back. Please. I'll do anything."

"Just like I'd do anything to get my husband back." Jessica slid open the drawer of a side table, emerging with a small tablet in one hand and a large pistol in the other. She aimed the pistol at Leah.

Leah stared at the gun. Jessica's husband? He died in Chicago—at least that's what Jessica had told Leah. Had Jessica lied?

Feeling as if she were skidding on black ice, spinning out of control, Leah hesitated, unsure of how to connect with this madwoman. Empathy? "I'm sure you miss him desperately."

"You have no idea. Gordan was a genius—much more so than your husband. Think of how many lives are better because of his work. Work that impacted real people in the real world, not just imaginary zeros and ones like your husband's fiddling on the computer."

Leah wanted to defend Ian but knew Jessica was baiting her. "You must have made the perfect team."

"We were," Jessica said wistfully. "We were. But you destroyed all that."

Did she mean Leah personally? No, impossible. She'd never met Jessica's husband. She remembered Jessica's work with the military and how passionate she was about it. "You wanted to use your husband's work to do more than program prosthetics, didn't you?"

Her guess hit home. Jessica's face flushed and her grip on the gun tightened. "That's why we were outside arguing in the parking lot, instead of inside watching the movie. He found out I'd given his designs to the army, said I betrayed him, accused me of—" She shook her head, stray bits of hair escaping their carefully coiffed French knot. "He would have seen the light, if I only had more time. But you stole that from me. He would have agreed with me, this is the best way to prevent what happened to our son from ever happening again. But then—"

Her gaze sharpened, an eagle homing in on its prey. "Now it's too late. All because of you."

CHAPTER 42

It was all over in a matter of moments. Luka watched on his laptop as ghostly figures of men with weapons surged through the house and searched each room.

As Luka and Ray waited for McKinley and his men to finish securing the house before they began their own search, Luka's phone rang. Krichek. "Just wanted to let you know the staties caught Cochrane," he said. "Brought him here to sober up. He's talking about some woman who paid him to post those videos and go after Leah Wright." He paused. "A woman *doctor.*"

"You're not questioning him, are you?"

"Course not, he's impaired. But we are taping him in the holding cell—for his safety, of course. And he keeps muttering about how he never should've listened to her, that it was her fault he was going to get sent back to prison, lose his kid for good. I think he's talking about Leah Wright. I think she paid him to help make her look more like a victim—while setting Cochrane up as a possible suspect, to take the heat off her."

"Has he mentioned names?"

"Nah. I'm wondering if he even ever met her or knows who exactly paid him, but we'll need to wait for him to sober up to be sure."

"Keep an eye on him. And start prepping warrants for his house and electronics." Luka hung up as McKinley waved to them. He and Ray climbed out of the warm SUV, hurried through the wind and snow to Broderick's house.

"Guess our guy rabbited," McKinley said when Luka met him in Brody's front room. Ray joined McKinley's men, who had lowered their weapons and were now executing the search warrant, looking for evidence that tied Broderick with the Wright killing.

"What about the kid?" Jericho asked.

"Come see for yourself."

Jericho followed McKinley into a bedroom at the rear of the house. It was decorated with photos ripped from magazines of kids' toys and cartoons and amusement parks and movies. The dresser was painted red, white, and blue with race car knobs on each drawer. Toys of all shapes and sizes filled plastic buckets and spilled out of stacks in the corners of the room. The bed was shaped like a race car with a race car themed quilt pulled up high over the pillow.

"Guy must've spent all his dough on this shit," McKinley said, toeing a bucket of wooden cars.

"His kid's sick," Luka said, somehow feeling defensive of Broderick—or at least of his kid. Charlie, Harper had said his name was. "Has cystic fibrosis. I don't see any breathing machines or medicines." He opened the closet doors. Empty except for the toys piled along the bottom. He yanked out the dresser drawers. Also empty. "They cleared out."

"Looks like it." McKinley's radio sputtered and he left Luka to answer the call.

Luka stood in the center of the room, turning slowly in a circle. Made sense. Broderick realized they were on to him and ran with the kid. And yet… The room didn't feel like it had been hastily abandoned—it felt as if it had never been lived in at all. He pulled back the race car quilt. The mattress below it was naked, no sheets, still sheathed in its original plastic wrapping. But on top of the mattress, smiling up at Luka was a large doll, the size of a toddler.

McKinley returned. "You mentioned your other suspect has a kid—think this was for them? Maybe he was prepping it as a hideout or something, getting ready to snatch them?"

Luka shook his head. "Leah's daughter is a girl. This wasn't for her." Since when had the widow gone back to plain Leah? "If Broderick is this obsessed and delusional, there's no telling what he might do."

"Are you saying she's his partner or his victim?"

"Not sure. Leah and her daughter are at Dr. Kern's. We need to warn them and get some men out there to protect the daughter and other civilians until we get some answers." He slid out his phone and dialed her number, but it went straight to voicemail as did Kern's.

"Give me the address and my guys will come up with a plan," McKinley offered.

"Hey, you guys are gonna want to see this," Ray said, motioning for them to follow him. He led Luka and McKinley out to the carport where one of the ERT guys stood beside a black motorcycle. He had flipped open the storage compartment below the seat. Inside was a stainless steel hatchet, covered in blood.

"We got him. This is definitely our guy."

Luka grunted in response. Broderick might be their guy, but they didn't have him. Not yet. He dialed both Leah and Jessica Kern again, leaving voicemails warning them. Some might argue that he shouldn't alert a possible suspect that they were coming, but he couldn't in good conscience not warn the women at Kern's house that Broderick might be targeting them. Not given how unhinged Broderick appeared to be.

McKinley was also on his phone. "ADA refuses to get a no-knock warrant for Kern's. Says unless we have proof that Broderick is there and is endangering lives, she can't."

Luka understood the ADA's reasoning—sending armed men charging into a civilian's house, a respected physician no less, without adequate evidence could be a career ender. But damn it, he knew in his gut that was where Broderick had gone.

"Ray, stay and finish the search," he ordered as he turned to leave.

"Can't hear you with all this snow," Ray said, striding fast to catch up to Luka. They both got into the SUV.

Kern's place was up the mountain, less than three miles away. Luka programmed the route into the SUV's nav system. He didn't have much of a plan other than protecting Emily Wright and the other civilians. If Broderick wasn't at Kern's, he'd apologize for waking everyone and drag Leah and Emily to the station house where they could safely wait for their damn lawyer and straighten all this out one way or the other. It was the logical thing to do.

But logic did nothing to quell the sudden feeling that time had already run out.

CHAPTER 43

Confusion added to Leah's panic. She'd barely met Jessica before today, never met her husband at all.

"You're such an idiot," Jessica told her. "You still don't see, do you? You have no idea the pain you caused, what I've suffered." She tapped her earbud, whispered something. A few moments later, Brody appeared in a doorway at the rear of the room.

"Brody?" Then Leah saw the knife in his hand. He was the man from the TV. It took everything she had to shove down her rage and fear. If Brody was delusional or psychotic—why else would a grown man be threatening a little girl with a knife? She had to remain calm, find a way to reach him on his level. "Is Emily all right?"

Brody's gaze was distant, as if he were listening more than seeing what was right in front of him. The overhead lights sparked off the array of electrodes covering his shaved skull, giving him the appearance of a modern-day Frankenstein's monster. He wore a tight-fitting tank top revealing an implanted device beneath the skin over his collarbone.

Leah recognized it as a drug delivery system. With it, Jessica could pump him full of anything—including the designer drugs that were used to torture Ian. She could dull his senses, fill him with psychotic rage, even wipe parts of his memory. His expression remained totally blank. He might not have any idea what he was doing now—or what'd he'd done last night. To Ian.

Jessica had reduced him to a drone, a puppet, capable of anything she commanded. Leah's body flooded with chilling terror as she realized two things. Jessica Kern was insane. And she'd had Ian killed.

When Brody remained silent, unable to answer her questions, she turned away from him to stare at Jessica. "What do you want? I never knew you or your husband. Why do you hate me so much that you'd take my daughter?"

"Maybe it's not about you," Jessica snapped. But then with the next breath, she regained composure. "At least not all about you. You gave Brody a second chance at life. Do you know what he did with it?"

"I don't understand."

"You saved the wrong life when you decided to play God and bring Brody back from the dead. What did you think Brody would do with the second chance you gave him? Did you think he might change? Reform himself, do something with his life? You have no idea what you did, the consequences, the pain. *My* pain. It's your fault, what I've had to endure!" Jessica was shouting now, her words ricocheting from the hardwood floors and high ceilings like bullets. "Do you know what he did? Do you?"

Leah didn't trust her words. All she could do in the face of Jessica's tsunami of fury was shake her head. There were no weapons in the room she could use, other than playing to Jessica's emotions. *Keep her focus on me*, she thought, *keep Brody here, away from Emily.*

"After you saved Brody, after he left the hospital, he killed my husband. Because of you, my Gordan is dead." Jessica's voice rose then fell until the last word was barely a whisper. Her shoulders slumped as if she'd exhausted herself with her outburst.

"I didn't…" Leah trailed off, at a loss to find words capable of untangling the snarled knot of Jessica's warped logic.

"I watched Brody kill my husband. Helpless. Powerless." Jessica took a deep breath and straightened, her posture ramrod, unforgiving. "Now you get to watch as everything you love is taken away. Forever."

Leah stared at Brody. There had to be a human component buried beneath the drugs and pain. One that she could maybe use to get to Emily, save her. "Brody, you don't want to hurt Emily. She's just a little kid, like your Charlie."

A strangled grunt emerged from Brody and one finger twitched, curling as if trying to make a fist. Leah took that as a good sign—maybe his mind was free even if Jessica still had control of his body.

"He won't listen to you. He can't." Jessica smiled at Brody—more than a smile, a triumphant grin of delight. "He can't disobey."

Leah watched, assessing her options—she couldn't run and leave Emily behind, and she couldn't fight Jessica without getting shot, which would also leave Emily unprotected.

"Why are you doing this?" She directed her words to Brody, remembering how kind he'd been to Emily. "Is she threatening Charlie?"

He remained motionless and expressionless, held in the thrall of whatever commands Jessica had given him.

Jessica laughed and Leah turned back to her. "You're both idiots. Haven't you figured it out yet?"

She stepped forward, tapped the drug infusion pump. "Took me months to rebuild his mind—poor thing was so lost, his memories fragmented after you brought him back from the dead. Permanent brain damage. Was like a lost child, shuffling in a haze through a world he barely comprehended." She turned to smile at Leah. "Until I gave him new memories, built him a new world inside his mind. One that I control."

"You brainwashed him?" She remembered what Jessica had said about her work for the military—this was what she'd meant. Not helping people find peace, but reshaping their reality, until they were under her control. "How?"

"Gordie's neurostimulation tech combined with my own unique drug cocktail. Including some synthetic scopolamine." Jessica acted as if she deserved the Nobel prize.

A wave of bile overcame Leah—she'd let Jessica use a form of that same tech on Emily. She'd even left Emily alone with Jessica. "You didn't—Emily?"

"No, dear." Jessica's tone turned pitying, enjoying Leah's pain. "Not yet, anyway. But let me show you what she can expect." Her thumb caressed the screen and Brody grimaced in pain, every muscle rigid. Jessica stood back, appraising her work.

"I lied," she whispered to Brody. "There's no saving your son. What you see now is the truth."

She clicked the tablet and the TV lit up, but it wasn't the view from before. This time it was a video loop, only a few seconds long, taken from a car's dashboard. A residential block on a steep hill. The sound of the car's engine revving, then a young woman appeared, stepping off the curb, an infant's car seat swinging from her hand. The car sped toward them, hitting them without warning, the noise of the impact heart-wrenching. The camera angle didn't show the bloody results, but somehow that made it worse. Then there was silence, followed by a woman's laughter echoing from inside the car. The whole thing was maybe six seconds long, looping over and over as Leah stared.

"Charlie and his mother were the first ones I killed." Jessica leaned in, hovering intimately close to Brody, her voice low, almost seductive. "But of course, I couldn't tell you. Had to give you something to care about, something to believe in—something I could threaten if you tried to disobey."

Brody stood frozen, unblinking as the carnage of his family's destruction played out on the screen. Not even that horror could break Jessica's control over him.

"It's time," Jessica said, turning back to Leah. "Shall we begin with your mother or your daughter? You've seen what Brody can do with a hatchet. It's nothing compared to his work with a knife."

Leah's body moved before she could make a conscious decision. She lunged toward Jessica, but before she made it halfway across the room, Jessica aimed the pistol at Leah's heart. "Stop."

Leah obeyed. Even if Jessica was a poor shot, there was no way she could miss at this distance. From the other woman's stance and unwavering hand, she had a feeling Jessica was very practiced with the pistol.

"That's a good girl." An alarm sounded like a doorbell on Jessica's tablet. She glanced at it, lips pressed in consideration, then touched a button. "Company."

A few moments later the sound of pounding footsteps echoed from the front room. Leah turned to face the newcomer, hope thrilling through her. Was it Jericho?

No. It was Radcliffe. He had a gun as well. Relief flooded over Leah. "Thank God you're here," she gushed. "They killed my husband."

Nobody moved. Then Radcliffe nodded to Jessica and lowered his pistol. "I told you, you were sloppy. Giving him your son's motorcycle? Helping Broderick get out of prison early. Not to mention the drug cocktail you used on Ian Wright. Same as in your DARPA research. Took me all of an hour to figure out it had to be you. But I can only cover up so much; the cops are on the way. Grab the proof of concept and your research. We're out of here."

"No. I'm not ready. Besides, the police will believe exactly what I want them to believe. That Leah coerced Brody to kill her husband. I even left them evidence—a photo," Jessica said, speaking as if Leah wasn't right there. "When she and Brody vanish, the cops will add two and two, get five, and I'll be free to continue mine and Gordie's work."

"Work?" Leah yelled and suddenly she had everyone's attention—except Brody, who still stood frozen, awaiting Jessica's next command. "In the name of research, you had my husband murdered? You kidnapped my mother and daughter?"

"Not research. Revenge."

Leah turned to Radcliffe. "She's holding them hostage, said she's going to have Brody kill them."

"Call it a signing bonus." Jessica beamed at Radcliffe, but he merely appeared exasperated.

"You're crazy if you think I'm going along with hurting a child. We're out of time," he told her. "Put away the gun. We're leaving. Now."

"No," Jessica told him. "You need to buy me more time. She needs to feel what I did, she needs to pay—"

"Lady, I said, grab your shit and let's go." The words cracked like a whip, but Jessica merely smirked.

"This project is too valuable—I'm too valuable. The research is all here, inside my head. Your bosses will want you to do as I say, let me finish. Then you can have everything, my research and Gordie's. I don't care what you do with it. As long as I get to see the people who stole Gordie from me suffer like I have."

Radcliffe frowned at that, seemed to be actually considering giving into Jessica's demands.

"What do you want from me?" Leah realized the government agent might not be her ally. She tried to think of any words that would convince Jessica to let Emily go, unharmed. Then she realized there was only one thing that would satisfy Jessica's pain, her need for retribution. "Take me with you, you'll have all the time in the world to make me suffer. Just leave Emily and Ruby. Safe and alive."

Jessica's eyes gleamed as she considered Leah's offer.

"We don't have time for this," Radcliffe argued. "Let's go. Now."

"Your job is to give me what I need. So, do it."

Radcliffe raised his weapon, aiming at Jessica. "Lady, I've had all I'm going to take from you—"

"Shut up. Do as you're told and help me finish this." Her tone sounded bored, as if instructing someone unwilling to listen to simple logic.

All Leah could think was how absolutely insane this woman was. How was she going to save Emily and Ruby? They were obviously in a wine cellar, and Brody had come from the rear of the house; the entrance must be there.

Jessica whispered something too soft for Leah to hear and thumbed her tablet. Brody grabbed Leah's arm, raising his knife in his other hand and pressing it against her jugular, ignoring Radcliffe's gun as the DIA man whirled to face him.

Radcliffe seemed more than intimidated by Brody; he actually stepped back as if afraid. The expression on his face was a mix of disgust and repulsion. The two men faced each other in silence, the only sound the huffing of Radcliffe's breath.

"Give me your gun," Jessica commanded.

Radcliffe glanced at Leah, his bravado crumpling, and slowly lowered his gun to the floor, kicking it across the hardwood to Jessica, who scooped it up. Brody's grip was bruising, but it was the blade against her throat that held Leah frozen, unable to fight back as much as she wanted to. She was Emily's only hope; she just had to wait and watch for an opening that wouldn't end up with all of them dead.

Jessica glanced up from her tablet, her eyes dilated with excitement as she met Leah's gaze. "Let's go pay your daughter a visit." Then she smiled at Brody.

CHAPTER 44

Brody's mind fragmented into more pieces than the kaleidoscope he'd given Charlie for Christmas. Shattered slivers sliced into view then spun away into oblivion. Dr. Jessica, her face warped like a blond gargoyle; the room smelling of woodsmoke and sweaty fear. The knife in his hand gleaming like a mirror. Leah, her face the only one in focus, so sad, so afraid, he wanted to step in front of her, protect her.

Pain surged through Brody, his limbs moving as if they had a life of their own. His fingers clenched soft flesh—Leah's. The other doctor. The other mother. The other wife… the widow. All Brody's fault. No—not Brody's fault. He'd had no choice; it was the only way to save Charlie.

But he'd failed. The bloody nightmares hadn't been dreams at all—they'd been real. The dream, the golden haloed dream that had saved him from the pain, that had been Charlie. Only a dream.

This time the pain was of his own creation as he howled with rage and sorrow, yet was unable to make a sound. The most Brody could do was create a tiny whimper, a dog whipped past caring enough to want to live. He would have passed that point a long time ago—if not for Charlie.

Charlie was gone.

He'd killed a man, destroyed a family for a dream, a wish. Make-believe. False hope of a life worth living. How could he have done that?

For Charlie. He'd do anything for Charlie.

Tears seeped from his eyes, but he couldn't raise a hand to wipe them away. They made the world seem blurry—almost as blurry as his memories were. The only thing that had felt real was Charlie, the sound of his laughter, the feeling of his weight against Brody's chest, snoring his little boy snores, smelling of bubblegum soap and pajamas fresh from the dryer. The rest of Brody's life, the rest of the whole damned world blurred into nothingness compared to Charlie.

As he marched Leah through the kitchen to the door leading to the wine cellar, his chest ached so bad he thought it might burst from the pain. *Charlie...* his son's name screamed through his brain, echoing, until it faded into oblivion.

Silent, he waited as Jessica unlocked the heavy door, swinging it open so he could pass through, forcing Leah down the steep stone steps. Down, down, down to an ice-cold hell where there was no sunlight, no laughter, only tears.

Her daughter's tears. The little girl Brody had once made laugh. So long ago. Leah would do anything to save her, even sacrifice her own life. He could feel that truth in the way her muscles tensed as she examined the stone walls, her gaze like a bird flitting from one possible escape route to another before slumping in defeat.

"Help me." Her whisper was for his ears only, undercutting his own mental screams of anguish. "Please. You loved your little boy—I know you loved Charlie. Please help me save Emily."

Was she real? Maybe this was all a dream? If so, then what he'd done to the man, that was a dream as well, wasn't real. What a relief that would be... but this time Brody couldn't convince himself, not with memories seeping through the crumbling walls Jessica had built to hold them back. The man was real. The way he'd cried and screamed and fought to save his little girl.

Her little girl.

"Please."

He'd tried to fight back so many times—but he'd been shackled by more than pain, by fear of what would happen to Charlie.

Charlie was dead. The thought hammered through his brain, a coffin lid slamming shut for the final time.

Charlie was dead. He hadn't saved him. Charlie was dead. Because of him.

CHAPTER 45

Luka pushed the SUV to its limits as he drove through near white-out conditions. Then, less than a mile from Jessica Kern's home, the storm eased off. Like the eye of a hurricane, the winds vanished and the clouds opened up to reveal a panorama of stars shining above the snow glistening undisturbed on the road ahead.

"You know," Ray said after checking in with Krichek via radio—cell reception was nonexistent up here even in the best of weather. "If Broderick is delusional enough to create an imaginary son, then he's the perfect foil for Wright. She's probably manipulating him."

Luka shook his head. "No. I still don't buy it."

"You're forgetting the picture we found on Wright's phone. It wasn't a selfie—someone was there with Broderick."

"Doesn't mean it was Leah. There's something we're missing. I just can't put my finger on it." Luka steered them onto Kern's private drive, but a pair of massive steel gates blocked their path. He tried the intercom twice. No reply. He climbed out of the car and waved to the security camera. Its light blinked red; it seemed to be working. Then he tried the intercom one last time. Still nothing and there was no override he could find.

"What's our play?" Ray asked as he joined Luka. "We still don't have a warrant."

"There's a child in there. And no one is answering repeated attempts to contact them in order to verify her safety."

"Sounds like exigent circumstances to me. I'll radio McKinley for backup."

Luka strode to the rear of SUV and opened the back hatch. He grabbed flashlights for both of them along with tactical vests. There was a shotgun and ammo—he handed those off to Ray, keeping only his Glock.

"We're not waiting for McKinley," Ray said as he checked the Remington's ammo.

Luka didn't bother with an answer, instead pivoting on his heel and striding to the gate. The newer section over the drive had steel struts too closely placed for them to get through, but there was no way Kern could have replaced all of the original fencing surrounding the entire estate. He remembered coming here as a kid for a school trip. The mansion had been cool, but what had really impressed him was the cavernous basement with its labyrinth of tunnels. He and his friends had evaded their chaperones and spent half a day exploring down there. As he plowed through the half foot of snow, stumbling against the brush buried beneath, finally reaching the old wrought-iron fence surrounding the property, he wondered if Tanya had ever been here.

Ignoring the snow that fell into his shoes, he shoved the thought aside. It felt as if he was shoving his little sister away, abandoning her, like he had at lunch. Damn it, he needed to focus. Lives were at stake with every choice he made. He walked along the ancient original fence until he found what he'd been looking for: a section rusted out, partially collapsed, leaving a wide enough space for him and Ray to climb through.

They exited the wooded area, then crossed through a section of shrubs, heading back to the flatter drive where they could move faster. There Luka spotted two sets of tire tracks. One set almost buried in snow, the other fresh and from a larger vehicle like an SUV.

Luka drew his weapon and quickened his pace, jogging up the road, the lights of the huge house beckoning to him. He slowed once he spied Leah's truck parked out front, used it for cover to reach the porch. Luka sidled to the front doors and Ray joined him. The left-hand door was ajar, a sketch of snow blown over the threshold, melting on the foyer floor, a man's boot prints visible against the white marble.

Not good.

CHAPTER 46

Brody and Leah led the way down the stairs to the cellar, followed by Radcliffe, and finally Jessica. As soon as they began their descent Leah felt suddenly claustrophobic. The walls were stone and so close together that she could reach her hands and brush both sides without straightening her arms. Brody kept prodding her along, but he no longer held her arm and he'd lowered his knife. Because she had nowhere else to go once they reached the bottom?

She whispered to Brody, pleading, her words masked by their proximity and the fact that Jessica kept pausing to fiddle with her tablet, turning lights on ahead of them and nudging Radcliffe with her pistol as they rounded one landing after another.

"The man who built this house was a mining engineer, owned most of the coal pits around here," Jessica said, sounding more like a chirpy tour guide than a deranged killer. "He was constantly afraid of his workers rising up against him, so he built escape routes, turned his basement into a labyrinth. Came in handy during the Civil War, I'm told."

Leah reached the final landing at the bottom of the stairs. The air smelled different down here, damp with minerals. Beyond her was only darkness until Jessica joined them and used her tablet to turn on the lights, revealing a vast stone-walled room with several tunnels leading off it. The walls were lined with shelves designed to hold wine, while in the center a surgical light had been hung over a dental chair outfitted with heavy-duty restraints. Tables with surgical equipment and special monitors flanked the chair.

But what grabbed Leah's attention and had her plunging down the final three steps and sprinting across the space was the wrought-iron cage in the far corner. The grilled walls were old, clearly intended to protect the most precious wines, but Jessica had turned it into a jail cell. Beyond the twisted rows of iron were Ruby and Emily.

Ruby stood over Emily, her expression fierce, a splintered length of shelving held in her hands like a baseball bat. Emily curled up in the corner, awake and clearly frightened, hands over her face. Leah rattled the cage's door. Its lock was modern, electronic. "It's all right, pumpkin. I'm getting you out of there."

She felt Brody's presence behind her but ignored him to focus on Emily, crouching down to her level. "You okay? No one hurt you, did they?"

"They didn't lay a finger on her," Ruby answered. "I wouldn't let them."

Jessica and Radcliffe joined them. The cage door buzzed. Leah tugged it open, placing her weight against it so that Ruby and Emily couldn't be locked in again. Ruby led Emily out, Emily hiding behind Ruby's legs, her eyes wide, tears streaking her cheeks. Leah gave Emily a quick hug, all she could afford before returning her attention to the threat they still faced. She straightened, edging her body between Ruby and Emily and the others.

A loud chime sounded from a speaker on the wall. Jessica glanced at her tablet. "Oh look. More company. Your friend, Detective Jericho."

Brody's grip on the knife tightened. His emotionless mask had vanished, replaced by sheer anguish as he fought the commands Jessica had programmed into his brain. Free will. The ultimate weapon against tyranny. No wonder Jessica needed to construct an entire alternative reality, keeping his son alive, burying his real memories, in order to take control, force him to kill.

Ruby of course had no idea what was going on; she merely saw an opening and tried to take a swing at Brody. Leah grabbed her arm and stopped her before Brody could respond—or rather, before Jessica could force him to respond. They stood no chance. Unless she could somehow get Brody to fight back.

Jessica laughed. Then she turned to Radcliffe, slipping her tablet into her pocket and drawing his pistol, so that she held a gun in each hand. "Let's cut to the chase, shall we? If the cops find them alive, you're in this as deep as I am."

Radcliffe's mouth worked as he stared at her, stunned. "What do you mean, exactly?"

"Brody will do the dirty work, take care of our guests. You just need to back him up. Save your job—and save your life. Or, shall I tell Brody to take care of you first?"

Radcliffe's expression crumpled, his shoulders drooped, and he nodded. Jessica handed him back his gun. Leah held her breath, expecting Radcliffe to jump Jessica, take control, but he didn't. He shuffled his feet, edged a glance at Brody, and avoided looking at her or Ruby and most especially Emily.

Jessica started up the stairs and then turned back. "Oh, don't worry about the noise—no one upstairs will be alive long enough to hear you."

CHAPTER 47

Leah waited for Jessica to move beyond earshot before making her play. It was clear Radcliffe was terrified of Brody—and she thought she could get through to Brody, or at the very least slow him down long enough for Ruby and Emily to escape. The one thing she couldn't do, though, was outrun a bullet. "Radcliffe, you have to go help Jericho—she's going to kill him."

The DIA agent didn't move. Instead, he finally raised his face to stare at her, his expression stony. "I never planned for any of this, you know. They said to bring Dr. Kern back, her and her research. No matter the cost. That's all. I'm just following orders."

"Fine, then let us go."

He raised his gun slowly, shaking his head as he aimed it—at her. "I can't risk anyone talking." He turned to Brody. "Go ahead. Do it. Let's get this over with."

"No!" Leah whirled to Brody. She tugged on his arm, but he threw her off effortlessly. His shoulders tensed with effort, biceps bulging as he raised his knife. Leah stepped in front of Ruby and Emily, holding Brody's gaze.

"Please, Brody." She spoke softly. "You don't want to hurt anyone. Please. I know you loved Charlie. I know how much it hurts now that he's gone. You wouldn't let that happen to another child. You're stronger than that."

"Don't listen to her," Radcliffe shouted. "The cops are here—we can't waste any more time. Go on. Do it. Now!"

Brody didn't move, frozen like a marble statue, each muscle chiseled in tense relief. Except for his face. His mouth twisted in anguish and a single tear shone against his cheek.

It was working. Leah was getting through to him. "Brody. Please. For Charlie."

Slowly his knife lowered.

"Damn it all. I'll do it." Radcliffe tried to shove Brody aside.

Instead of yielding, Brody spun on the government agent, the knife now aimed at Radcliffe. His struggle as he forced his body to take another step away from Leah and the others, despite Jessica's orders, showed in his ravaged expression and sharp grunts of pain.

Radcliffe backed up awkwardly, totally off balance as he raised his gun almost as an afterthought. Brody stood between Radcliffe and the women. Leah used the opportunity to motion Ruby to get Emily ready to run. Ruby handed off her makeshift weapon to Leah.

"Stop or I'll shoot," Radcliffe shouted as Brody marched toward him, each step stiff and ponderous. Radcliffe's voice was reedy, pitched high with fear, but his gun didn't waver. He also didn't pull the trigger.

He'd never shot anyone before, Leah realized. Had probably never encountered violence in real life. But still, the instinct of self-preservation would kick in—and once Brody was down, Emily and Ruby and Leah were next.

"Run. Take Emily down the tunnels," Leah implored her mother. "Don't stop until she's safe. I'll keep them from coming after you."

For once, Ruby didn't stop to argue. Instead, she grabbed Emily's arm and fled down the closest tunnel. It didn't matter where it led—there was no way in hell Leah was letting anyone go after them. This ended here. Tonight. She hefted the broken piece of wood, splinters gouging her palms, and whirled.

Brody had closed in, backed Radcliffe up against the stone wall, stood close enough to grab Radcliffe's wrist. Radcliffe struggled to take aim at Brody, but Brody held his arm tight, forcing his aim away from Brody's body, over his shoulder. Brody still clutched his knife in his other hand, but that arm dangled loosely, as if he'd forgotten it—or maybe it required all his focus and strength to resist Jessica's commands and attack Radcliffe.

Leah took a step toward Radcliffe, and raised the length of shelving, ready to strike. "Drop it, Radcliffe."

His gaze flicked toward her but so did Brody's. The break in concentration was enough for Radcliffe to wrench his arm free. He pivoted toward Leah. She swung her makeshift bat in a chopping motion, bringing it down hard on his gun arm. The pistol went off. Leah felt the rush of the bullet as it raced past her before burying itself in one of the wooden shelves behind her.

Brody pounced before Radcliffe could adjust his aim. The two men struggled for the gun, buying Leah the time she needed. She ran toward the stairs—the only way her family would be safe would be with Jessica in custody, plus she had to warn Jericho that he was walking into a trap.

Two more gunshots were followed by the thud of bodies hitting the ground. She looked back. Brody straddled Radcliffe. His knife flashed, dripping blood. He rolled off Radcliffe, panting with exhaustion. Radcliffe lay face up, covered in blood from a variety of stab wounds, not breathing.

Leah hesitated. Radcliffe's final shot had torn through Brody's abdomen. Left upper quadrant through and through—no way the bullet could have missed the spleen. Brody was a dead man unless she could get him help and soon.

Following well-honed reflexes more than thoughts or emotions, she rushed over to him, placed pressure on his wound. Ian's body flashed before her eyes—Brody had done that. He should die. She should let him die.

Except... that wasn't the real Brody. The real Brody had just risked his life to save Emily.

"No. Leave me." His head arched back, neck muscles taunt, as pain seared through him. Not pain from the gunshot wound—it was more like a Taser hit ripping through his muscles. Jessica's electrodes, misfiring, shocking him over and over. He flailed one hand up, grabbing Leah's arm. "Go. Stop her. Please."

"Let me help." He saved Emily—Leah wasn't about to let him die.

"She killed me a long time ago." He gasped as another shock-wave hit. "At least this time, I die on my terms."

"I can't—"

"She'll do it again. She'll steal more lives. Do it, please. Stop her. Before it's too late. Plea—" Pain choked off his words, his entire body spasming.

Leah hesitated. It would be easier to try to save him and fail. So much easier than making the decision to walk away, do nothing. Andre Toussaint had been right about her: the truth was, when it came to making the tough choices, she was a coward.

"Go." Brody thrust the word through clenched jaws. "Please. For Charlie."

Brody's wasn't the only life at risk. Somewhere upstairs was Luka Jericho, who had no idea he was walking into a trap.

Leah turned to leave. Brody grabbed her arm, pulling her down, close to his lips.

"So-s-s-sorry…" he said.

She wanted to forgive him, give him that solace in his final moments, but the memory of Ian's body held her heart hostage. How could she ever forgive the man who'd destroyed everything she held dear? Leah rocked back on her heels, her eyes shut tight against the tears that threatened. She was so angry—and terrified—and for the first time in her life she felt true hatred in her heart.

It wasn't Brody she hated.

She opened her eyes and gazed into his, nodding her under-standing.

"I'll stop her," she promised. Then she laid her palm against his cheek. "Thank you."

Exhaustion trembled her muscles; she could barely stay upright. Weary. Drained. Not only her body, her soul. Leah honestly no longer cared what happened to her—as long as Emily was safe.

She had to buy time for Ruby to get Emily to safety. Had to trust Ruby to save Emily. Her mind rebelled against the idea but quickly surrendered the fight.

Leah pried Radcliffe's pistol from the agent's dead hand and raced up the steps. She had no idea how to use a gun, no idea if she could even take another person's life, no idea if the cops had seen through Jessica's lies or if they were already upstairs, lying dead in their own blood.

CHAPTER 48

Luka radioed their situation to McKinley. There was a kid inside and they had no time to wait for backup. "We're going in."

He met Ray's gaze as they stood before Kern's front doors. Ray nodded his readiness. Luka guided the door fully open, bracing himself for what might be waiting. The foyer was empty and Ray moved past Luka, hugging the righthand wall, glancing into the well-lit living room, while Luka shone his flashlight into the darkened dining room on the left. Empty.

"Clear," Ray whispered. "Lights are on in the rear, but I don't see any movement."

The house was silent. Too silent. There was a hallway leading to the back of the house behind the righthand set of stairs. Luka motioned to Ray to clear the living room side while he approached from the foyer side. As much as he hated splitting up, with a space this large they had little choice if they wanted to avoid an ambush.

Luka pressed his back to the wall and began down the narrow corridor. A servant's passage, he guessed, since all the doors he opened led to a variety of different pantries: one for dishes, one for pots and pans, one devoted to glassware. Then a small half-bath, which, given its sparsity of decor and utilitarian design, was meant for servants, not guests. Followed by a final door that led to a kitchen.

Ray's passage had been more direct, because when Luka arrived, he was helping a woman out of a narrow broom closet on the far end of the expansive kitchen. Jessica Kern, her hair astray, tears washing rivulets in her makeup.

The overhead lights reflected from gleaming marble and steel, all polished to a mirror finish. In the center of the space stood a large island, marble on top, brushed steel surrounding the base. Beside the door Ray had entered through was a taller door, arched at the top, crafted out of heavy, dark-stained wood.

"Don't open that," the woman cried out as Luka reached for the door. He turned to her. "That's where they went. I hid. Maybe I should have tried to stop them." She hauled in a sob, sagged in Ray's arms, her weight forcing him to set his shotgun aside as he walked her over to a stool at the island. "They took the little girl, Emily. They had guns."

"Who?" Ray asked. "Broderick?"

"And Leah." Her head bobbed up and down in a nod. "She let him in. He had a gun. He hit Ruby, and I, I ran. I'm sorry, I didn't know what else to do." Her shoulders shook and she grabbed Ray's arm with both hands. Then she lunged from the stool toward the sink, hauling him with her. "I'm going to be sick."

Luka eased the door open a crack. Stone walls, stone steps, well lit—but that could be a disadvantage, coming from above, moving down what was a classic fatal funnel. One time when the high ground was not an advantage. "What's down there?"

Jessica was dry-heaving, Ray supporting her, holding her hair away from her face. "Wine cellar. Tunnel leading out," she gasped. "Maybe they left?"

The faint echo of gunshots—no way to tell how far away they were—bounced off the stone walls. "Maybe not. Ray, watch her."

"No, I'm coming—"

"Only room for one on the steps. I'll get eyes, see what we're up against and then retreat to wait for ERT." Luka could tell Ray was pissed off about missing any potential action, but if Luka did this right, there would be no action. He hoped.

He considered taking the shotgun, but the stone steps were steep and narrow. The Glock would be better, he decided. As he edged his way down the first flight, he tried to imagine Leah putting her daughter in harm's way. It didn't seem in character—had she fooled him so thoroughly?

He reached the first landing and turned past it, keeping his back to the rough-hewn wall as he began down the next flight. Only four steps to the next landing. Steps echoed from below, getting closer. He stopped, edged his gaze around the corner. Leah, running up, carrying a pistol. Luka planted himself and raised his weapon. He'd never shot anyone before, never even had to draw his weapon before, and he hated that hers might be the first life he took.

But he didn't let that slow him down. "Stop," he ordered. "Or I'll shoot."

CHAPTER 49

Leah sprinted up the steep steps, her heart racing with adrenaline. She'd forgotten how many landings there were, each with a short flight of slippery stone steps staggered between them, but she thought she was getting close to the top. She rounded a corner and came face to face with Luka Jericho, aiming his weapon at her, his eyes wide.

"Stop!" he shouted. She didn't hear much after that, all her attention was on his gun, but the essence of his commands filtered through the thunder filling her mind. Slowly, she turned her back to him, keeping her hands out wide, and placed Radcliffe's gun on the ground, stepping away from it. He grabbed the gun, then pushed her against the wall, his hands patting over her body. "Who else is down there?"

"Radcliffe. Dead. But Brody is injured. He needs help."

"Broderick's here?" She felt him tense behind her.

"He's no threat. It's Jessica. She's behind all this. And she has a gun. Did you arrest her?"

"Arrest her?"

"She said she was going to kill you, fool you into thinking she's the victim—" Before she could finish, he was racing up the steps.

Leah followed after him, no idea what she could do, but it was the best way to get Brody help and make sure Jessica didn't go after Emily and Ruby.

They reached the last flight of steps. Two loud pops came from above, sounding small and tinny compared with the loudness of the shots Leah had heard in the confined space of the stonewalled cellar. Or maybe it was just the pounding of her heart and rasping of her breath muffling the noise. Jericho pushed off the steps, sprinting even faster. He stopped at the top, using the partly open door as cover, glancing around it. Then he sprang forward, shoving the door aside.

Leah reached the top in time to catch the door before it closed on her. She pushed it all the way open. The window above the sink was shattered, cold air whistling through like the soundtrack of a horror movie.

Jericho aimed his gun at Jessica, who was crouched over a man's body. It was the other detective, Acevedo. He was alive, gasping for breath, his hands clutched over his groin. A thin stream of blood flowed out from beneath his leg, not stopping until it hit Jericho's shoe.

Jessica held her gun at Acevedo's temple. "He'll die unless you let me go." Her voice was calm, certain. "Put your gun on the floor and kick it to me."

"You know I can't do that, Dr. Kern." Smart of Jericho to use Jessica's title, Leah thought. Treat her with respect, play into her ego. "What do you want?"

Leah moved around the island, hoping to distract Jessica, give Jericho a chance to grab her gun or tackle her. But Jessica didn't take her eyes off Jericho. "Stay where you are, Leah," she said in a level tone. "Unless you want one more man's death on your conscience."

Leah raised her hands and stood still.

"Good girl. Now, Detective, here's what you're going to do—"

Before Jessica could finish her sentence, Leah felt movement behind her. Brody barreled through the door, pushing Leah out of the way, a blur of bloody motion, charging Jessica.

Jessica turned her gun on him, firing over and over, Brody's body falling, falling as if in slow motion.

Everything was blurry around the edges as Leah realized that Jericho was also shooting—not at Brody, but at Jessica. The shots reverberated like thunder, quaking through Leah, making her cover her ears and cower below the island, gagging against the smell of gunpowder and blood.

Her own breath echoed through her skull loud enough to drown out all sound. But then the echoes fell away, leaving behind an awful, empty silence. She raised her head to peer over the island. Brody had fallen to the floor on the other side. Leah rushed to him.

Jericho still held his weapon, trained on Jessica's body slumped beside Acevedo. Jessica's breath came in loud, raspy gasps. Jericho bent over to grab Jessica's gun from her limp hand. Only then did he kneel to check on his friend.

Leah felt for Brody's pulse. Weak and way too fast, but there. She couldn't believe he'd managed to make his way up the steps, much less rush at Jessica. Jessica's manipulations, the drugs and stimulation—they must have blocked his pain, given him the surge of adrenaline Brody needed. Jessica's own warped experiments had been her final undoing.

"I need you here," Jericho shouted to Leah. "Help Ray."

Leah was torn. "Brody? Can you hear me?"

His eyes fluttered open, his lips parted as if he was trying to say something, but then he sighed, his breath escaping him one final time as he sagged in her arms. He was gone.

"Help Ray," Jericho commanded.

Leah scrambled around the island and turned her attention to Acevedo.

"Ray." Jericho joined her on the floor after calling for help on his radio. "Stay with me, you stubborn bastard."

"Hold pressure," she told him, pressing both his hands over the entrance wound on Acevedo's thigh. She checked for other wounds: nothing. The man was lucky—luckier than Jessica, who had taken two shots in her chest and one low in her belly.

Jessica stared at Leah, her gaze both imploring and filled with hatred. "Help. Me."

Leah hesitated. She could still save her—save them both. If she worked fast enough.

"Forget her," Jericho shouted. "Save Ray."

Saving Jessica—Toussaint would tell her to look at the big picture, Jessica standing trial, suffering the rest of her life in jail… but never suffering as much as Ian had. And what if Radcliffe's bosses somehow cut a deal for her?

But it wasn't all those thoughts that made up her mind. Instead, it was Brody's voice. Pleading with her, despite the pain tormenting him, begging her to stop Jessica. Forever.

"Give me your belt." Leah examined Acevedo's wound. She grabbed a dish towel and shoved it into the exit wound. She was rewarded by a sudden gurgling gasp. Acevedo's eyes fluttered, then closed again.

"More pressure," she ordered Jericho, who leaned his body weight against Acevedo's wound as Leah slid his belt around the leg and pulled it as tight as possible. The blood slowed to a trickle.

She rocked back on her heels. "He needs fluids and an OR."

She'd kept her back turned to Jessica during the few seconds it took her to tend to Acevedo, but now there was no choice but to face her other patient. Leah pivoted, turning to Jessica's still form. Blood puddled on the floor, spreading out beneath Jessica, two drooping, shredded, scarlet wings.

"Leah." Jessica's voice rattled with blood and the effort to breathe. She batted a hand at Leah's ankle. She was suffocating, drowning in her own blood. An agonizing and painful death.

"You. Just like. Me." Her chest heaved with effort. "Killer."

A sound that was a cross between ghastly laughter and a death rattle emerged, accompanied by blood gurgling from Jessica's mouth. The bright red color matched her lipstick, Leah noticed, fighting a wave of hysteria, trying to pretend she hadn't heard

Jessica's accusations. Her chest was still, eyes open, staring at Leah. Leah checked the other woman's pulse, leaving her own bloody handprint on Jessica's neck and chest. Nothing. She was gone.

Leah sucked her breath in, ambushed by a host of emotions too tangled to name. Tears blurred her vision, her throat tightened, strangling her scream as Ian's face filled her vision. Not the Ian from last night, battered and broken. No. *Her* Ian. The man who had died to save their daughter.

A sudden pounding shook the house. Men in SWAT uniforms thundered in, a herd of bison ready to mow down anything that stood in their way—except only Leah, Acevedo, and Jericho were left alive.

Once the SWAT team realized that, they stood aside, as their medic took over for Leah. She heard her name called and turned, and then began laughing and crying, not caring at all about the men with guns who surrounded her.

Because there, safely ensconced in one of the large, black SUVs outside the door, were Ruby and Emily.

CHAPTER 50

After the initial rush of the ERT entrance, followed by the medics, Luka finally found himself alone, sitting at a banquet table that could seat twenty, his bloody clothes and hands staining the silk upholstery and walnut wood.

He sat in silence, counting the crystals in the nine-tiered chandelier, losing track every time images of the night intruded, replaying themselves as he tried to understand where he'd gone wrong, how two of his team were in the hospital, one of them barely clinging to life. If not for Leah Wright, Ray would have died on that kitchen floor.

He had no idea how long he'd sat there, waiting for the state police's Officer-Involved Shooting team to arrive, when Maggie Chen entered through the archway on the far end of the room. Why was she here? The team from the coroner's office had already collected the bodies. And she wasn't even on duty tonight.

"You're here for Ray?" He stood, pushing the chair out of his way, his vision swimming, stomach lurching.

"Ray's still in surgery, but stable. Commander Ahearn is notifying his family in person."

"He should have waited for me. I'm his commanding officer, I'm—" His voice caught. What if Ray died—he'd looked gray as death when they'd carried him out. How the hell was he going to run his squad without Ray? If Ahearn didn't fire him or demote him to traffic control. "I'm his best friend."

Then a sudden jolt of terror raced through him. "If you're not here for Ray—is it Harper? Don't tell me—"

"Naomi's fine."

He sagged with relief. "Sorry, I'm juggling too many—" Then it dawned on him. She waited as he took a breath, swallowed, took another, filling his lungs but the oxygen tasted of blood, was lifeless. Finally, he found the strength to speak, somehow forcing his voice to sound professional, maybe even calm, despite the fact that he felt anything but in control. "You found Tanya. Let me guess, county lockup? Give me a little while, I just need to wrap up things here and then I can go—"

She laid her hand on his arm; his wall of denial crumbled beneath her touch. "There's no rush."

And with those words he knew. He stumbled back, searching for a chair, he needed to sit, but his body lurched into the wall. He slid to the parquet floor. "She's—"

Maggie joined him on the floor. "She checked into the Kingston Hotel over near the park."

Tanya was still here, hadn't left Cambria City? After he'd wasted all that time looking for her in Baltimore… Well, not his time wasted; all he'd done was make a few calls to the Baltimore police. He should have gone looking for her himself, maybe… "The Kingston Hotel? Where all the rich people go? My—our—gran took us there once for tea. Said she wanted us to see what it felt like having people wait on us, wanted us to remember being treated special but also how to treat the hardworking men and women serving us like they were something special as well." He and Tanya in their best Sunday clothing, Gran wearing her gloves and special Easter hat. "Tanya never got the lesson—instead she just learned how to yearn for something she could never have, a life she never stopped chasing after, even if it was only a drug-induced fantasy." He sighed, let Maggie take his hand even though he barely felt hers. "How?"

"OD. Fentanyl. It was quick."

He nodded, not sure what to say. Beyond the room, patrolmen and CSU buzzed around but for the life of him he couldn't remember what they were doing or why. It all seemed so pointless and very far away. Was this how Leah Wright had felt last night?

He remembered the video the patrolmen had taken of her, rescuing her daughter from under the bed her dead husband sat in front of. The determined look in her eyes—and the pain that shadowed the rest of her face.

Luka pushed up to his feet, still leaning against the wall. Maggie mirrored his movements. "Would you like me to come with you to tell your family?"

He shook his head. What was the rush, bringing this hell into his home? He thought of Nate's face, the kid already expecting the worst from life. His responsibility now. "No. I'll do it myself." He spotted the state police signing in at the foyer. "Later. Right now I have work to do. If I want to save my job."

And suddenly, more than anything, Luka did care, he did want to save his job—if not for himself, then to honor Ian and his wife, both willing to sacrifice their lives to save their daughter.

To honor Cherise, killed so many years ago, yet still a guiding force in his life, haunting Luka at every crime scene.

Even, in some strange way, to honor his lost sister, Tanya.

CHAPTER 51
Two weeks later

March hadn't come in like a lion at all. If anything, after February's storms, it had limped in with barely a whimper. This morning the temperatures hovered around sixty while the sun teased plants eager for winter to be over.

For the first time, Emily had slept through the night without waking up in terror, which meant it was the first night since Ian's death that Leah had gotten more than a few hours' sleep as well. To celebrate, she'd made them all French toast for brunch; and now, as Emily explored the garden's treasures guided by an old notebook of Nellie's, Leah sat out on the porch swing with a cup of cinnamon tea, listening to the birds and Emily's singsong monologue. She could almost imagine Nellie stepping through the screen door, its hinge sighing as it closed behind her.

But the woman who took the rocker beside Leah wasn't Nellie. It was Ruby. They'd spent the last few weeks tiptoeing around the farmhouse, making too-polite conversation, talking to Emily, but not to each other. Leah shifted in the swing, the creaking of the chains drowning her sigh. All she wanted was a single moment of peace, but of course Ruby had intruded, no doubt wanting something from Leah.

Yes, Ruby had protected Emily and helped to save her. But that did not mean Leah should trust the woman. They were living under the same roof and Emily was becoming more and more attached to Ruby with each day. Leah knew it would break Emily's heart when Ruby finally showed her true colors and betrayed Emily. Leah could not—would not—allow that to happen.

"You still don't trust me, do you?" Ruby said as Leah kept her eyes closed, rocking harder, the chains squeaking in protest, hoping Ruby would get the hint and leave. "Is that because you're not sure if Ian had an affair or not? Because you lost trust in him?"

Leah sat up, planted her feet on the ground to halt the swing's motion, and glared at Ruby. "What business—"

"Like it or not we're family," Ruby cut her off. "And I know how you are. The tiniest little thing goes wrong and you just need to grab hold and fix it, make it right."

"Just say it. I'm a control freak."

"It's the truth. Been like that since you were younger than Emily." Ruby tucked her ankles under her on the seat and sipped her tea.

"Right. And you had nothing to do with it."

"I never abandoned you. You always had food, shelter, clothes on your back. Maybe not a lot, but enough. It's not my fault that you grew into the kind of woman who—" Ruby clamped her mouth shut.

"You think I'm not thinking the same thing? If I wasn't who I am, always trying to control everything, fix everyone, Ian would still be alive. Think I don't know that I got Ian killed? And now I have to live with that fact for the rest of my life. Not to mention never knowing if he betrayed me or if he ever even loved me at all." Leah's voice lowered to a hoarse whisper, barely able to choke the words out. Still, they screamed through her head, a chorus that had been repeating in an endless loop of guilt and recrimination. All her fault. Everything was all her fault. And the worst thing? Someday Emily would know that truth.

"Ian wasn't having an affair," Ruby said, her tone certain.

"How the hell would you know? I saw the drawings—the girl, she's beautiful. And there was ten thousand missing that Ian withdrew in cash."

"Ten thousand?"

"Yeah. I don't know. Maybe he was planning to run away with her or something."

To Leah's surprise, Ruby rocked back in her chair, her body convulsing with laughter, almost spilling her tea. "Ian wasn't going to run away. He took that money out for me. My truck broke down and he helped me buy a new one. He didn't tell you because—"

"I'm a control freak." Even as relief swirled over Leah, her guilt quickly stomped it out.

They both sat quietly for a moment, the cinnamon scent of the tea floating between them.

Ruby broke the silence. "You were better off here, with Nellie."

"Excuse me?"

"All those times I tucked my tail between my legs, came crawling over here, it wasn't only about money. It was to see you. But every time, every single time, you'd come running down those stairs with a smile brighter than the sun filling your face, and I knew, I just knew I'd done the right thing, leaving you here."

Leah's mouth fell open as she stared at her mother. "Only you could twist that—I was smiling because every time you came, I hoped you'd come to take me back, that I'd finally done something good enough to make you want me back."

"Want you back? You think I didn't want you?"

"You said—"

"I was upset. You have any idea how hard it is for a mother to leave her daughter, admit that she's no good for her little girl?"

Leah stood, the swing twisting violently against its chains with the sudden motion. She stalked toward the door, then stopped. Where did she and Emily have left to go? Move across the country with Ian's parents, leave everything they knew behind? Try to live in the house that would forever be haunted by Ian's death? Like it or not, Ruby was the only family Leah had left.

She took a deep breath and turned. Ruby watched her, a strange emotion playing across her features, one that Leah had never seen in her mother before. Fear.

"Do you have any idea how hard it was, thinking you didn't love me, that I was the kind of kid, so awful, so terrible, not even her own mother could love her?" Leah shocked herself with her words—she'd never dared to think them before now. "And now, to hear, decades later, that it wasn't me, wasn't my fault?"

Ruby stretched out both hands, palms up, empty, waiting for Leah to fill them—just like it'd always been up to Leah to fill her mother's empty heart. Yes, now she understood that it was more than a personality disorder, but knowing the facts did little to assuage decades of emotion.

"I don't know how many times you can expect me to say I'm sorry," Ruby said, her tone wounded.

"That's just it. You haven't. You've explained why you did what you did. You've told me how it wasn't your fault. But you've never actually apologized," Leah snapped, instantly feeling ashamed for allowing her fury to rule her. Ian never cared about the words, apologies. He needed to understand why things happened and why people did what they did, but then, once he understood, he could move on. Leah wished she was more like him. "It's not even that I need to hear you say it. It's more that I need to see you live it."

Ruby sighed, then gripped Leah's hands, pulling her down until their foreheads touched, their gazes locked. "Maybe I've never said the words because I have no right to ask for forgiveness," she said in a hoarse whisper. "All I can hope is you'll let me in your life, let me help." Then she dropped Leah's hands. "But if you want me to leave, I will."

Leah sank down into the chair beside Ruby. They were both silent, both watching Emily as she played with dried lavender stalks, weaving them into a crown. Leah didn't want to be anywhere else. And she wanted what she'd had with Ian, a home, a family. She glanced at Ruby, who leaned forward, elbows on her knees, waiting, eager for an answer Leah didn't have. Could that family ever include Ruby?

"If we stay—"

Ruby bounced halfway out of her seat, caught Leah's eye, then sat back down again, clasping her wrists as if restraining herself.

"*If* we stay, I need to see you think about someone else for a change. Namely that little girl. Because so help me, if you ever betray or abandon her, or make her feel like she's somehow responsible for your passive-aggressive nonsense, then you will never see us again. We'll leave without looking back."

"But you want to stay? Here? With me?" Ruby's tone was hushed as if they were in church.

Before Leah could answer, Emily raced up the porch, clutching Nellie's old notebook in one hand and her flower crown in the other. "Did you know you can make candy from flowers?" She bounced onto Ruby's lap. "Can we do that, Ruby? Please? I want to learn how." She turned to Leah. "Mommy, don't you want to learn how?"

Words tangled in Leah's throat, as twisted as her emotions. Joy at seeing Emily's smile again. Sorrow that Ian wasn't here. Bitterness at the way Emily embraced Ruby, inviting her into their world so easily. "I already know how," she finally said. "I know all the secrets of this farm. More than Miss Ruby even."

"You do? How?" Emily squinted at her as if she might be lying.

"I grew up here, silly."

"You know…" Ruby told Emily, although her gaze slanted to meet Leah's—it was difficult to ignore the yearning that filled it. "If you and your mom want to, you could stay here. With me." She gave Leah a tentative smile. "After all, it's your home, too. I think Nellie—and Ian—would have wanted it that way."

Emily bounced up and down. "Can we, Mommy? Stay here? Please?"

Typical Ruby. Pushing things too far, too fast, so that Leah was suddenly backed into a corner, her daughter's emotional well-being used to blackmail her into doing what Ruby wanted. When would she learn? And yet, a glimmer of an image teased her: Leah and Emily, making Nellie's home their own. It was tempting, so tempting.

A red pickup truck appeared on the lane. Luka Jericho. He parked and Nate jumped out of the passenger side like a prisoner sprung from jail. He and Luka still didn't get along—Nate blamed Luka for his mother's death. But they were working things through with the help of a child trauma counselor, which was where Emily and Nate had met, in his waiting room.

Nate stood pressed against the truck's door, one hand shielding his eyes from the morning sun, scanning the environment warily. Until he met Emily's gaze. She waved, bouncing on her toes with excitement. "Nate!"

Without a backward glance at Leah—which Leah knew was a good sign, as much as it stung—Emily raced to her new friend and they took off, vanishing around the side of the house.

Luka strode to the truck's passenger side. Leah joined him. "How's Ray?" she asked.

"Home. Driving his wife nuts." He slid a large flat package out from behind the passenger seat. "Thought you might want this. Got it released from evidence."

Leah glanced at Ruby, who stared with unabashed curiosity from her rocking chair on the porch. She and Luka climbed the steps to the front door and Leah held it open for him. "Let's go inside where we'll have some privacy."

They'd talked a lot over the past couple of weeks, mostly about pain and healing. She'd learned from Luka that Jessica had been planning her revenge on Leah for years—had met Brody through an offender/victim reconciliation program, even arranged for his early release and offered him a job as her research assistant. Poor guy never had a chance.

Her and Luka's conversations had all been over the phone or while sitting in the counseling center waiting for Nate and Emily—neutral territory. This was the first time she'd invited anyone, as a friend, inside her home.

Her home. Leah stopped, took a breath to recognize the thought. It felt good—yet also dangerous, a painful risk, investing so much, maybe too much.

"We found it at Kern's," Luka told her as he set the package on the dining room table. "From the video she shot that night, Valentine's, she took it from your house. Your husband had it all wrapped up, waiting for you."

Leah remembered the last words Ian had said to her. "He said he had a surprise, wanted to see my face when he gave it to me." Leah stared at the package, her hand hovering as she hesitated. "I guess this is it."

Luka shrugged. "Won't know until you open it."

Leah took a deep breath, then carefully removed the heavy brown paper. She felt the outline of a frame. Glass shimmered as she folded back a layer of tissue paper, exposing a large drawing.

Leah. Cradling Emily in her arms, reading her a bedtime story. Both drawn with loving precision, every detail so fluid the image felt as if it might come alive.

Scrawled at the bottom was Ian's signature.

"Guess Balanchuk wasn't lying about those art classes after all," Luka said as he studied the portrait. "Your husband, he did good work."

Tears ambushed Leah but for the first time in weeks they weren't tears of grief but rather of joy. Ian may have had his secrets, but he'd never betrayed her, never abandoned his family.

"I'm not sure how I'm going to do this without him," she confessed. "I don't know if I can."

"You can. We both can." She wished she could be as certain as he was. Laughter drifted in from the open front door. Luka jerked his chin in the direction of the delightful noise. "For them."

They stood in silence for a moment, listening to Nate and Emily as they played Space Aliens and Pirates. Nate was the pirate, swinging an imaginary cutlass, while Emily zapped him with her ray gun.

Then Luka shook himself. "Sure it's okay for him to stay the afternoon? I've got another meeting with the social worker and the judge. Think they're ready to sign off."

"Good job, *Dad*," she told him.

"It doesn't feel real. Not yet." He took his keys out and stepped to the door, then stopped. "Almost forgot. The feds finally released your house—the cleaners can get in there tomorrow. If you want, I can set it up for you. I know some good guys, won't rip you off."

"Thanks, Luka."

Then he was gone, leaving her alone with Ian's final gift. She took a deep breath, filling her lungs with one of her oldest, warmest memories: the scent of dried lavender and roses. She touched her fingers to her lips and pressed them against the glass above Ian's signature. Gratitude surged through her. It was Ian who'd taught her how to trust, to risk letting someone get close enough to love. Now, thanks to his lessons, she knew what she needed to do next.

She rejoined Ruby on the porch. They both turned their chairs to watch Emily and Nate as the kids ran through the fields near the woods. It wouldn't be easy without Ian to help, but Leah wasn't in this alone. And most importantly, neither was Emily. Leah would make sure of that.

Her daughter would always know how much her father loved and cherished her. The pain of his death was a pain they'd share and carry and someday heal.

Together.

"We're staying," she told Ruby, feeling light, unfettered, as if she could finally breathe. "I'm taking the job at the Crisis Intervention Center."

A shadow moved in the corner as a stray breeze rustled the empty porch swing. Leah swore she saw Ian there, his smile brighter than the sunshine as he gazed down upon his family.

No. Leah wasn't alone. She was home. Finally home.

A LETTER FROM CJ

Thanks so much for reading *The Next Widow*. Want to follow more of Leah and Luka's adventures? Then sign up at the following link to receive updates on the next book in the series. Your email address will never be shared and you can unsubscribe at any time.

www.bookouture.com/cj-lyons

The inspiration for *The Next Widow* came from what is any ER doctor's worst nightmare: having absolutely no control over the fate of a loved one.

When my niece was born, I diagnosed her with a life-threatening heart condition, which enabled her to start treatment before she was even a few hours old. I watched her grow and thrive, refusing to allow her condition to hold her back, and she became a gorgeous young woman attending university.

Until the night when she died… for nine minutes. Thankfully, two nursing students began CPR immediately and the ER team who treated her refused to give up. Her parents and I rushed to the ICU where she was in a coma, unsure—*if* she ever woke up—how much of the "old" her would remain intact.

As you could probably tell from *The Next Widow*, those of us drawn to emergency medicine tend to be control freaks (and proud of it, lol!) During those long, empty hours of not knowing my niece's fate, standing helpless, powerless by her side, my imagination couldn't help but travel down some dark and twisted paths, wondering… what if?

What if an ER doctor saved the wrong patient? What if this led to someone's death? What if a loved one sought revenge by taking control in every possible way, body-mind-soul, orchestrating a living hell for the doctor and the patient she saved?

Thankfully, my niece not only recovered, she's stronger and more fearless than ever before, back at her studies (and on the Dean's list despite the time lost from her hospitalization and recovery!) and doing great.

And, of course, being a thriller writer, I used all those nightmare ideas conjured at her bedside to create *The Next Widow*.

I hope you enjoyed Leah and Luka's first story! If you did, I would be very grateful if you could write a review. I'd love to hear what you think, and it makes such a difference helping new readers to discover one of my books for the first time.

I love hearing from my readers—you can get in touch on my Facebook page, through Goodreads or my website.

Thanks for reading!
CJ

www.cjlyons.net

cjlyons

@cjlyonswriter

cjlyons

Printed in Great Britain
by Amazon